Praise for *New York Times* bestselling author B.J. Daniels

"You won't be able to put it down."
—*New York Times* bestselling author Jodi Thomas
on *Heartbreaker*

"Daniels is a perennial favorite on the romantic suspense front, and I might go as far as to label her the cowboy whisperer." —*BookPage* on *Luck of the Draw*

"Daniels keeps readers baffled with a taut plot and ample red herrings, expertly weaving in the threads of the next story in the series as she introduces a strong group of primary and secondary characters."
—*Publishers Weekly* on *Stroke of Luck*

"Daniels again turns in a taut, well-plotted, and suspenseful tale with plenty of red herrings. Readers will be in from the start and engaged until the end."
—*Library Journal* on *Stroke of Luck*

"Readers who like their romance spiced with mystery can't go wrong with *Stroke of Luck* by B.J. Daniels." —*BookPage*

"Daniels is an expert at combining layered characters, quirky small towns, steamy chemistry and added suspense."
—*RT Book Reviews* on *Hero's Return*

"B.J. Daniels has made *Cowboy's Legacy* quite a nail-biting, page-turner of a story. Guaranteed to keep you on your toes." —*Fresh Fiction*

**Also by *New York Times* bestselling author
B.J. Daniels**

Look for B.J. Daniels's next novel
available soon from HQN.

For additional books by B.J. Daniels,
visit her website, www.bjdaniels.com.

B.J. DANIELS

NEW YORK TIMES BESTSELLING AUTHOR

Before BUCKHORN

HQN

ISBN-13: 978-1-335-63988-2

Before Buckhorn

Copyright © 2022 by Barbara Heinlein

Out of the Blue

Copyright © 2022 by Barbara Heinlein

Recycling programs for this product may not exist in your area.

This edition published by arrangement with Harlequin Books S.A.

For questions and comments about the quality of this book, please contact us at CustomerService@Harlequin.com.

HQN
22 Adelaide St. West, 41st Floor
Toronto, Ontario M5H 4E3, Canada
www.Harlequin.com

Printed in Lithuania

CONTENTS

I've always loved a little weird and spooky,
so I had such a good time writing this book.
This one is for all of you who are like me.

BEFORE BUCKHORN

CHAPTER ONE

SATURDAY EVENING THE crows came. Jasper Cole looked up from where he'd been standing in his ranch kitchen cleaning up his dinner dishes. He'd heard the rustle of feathers and looked up with a start to see several dozen crows congregated on the telephone line outside.

Just the sight of them stirred a memory of a time dozens of crows had come to his grandparents' farmhouse when he was five. The chill he felt at both the memory and the arrival of the crows had nothing to do with the cool Montana spring air coming in through the kitchen window.

He stared at the birds, noticing that all seemed to be watching him. There were so many of them, their ebony bodies silhouetted against a cloudless sky, their shiny dark eyes glittering in the growing twilight. As this murder of crows began to caw, he listened as if this time he might decode whatever they'd come to tell him. But like last time, he couldn't make sense of it. Was it another warning, one he was going to wish that he'd heeded?

Laughing to himself, he closed the window and finished his dishes. He didn't really believe the crows were a portent of what was to come this time—any more than last time. His grandmother had, though. He remembered watching her cross herself and mumble a prayer as if the crows were an omen of something sinister on its way. As it turned out, she'd been right.

At almost forty, Jasper could scoff all he wanted, even as a bad feeling settled deep in his belly. That feeling only worsened as the crows suddenly all took flight as if their work was done.

Over the next few days, he would remember the evening the crows appeared. It was the same day Leviathan Nash arrived in Buckhorn, Montana, to open his shop in the old carriage house and strange things had begun to happen—even before people started dying.

CHAPTER TWO

MONDAY MORNING, THE Buckhorn Café was packed. Most of the customers though weren't seated in the booths or even at the counter. Instead, they were lined up at the front window waiting for something to happen across the highway at the old carriage house.

All the mystery surrounding Leviathan Nash and the new shop had dropped an expectant air of excitement over the tiny isolated town. It had been a while since any new businesses had opened in Buckhorn, so watching the building had now apparently become a town pastime.

With the café located just kitty-corner across the main drag, business had been brisk, the owner Bessie Walker Caulfield said, clearly tickled. "The new shop and its owner are all anyone's talking about," she told him as she filled a cup of coffee for him before handing off the coffeepot to the young waitress and heading back to the kitchen. Bessie, a woman in her late fifties with a long gray braid that fell over one shoulder, loved nothing better than being busy.

Jasper had always enjoyed his early morning weekday breakfasts at the café. Usually, the place was empty this early unless it was the day that Bessie made her famous cinnamon rolls. It was why he avoided weekends at the café. He liked the peace and quiet visiting with his older friend while the small town in the middle of nowhere was waking up.

But that wasn't happening this morning as some of the early-morning patrons took their seats again. As was with most news in Buckhorn, word had spread like wildfire through town that Leviathan Nash, the man who'd rented the old carriage house, had arrived—and gotten to work on the place.

Bessie told him the latest scuttlebutt in between bringing out food for her customers to help her teenaged waitress. According to Mabel Aldrich, who lived behind the old carriage house, she'd seen his large truck backed up to the shop late Saturday night. She'd claimed she'd seen a waif of a man dressed in all black moving around in the shadows, however she hadn't been able to get a good look at him.

Not only had no one else claimed to have seen Leviathan Nash, they also hadn't had a peek into his shop. The arched windows in the double doors that had gleamed clean and clear when landowner Melissa Herbert had leased the space, were now covered with black paper and had been since his arrival.

Even Melissa hadn't apparently laid eyes on the man, according to Bessie, who Jasper considered a reliable source. Melissa, who had only talked to him on the phone since the arrangements had all been made online, said he had an unusually low voice. "How long is this going to last?" Jasper said more to himself than Bessie on one of her update stops by his booth.

She shrugged as she delivered his breakfast on this particular stop. "Probably until his lease is up at the end of the month."

Suddenly all customers were on their feet again to rush over to the front window, although he couldn't see what was going on from where he sat. He missed his normal view of the highway that cut through the middle of town.

Jasper concentrated on his breakfast. He always had the same thing every weekday when he came in early. Ham, eggs over easy, toast and coffee, black. He liked routine and resented having that routine interrupted like right now. Maybe Bessie was right, he thought now, remembering an earlier conversation.

"You're getting set in your ways like an old man," Bessie had warned him and then lowered her voice. "You want to be like some of these cantankerous old bachelors who come in here?"

"I can think of worse things," he'd said.

Bessie had shaken her head in defeat, but then grinned. "Let's just see if Darby Fulton changes your mind," she'd said with a wink. Darby was the new online newspaper publisher, editor and reporter who'd moved to town a few weeks ago.

Since arriving in town Darby had interrupted more than his thoughts. Saturday night, after seeing the crows, he'd had a very disturbing dream about the young woman. What Bessie didn't know was that there was much more to the story of him and Darby—something he planned to keep to himself.

"What's Leviathan Nash done now?" he asked, motioning to the activity at the window as Bessie peered over heads to see what was going on.

"Seems he's putting up a sign in the front window," Bessie said before sitting down to have a cup of coffee with him—and banishing his thoughts of Darby for the moment.

As much as Jasper had tried to ignore the goings-on, he had to admit the mystery of Leviathan and his shop definitely had caused a stir. Everyone wanted to be the first to see the man and what he was selling. If Leviathan Nash had only arrived late Saturday night, he'd certainly gotten busy quickly and without any apparent help, Jasper noted.

Unable to take it any longer apparently, Bessie got up and wormed her way through her customers to the front window to see for herself. She came back to the table shaking her head. "Apparently the name of his shop is GOSSIP. Well, he's certainly gotten that started. Can't imagine what he sells, though. What is it he doesn't want people to see by keeping the windows covered? It makes a person wonder. I guess that's the idea."

The café patrons returned to their seats when nothing more happened and Bessie went to check her blueberry muffins. Muffin day had never been this busy in the history of the café, he thought.

Across the highway, he could now see the sign reading GOSSIP in large gothic type perched in front of the black paper in one window of the shop. But there was still no open sign.

"If mystery is what he's after, he's certainly achieved his goal," Jasper commented when Bessie returned. "The entire town can't wait to see what's inside."

"Well, they'll have to," she said, lowering her voice conspiratorially. "I've just heard that several residents have received engraved invitations with a date and time for a 'special showing.'"

"The man has interesting marketing skills," Jasper commented as everyone jumped up again. Just before they blocked his view, he saw Vivian "Vi" Mullen walk up to the front door of GOSSIP. She tried the knob and a gasp went up in the café as she opened the door and disappeared inside.

CHAPTER THREE

Vi CLUTCHED THE invitation in her hand as she stepped through the door. She knew already that whatever she would find inside was going to make her even more furious than she already was. The nerve of the man inviting her to see what he had. Was he planning to rub it in her face?

Buckhorn had an antique barn and a general store that sold most everything anyone needed in this town—thanks to her and her family. Why someone would want to open a shop that duplicated that was beyond her. It was just wrong.

She planned to let Leviathan Nash know that he should move on or her name wasn't Vi Mullen. Also GOSSIP was a ridiculous name. She figured the shop wouldn't be in business for even the month he planned to be here—especially if she had anything to do with it.

But as she stepped in, she was momentarily at a loss for words. She'd expected to see the old carriage house full of junk. Or worse, antiques that would rival her own at the barn.

Instead, the space wasn't full at all. There was so little on the shelves that she felt a sense of shock. Was this a joke? She realized he had to be waiting on a shipment because this smattering of stuff was absurd. He couldn't stay in business a week at this rate.

She started to turn around and leave, telling herself she

had better things to do. And to think the man had sent her an engraved invitation for this?

But something caught her eye and stopped her cold.

The beautiful blue crystal vase sat at eye level, a light shining on it, making it even more exquisite. Vi moved toward the vase as if no longer in control of her feet. Her pulse drummed in her ears. It couldn't be. She tried to catch her suddenly ragged breath as she stopped in front of the amazing piece of art, afraid to touch the vase for fear it was a mirage.

"Beautiful, isn't it?" a low, deep voice said from a shadowed far corner of the room.

She could barely pull her gaze away from the vase to look at the man. She realized as she turned that he must have been seated behind the antique desk this whole time. Because of his diminutive size, it was no wonder that she hadn't noticed him when she'd entered the store.

For days she'd been dying to see Leviathan Nash, but right now it was the vase that pulled her attention back. Everything about the light glowing in the crystal broke her heart and healed it all at once. She desperately wanted to own this, but she knew the vase would be horribly expensive. Did she dare?

The one her mother had prized so dearly had been a family heirloom. After Vi had broken it, she'd spent years searching for a replacement without any luck. And now here it was.

"It's very old," Leviathan said suddenly next to her, startling her. The top of the man's head only came to her shoulder. Had his hair not been gray and his face wrinkled with obvious age, she would have thought him a child. And yet his features were full-sized and masculine. It was difficult to gauge his age. Somewhere in his sixties? He wore all black; his gray hair, much too long, grazed his shoulders. But it was his deep-set dark eyes that gave her a start. Vi would have sworn that she'd never seen him before in her life, but there was something about him that was strangely familiar.

"How…" Her voice broke. "How much is it?"

"Since you're my first customer, fifty dollars."

She stared at him, her mouth hanging open. She knew how rare the vase was. Had she been able to find one during her last search, it would have cost her over a thousand dollars.

"Go ahead. Pick it up. You can hold it," Leviathan said in his low, soothing voice.

She swallowed and carefully reaching out, took the vase in both of her hands. The moment she did, she knew. The weight was right, everything about it was right. This was exactly like the one her mother had loved so much.

"I'll take it." When she looked over at him he was smiling, exposing perfect little teeth that reminded her of corn on the cob that wasn't fully ripened.

"An excellent choice," he said and walked back to his desk. "Let me wrap it for you."

She hesitated, not wanting to give it up even for a moment. But at his insistence, she handed the vase over. She watched him carefully wrap it in white tissue paper with surprisingly large strong-looking hands.

"I'm putting my card in here. You'll want to keep it because it will allow you to come back in case there is a problem or there is anything else you would like," he said as he put the tissue paper–wrapped package into a white bag.

She quickly dug in her purse, pulled out two twenties and a ten, and handed them over. Reaching for her package, she met his dark gaze and felt that uncomfortable stirring again at the edge of her memory.

But as she headed for the door, she quickly forgot about

Leviathan Nash. She stepped outside, passing elderly Anita Berg who was studying her invitation and checking her watch impatiently. "What did you get?" Anita asked, but Vi didn't answer.

She was too anxious to go home with her find. Although she was half-afraid that when she got home the vase wouldn't be wrapped in the tissue paper because this whole experience was a dream she would awake from at any moment. Or worse that she would open the bag and lying in the tissue paper would be dozens of broken pieces like the one before it.

The heat of shame flushed her cheeks as she remembered the day her mother's vase had been shattered. She'd been fifteen and playing outside with her friends when she'd heard her mother scream. They'd all run inside to see what was wrong. Her mother stood, head bent next to the table, sobbing hysterically.

Vi had stepped closer and seen the shattered vase on the floor. But it was the baseball beside it that made her eyes widen in alarm and her heart drop. She and her friends had been playing baseball outside earlier. Her gaze went to the open screen-less window next to the dining room table.

She knew at once what must have happened. She and her friend Karla had gotten into an argument. Vi had thrown the ball at her as hard as she could and then stormed off in anger. She'd thought that she'd heard the ball hit the side of the house near Karla, but apparently it had ricocheted into the open window.

Her mother hastily wiped her tears, reached down and picked up the ball from the floor among the pieces of broken blue crystal. With heartbreak in her face, her mother had handed her the ball. The only thing Vera Mullen had said was, "Clean up this mess."

Vi had taken the pieces to her room and tried to glue them back together. But there was no saving the vase. It was ruined and she had never forgiven herself.

Rushing inside the house now, she put the package down gingerly on the table her mother had left her and carefully unwrapped the new vase. She knew it couldn't make up for what she'd done all those years ago. Her mother had been dead for some years now, but Vi still felt that somehow this new vase made amends for the past.

As she placed the vase in the center of the dining room table in the spot where the other one had always sat, she felt her heart lift. She'd needed this. Last year had been awful. This, she told herself, was a sign that her luck had changed. From now on, things would get even better.

But as she went to throw the tissue paper and bag away, Leviathan's business card fluttered to the floor. She doubted she had any reason to go back to the shop, but still, she bent down to pick it up. As she did, she saw the words neatly printed on the back side of the card.

She read the words twice, her pulse a deafening roar in her ears. Her vision blurred bloodred. Her hands shook. She stumbled back, hitting her hip on the edge of the table. The vase rocked for a moment before tumbling over, then rolled toward the edge of the table and dropped over the edge. It hit the floor and shattered, the sound as loud as a gunshot.

But Vi Mullen hardly noticed. She stormed toward the door with only one thing on her mind. Murder.

AT THE SOUND of someone at the door, Karla Parson wrapped her robe around her and stumbled out barefoot. She glanced over her shoulder to make sure the bedroom door was closed before she opened her front door to find Vi Mullen standing there.

She blinked. Vi was the last person she expected to see. They hadn't been close in years. Neither traveled in the same small circles in Buckhorn nor had they said two words to each other the few times they'd crossed paths. Karla knew that Vi wouldn't spit on her if she was on fire, so what was the woman doing on her doorstep at this time of the morning?

Before she could ask, Vi lunged at her, going for her throat. Bony, strong fingers closed around her neck. Karla was so surprised that she didn't even try to protect herself. She fell back, stumbling and falling to the floor, landing hard. Vi fell with her, those hands still clutched around her throat, the nails digging into her flesh as Vi screamed something unintelligible in her face.

Karla's first thought was that Vi had finally gone bonkers. Everyone in town had been expecting it. The woman had been teetering on the edge for years. But nuttier than her grandmother's fruitcake or not, Vi was cutting off all her air supply. Unable to breathe, Karla realized that the woman was going to kill her if she didn't do something to stop her.

She fought to pry the woman's hands from her throat, surprised at just how strong Vi was. Stars sparked in her eyes as darkness began to leak in at the edges of her vision. As the words the woman was screaming in her face finally registered, Karla felt a start. This was over that ugly blue vase Vi's mother thought was worth something?

As the darkness shouldered its way in, Karla realized she was going to die over some old broken vase. Wouldn't her mother be surprised that her death came at the hands of her former childhood friend and not one of Karla's loser boyfriends.

CHAPTER FOUR

JASPER HEARD ABOUT Vi Mullen's arrest for assault the next morning at the café. The news had swept through town. But it wasn't until Bessie sat down to join him in his booth that he heard the whole story.

"Everyone is saying that Vi lost her mind and attacked Karla Parson and would have killed her if Karla's latest boyfriend, AJ something or another, hadn't pulled her off," Bessie said.

"When did this happen?" Jasper asked.

"Yesterday morning. Not long after you were in the café. Apparently, it had something to do with her mother Vera's crystal vase that Karla had purposely broke when they were kids—but that Vi had been blamed for breaking all these years."

Jasper thought about seeing Vi that morning going into the new shop and coming out with a package. It made him wonder if the attack had anything to do with what she'd bought in Gossip's yesterday.

Bessie voiced the same thought a moment later. "Why would Vi suddenly decide to settle the score now after all these years?" She shook her head. "The marshal had to be called for a half dozen other disturbances as well since yesterday. Fistfights in the street, people threatening to shoot each other, husbands and wives getting thrown out on their ears."

He was surprised to hear this. There was always some-thing going on in Buckhorn, but never to this extent.

"You'd think there was a full moon or something got into the water." Bessie leaned toward him and dropped her voice. "Anita Berg took a baseball bat to her husband. Al-most killed him before he got away. Heard she threw all his things out in the yard and set them on fire. Volunteer fire department had to be called. The woman is almost eighty. The rumor is that she found out he'd had an affair fifty years ago with one of her bridesmaids."

"It *is* strange," Jasper agreed and glanced across the street at the new shop. Whatever Leviathan Nash was sell-ing, it seemed to have gotten the whole town riled up. "Been to Gossip yet?"

Bessie shook her head. "Nothing I need. Not that I got an invitation. You?"

"Me neither." He was curious about the man since all this seemed to have started with his arrival, but not curi-ous enough to want to see the shop or the man. "Have you seen him yet?"

"Only a glimpse when I ran over to drop off his to-go order at about five," she said. "He barely opened the door. He looks harmless enough from what I could see of him. He's small for a man, gray and wrinkled." Short and old had been the description Jasper had heard so that pretty much matched it.

"It's funny, though," Bessie continued. "There was al-most something familiar about him. But I can't put my fin-ger on it. Makes you wonder why he chose Buckhorn for his shop. You think maybe he has kin around here?"

"Don't remember anyone named Nash. Have you heard what he sells?" Jasper asked.

"Not much from what I've seen of those coming out after their 'special showing.' Can't see anything with the windows covered like that." She grinned. "Okay, I was curious. I might have tried to peek in, if there had been even a little space between the black paper and the window frame. There wasn't. What do you make of the name? Gossip?"

"It certainly has people talking so I suppose that's the purpose." But if Leviathan was behind the latest incidents in town, then he was apparently dispensing the gossip. But why would anyone believe him since he'd only just arrived in town and wouldn't know all the scuttlebutt unless like Bessie said, he was related to someone in the area.

The timer went off in the kitchen. "That will be my apple coffee cake," Bessie said as she took her coffee and left. Her baking was legendary and clearly she enjoyed it and running the café. People knew what day of the week it was by what Bessie was baking.

He glanced at his plate and his half-eaten breakfast and realized that he'd lost his appetite. It didn't improve when Buckhorn's new newspaper owner, editor and reporter slid into the booth across from him.

Darby Prudence Fulton dropped her notebook on the table, flipped it open it to a blank page and picked up her pen. "I'm doing a piece on the new shop," she said without preamble.

"Good morning to you too, Darby," he said. She had a cute button nose with a sprinkling of freckles that always made him smile against his will.

She mugged a face before motioning to the teenaged waitress that she was good, waving off both breakfast and coffee. Energy radiated from her. Darby had only recently moved to town to start a weekly online newspaper that would cover the county. Most of the locals were already laying odds as to how long she would last.

"So, Jasper, what do you think of Gossip?" she asked, pen poised above the paper.

"Gossip in general?" he asked. "I don't encourage it."

She rolled her eyes. "Help me out here. I'm having trouble getting anyone to talk who's been inside the shop."

"Well, don't look at me," Jasper said. "I didn't get an invitation."

"Me neither," she said and glanced around the café. It was still early so the place was almost empty. Apple coffee cake was good, but didn't pack residents in early. Also, the frenzy of staring out the window at Gossip with its blacked-out windows was apparently beginning to wane some. Though he did notice that the town's worst gossip, Marjorie Keen, was sitting by the window where she couldn't miss who came and went. He wouldn't be surprised if she was taking notes.

He turned his attention to the woman across from him, remembering the party at Montana State University in Bozeman where they first met. It had been a night he'd never forgotten. So, imagine his shock when she turned up in Buckhorn—and acted as if they'd never met before.

He'd mentioned that they'd met in college, but she'd said she didn't remember him—or what they'd shared that night, for that matter. He didn't bother reminding her since apparently it hadn't been that memorable for her, which had been a direct hit to his ego. Worse, he'd been disappointed since he'd never forgotten her or that night.

But at the same time, he was relieved. The last thing he wanted was a trip down memory lane. He wasn't interested in seeing if the chemistry he'd felt that night so long ago was still there—or worse that it had never even been real.

Darby was still too appealing as it was. Her blond hair was shorter now, cut in a tousled pixie that made him want to run his fingers through it. Her brown eyes were still that warm honey he remembered. Everything about her was the girl next door, the one you wanted to protect at the same time you wanted to ravage.

Good thing he wasn't in the market. But whatever it was about Darby, she was the first woman in a long time to even tempt him. The thought did nothing for his appetite. He pushed his plate away.

"Don't you think it's odd that anyone who got an invitation doesn't want to talk about the shop or what they bought? Or maybe more to the point, what they did once they left the shop?" she asked.

"Haven't really given it any thought." Which wasn't quite true, he knew. But he didn't want to see any speculation on his part in the newspaper.

The waitress came to take his plate. Darby snatched a slice of his uneaten toast before it was taken away.

"You have to have heard about the strange things that have been happening around town," she said between bites. She lowered her voice. She was sexiest when she wasn't trying. "Everyone involved in the 'incidents' received an invitation to Gossip. Even you have to admit that's odd."

"*Even* me?"

She finished his toast and borrowed his napkin to wipe her mouth. "I would think a former homicide detective would have more of an interest in what was going on than you seem to." She eyed him speculatively. "But maybe that's why you retired before forty. You just weren't cut out for it."

He smiled, aware of what she was trying to do. He thought about the night they'd met in college. Had she challenged him that night too? Was that why he'd kissed her? Or was kissing those bow-shaped lips just something he felt he had to do? She'd looked surprised, shocked actually, by the sudden kiss. She'd opened her mouth, closed it, and then their gazes had met and that had been his downfall.

He was graduating the next day, but still he'd tried to find her. She'd left campus and without a number or even her last name... He'd told himself it wasn't meant to be even as he'd wished he was wrong.

Now here she was, messing with all his instincts that told him this woman was trouble. She threw him off balance. Worse, she made him wish for things he refused to even consider.

"Are you trying to bait me, Ms. Fulton?" Even as he deflected her gibe, he worried about the look in her eye. The last thing he wanted was her digging into his past. He knew that she'd been a damned good reporter, having won numerous awards for investigative reporting at several prestigious large newspapers. It crossed his mind that she might have a past she didn't want dug into as well. Why else had she quit a good job to strike out on her own here, of all places?

"Why Buckhorn?" he asked, hoping to get that gleam out of her brown eyes—and throw her off him as the subject—especially if there was something in her past she didn't want him to know. "You worked at some good papers. Just curious what would make you give that up?" He laughed, seeing something cross her expression before she covered it. "Don't like having the shoe on the other foot, do you?"

He could see that she got his point. He liked that about her. She was smart and quick witted and tenacious, all things he admired. But even as he returned her jab, he knew he was also curious about her and the years since he'd last seen her.

"Well? You like to ask people personal questions. How about answering mine?"

For a moment, he thought she would tell him it was none of his business.

"I wanted my own business. I needed a new challenge. What about you? What's your excuse for being in Buckhorn?"

"I'm from here so not unusual to return home. Also, I like ranching." He saw that gleam in her eye again. "Which reminds me. I've got cattle to feed." He slid out of the booth and stood. What had made him think he could throw her off the scent? This woman was much better at jousting than he was.

Darby slowly closed her notebook, picked it and her pen up and rose as well. He was momentarily distracted by how well her sweater and jeans fit her curvy petite frame. This, he reminded himself, was why he did his best to avoid her. The woman seemed to be awakening something in him. He'd been perfectly happy with it hibernating. But spring had come in more ways than one. He was beginning to feel again and he hated it.

"Something weird is going on in this town, whether you want to admit it or not," she said with a shake of her head. "What do we even know about Leviathan Nash?" she asked as she followed him to the counter.

"I'm assuming you've dug up his past from birth to present, leaving no stone unturned," Jasper said, just wanting to get home. "You tell me."

She shook her head. "That's the thing. I haven't been able to find *anything* on him. No social media, no last known address, no nothing. It's as if he doesn't exist. At least not as Leviathan Nash."

That surprised him as he dug out his wallet and dropped a twenty on the counter with his bill. Bessie was in the back so he had to wait for her to take it. The man had lied about his name? Jasper just hoped he didn't stiff Melissa on the rent.

"Clearly the man has something to hide," Darby said as a slow smile curved those irresistible lips. She had his attention and she knew it. "I need his prints or his DNA to prove that he isn't the man he claims to be. I thought that if you'd gotten an invitation, you'd help me."

Jasper shook his head. He didn't want to get involved. Not with Darby. Not with the mystery of Leviathan Nash. He'd come back to Buckhorn to avoid everything about his old life. "More than likely he's exactly who he appears to be, an old man just trying to make a living."

She looked at him as if she had expected as much from him. The disappointment he saw in her expression hurt, though, even as he told himself he didn't care what she thought of him. She didn't even remember the kiss and what they'd shared that night. Even if he got the chance to kiss her again…

"I have to go," he said to her. "Bessie, I'm leaving my money here on the counter," he called through the pass-through. She nodded in answer as she took a large pan from the oven.

"Something is wrong," Darby said defiantly as she started to follow him.

He stopped and she collided with him as he reached back and picked up the keys she'd left on the counter. "Here, you might need these."

She rolled her eyes and snatched them from him. "I'm always losing my keys, believe me it's no big deal—unlike what is going on in this town." She shook her head as she dropped the keys into her purse. "I shouldn't have expected any help from you. Don't worry. I'll get to the bottom of it without you."

He saw the stubborn determination in her jutted jaw and fiery glint in those brown eyes. Suddenly he felt real concern for her. She was right. The man was probably hiding something or he wouldn't be using a fake name. Add to that, a lot of weird things had been happening since Gossip had opened. Jasper was suddenly reminded of the crows he'd seen the evening Leviathan had come to town. He realized that he hadn't seen them since.

He stopped on the sidewalk in front of his pickup, not surprised that she'd followed him out. "Just be careful, okay?"

She brushed a lock of blond hair back from her forehead and settled those honey-brown eyes on him. "Don't tell me that you're worried about me. Why would you be if Leviathan Nash is merely some old man just trying to make a living?"

"Because, as you said, weird things have been happening. If he finds out that you're investigating him and he really does have something to hide, then it could be dangerous."

Darby scoffed. The tip of her tongue poked out for an

instant to trail across her upper lip, distracting him for a moment. She stopped whatever she'd been about to say until she could see that she had his full attention again. "I can take care of myself, but it's good to know that you aren't as disinterested in other people as you pretend to be. That gives me hope that whatever made you a homicide detective is still in there." With that, and a toss of her head, she walked away, calling back over her shoulder, "Thanks for the toast."

CHAPTER FIVE

DARBY WALKED DOWN the street trying to catch her breath. Being around Jasper set so many emotions in motion. She heard him drive by, but she pretended not to look. Had she really thought he would help her?

She shook her head as she watched the pickup disappear down the highway. The man infuriated her as much as he attracted her on some primal level. It was her own fault, she told herself, that she'd let him get under her skin again.

Taking another breath, she let it out and walked the rest of the way down the street to her office. The man was impossible. How could he ignore what was happening in Buckhorn? She couldn't believe he'd been a homicide detective. And yet she could. Something had happened to make him quit, to make him come here, to make him build a stone wall around him. He was definitely not the man she'd met that night at college.

But what had happened to him? He could pretend he wasn't hiding out here in Buckhorn, but she knew better. She was doing some hiding herself. She'd dug into his past, but had hit a brick wall. Whatever had made him quit was big enough that it was buried deep.

She thought about the man who'd come to her rescue all those years ago. Her friend had insisted they go to the last college party of the year when Darby would have rather been at home packing and then reading a good book. The next day she would be leaving and a few days after that, she would be starting her first real job at a newspaper.

Jasper had found her behind the party house alone, staring up at the moon and thinking about her future. She quickly realized that unlike most of the young men at the party he hadn't sought her out to try to seduce her. He'd come to the party with friends and had been looking for a place to hide until his friends were ready to leave. They'd realized that they were kindred souls. Talking to him had been so easy. They'd bonded, growing close quickly.

When he'd leaned in to kiss her, it had felt more than right.

Now she chided herself for pretending she didn't remember him or that night. It had been everything she'd ever dreamed for her first time—until the police had busted up the party. A girl doesn't forget her first real kiss, the kind that curled her toes, or her first time with someone gentle and sweet and loving.

She'd never known true desire until then. She'd never wanted a night to last forever. She'd dated in high school and college, but she'd been more interested in her career than any of the men she'd met. Until Jasper.

She'd always wondered what would have happened if the police hadn't come and broken up the party. She remembered hurrying to get dressed as people were fleeing the house. She'd been so shocked by the tsunami of emotions Jasper Cole had evoked in her—to be so rudely interrupted. She'd looked into his smoky gray eyes and had felt as if she might cry at how beautiful it had been.

Jasper, who was a senior and about to graduate, had tried to talk to her, but a policeman had stuck his head in the door and told them to get moving. Once out in the hallway, they'd gotten separated. They didn't see each other again—until a few weeks ago.

That's why it had felt like fate when she'd stopped for gas in Buckhorn, Montana, and had seen him again. She'd recognized him right away. His dark hair was longer now, curling at his neck, but his eyes were the color of twilight framed by thick dark lashes. He wasn't classically handsome with his strong jaw and that scar under the lock of dark hair that fell over his forehead. He was a man with rough edges and strong-looking hands and a strength in more than those broad shoulders of his. Everything about him now was even sexier than when he'd been in college.

Why Buckhorn, he'd asked? She sighed as she reached her office, unlocked the door and stepped inside. Darby told herself it hadn't all been about Jasper Cole. Nestled in the mountains in the middle of Montana, Buckhorn had its appeal. Also, she'd gotten a deal on a combo office downstairs and apartment space upstairs.

So why not Buckhorn? Maybe she'd hoped that Jasper would remember her and what they'd shared and tell her that she hadn't been wrong about the chemistry that had practically set her on fire that night. But it *had* been years and only that one night. Everyone said he was a loner, destined to be one of those old rancher bachelors. Maybe it was true since he certainly hadn't shown much interest since she'd come to town.

Not that she was giving up, she thought with a smile as she looked around her tiny office. She was here to stay. The room was just large enough for a desk, two chairs, a mini refrigerator and a large plant. The plant might have been a mistake, she thought now. It towered over the corner next to the front window. The darned thing was so huge that it dominated the room. She could easily hide behind it and had actually done just that a few times to avoid those she didn't want to see.

Slipping behind her desk, she opened her laptop, determined to go to work and get her mind off Jasper. In retrospect, she probably shouldn't have lied about not remembering him. But she hadn't wanted him to think that he was the only reason she'd chosen Buckhorn as her base. It was embarrassing that an encounter interrupted by the police back in college might have influenced her when she'd chosen Buckhorn. She shook her head, realizing that her thoughts had gone right back to him, straight as an arrow.

Darby considered herself too sensible to have moved here—let alone stayed—because of some man. Even Jasper Cole. Her online newspaper was actually doing fairly well. The Buckhorn area was quite picturesque, so every week she uploaded photos she'd taken of the mountains, the sunrises and sunsets, the main drag filled with tourists.

The paper had caught the attention of advertisers throughout the state because of the interest of those wanting to come to a unique part of Montana. Locally, she'd picked up some ads as well. She'd even talked Vi Mullen, who'd openly ridiculed her newspaper at first, into buying several large ads highlighting her businesses.

What she hadn't had was any luck selling an ad to Leviathan Nash. He was a hard man to get in to see. The front door of his shop was always locked—until someone with an invitation was let in. The door quickly locked behind the person. Too quickly, she'd learned.

She was dying to find out what happened once the residents got inside. Maybe he hypnotized them, forcing them to do random acts. Were the acts of violence random? If she could just get Vi to talk to her about her visit—and the assault charge against her. Vi was out of jail on bail and back at her job as postmistress in the back of her store. Her family ran the store and the antique barn. Her daughter, Tina, helped out when she could since she had Chloe, who was still a toddler. Tina's husband, Lars, worked for Vi as well. But apparently Vi hadn't confided in them about Gossip or why she'd come out of the shop ready to kill Karla Parson.

After grabbing her purse, Darby hit the street. The rest of the day, she did her best to talk to people about Gossip. Vi still flat out refused to say a word. Darby canvassed the whole town. By nightfall, she was exhausted and hadn't found anyone willing to talk who'd been inside Gossip and she knew she would do it all again the next day.

CHAPTER SIX

WEDNESDAY MORNING, DARBY woke more determined than ever. She'd awakened in the middle of the night with an idea and had gotten out of bed to explore it. Back in bed, she'd been more convinced than ever that she was onto something.

The sun rose in a cloudless blue sky making the snow-capped mountains glisten like fields of diamonds. The air smelled of evergreen and a Montana spring. After grabbing her camera, notebook and the handful of tiles from her old Scrabble game that had been in the family for years, she headed for the café where she knew she could find Jasper Cole having breakfast with Bessie. She felt a surge of hope. Her newspaper had to be about more than pretty pictures and what Bessie was baking at the café this week and the drink specials and music at Dave's bar Friday and Saturday nights.

She knew she couldn't bust this story wide-open without help. The problem was getting that help. Not that she didn't enjoy seeing him, she thought with a grin. Too bad he didn't seem all that thrilled to see her.

JASPER GROANED INWARDLY as Darby slid into the booth across from him. Was this going to be an every weekday occurrence now? He did fairly well when he could avoid her. But this…

"I think Leviathan Nash's name is like an anagram," she said, her face animated, eyes bright.

He stared at her as she reached into her pocket and dropped a handful of Scrabble tiles onto the table. He watched as she began to make words. She turned the first word so he could read it. AVENTAILS.

"Aventails?" He frowned. "What is that?"

"It means *avenger*." She began to scramble the letters again.

He watched as she put together SHAVETAIL and turned it with a look of told-you-so on her face. He shook his head. "I wouldn't even venture a guess."

"One of the meanings is *shattering*."

"Fascinating," he said and took a bite of his breakfast. Bessie was back in the kitchen, seeing to the giant biscuits she made that practically floated they were so light. "Darby, you seem to have a lot of free time on your hands." She mugged a face at him as she began to pick through the letters again.

As he chewed, she made another word. "You're assuming that Leviathan might know the meaning to any of these words, right?" he asked.

"It could be subconscious on his part," she said with a knowing look as she turned the letters so he could see.

He stared at the word ANNALIST. "I'm guessing annihilate."

"Good guess," she said, smiling, and picked through the tiles yet again until they read INHALANTS. "*Ingratitude*. Don't you see it? Revenge that will shatter the ungrateful. And his final goal, to destroy those he feels have wronged him."

"Wow." He laughed. He couldn't help himself. "You got

all of that from the letters of a name you said isn't even really his?"

She scooped up the tiles and stuffed them back into her pocket like a magician finishing her final act. "Leviathan Nash is here to get revenge. He didn't just randomly pick Buckhorn, Montana, out of a hat. He didn't just make up his fake name. It means *something*."

Jasper couldn't help but smile at her. "It probably does mean something to him. But you can also use those letters to make the word *aliens*."

She glared at him.

"The point is this doesn't prove *anything*." He pushed his plate toward her. "Toast?"

She clearly grudgingly accepted a half slice and took a bite, chewing as she continued glaring at him.

"I'm not arguing with you, okay? I'm just not getting involved."

"Even knowing what we know now?" she demanded, waving the piece of toast around.

"The only thing we *know* according to you is that Leviathan Nash isn't his real name. It's more like a stage name, which isn't illegal."

"What about the trouble he's causing?" she demanded before taking another bite of toast.

"Also not illegal—even if you could prove it."

"So, you aren't going to help me," she said as she tossed the remainder of the toast back on his plate. He saw that he'd hurt her feelings. He wanted to pull her into his arms and hold her. He really wished she wasn't so darned nearly irresistible. Or that he didn't feel such a pull toward her whenever she was around. Worse, that pull just kept getting stronger. "Then what *are* you going to do?" she demanded.

"I'm going to take my dog home and work on my trac-
tor." He pushed to his feet.

"How can you just ignore what's going on?" she said as
she rose from the booth.

"Because it's none of my business."

She scoffed at that. "I believe some Germans said that
when Hitler was coming into power."

Jasper laughed. "Not even a close comparison." He
turned and walked to the counter to pay. Out of the corner
of his eye, he watched Darby leave and shook his head. *That
woman's going to be the death of you.* Where had that come
from? he wondered, and felt growing unease as he stepped
outside. A chill rippled across his skin as if someone was
watching him. He hadn't experienced that feeling since he
was working in homicide.

He glanced toward Gossip and noticed a corner of the
black paper covering the window fall back into place.

CHAPTER SEVEN

On the way to the ranch later that afternoon after picking up feed, fencing and dog food in the next town, Jasper found himself trying to recall a local family by the name of Nash or anything close to it. He came up empty.

But then again, if the man was using an assumed name... Jasper had spent his first eight years in Buckhorn. Then one day his father had packed them up, leaving the family ranch and Buckhorn behind. He'd never understood what had happened, but his parents had been different after that. They still seemed to love each other and him, but the light had gone out of his mother's eyes and his father had tried too hard to pretend that nothing had changed.

When his grandmother died and six months later his parents were killed in a car wreck, he'd gone back to Buckhorn to live with his grandfather. After graduating, he'd gone into the military and then worked his way up in law enforcement to a homicide detective. When his grandfather passed and there was no one to take care of the ranch, he'd inherited it. But he'd been young and broke so he'd sold it.

When things had gone south with his job, he'd had nowhere to go. Buckhorn had come to mind. He'd saved some money over the years and realized that he needed peace and quiet as well as the hard work that went with running a small cattle ranch. There was always work to be done.

Other than sneaking off to have an early breakfast with

Bessie at the café five days a week, he saw few people except for her husband, Earl Ray. Jasper told himself that he'd been just fine with that.

But then Darby had shown up and distracted him with thoughts of her too much of the time. Now she had him thinking about Leviathan Nash when he was adamant about not getting involved. But she was right. There had to be an explanation for the odd things that had been happening in town. It was too much of a coincidence that the trouble had begun the same time Leviathan Nash had opened Gossip.

Bessie had said something about Leviathan Nash had seemed familiar. If his name wasn't Nash at all as Darby suspected, then who was the man and why Buckhorn? If Leviathan was dispensing gossip as Jasper suspected, then how did he know so much about the people here unless he had kin here?

As he pulled up to the ranch house, he tried to shake off his thoughts. He wasn't getting involved. Leviathan Nash, or whoever he was, would be gone by the end of the month. Jasper was assuming that the man only had so many secrets to dispense—if he was actually responsible for the havoc in town—and might even leave sooner.

He started to get out of his truck when he realized something was wrong. *Someone had been here.* He lived far enough out of town that he didn't get many visitors. That and his usual unfriendliness kept people away. But there was no doubt that he'd had a visitor. Something was hanging on his front door. It appeared to be a small white bag now fluttering in the breeze.

Next to him on the passenger seat his dog, Ruby, spotted the bag and began a low growl. The black-and-white springer spaniel was six months old, a present from Bessie. Had anyone else tried to give him a puppy, he wouldn't have stood for it.

"You need a dog," Bessie had said one morning at the café after they'd had breakfast together. She'd said the words as if that settled it. "The Urdahls had a litter and I thought of you." She'd stepped outside, come back into the café and shoved the round fur ball into his arms. "I call her Ruby." Ruby had cut her dark eyes at him as she'd wagged her unbobbed tail and licked him in the face. "You need the company and she needs a good home. Now get that dog out of my café."

Bessie had said the last as she'd disappeared into the kitchen, leaving him holding the puppy. He told himself he'd find a good home for the dog. In the meantime, he took Ruby home. He should have known that was a bad idea—even temporarily. He hadn't wanted the responsibility since he had little faith that he could even take care of himself some days.

But something about Ruby had ensnared his heart and as time passed without trying to find someone to take the pup, he'd realized that Bessie was right. He'd needed Ruby more than she'd needed him. She was good company. She didn't have much to say, didn't get mad at him even when he scolded her and she was always happy to see him. He'd never found a woman like that. If he had, he joked to himself, he would have hung on to her.

Opening his pickup door, he stepped out into the cool spring air. The sun lolled in the big blue sky. The breeze stirred the nearby pines. Ruby came flying out with him and raced to the front door, barking. He slammed the truck door and followed her to see what someone had left him. Telling Ruby to hush, he climbed the steps to the porch and reached for the bag. It looked familiar and it took him a moment before he remembered where he'd seen one like it.

Vi had been carrying a bag the same color when she'd exited Gossip—before she'd gotten arrested for assault. The only difference was that this bag was smaller. The way it fluttered in the wind, he could see that it didn't hold much—if anything.

Unhooking it from the doorknob, he took a moment to look around. He couldn't shake the feeling that he was being watched. He rubbed the back of his neck for a few seconds before he looked inside the bag.

At first, he saw nothing. Why would someone hook an empty bag on his front door? Then the wind caught the bag and made a fluttering sound erupt inside it. He saw the small card with the neat script.

Widening the drawstring opening to get his hand inside, he caught the card in his fist. As he plucked it out, he saw that it was an engraved invitation to Gossip. His "special showing" was next Monday morning at eight. The date and time struck him like a fist. It was as if Leviathan Nash knew that he would be just across the street at the café and would have probably finished his breakfast by then.

The hair prickled on his neck. This man knew way too much about the goings-on in Buckhorn—past and present. Jasper fought the urge to go over there, bust down the door and—

He shook his head, reminding himself that he wasn't a cop anymore. He was a civilian. He'd promised him that he'd put that other life behind him.

WHEN DARBY WENT by the post office in the back of the general store to try to question Vi once again, the woman saw her coming. Approaching the small gated opening in the wall marked Postmistress, Darby barely reached her before Vi pulled down the closure with a bang and locked it.

Darby clearly wasn't going to get anywhere with Vi right now. She stood there for a moment, then decided maybe the best approach would be to visit Karla Parson. She'd asked around for directions before driving to the outskirts of town and down a dirt road to what had once been a trailer park. Only a few trailers remained, Karla's and several abandoned ones that appeared to be used for storage since the doors hung open. A stripped-down motorcycle leaned against a post beside the one trailer that looked occupied.

As Darby got out of her car, she took in the view of the mountains. This was a beautiful spot with the dark green of the pines and the golden of the rocky cliffs as a backdrop. Unfortunately, it wasn't that far from the dump, which could explain why most everyone had moved on.

She climbed the steps to a small wooden deck and knocked. Inside came the sound of movement, then nothing. She knocked again, knowing that Karla would have heard her drive up.

Finally, the door opened a crack. "Yes?" asked a woman who looked as if she'd been awakened by the knock—even though it was well after noon. Darby reminded herself that according to the police report, the last time Karla had been awakened she was almost killed by Vi Mullen. That could explain why she looked so leery.

"I'm Darby Fulton. I don't believe we've met. I own the newspaper in town."

Karla frowned. "I don't want to buy no newspaper." She started to close the door.

"I'm not here to sell you one," Darby said quickly. "I need your side of the story about your attack."

The door stopped closing. "I don't know what Vi told you, but if it's 'bout that ugly vase again…"

"I just want my readers to have the whole story, the *true* story," Darby added, and the door opened.

Karla Parson pulled her threadbare pink chenille robe around her and motioned Darby into the trailer. As she stepped in, the woman got busy clearing a place for her to sit on the cluttered couch. "I need coffee. You want some?" Karla was already stepping into the kitchen just off the living area, her bare feet slapping the worn linoleum floor.

Darby took a seat on the edge of the couch and looked down the hallway toward the closed door. She thought of the motorbike parked outside. There'd also been a couple of old cars parked nearby. One looked as if it might run. Which meant Karla might not be alone. Hadn't a boyfriend, AJ Rasmussen, pulled Vi off her during the attack? She could see Karla stirring spoonfuls of instant coffee into two mismatched cups.

"Whatever Vi told you, it's a lie," Karla said as she brought over both coffee cups and handed one to her.

Darby set it on the scarred end table next to her and pulled out her notebook and pen. "Why don't you tell me your side of it."

Karla drank a large gulp of her coffee, shuddered and then settled herself into the recliner with a groan, both from her and the chair. "Vi always thought she was somethin' special. So did her mother, Vera. You'd think that vase was made a gold. It was cheap and ugly. My mother said she'd seen a much prettier one at a garage sale for a dollar." She took another gulp of coffee.

"I'm sure you didn't mean to break it," Darby said.

That got a howl of laughter from down the hallway. "Like hell she didn't," hollered a male voice.

"You stay out of this, AJ," Karla yelled back, then returned her attention to Darby. Darby recalled the report. Alan John Rasmussen, address unknown, unemployed, rap sheet full of small crimes including involvement with a biker gang in California, now out on parole. He apparently owned that stripped-down motorcycle outside.

"Where was I?" Karla asked irritably—loud enough for her boyfriend to hear.

"You were going to tell the truth," AJ called.

Karla flipped him off, although as far as Darby could tell, AJ couldn't see her through the closed door of the back bedroom.

"What if I did do it on purpose?" she continued sounding defensive. "I was sick of Vera always going on about how special it was as if the rest of us didn't have nothing special on our dining room table at home."

"You didn't," AJ yelled. "Hell, you didn't even have a dining room let alone a table." His laugh echoed down the hallway.

Karla gritted her teeth for a moment. "Don't pay no attention to him. He doesn't know nothing. Vi was always lording stuff over us. I was sick of it. I threw a ball better than she did. She tried to hit me, but the ball missed by a mile. I picked it up…" The woman smiled, eyes narrowing. "I saw that vase sitting there past that open window and I wound up and I threw it as hard as I could." She let out a laugh. "I hit it smack on. Sent it flying off that table. When it hit the floor…" She looked at Darby and wiped the smile off her face. "Okay, it was a mean thing to do, but how was I to know that Vi got blamed for it? No vase is cause to be killing someone. I hope Vi gets the chair."

"They use lethal injection in Montana now, but since she didn't kill you—"

"She would have if I hadn't pulled the bitch off of her," AJ called.

Karla nodded in agreement. "I'd be dead as a doornail if it weren't for him and all because of that ugly-ass vase." She shook her head. "Strange what sets a person off, huh?"

Darby agreed. "I'm also doing a story on the new shop in town, Gossip. Have you been inside it yet?"

Karla shook her head. "My mother got an invitation. She was goin' this morning. I ain't talked to her. Doubt she'll buy nothing much."

"Your mother is…" She poised her pen over her notebook.

"Nancy Green. She's retired. Used to babysit most of the kids in this county until my stepfather keeled over and now she don't have to work no more since he left her his house."

Darby got the woman's address. "Have you seen the owner of the shop?"

Again, Karla shook her head. "I don't get to town much."

Closing her notebook, she rose. "Well, thank you for your time."

"How do I get a copy of the paper?" Karla said as she drained her coffee cup, set it aside and rose.

Darby hadn't touched hers so she quickly picked up her full cup. Stepping into the kitchen. She turned on the faucet, poured out the coffee as she rinsed her cup and set it in the sink. "You can read it online on your computer or your phone." From the woman's expression, she had neither. "Or if you stop by my office in town I'll print out a copy for you." She could see that Karla probably wasn't that interested if it meant going to all that trouble.

"Thank you again," Darby said and left. As she drove away, she could hear an argument break out in the back of the trailer.

JASPER WAS STILL holding the invitation when he heard a vehicle coming up his road. He looked in that direction, but couldn't make out who it was yet. The spring day was all sunshine now. He could feel the heat of it against his back. It was the kind of day that he loved. He realized he hadn't noticed how beautiful the day was until that moment—and blamed Darby, who he suspected was his visitor.

He quickly pocketed the card and pulled the bag from the door. If it was Darby coming up the road, she was the last person he wanted to know that he had gotten an invitation to Gossip. She'd nag him to death over it when he had no intention of going. Leviathan Nash was a fool if he thought he had any interest in showing up next Monday or any other day.

To his surprise—and admittedly a little disappointment— he saw the marshal's vehicle headed his way. Balling up the bag, he opened his front door, sent Ruby inside and closed the door. He stuffed the bag into a corner of the porch chair.

Then he tried to relax as he watched Marshal Leroy Baggins park and climb from his cruiser. Leroy was tall and slim with wide shoulders and big hands. He looked like a man who could take you down without any trouble—and would—at the least provocation.

Unless you looked at his face. It was so darned pleasant that it seemed inconceivable that he could be one of the toughest marshals in the state.

Leroy stopped on the bottom porch step, resting an elbow on the railing. "'Suppose you've heard about the goings-on in town lately," the marshal said.

"Heard something to that effect," Jasper admitted. "Would you like to come in? I just got home, but I could rustle up some coffee pretty quickly."

"Thanks, but I won't be staying that long," Leroy said. "I was just in town. Happened to run into Darby Fulton. She said if I wanted answers as to what's causing the problems, I should talk to you."

Jasper swore silently and looked out at the mountains for a moment. Damn that woman. She was determined to involve him in this as if she thought it was for his own good. "Not sure why she'd say that. Saw her at the café earlier. She has her own theories."

"I'd like to hear yours," the marshal said and settled his gaze on him.

Leroy didn't look quite as pleasant when those blue eyes narrowed like they were doing right now.

Taking off his Stetson, Jasper ran his free hand through his too-long dark head of hair. He could use a haircut, he realized. Probably could use a shave too. His hand dropped to the stubble on his jaw. He couldn't remember the last time he'd looked in a mirror.

"Marshal, I don't know enough about what's been going on in town to really offer an opinion."

Leroy narrowed his eyes. "No opinion on the new shop in town or its owner either?"

"I haven't been in the shop or even seen its owner." True enough, but he couldn't help thinking how different this conversation would be right now if he'd gone to Gossip and broken down the door as he'd wanted to.

The marshal looked away for a moment. "I know you're no longer in law enforcement, but I'd appreciate it if you let me know if…" His gaze came back to Jasper. "If you hear or see of something that might be of concern. This is a large county and with tourist season about to start, I'm stretched pretty thin. I don't know if you heard or not, but a deputy marshal position just opened up. I was thinking you might be interested."

Jasper put his Stetson back on his head. "I'm a rancher now, but thanks for thinking of me." He could feel Leroy eyeing him intently, looking not quite as disappointed as Darby had been.

He couldn't shake the feeling that Leroy knew exactly why he was no longer a homicide detective. But it was nice of him to still want him on the force—as misguided as that would be.

"I'm sorry you had to make a wasted trip out here," Jasper said and swore silently at Darby even though he figured it was just a matter of time before the marshal would have ended up at his door anyway. People seemed to just assume since he was a former lawman, that he had an interest in being the law again.

"It was a nice drive and it's always good to see you, Jasper," the marshal said as his radio squawked. "You have a nice day." Tipping his hat, Leroy headed back to his patrol SUV as he took the call. Jasper heard enough to know that something had happened in town with a woman named Nancy Green. He also heard Gossip mentioned.

As he watched the marshal drive away, he thought about the invitation in his pocket. When the SUV dipped over the rise and disappeared from sight, he pulled out the card and ripped it into a dozen pieces. Watching the spring breeze take the scraps of paper and spread them like confetti across the ranch yard, he told himself that staying out of it was his best option. Now maybe, Leviathan Nash would stay out of his business.

Turning back to the house, he breathed in the beautiful spring day. Whatever was happening in town had nothing to do with him. Maybe if he said it enough, it would be true.

CHAPTER EIGHT

AFTER HER TALK with Karla, Darby drove back into town, stopped for a very late lunch at the café, had her usual—cheeseburger, fries and a chocolate milkshake—and headed for Nancy Green's house. She'd thought she might see Jasper and smiled to herself as she thought about the marshal's visit this morning to her office. She didn't even feel a little guilty about mentioning Jasper Cole's name to him. By now Leroy would have gone out to the ranch to talk to him. She could well imagine what Jasper thought about that.

Jasper had made it abundantly clear that he didn't want to be involved. But Buckhorn needed him. *She* needed him. She couldn't stand the fact that one of the former top investigators in the country was living just outside of town and refusing to help. All her instincts—which were damned good, if she said so herself—told her that this was far from over. Her fear was that things would get worse.

So far all Leviathan Nash had done was stir up the town. No one had died. Yet. But it felt as if he'd just been playing so far and would soon be winding up for something big. She'd thought about sharing this with Leroy, but she knew how far that would have gotten her. But if it came from former homicide detective Jasper Cole? That, she believed, would be a different story.

Darby sighed, knowing that all she'd probably done was

made Jasper mad. Now he'd dig his heels in even more. As she drove down the street, she was almost to the end when she saw Marshal Baggins's patrol SUV parked in front of Nancy Green's house. Her heart fell.

She slowed and put down her window as he came out on his radio. She heard him call for the coroner. When he saw her, he waved her away. She stopped and got out of her car, but he continued waving her back. Another patrol car rolled up. Leroy barked orders to the man to seal off the area—starting with her.

As the lawman approached, she climbed back into her car and backed away. Her hands were shaking. Hadn't she just been thinking that no one had died? Had Nancy Green gone to her appointment that morning at Gossip? Was that why she was now dead? If she was right, Leviathan Nash had just taken his revenge to another level.

She shook her head and checked the time. What she desperately needed was someone who'd been in the store to tell her on the record what Leviathan Nash had given her to cause what happened next.

It was late enough that Vi Mullen would be leaving for home before very long. Darby drove back to her office, parked and grabbed her notebook and pen, thrust both into her satchel and headed for the alley behind the store and post office to wait for Vi.

From the moment she'd come to town, she'd been warned about Vi. It was no secret that the woman intimidated most everyone in town.

She's the kind who would eat her young, she'd overheard one woman say about Vi.

Darby had heard rumors about all kinds of things that had happened recently to the woman. But she clearly hadn't eaten her young. She had a daughter, Tina, and grand-daughter, Chloe. Although she had lost her only brother and her husband last year. The brother had died, the husband had left her.

Darby sat down on some plastic boxes stacked up in the alley to wait. It was Wednesday so she knew the post office closed at four. Vi might decide to stay until the store closed at six, but Darby was determined to wait. She hoped to catch Vi at a weak moment as she left by the back door. If Vi still wouldn't talk to her, she'd try again tomorrow. Perseverance was her middle name. Actually, it was Prudence. Darby Prudence Fulton.

"Ms. Mullen?" Darby hopped off the boxes and hurried after Vi who appeared to be sneaking down the alley, carrying a heavy grocery bag.

To her surprise, the woman stopped and turned to face her. "It's *Mrs*. Mullen," Vi snapped. Darby caught a whiff of pure alcohol. "*Mrs*. I'm still married and until I sign the divorce papers he sent me, I'll remain *Mrs*. Mullen."

"Mrs. Mullen," Darby said, realizing that Vi had gone down to Dave's bar for at least one drink, probably more. "Can I help you with your bag? It's a long walk home."

Vi lived a mile back toward the mountain, but often walked. People in town said she was too cheap to drive. Vi told everyone she did it for the exercise.

"I'm not walking. I drove today."

Darby looked down the alley to where a white SUV sat parked as if for a fast getaway. She wasn't sure Vi should be driving. She didn't seem all that steady on her feet. "Then I'd love to ride with you," Darby said and smiled. "Please, let me carry that for you." She reached for the bag. Vi pulled it back with some effort. Whatever was in there was heavy, Darby realized. "At least let me carry it as far as your car."

Vi sighed and relenting, shoved the bag at her. Bottles rattled inside it. Darby took the handle and didn't have to look inside to know that it was filled with bottles containing alcohol.

They walked the rest of the way down the alley, neither talking. At the SUV, Vi remotely unlocked the doors.

"I think I'd better hold this while you drive," Darby said. "I'm afraid the bottles will get broken otherwise." Vi hesitated a moment before she opened the passenger-side door, and Darby slipped in with the bag in her arms, letting it close behind her.

Once behind the wheel, Vi said, "Don't think I don't know what you're up to."

Darby said nothing as the woman started the SUV and drove down a side street before heading out of town toward her mountain home. She looked out the window, thinking that she should be able to see Jasper's ranch once Vi started up the mountain. When she looked at the road ahead, she could feel Vi looking at her curiously. Darby knew that the woman would probably just dump her out on the mountain and still refuse to talk to her when this little trip ended. She reminded herself that she'd have to walk back to town at some point. It was a beautiful afternoon, but still spring in Montana. Once the sun went down, it would be chilly if not downright cold.

But Darby had been cold, hungry and even drenched in the rain trying to get a story before. It would be worth it if she could get Vi to talk.

The modern house of stone and glass appeared out of the pines. Darby had heard that Vi had had the place built after her husband, Axel, left her. Before that, she and Axel had lived over the store on the main drag. Darby wondered why they'd split. Then again, she had to wonder about the man who could love someone as bristly as Vivian "Vi" Mullen for as long as he apparently had.

Vi parked at the side of the house, got out and started toward the front door. Hugging the bag to her, Darby climbed out as well. "I suppose you're coming in," Vi said over her shoulder. Darby noted that she didn't bother to use a key to open the front door. As Vi stepped inside, she left the door hanging open. Darby followed her as Vi went straight to the kitchen. Darby placed the bag on the island.

Still without looking at her, Vi pulled one of the bottles from the bag, grabbed the opener already on the countertop and pushed both toward Darby. "Make yourself useful and open this while I go change," her hostess said. "The glasses are…oh, just look, you'll find them." With that the woman left her alone in the kitchen.

Darby looked around for a moment before she opened the wine and found the glasses. The house had a view of the town and if she stood close to the glass, she could see where Jasper's ranch was on the horizon to the south. Pouring herself some wine, she wandered around the living area. The place was exceptionally neat and nice. That didn't surprise her given what little she'd seen of Vi Mullen.

When she heard the woman coming, Darby returned to the kitchen and poured Vi a glass of wine. She could feel the woman studying her as she took it.

"Like my house?" Vi asked as she snatched up the wine bottle and her glass and headed for the living room.

"I do," she said following her.

"It was my present to me," Vi said as she dropped into one of the large leather chairs in front of the fireplace.

Darby took a seat on the couch nearby. "It's beautiful."

Vi picked up a remote and turned on the gas fireplace. It burst to flame, casting the room in a golden warmth. "You'd think I'd get lonely out here," she said after taking a healthy drink from her glass. "I don't." She looked at Darby as if expecting her to argue the point.

"I would imagine it is especially enjoyable during tourist season when the store is open longer hours to be able to get away from all of that," Darby said.

Vi made an indistinguishable sound and took another drink of her wine before refilling her glass. "You want to know why I attacked Karla Parson." Darby held her breath and waited. "Hasn't Karla already told you?"

"She told me her side," Darby said.

Vi scoffed. "*Her* side? What did she say? That she's the victim here? That breaking the vase was an accident?"

"No, she admitted she did it on purpose."

The woman froze, the wineglass halfway to her mouth. For a moment, Vi looked as if she was about to have a conniption fit. She sputtered before she downed the wine in her glass in one gulp.

Setting down the glass with what appeared to be extra care, she said, "She admitted it to a reporter on the record?" Darby nodded. Vi sniffed and refilled her glass. "It was a family heirloom. It broke my mother's heart when it was destroyed and Karla let me take the blame for it all these years. That may seem petty to you, but when I found out that she was the one who'd broken the vase and never admitted the truth..." Vi took a gulp of her wine, her mouth twisting in pain, eyes filling with tears.

"You only just found out recently?" Darby asked. The woman nodded and took another drink. "Leviathan Nash told you, didn't he?"

Vi met her gaze for a moment. She seemed almost afraid to answer. Her nod was so subtle, Darby wasn't sure she'd really seen it.

"How did he know?"

The woman shook her head.

"What made you so sure it was true?" Darby asked.

Vi frowned. "I didn't question it. I just knew it was true and then when her boyfriend pulled me off her…" Vi's face was a mask of rage. "She said it was an ugly cheap vase and she was glad that she'd broken it, but now I know that she broke it on purpose."

Darby sipped her wine, afraid she'd made things worse. "You aren't the only one Leviathan Nash has been sharing news with, I've heard. After Anita Berg left his shop, she went home and beat her still sleeping husband with a baseball bat, kicked him out and burned his belongings in the yard." She figured Vi already knew this, but she wanted to get the subject off Karla Parson.

"He had an affair with her best friend fifty years ago," Vi said as if her tongue was loosening again. "Margaret Fletcher was her best friend. Good thing Margaret is dead."

"So it was true about the affair?"

"Just as it was true about the vase and Karla's part in it," Vi said.

"Where is Leviathan Nash getting his information?" Darby asked.

Vi frowned and shook her head as if it was the first time she'd questioned it. "I have no idea. Unless…"

"Unless…?" she prodded.

"Unless he somehow knows all of our secrets. Maybe he's psychic," Vi suggested. She fingered her wineglass for a moment, staring at the liquid in the firelight. "I once went to a fortune-teller at the state fair. She knew things about me that I'd never told anyone."

Darby had her doubts about Leviathan being psychic. "Even if he is clairvoyant, why share this painful information? Does he have something against Buckhorn?"

Vi was frowning again as if she hadn't asked herself any of these questions until Darby had raised them and wasn't happy to have to consider them now. "That's what was so odd about him," she said. "Leviathan looked…familiar."

"As if you knew him? As if he used to live here?"

Vi shook her head. "No, he just looked…familiar." She finished her wine and put down her empty glass.

Darby got up and moved to where Vi had put down the wine bottle to refill the woman's glass. There wasn't much left. Darby had barely touched her first glass. "I've heard that he is still sending out invitations to people. *When* does it stop? Will he ever open the store or just disappear as quickly as he appeared? *Where* does it stop? I mean, if he's come here to get revenge against the town, don't you wonder how far he's willing to go?"

She turned with the bottle in hand to see that Vi had dozed off in her chair. Taking the wine, her own glass and Vi's empty one, she went into the kitchen and rinsed out the wineglasses and corked the almost empty bottle. She could hear Vi snoring as she let herself out.

On the walk back to town, Darby kept asking herself the same questions she'd put to Vi. Now at least she had verification as to where the information was coming from. But what to do about it, if anything? As Jasper had said dispensing gossip wasn't illegal, though obviously morally wrong. Nancy Green was dead, not that Darby knew for a fact that Leviathan Nash and Gossip had played a role in her death. But if he had, the question was what did Leviathan Nash get out of it?

Sick satisfaction? Or something more? Revenge, just as she theorized? But for what? And why Buckhorn?

CHAPTER NINE

BESSIE CALLED FROM the café when Jasper didn't show up on Monday. He also hadn't come into town Thursday or Friday of the week before. "I was worried that you were sick."

"I'm fine. I've just been busy." He could hear in her silence that she didn't believe him.

"How's Ruby?" she asked after a moment.

"Fine. Great. You were right. She's good company."

More silence. "Well, if you're sure you're all right. But I'd better see you tomorrow or I'm going to come out there and see how you're doing for myself." With that she hung up.

Jasper hadn't been to town since getting his "special showing" invitation to Gossip. He told himself it wasn't cowardice on his part. He really had been busy. But he'd missed his breakfasts with Bessie. Hell, he missed his routine and cursed Leviathan Nash, or whatever his real name was, for interfering in his life.

Idly, he wondered what Leviathan would do when he didn't show.

A part of him *was* curious about the man and his shop. He'd received an invitation… Well, he had one, but he could no longer even see the confetti in his yard thanks to the breeze. So why hadn't he jumped at the chance to squelch that curiosity once and for all?

He could have gone to the shop, checked it and the man

out. But that would have been the old him who had to act on that curiosity. This him, the man who'd come back here to ranch, was determined to live a peaceful, quiet life as far from being a lawman as he could get. He refused to be responsible for anyone's life ever again.

But he knew it was more than that. Whatever Leviathan was selling, it was causing the problems in town, Jasper had no doubt about that. By getting an invitation, it meant that Leviathan Nash knew something he wanted to share with him. About his family? Or someone he knew? Or his parents before they moved away? Or even his grandparents?

Just the thought that the man could know something that far back about someone in his family chilled him to the bone. But it was possible since Leviathan had known about the broken vase when Vi was fifteen. Which meant Leviathan had to know someone who had lived in Buckhorn at least that long ago or maybe longer.

Hadn't Jasper always wondered what had happened to make his father leave the ranch, take his wife and son away, change everything and destroy what had been good in their lives?

He had a bad feeling that Leviathan not only knew, but also was determined to tell him whether he wanted to hear it or not.

CHAPTER TEN

WEDNESDAY UNDER DEADLINE and determined to get the whole story, Darby did something impulsive. Clearly, she wasn't going to get any help from Jasper. So she'd have to do the investigating on her own.

Through a crack between the black paper and the windowsill, she could see the lights were on at Gossip. Earlier, she'd seen one of the locals go inside and then hurry out not fifteen minutes later in tears.

Maybe no one else cared what was going on, but she was going to get to the bottom of it. She knew better than to try the front door of the shop. If she wanted answers she was going to have to go out on a limb, so to speak.

She left her office and walking across the highway, down a block and up an alley, she came out on the street that ran behind the old carriage house—and the cabin where Leviathan Nash now lived. His large old truck was parked behind it.

Darby surveyed the street as she walked. It was late enough that she didn't see anyone around. As she reached the edge of the small cabin behind the Gossip shop, she slowed. The light was still on in the shop. But as she started to step around the corner of the cabin, the light in the shop went out.

Hurriedly, she ducked back into the shadows and held her breath. She heard him come out, close and lock the door behind him. As he headed toward the cabin, she cursed her bad luck. Maybe if she'd come over earlier, she could have gotten into the cabin while he was in the shop. She'd waited too long.

But to her surprise, he entered the cabin and didn't even bother turning on a light before he came right back out. She stayed pressed against the side of the cabin, listening. She heard him walk to the truck. The driver's-side door groaned open, seat springs creaked, the door slammed shut and a few moments later the engine turned over.

Darby edged back along the cabin wall and slipped around the corner. She waited to see which direction he was going. If he headed toward her, she'd have to move or he'd see her as he passed.

Her luck improved. Not only was he leaving, he turned the opposite direction, going down the street away from her. She had no idea where he was going or when he would be back. The only person who was here on this street this time of year was Mabel and her lights were out since she went to bed early every night.

There would be no one to see her, Darby realized. Just as there would have been no one to see Leviathan leave. Sneaking back around to the entrance side of the cabin, she tried the door. She held her breath as she gripped the knob, surprised when it turned in her hand. She told herself at least she wouldn't have to cross the line to breaking and entering.

The door swung open—almost like an invitation. She pulled the penlight from her pocket and quickly stepped in. Listening for the sound of his truck returning, she shone the penlight around. She didn't know what she was looking for. The cabin was almost as small as her studio apartment over her office.

The living room consisted of a couch and large recliner separated by a small end table. Past it was a kitchenette of sorts that didn't look any more used than her own. Through a doorway was a bedroom with a double bed and a dresser. She hurried to it and opened the top drawer. It was empty. It didn't take long to realize that none of the drawers had been used.

She spotted a trunk on the floor beside the bed. It appeared to contain a mixture of black clothing neatly folded. She reached through the clothes to the bottom of the trunk and checked the sides and top. Nothing of interest.

The only other room was the bathroom. It was even smaller than hers. There was a shower, sink and toilet. Her light caught on the hairbrush next to the sink. She quickly used one of the plastic bags she'd brought in her pocket to pluck out as much hair as she could. After closing the bag, she checked the medicine cabinet, hoping to find a prescription label with a name and address on it. Nothing but a bottle of ibuprofen and some antacid tablets.

Closing the medicine cabinet, she stopped to listen. Still no sign of the truck. She knew she was spending too much time with this and had to get out of there soon or she would get caught. He couldn't have gone far. She really doubted he'd drive an hour to the next town this late.

In the living area, she swung the beam of the light around until it fell again on the tiny kitchen. She stepped to the coffee cup sitting on the edge of the sink. There was still a little coffee in it.

Using one of the plastic bags again, she opened the cupboard, took out a clean cup and poured a little coffee into it from the dirty cup. She bagged the dirty one and placed the new dirty cup where the other one had been.

She took one look around the cabin and was about to

leave when she saw a book sitting beside the couch—and what looked like a photograph sticking out of the pages. She hurried to it, opened the book and took out the photo. It appeared to be an old family picture. Flipping it over, she hoped for writing on the back. No such luck. Whipping out her phone, she snapped a shot of the family—the only thing personal in the entire place.

As she was dropping her phone back into her pocket she heard the sound of the truck returning. Leviathan Nash was coming. She snapped off her penlight and looked toward the door, wondering if she could get out of there quickly enough. But the truck was coming fast. The headlights flashed through the window beside the door. She ducked. He would park on the side of the cabin with the only exit, and he was too close already.

She kept down as the truck's headlights swept across the room. Too late, he'd already turned in and parked. She heard him cut the engine. The truck door groaned open. A moment later it slammed closed.

Any moment he would be opening the cabin door. *Hide!* But where? Her frantic gaze took in the too-tiny kitchen, the equally small bathroom and the bedroom. She could just imagine herself getting caught in the closet all night.

By the time the door came open, she was crouched behind the recliner in the corner and trying not to breathe, let alone move.

He came into the cabin, turned on the overhead light and stood for a moment as if sensing something wrong. Darby held her breath. Did he know she was there? She listened, afraid he might be moving toward the recliner at any moment.

But when she heard the door close and floorboards creak, she realized he was headed for the bedroom. Relief at not choosing the bedroom washed over her. She let out the breath she'd been holding, but she wasn't out of trouble yet. She would have to go by the bedroom doorway to get out of the cabin.

Listening hard, she heard the sound of the bedsprings. Was he sitting down? Lying down? Was he facing the doorway? No, she realized. He had to be sitting on the side that didn't have the trunk on the floor next to it.

Which meant with luck, he was facing the other direction. She knew he could come back into the living room at any moment. She had to move.

She eased out from behind the chair, trying hard not to make a sound. She couldn't hear what he was doing in the bedroom. She listened for the telltale creak of the bedsprings should he rise. Hearing nothing, she took careful steps toward the door, fighting the urge to run, fling open the door and keep running.

Instead, she practically tiptoed, willing the old wood floor under her feet not to make a sound. As she passed in front of the bedroom doorway, she finally dared look. Just as she'd thought, he was sitting on the bed facing the opposite direction.

She took the last few steps to the door, grabbed the knob and opened it just wide enough to slip through. Carefully, she closed it behind her, fearing that he would feel the spring night air rush in. Then she ran. She didn't stop until she turned the corner through an opening between the buildings out of sight of the cabin. She stopped just long enough to catch her breath, then raced through the dark, sprinting toward the highway.

She'd done it. She grinned as she reached the two-lane blacktop. No traffic. She jogged across to the other side before she looked back. There was no sign of Leviathan Nash. No sign of anyone. She'd gotten away with it.

Back at her office, she ducked in, locked the door and hurried upstairs to her studio apartment. She pulled out the bags with the hair and the coffee cup. Then checked her phone. She was half afraid that the photo wouldn't be there, but there it was. She made it larger, but none of the faces looked familiar to her. She studied it for a moment before she knew what she had to do. Pocketing everything, she headed out the door again.

JASPER STARTED AT the sound of a vehicle coming up the road to the ranch house this late at night. He'd been jumpy and on edge all day—since waking up this morning to find another small white bag hanging on his front door. Like before, it held only one thing: another invitation. This one for Wednesday at 8:00 a.m. since he'd missed Monday's.

He had crumpled the card in his fist and looked around, wondering why neither he nor Ruby had heard someone come up on the porch in the wee hours the night before to leave it. The bastard had trespassed on his property. Jasper wished he'd caught him. He would have loved to have scared the shit out of the little schemer. He hoped that was all he'd do.

That he didn't trust himself scared him. All this time, he'd been trying to learn to control his anger. The only things that had kept that boiling rage from bubbling over was being back here in Montana on this ranch, and Ruby, he thought with a smile. While realizing how much the damned dog had added to his life, he wasn't about to admit it to Bessie. She probably knew anyway since he was seldom without the dog.

As he watched the lights of the vehicle approaching the

house, he told himself that if Leviathan Nash had the nerve to come back out here again…

But as the car pulled up in his yard, he saw that it was Darby Fulton. When it came to unwanted guests, she wasn't at the top of the list—but pretty darned close.

He folded his arms over his chest and leaned against the porch railing. Whatever she wanted, it wouldn't take long to send her on her way. Even as he thought it, a part of him was actually glad to see her. What was it about this woman? She annoyed the devil out of him and yet he often found himself smiling in spite of himself.

The car door opened. He watched her step out and wished that just seeing her in his yard didn't make his heart beat a little faster. Ignoring her wasn't working. The woman got to him in a way he told himself he didn't want or need. Not that it stopped his body from reacting even at the sight of her. He tried to ignore it as she came hurrying up the steps toward him.

"I found something you need to see," she said without preamble.

"Good evening to you too, Ms. Fulton. A little late for a visit, though, don't you think?"

She ignored him as she stepped past and walked right into his house. Shaking his head, he followed her to find her petting his dog.

"Please make yourself at home," he said and saw that his sarcasm was wasted on her. "Oh, and thanks for sending the marshal out here to see me."

She waved a hand through the air, ignoring both comments. "I found this in Leviathan Nash's cabin," she said and thrust her phone at him.

He frowned. "You found a phone in his cabin? Wait, what were you doing in his cabin?"

"Just look at the photo, Jasper," she said impatiently and squatted down to talk to Ruby. The worst part was that Ruby was eating up the attention. Definitely not a watchdog. *Traitor*, he thought.

He glanced at the photo on the screen, frowned and then looked at Darby. "What is this?"

"It's an old photograph of a family," she said, her attention on the dog. "It was tucked in a book in Leviathan's cabin—the only personal thing in the entire place."

He didn't bother to glance at the photograph again. "Well, as fascinating as this is, I have no idea why you drove all the way out here to show me this." He handed the phone back.

"You don't recognize any of the people?" she asked with obvious disappointment as she rose.

"Why would I?" He didn't like letting her down, but then again he had no idea why she would think he would know those people.

"You're from here. I knew it was a long shot, but I thought maybe if Leviathan had family here…"

"I left here when I was five, came back after losing both my grandmother and my parents, and left right after high school. The photo is in black-and-white. I'm old, but not that old."

She shook her head, clearly exasperated with him, but not half as much as he was with her.

"I thought I warned you about this. What were you doing in his cabin?"

Darby met his gaze with a steely one of her own. "Someone needs to find out who this man is. We know he's dangerous. What we don't know is how dangerous. Nancy Green is dead. She shot herself after going to Gossip. I suspect this is just the tip of the iceberg. And since you weren't going to help me, I had to do something."

"Tell me you didn't break in."

"I didn't. The door was open."

"So he doesn't know that you were there," Jasper said with a wave of relief.

"Not that I know of. Like I said, the door was open."

"Kind of like my door was open," he said.

"He left in his truck so I had a look around his cabin."

"Where did he go?"

She mugged a face at him. "I have no idea, but he wasn't gone very long. He keeps all his clothes in a trunk on the floor by his bed as if he isn't planning on staying long."

"Probably leaving when his lease is up in a couple of weeks." He could see her frustration.

"Someone needs to find out the truth about this man before he goes on to the next town."

He didn't think the man would be going on to another town to cause trouble. Just a gut feeling that this was all about Buckhorn. All about the residents who lived here, including Jasper's family. "We don't know that Leviathan Nash is planning—"

"That's just it," she interrupted. "We don't know *what* he's planning. Look what happened to Nancy Green."

He argued that those left behind seldom knew why a person died by suicide and that there were often other factors.

Darby scoffed. "She goes to Gossip in the morning and shoots herself in the afternoon."

"Still, you don't know—"

"Yes, I do," she snapped, cutting him off. "I talked to Vi Mullen. She told me exactly how she learned about the broken vase. *He* told her. He told her that Karla Parson broke it and let her take the blame. He incited this violence. But come on, don't you wonder how he knew? Or why he's doing this? What he hopes to accomplish? And when does it end?"

"Wait, Vivian Mullen told you that Leviathan Nash was the one who—"

"He wrote her a note on his card in the bag with the vase she bought."

He thought of his own invitations he'd received and the too-neat handwriting in black ink. "And she believed it." He shook his head. "Why would she?"

Darby shrugged. "She said she knew it was true because of the vase. Leviathan had the exact same vase that had gotten broken. If he knew that, then she believed he knew who had broken it. *And he was right!* Karla admitted it. And apparently he's been right about the others he's broken bad news to. Or at least they had reason to believe it."

"Even if he caused some of these incidents, as far as I know there's no law against telling people things they don't want to hear."

She rolled her eyes. "So you keep saying. Tell me you really don't want to find out who this man is and why he's doing this, because I don't believe you." She reached into her coat pocket and withdrew a plastic bag that appeared to hold a cup and from the other pocket a bag with something gray in it.

"What is that?" he asked with concern as she thrust the bags at him. He took a step back. "Is that hair?"

"It's Leviathan Nash's hair from his brush. I need you to get the prints off the mug and his DNA from the hair. One or the other is bound to tell us who he is."

Jasper held up his hands as he shook his head without touching either bag. "I already told you—"

"I risked getting caught to get this and now you're telling me that you won't help find out who this man really is?" she demanded, settling those honey-brown eyes on him. Her look would have melted even the darkest of hearts, and that it was doing a number on his really pissed him off. How many times did he have to tell her he didn't want to get involved? He couldn't.

"I didn't tell you to risk anything," he snapped. "In fact, I told you not to because it could be dangerous. I would suggest giving your ill-gotten evidence to Marshal Baggins except he can't do anything with it because it was illegally obtained. He'd probably throw you in jail."

She waved off his logic as if it was of no consequence. "Surely you know someone who would help behind the scenes."

He studied her for a moment. Had he really thought she'd take any advice from him? Or that she would give up on this? He groaned. What was it about a strong, determined woman that attracted him, especially this one? He considered for a moment what she would do if he didn't help her and swore under his breath. "You seem to think that I have more power than I do. I'm not a cop anymore. I'm a rancher." Another eye roll. He swore under his breath. "I might know someone, but I'm not making any promises."

Her grin was like a shaft of sunshine on a rainy day, all rainbows and pots of gold. It made him all the more irritated with her. She thrust the bags at him. This time, he took them, though shaking his head even as he did. "I'll have to get back to you." He put the bags aside.

"Okay," she said and stuffed her hands into the pockets of her jeans. She looked relieved. She also looked as if she wasn't anxious to go. "Once we find out who he really is…"

"I'm sure you realize that neither his fingerprints nor his DNA might be in any of the databases. Unless there is something to compare his fingerprints or DNA to..."

"He has to have been arrested for something."

"We don't know that. Like I said, what he's doing isn't illegal. You need to accept the real probability that you'll never know who he is or why he came here." Darby gave him a smile that argued differently. He could see that it was inconceivable to her that she might never know. She wouldn't rest until she got to the bottom of it. She was certainly in the right profession, it seemed.

She gave a determined shake of her head. A lock of hair fell over her forehead. He fought the urge to reach out and guide it back into her pixie cut.

"You know I'm not wrong about him," she said. "He's in a database somewhere. He's going to pop up because this man has had a brush with the law." She pulled out her phone. "I'm sending you the photo so maybe later you'll take a better look at it. Or show it to the person you give the hair and cup to." Glancing up, she asked, "What's your number?"

He could see that arguing with her was a waste of breath. He gave her his mobile number with a silent groan.

"If you still don't recognize anyone in the photo, maybe you could show it to Bessie or one of your other friends. You do have friends, don't you?" He ignored that. "I'll be waiting to hear from you. Every day that man dispenses his poison—"

"I'll do what I can. No promises, remember?"

She shifted on her feet as if there was more she wanted to say before she seemed to realize that she'd said enough and headed for the door. "I'll see myself out."

"You saw yourself in, so I'm sure you can find the way," he said.

Darby shot an amused look over her shoulder. "Good to see you too, Jasper." And she was gone.

He waited until he heard her drive away before he picked up the phone and made the call.

CHAPTER ELEVEN

EARL RAY CAULFIELD considered the bags with the gray hair and the dirty coffee cup before looking at the man sitting at his kitchen table. He'd been busy for months with the house. He and Bessie had bought an older house in Buckhorn that desperately needed remodeling. He was overseeing the remodel, doing a lot of the work himself.

He'd waited until Bessie had gone to the café before he'd told Jasper to come over. After a tour of the house, he'd gotten them both a cup of coffee and they'd settled at the kitchen table he used as a desk. Jasper had said on the phone that he had a favor to ask. Earl Ray had heard the tension in the man's voice. Whatever it was, he'd had no doubt that it was something important.

But he hadn't expected to be handed a bag of gray hair and a dirty coffee cup first thing in the morning.

"I figured if anyone could help…" Jasper said. "It would be you."

That made him smile. It also made him wonder how much Jasper knew about him to think that. Earl Ray kept a low profile. People in town thought he was a war hero. He'd never considered himself a hero of any kind. But he'd done what needed to be done in the military and still did that for the town of Buckhorn.

He was pretty sure his military service was under top security protection—just like Jasper's record with the big-city police department where he'd worked as a homicide detective. Earl Ray hadn't had any trouble finding out what he needed to know about the man when Jasper had moved back to Buckhorn. He'd taken on the job of protecting the town. That meant knowing the people who came and went. What he learned he kept to himself—as long as there were no problems that needed to be dealt with.

"Like I told you, I hate to ask," Jasper continued. "But our new publisher, editor, reporter in town isn't going to stop until she finds out who Leviathan Nash really is."

Earl Ray smiled. "Nice of you to help her."

The former lawman shook his head. "It wasn't at gunpoint, but damned close. That woman... Trust me, you've never seen such dogged, stubborn, pigheaded determination."

He laughed. "Did you forget that I'm married to Bessie?" They both laughed. "Why did Darby come to you with this?"

Jasper looked embarrassed. "She thinks I'm more...capable than I am."

Earl Ray would question that, but he let it go.

"Also, she got a copy of a photograph she found." He watched Jasper pull out his phone, find the photo and pass it over. "She thought maybe someone might recognize the people in it."

He took the phone and studied the old photograph for a few minutes before shaking his head. "You might show it to Bessie. She's better with faces than I am. I guess it's all those years running a café." He handed the phone back.

"I'm sure you've been following the incidents in town. Vi Mullen told Darby that they're tied to the new shop owner."

Earl Ray had expected as much. It was no coincidence

that the trouble had started when Leviathan Nash came to town. "I won't ask how Darby got these…personal items."

"Best not to," Jasper agreed. "I told her that his DNA might not be in any of the databanks. But if it doesn't get a hit, I'm afraid she'll go back to find more evidence."

Earl Ray had met Darby. He thought Jasper was right. "I'll see what I can do." He hesitated. "Have you gotten an invitation to Gossip?"

"Two so far. I threw both away. How about you?"

He shook his head. "I'm surprised you didn't go. You aren't curious?"

Jasper shook his head. "Not at all."

Laughing, Earl Ray studied him. "I don't even think you believe that, but I don't blame you. I would be hesitant as well. But you have to wonder what information the man has and how he got it—and what he has on us, if anything."

Jasper laughed. "You sound like Darby." Their gazes locked for a moment, both of them men of secrets—and regrets. Regrets were just part of it. He finished his coffee and stood to go. "I should get going. Ruby's waiting."

Earl Ray smiled, remembering his wife's plot to get Jasper the puppy for companionship. He'd advised against it. One of the many times he'd been wrong, he thought. Thinking of Bessie… "You happen to notice all the crows lately?" he asked, looking toward the window and the now-empty phone lines. "Fascinating birds. Wicked smart. Proportionally, some crows have bigger brains than we do."

"I feel like you're getting at something here," Jasper said.

He smiled and nodded. "Do you know why crows gather like they have been?"

"My grandmother would say because something bad is coming."

Earl Ray laughed. "Crows gather to fight off their predators, safety in numbers, or to share facts like where there is abundant food—or where there is danger. Mass gatherings can also be for a funeral of one of their own to let others know this is not a safe place for them."

"If you're trying to spook me—"

The older man shook his head. "Humans gather for the same reasons. We're safer not being alone. Crows are smart enough to know that."

Jasper chuckled. "I get it."

"Good, because Bessie misses you at breakfast," Earl Ray said as he walked Jasper to the door. "She thinks you're avoiding her."

JASPER GROANED. EARL RAY knew why he'd been avoiding the café and town in general. But it bothered him that Bessie thought he was avoiding her. In truth, he'd been avoiding Gossip, avoiding running into Leviathan Nash and keeping his distance from Darby.

He was a lone crow. And it was all out of nothing more than cowardice, he told himself as he left. Was Earl Ray worried that like a lone crow, he was in danger because of it?

Shaking his head, he told himself that nonetheless, he was glad to hand off the bag full of hair and the cup. He felt relief—and anxiety. He found himself hoping there would be a match on one of the databases. At least that would put an end to Darby's investigation if she knew the man's real name.

If the man calling himself Leviathan Nash was a known crook and Darby exposed him, maybe residents might lose interest in what the probable con man had to "sell" them. But at the same time, it would put Darby in danger when she wrote about it—depending on exactly what kind of criminal record the man had.

Even though Jasper had told Darby not to expect much, he realized that he was anticipating the man would have an extensive criminal record. Which meant Leviathan Nash might be more dangerous than even he feared.

He tried to tell himself that once exposed, Leviathan would probably disappear as quickly as he'd appeared—and take the rest of his secrets with him.

Including whatever secret the man had for him.

That thought disturbed him more than he wanted to admit. He would never know whatever Leviathan Nash had to tell him. All his instincts warned him that he didn't want to know.

But how badly did the man want—or was it *need*—to tell him? The bigger question was what Leviathan would do if he kept refusing.

AFTER EARL RAY got the DNA sample sent to a friend, he put it out of his mind. He was determined to get his and Bessie's house ready so they could finally move in. Since they'd gotten married, their lives had been up in the air. He'd sold his house that he'd shared with his now deceased wife, Tory, and bought this one and gone to work.

It had been hard to sell the house, feeling like another betrayal. He'd told himself that Tory would be glad he'd found love again. He hoped it was true.

Bessie had kept her little house for the time being. She also had her café and bakery, both of which had kept her plenty busy. He knew she needed a familiar routine. Not that she didn't love baking. Also the town loved her baked goods. If the day ever came that she quit… He hoped it would be her choice.

He had Bessie on his mind, which had been the case for years. He loved her and marrying her had been the smartest thing he'd ever done. He just wished he'd done it sooner. But for years, he'd felt he was betraying his late wife, Tory, by falling in love with Bessie. When he'd realized that he might lose Bessie… Well, he'd smartened up and told her how he felt. Proposing had been a no-brainer. He wanted her for keeps.

With Bessie and the house remodel on his mind, he hadn't noticed the small white bag hanging on his front door until he returned from the hardware store. He had a large sack filled with hinges, screws and nails and was pushing open the door when he saw it.

He frowned and pulled the small white bag free. As he did, the sack in his other hand clattered to the floor, spilling boxes of screws and nails and hinges on the wood porch.

Earl Ray stared at the small bag almost in disbelief. Bessie had been keeping him abreast of the goings-on at Gossip and the rumors circulating through town. That was why he was so shocked. He'd heard about the invitations, but he hadn't expected to get one. Any secrets he had weren't the kind a con man could uncover. What could Leviathan Nash have to share with *him*? It made no sense.

Scooping up everything he'd bought at the hardware store and the small white bag, he stepped into the house, letting the door close behind him. In the kitchen, he put down everything on the table, surprised how scared he suddenly was. He could understand how the locals had felt when they'd gotten their invitations—especially after the rumors had started to circulate. They might have been excited, honored to be singled out—until they'd realized why.

What could Leviathan Nash—or whatever his name was—have to tell him? He'd come to Buckhorn in his twenties on a trip through the state while on military leave and met Victoria "Tory" Crenshaw as she was getting off a bus. It was by chance that they'd settled here. It wasn't like he'd grown up here.

His stomach sank as he realized who had grown up here. Bessie, the woman he loved and had only recently married.

Earl Ray pulled out a chair and dropped into it. He thought he would be sick. For years, he'd held Bessie in the highest esteem… The last thing he wanted to know was anything bad about her. He would have sworn that they had no secrets from each other.

But Leviathan Nash's calling card, so to speak, was bad news that turned people's lives upside down. Earl Ray was happy. He didn't want his life upside down or inside out.

He thought about Jasper throwing his invitations away as he picked up his own. He didn't want to know. Whatever it was, he told himself that there was nothing he needed to know about Bessie. He already knew everything he needed to know about her. He hated to admit it, but he'd done a full background check on her a long time ago. There was nothing to find.

Or was there? Swallowing, he turned the business card over in his fingers. At heart, he was an investigator. He could feel the need to know pushing aside the fear of what he might find out. He wasn't that much different from Darby and it was one reason he respected her.

He tried to assure himself that whatever Leviathan Nash had to tell him was a lie. But unfortunately that hadn't been the case apparently with what the man had told other Buckhorn citizens. Just the thought that this con man would try to besmirch Bessie's good name…

Earl Ray prided himself on his ability to stay calm in the worst of circumstances. He drew on that ability now.

He thought of Jasper, who'd thrown away the two invitations he'd gotten. Ignoring the invitation was a thought.

But unfortunately, Earl Ray knew he could not. Had he known what he would do even before he'd seen the bag hanging on his door? He'd been invited inside the lion's den. How could he pass up the chance to make his own assessment of the man calling himself Leviathan Nash? Didn't he owe it to the town he'd sworn he would protect?

He realized that he'd been falling down on his duty to the town since the man had arrived with his poisonous gossip. Earl Ray should have been the one to find out that there was no one by the name of Leviathan Nash before the local newspaperwoman did. He should have protected the town and its residents. He couldn't turn a blind eye anymore.

Both angry and scared, he picked up the invitation to check the time of his "special showing."

CHAPTER TWELVE

MONDAY MORNING, DARBY leaned an elbow on her desk and stared at her computer. She needed more on Gossip and its owner. She'd written about the so-called opening of Gossip the first week. The second she'd written Vi's story and more about Gossip and Leviathan Nash. She needed something new if she was going to keep writing about the man and his shop.

She still had more questions than answers. Unless she heard about the DNA on the hair, the fingerprints on the cup, she had nothing new to say about Gossip or Leviathan Nash.

Last week she'd debated holding the story, but had ended up running it. She'd hoped that locals would read Vi's story and keep their distance from Gossip, but that hadn't happened. More people had gone. Unfortunately, none of them wanted to talk about it after they'd gone inside.

She sighed and looked up, startled to see a man standing on the street in front of her office window. More startling was the fact that he was the last person she'd expect to see in Buckhorn—not to mention the last person she ever wanted to see again.

Just when she was about to duck behind her large plant, he stepped closer, cupped his hands around his eyes and leaned into the glass to stare right at her. She froze as he smiled, stepped back and headed toward her front door. It was unlocked and there wasn't time to reach it and bolt it shut. She held her breath as he stepped into her tiny office.

"Aiden? What are you doing here?" she demanded, surprised how angry and scared she was to see him again.

"What are *you* doing here is more the question," he said as he sent a disparaging glance over her office. "This is..." He seemed at a loss for words.

"My newspaper office," she said, gearing up for a fight. "So you can just wipe that look off your face because I don't like it."

He settled his gaze on her. "There seems to be a lot of things you don't like. Me included."

Darby looked away. She just wanted him out of her office. What was he doing in Buckhorn anyway? What were the chances that he'd just been passing through town? She got to her feet. "We've already had this discussion. There really isn't anything left to say."

His laugh had an edge to it. "*You* had your say, that's for sure." He glared at her. "But I didn't. You never gave me a chance."

"Aiden, I really don't have time for this. I have a newspaper to get out." She could see that he had to bite his tongue not to say something demeaning. She wasn't going to argue with him, even if he hadn't scared her the last time she saw him.

"I'm not leaving town," he said. "Where would you suggest I stay?"

He looked as if he thought she might offer her apartment upstairs. Was he that delusional? "It's early spring so not a lot has opened yet for the season. Perhaps someplace in the next town."

He mugged a face. "I'm staying in Buckhorn."

"Then your best bet is a room at the Sleepy Pine Motel.

It's right down the highway on the way out of town. I really don't see any reason for you to stay since—"

"I came a long way to see you," he interrupted. "I'm sure you can spare a few minutes. After all, we *were* engaged to be married. If you're too busy to talk now, then why don't you stop by my motel room later."

"No."

He looked at her as if he couldn't believe she'd just said that.

"If you're determined to talk, let's meet at the café. It's just down the street. I could be there by…six." She didn't want to meet him, but she told herself she'd let him have his say and then maybe he would leave town. She wasn't going anywhere near his motel room, though.

"Fine." With that he turned on his heel and left.

The moment he closed the door, she jumped up and locked it. She tried to breathe. Aiden. She had hoped to never see him again. She'd never dreamed that he would track her down. That he would show up in Buckhorn. That he would think there was anything he could say to make her change her mind about him.

Still shaking inside, she sat back down at her computer. She had to get the newspaper out. Pushing all thoughts of him from her mind, she began to do a last edit on what she'd written. She thought of Jasper. Had he done something with what she'd taken from Leviathan Nash's cabin? She thought about calling him, but didn't have the time to rewrite her entire article on Gossip.

Anyway, when he found out something, he would let her know—especially if the DNA sample didn't provide any answers. She hated to think of how he would gloat if it turned out that Leviathan Nash was just an old man trying to make a living with a stage name. But she didn't believe that for a moment.

Surely if the man's DNA got a match on some criminal database Jasper wouldn't try to keep it from her to protect her? No, she told herself. He was worried about her. If Leviathan was as dangerous as she suspected, Jasper would warn her. She thought of what they'd shared so long ago and sighed.

Meanwhile, she had problems of her own, she thought with a shudder. Aiden. Why had she agreed to meet him at all? Because she got the impression he wouldn't leave until she did. Better in a public place.

First the newspaper, she told herself, pulling herself back from those dark thoughts. Then she would deal with Aiden. But even as she thought it, she had to admit that she was scared of him. What had possessed him to follow her to Buckhorn? His reasons for being here made her uneasy. He wanted something from her for him to come all this way. It was over. He knew that, didn't he?

She thought about what had made her finally break up with him. She'd been trying to put distance between them, having realized that they were all wrong for each other. He wasn't the man she wanted to spend even the next date night with—let alone the rest of her life. Since the engagement, he'd become too possessive, too controlling, too much of everything she didn't need or want.

She'd decided to break up with him that Friday night. But he'd showed up unexpectedly at her door Thursday night late. He'd been drinking. She could smell the liquor on his breath when she'd opened the door and tried to send him away.

But he'd pushed past her, knocking her aside. She'd never seen him like that, but as she'd stared after him, she'd realized that it hadn't come as a surprise. She had sensed something just below the surface as if he made a special effort to control his temper around her.

Until that night.

"You've been avoiding me," he'd said, raising his voice. "What the hell is going on?"

"It's late. Let's not get into this now," she'd said, trying to lower the heat she saw in his glazed eyes.

"No, we're going to do this now," he'd insisted, taking a step toward her. "You tell me what's going on right now or I'll—" He'd stopped when he'd seen the cell phone in her hand and her finger on the send button. "Tell me you aren't calling the cops," he'd said between gritted teeth. "That would not be smart on your part." He took a threatening step toward her.

"Leave now," she said and pushed Send.

He swore and started to launch himself at her. She grabbed the back of the chair nearest her and hurled it into his path.

"911. What is your emergency?" came the voice over the phone. She'd put it on speaker.

"My boyfriend has been drinking and has forced his way into my apartment. I've asked him to leave and he won't. He just threatened me."

"What is your name and address?"

She rattled it off as Aiden took a step back, raking a hand through his hair and swearing.

"What is his name?" the operator asked.

"I'm leaving!" Aiden yelled as he righted the chair and started past Darby. "Hear that, bitch? I'm leaving. But this isn't over. You'll pay for this." As he passed Darby, he slapped the phone out of her hand. It skittered across the floor. She could hear the operator asking if she was all right. "I'll be back," he whispered before slamming the front door behind him.

She'd locked the door before picking up the phone. The operator was still there, asking what was going on.

"He left and I locked the door," Darby had told her. She was fighting tears. "I don't think he'll be back."

"I wouldn't count on that," the operator had said. "Is this the first time he's been violent?"

"Yes."

The operator lowered her voice. "It won't be the last. Honey, cut him loose and save yourself a lot of grief."

She realized that her hand holding the phone was trembling. "I was already planning to."

"You might consider getting a restraining order. But don't hesitate to call and don't let him in your apartment again."

She'd thanked the operator and burst into tears.

The next morning she'd called Aiden and told him it was over. He'd pleaded with her not to break things off, saying how sorry he was, that it had been alcohol talking not him.

But she hadn't weakened. She'd had the engagement ring sent by special courier, forcing him to sign for it so she knew he'd gotten it.

She'd been so sure it was over and they both knew it. Only apparently she'd been wrong. Aiden had tracked her down here in Buckhorn and was refusing to leave until he had his say. She didn't trust him. Something must have happened for him to come all this way. She'd sensed his anger just under the surface ready to come flying out at the least provocation.

Darby shuddered as she looked toward the window at

the fading light. She should never have agreed to meet him. But he'd been in her office, with no way to get away from him. She much preferred a public place to meet. Even as she thought it, she considered calling the marshal, but Aiden hadn't really threatened her. Yet.

Turning back to her computer and her weekly newspaper, she hit Send. All her instincts told her not to go alone to the café this evening to meet Aiden.

JASPER HEARD A text come in on his phone and was surprised to see a copy of the *Buckhorn Independent Press*. He felt his pulse jump. What had Darby written about Gossip and Leviathan Nash now? He'd already read about the opening and Vi's story.

He saw that there didn't seem to be anything new—just more on the marshal's report on the incidents that had been happening in town. She asked readers who'd been inside the shop to contact her and share their experiences.

So, she hadn't gotten anything new, it seemed. He felt relieved although it surprised him that she hadn't called to badger him about the DNA sample. He told himself it was just a matter of time. He'd started having breakfast with Bessie again this week, telling himself he could only avoid Leviathan so long—or Darby for that matter. Just a little over a week and Leviathan's lease would be up. With luck the man would leave and be forgotten.

So far Jasper hadn't found another bag hung on his front door. Maybe the man had gotten the message. But even as he thought it, he had a bad feeling that it wouldn't be the last he heard from him.

That was why he started when his cell phone rang. He checked. Darby. He thought about not taking the call, but feared she would just continue to call if he didn't.

"No, I have nothing to report," he said without preamble as he picked up.

"Nice to hear your voice too," she said.

"I told you I would let you know if and when I had information for you."

"That's not why I'm calling," Darby said. Something in her voice sent a sliver of worry burrowing under his skin. "I have a problem." He heard the hesitation. She sounded... scared. He'd actually thought that nothing *could* scare this woman. His first thought was Leviathan Nash. Had he found out what she'd done? Was he threatening her?

"What's going on, Darby?" His voice sounded tight, scared.

"I don't want to involve anyone I really care about in my personal problems. That's when I thought of you."

"I wish I wasn't sure how to take that," he said, waiting impatiently for her to tell him what was wrong. She'd said *personal* problems. For her to call him sounding the way she did, it was serious.

"You know what I mean." He feared he did. "My former fiancé is in town. I don't know how he found me, but he scares me. I don't want to be alone with him. He's determined that the two of us have to talk and he won't take no for an answer. I told him I'd meet him at the café in twenty minutes, but I don't trust him and the last time I saw him..."

"Are you telling me he hurt you physically?"

"No, but I could tell he wanted to. He was drunk and he threatened me. If I hadn't gotten away from him when I did... I broke off the engagement, quit my job and moved here. I hadn't seen him since—until he came into my office."

Well, that explained why she'd left her job to start her

own weekly online newspaper. He glanced out into the growing darkness. "Where are you now?"

"In my office with the door locked, lights out and the blinds closed."

"Sit tight," he said without hesitation. "I'm on my way."

CHAPTER THIRTEEN

JASPER WALKED OUT to his pickup only to see one of his tires was almost flat. He didn't have time to change it. He hoped it had just a slow leak. Driving it over to the barn, he plugged in his compressor and aired up the tire. That would have to do since he had to get to town. It wasn't what Darby had said so much, but what she hadn't. This was one woman who didn't scare easily. He thought about how she'd braved getting into Leviathan Nash's cabin to try to find evidence. He also knew from her award-winning articles that she'd taken all kinds of risks to get a story. If she was scared, it was for a good reason.

As he climbed behind the wheel, Ruby began to wag her tail. The pup really did like going—didn't seem to matter where. He was almost to the main highway into town when he saw that his neighbor was moving cows.

Jasper swore and looked at his watch. Hopefully, Darby would wait for him, but even as he thought it, he had a bad feeling she wouldn't. He suspected she was one of those people who was always punctual when it came to time management.

Finally getting through the cows, he turned onto the highway and raced into town. The sun had set, casting a blue-gray twilight over the small town. Town was still pretty much dead with a lot of the businesses waiting until Memorial Day to open—the official start of tourist season—and that was still weeks away.

A semi went past, choking out diesel fuel as the driver shifted down. As its red taillights disappeared into the growing darkness beyond town, Jasper saw Darby. She'd left her office and was walking down the street toward the café.

He swore. Of course she hadn't waited. But that wasn't the worst part. His not showing up on time would have rattled her faith in him and that bothered him more than he wanted to admit.

Just as he was about to pull over and give her hell for not waiting for him, he saw movement out of one of the narrow alleyways between the buildings. The figure that came out of the shadows of the alley was large and male. The man moved swiftly, grabbing her arm as if to pull her back into the alley with him.

Jasper swung the pickup to the curb, cut the engine and jumped out. "Let go of her!" he yelled as he stormed toward them.

"This is none of your business!" the man yelled back and continued to drag a struggling Darby, who was fighting to free herself of his grip.

"I said let her go." Jasper moved in swiftly, wrenching the man's hand from Darby's wrist. His fist shot out, snapping the man's head back as his knuckles connected to jawbone. The ex-fiancé let out a curse and, stumbling back, took a wild swing at him that missed by a mile.

As the man started to reach for something in his pocket, Jasper lunged, taking him down in the alley and pressing him to the ground. He raised his fist, wanting to pummel the man, but he stopped himself even before he heard

Darby screaming his name. "Jasper! Stop!" she hollered. "Jasper! Please stop."

He felt her hands pulling at his arm as she tried to drag him off the man. It took him a moment before he backed off. He couldn't believe how close he'd come to beating this man into the earth. His breath heaved, heart hammering, blood pressure up and pounding in his temples. Looking through a cloud of red, he still ached to hit the man again. He'd seen him hurting Darby. But he'd stopped himself, something that surprised him and left him shaking from how close he'd come to not stopping.

He took a breath and let it out before pushing himself up from the ground and off the man.

"I could have you arrested for assault," the man threatened as he got awkwardly to his feet. "This is none of your business, *Jasper*. I have the right to talk to my fiancée."

"She's not your fiancée and you weren't just trying to talk to her," Jasper said, his anger still running wild inside him. He took a few steps back, not quite trusting himself.

The man rubbed his jaw. "I don't know who the hell you think you are—"

"Aiden, he's a cop," Darby said.

"Former cop," Jasper corrected.

Aiden had been dusting himself off, but now narrowed his gaze at Jasper. "I just want to talk to Darby."

"I believe that's why she agreed to meet you at the café," Jasper said. "Apparently you had other plans, though, since you were waiting for her in this alley."

"I was just planning to walk her down to the café."

He scoffed at the man's lie, his fist itching to connect again with that arrogant face. He'd seen the way the man had grabbed Darby. What if Jasper hadn't come to town?

What if he hadn't got here when he did? He knew his reaction was a hundred times more complicated.

No one said anything for a moment as the tension waned some. "Do you still want to go to the café?" Jasper asked, turning to Darby. Even in the growing darkness he could see how pale she was. There was still a red mark on her wrist where the man had grabbed her. He felt his anger hunkered down just below the surface and Darby saw it too.

"Jasper," she said in warning.

He realized that Aiden hadn't been the only man who'd scared her and mentally kicked himself.

"All I want is a chance to have my say," Aiden said to her. "I came all this way. You didn't give me that chance when you broke off our engagement. Don't you at least owe me a few minutes of your time so I can move on like you have?" The man shot Jasper a hateful look as if he thought Darby had moved on with him.

Jasper looked to Darby. He could see her making her up mind. It was clear that she was afraid of Aiden and apparently with good reason.

She nodded slowly. "But don't touch me again."

Aiden looked as if he wanted to argue the point, but changed his mind. Darby's fear was only matched by Aiden's anger. Jasper knew that kind of fury. It scared him in himself. It really scared him in this man who'd professed to love Darby.

After Aiden finished making a show of dusting himself off, the three of them walked in the direction of the café. The highway next to them was inky black in the glow of the streetlights as they came on. Dusk had fallen over the town, taking the heat of the sun with it. Spring in Montana was often fickle. One day it could be warm and the next it could snow. Tonight was mild and yet Jasper could see his breath as they walked.

They were almost to the café when, across the highway that cut through the middle of town, he heard a door open and close. He glanced in the direction the sound had come from. Gossip. A moment later, the light inside the shop went out. Jasper wondered how much Leviathan Nash had seen and heard.

His pulse was only now returning to normal. He hated that he'd gotten so angry. Worse, that he'd scared Darby. It took him back to that other time in his life that he'd been trying so hard to forget.

Out of the corner of his eye, he could see Aiden rubbing his jaw and scowling as they reached the café. Jasper couldn't help but wonder about this man she'd once agreed to marry.

"You really don't need to go any farther with us," Aiden said, still scowling.

"I think I do," Jasper told him. "Consider it a personal escort through our town. Anyway, I'm hungry."

"Not exactly a friendly reception to your town, Darbs," Aiden said.

Darbs? Seriously? "Don't worry, I won't be sitting with you," Jasper assured him as he opened the door to the café and let Darby and her "date" go in. As Darby passed him, she shot him a look that could have been grudging gratefulness. He knew she was glad that he hadn't let Aiden pull her back into that alley. But at the same time, she wasn't happy about the way he'd handled it. Or maybe it was his own emotions he was seeing in her brown gaze.

He gave her a slight nod, pretty much agreeing with her assessment of the situation as he saw it. Aiden on the other hand glared at him and rubbed his jaw with a look that appeared to warn him not to walk near any dark alleys as long as he was in town.

Jasper headed for his usual booth, but sat on the opposite side so he could keep an eye on Darby and her former fiancé. All his instincts told him that she would need protecting as long as this clown was in Buckhorn.

AIDEN BOILED WITH fury inside even as he smiled across the table at Darby. She would pay for this humiliation. Clearly she'd called that former cop. Otherwise how had he known that they were to meet at the café? How dared she betray him like that.

He tried to rein in his anger. The night already hadn't gone as he'd planned it. Darby had sat on the side of the booth with her back to Jasper, leaving Aiden a good view of her Good Samaritan sitting only two booths away, watching him. He swore silently.

"Let's not stay here," he said and started to get out of the booth. "There must be some other place in town to eat."

She didn't move. "This is the only place open this time of year. Actually a lot of the year. Also it's here or nothing." She didn't even bother to look at him as she said it. Instead, she reached for the two menus leaning against the wall behind the salt and pepper shakers, napkin holder and large ketchup bottle. She tossed a menu over to him and opened hers, disappearing behind it.

He lowered himself back into the booth, feeling his ire fire on all eight cylinders now. He wanted to break something, anything to let out some of the rage building inside him. He'd planned this for so long and now it had all gone to hell. "I'm really not hungry."

"Well, I'm starved," she said behind her menu. "And

I'm not going anywhere else with you. If you have something to say to me…"

As the waitress approached, she lowered her menu. "I'm going to have the chicken fried steak special. Tell me you still have some of Bessie's red velvet cake back there." The teenaged girl said they did. "Great. Bring me one piece after dinner and the other to go for breakfast in the morning." She put her menu back and finally looked at him.

He could see that she was standing her ground, stubbornness behind her expressionless face and something more. Anger? He realized that she might get up and leave at any moment unless he played along. He could feel the waitress looking at him, waiting. He'd never minded letting waitresses wait. It was their job. But he could also feel Darby's gaze on him and he knew how much she hated it when he was rude to waitstaff.

"Just bring me what she's having," he said, slamming his menu closed, "but no cake. I'm watching my weight." He looked straight at Darby as he said it. She'd always been curvier than other women he'd dated and he knew that it had bothered her when he'd commented on her food selections.

As the waitress left and he put his menu back where Darby had gotten it, he asked, "So who's the wise guy who slugged me?" he asked. His voice sounded strained, no doubt from fighting hard to keep his temper in check. Why had he ever agreed to talk here? And when had Darby started calling the shots? "I might press charges against him."

To his surprise Darby laughed. "Against a former big-city homicide detective?" She didn't say anything else, just kept smiling, which infuriated him even more. Did she think he wouldn't press charges against a former hotshot cop? *The man had assaulted him.*

"So what is it you have to say to me that is so important you came all this way?" she asked, folding her arms in front of her on the table and looking him in the eye.

He let out a snort. "It isn't anything I intend to talk about here with your...friend watching."

"Well, this is the only place we'll be talking," she said, looking around at the other people having dinner. None of them were close, if that was her point.

His already aching jaw popped as he ground his teeth hard. "I thought we could go back to my motel room and talk like adults."

She shook her head. "That isn't going to happen." She said it with such finality that he swore under his breath. When he looked up he could see the former detective watching them. The man was Darby's protection? Or something more?

Aiden leaned over the table and lowered his voice. "You screwing that guy?"

Darby glared at him. "Even if I was, it wouldn't be any of your business. You and I are done and have been for several months."

He leaned back and tried to calm down. This was not the way he'd planned this at all. He'd had this crazy idea that she'd be glad to see him. It had been long enough that they'd been apart that he'd thought she might throw herself into his arms and agree to just about anything. He'd figured living in a dinky town like this she'd be desperate for male companionship. Then again, he hadn't anticipated that she might have found someone else in this short of a time.

Glancing at the former cop, he recalled how she had pulled the man she called Jasper off him. She'd seemed angry. Jasper, however, had seemed awfully protective of her. There was something there between the two of them. But maybe it wasn't serious.

Reaching into his pocket, he took out the ring case and set it on the table between them, thinking it would tempt her. "I'm only going to ask this once."

"Don't." She shook her head. "Nothing you can say can make me change my mind—especially after what you did earlier. You were waiting for me in that alley. You grabbed me hard, hurting my wrist. What were you planning to do? Drag me back in there and…" The words stopped as abruptly as they'd started, all the heat and anger fizzling down to a look of horror. "There is nothing you can say or do. I want nothing to do with you. That's why I broke off the engagement. I thought I made that clear. We're done."

"How can you say that? We were so good together. My family loved you. Our friends all thought we were perfect for each other." His voice broke and he looked away for a moment. He felt as if everyone in the café was listening—especially her new boyfriend. Heat rushed to his face and he felt his insides begin to boil to the point that he might not be able to control himself. He took a deep breath and let it out. "My life has been hell without you," he said in a hoarse whisper. He swallowed and tried again, hating that his eyes filled with tears. "I miss you so much." He couldn't look at her for fear he would cry. He'd rather die than cry in front of these people, especially Jasper. "I can't live without you."

"I'm sorry you feel that way," she said. "I would have thought by now that you would have found someone else."

"She wasn't you."

Darby chuckled. "She dumped you that quickly?"

"I dumped *her*," he spat, grabbing the ring box and shoving it back into his pocket as he blinked back the tears. He was trembling with his sudden intense hatred for this woman. How dared she laugh after he'd poured out his heart to her?

"Aiden, you need to see someone about your anger issues," she said quietly. "I'm serious. You're scary. That night at my apartment—"

"When you broke off our engagement."

"When you were drunk and so abusive..."

"You're going to hold that against me? You called the cops on me. Am I holding that against you?" he whispered angrily. "Do you have any idea how humiliating that was for me?" He was breathing hard and had to battle back the urge to reach across the table and grab her by the neck and shake some sense into her. "Do you have any idea how humiliating *this* is, sitting here begging you to come back to me with half the town and your boyfriend watching?" he demanded through gritted teeth. He waited a beat for a reaction from her and was rewarded with nothing. "You're making a huge mistake."

The waitress came up to the table to deposit a large plate of food in front of him. He felt as if he might throw up. He watched Darby dig into hers as if she hadn't eaten all day. She didn't seem to care that he hadn't touched his. He scoffed at that thought. She didn't seem to care about him at all.

He crossed his arms and watched her, thinking he could at least make her feel guilty. But she didn't seem to notice. When the waitress stopped back by again, she asked if there was something wrong with his meal he hadn't touched.

"I guess I'm not that hungry," he snapped. "My jaw hurts."

Darby smiled at the girl. "Mine's delicious. Please tell the cook that my steak is cooked to perfection."

The girl brightened. "I will." She left and Darby went right back to eating. He couldn't believe the amount of food she was putting away. He could see that she'd put on a few pounds. Not that it hurt her figure. Yet.

He looked past her to the cop. He also seemed to have a healthy appetite. Aiden had to look away. He realized that the food actually smelled good. He felt his stomach growl. He hadn't eaten all day, too anxious to stop for food. But he wasn't about to touch it now.

"I'll be leaving first thing in the morning," he said.

"I think that's best," Darby said as she carefully cut off another piece of her steak and popped it into her mouth.

He watched her chew. "I suppose breakfast is out of the question."

"Yes, it is," she said after swallowing. "I don't want to see you again. If I do, I'll do more than call a friend." He scoffed, but when she glanced at him, he saw the look in her eye. "I bought a gun after the last time I saw you and I learned how to use it," she said, her gaze again on the steak she was cutting into a bite. When she looked up, he saw more than determination in her brown eyes.

With a shock, he realized that she would actually shoot him. Hell, she might not stop with one shot. She'd kill him. It made him want to hurt her badly even as he feared he wouldn't get the chance now.

He leaned toward her, wanting her on her knees, begging him for mercy. "Someday, I am going to make you pay for this," he whispered. "Enjoy your dinner." He leaned back and, sneering, started to reach for his wallet.

"My treat," she said. "I wasn't going to let you buy mine anyway."

"Fine, pay for mine as well." He shoved noisily out of the booth, making the dishes on the table clatter. Moving to her side of the booth, he leaned down. He could feel the former cop watching him as if ready to spring up in an instant if needed. "Better watch your back," he said, his voice rising with each word. "Because this isn't over until I say it's over. The next time you see me, you're going to live just long enough to regret it."

CHAPTER FOURTEEN

DARBY TRIED TO catch her breath as Aiden stormed out. She could feel everyone in the café looking at her. The man had just threatened her in front of a lot of people. Tonight, she'd seen everything about the man that she had feared. Thank God she hadn't married him.

Her hand holding her fork was shaking. She set down the fork a little too hard and fought tears. He scared her because she feared that she would see him again. How was it possible that she'd ever loved this man? Because he'd hidden this side of him—until he hadn't.

She looked up, scared for a moment that Aiden had come back. But instead, Jasper took the seat across from her. He'd brought his plate and utensils. As the waitress rushed over, he said, "Can you get rid of all of this." He motioned to Aiden's uneaten meal.

As the waitress hurried away with it, Jasper said, "You okay?" She nodded as she felt the people in the café were no longer watching, as if they knew she'd be safe with Jasper. "I'm sorry about earlier," he continued. "I have a real problem with any man abusing a woman." He shrugged. "Also Aiden is a jerk. I wish you'd have let me hit him again."

The last made her smile. It was over, no matter what Aiden said. She was just relieved that he hadn't made a worse scene. But even more relieved that she hadn't foolishly agreed to meet him anywhere but here. It scared her to think of what might have happened. What might have happened if Jasper hadn't shown up when he did. The hate she'd seen in Aiden's eyes when he'd looked at her still chilled her to her core.

Taking a deep breath and letting it out, she picked up her fork. She wasn't hungry, but like earlier, she was determined not to show it. She took a bite and then another.

"I got the newspaper before your call," Jasper said. "Good article on Gossip. I took care of that other thing as I'm sure you knew I would. Still waiting to hear." She felt herself relax, which she knew was his plan. "I heard another business is going to be breaking ground soon here in Buckhorn. Heard anything about it?"

She hadn't, but her interest was piqued. Mostly, thanks to Jasper, things were feeling normal again and she needed that right now. "Where?"

He described a spot on the other side of town that had a large condemned building on it. She thought someone had told her it had been an apartment house at some point in Buckhorn's history.

She realized that Jasper had been more upset about what had been going on with Aiden than even she had. That comment about him having a problem with men abusing women. She would have loved to have asked him about that, but this wasn't the time. Still, she felt as if he'd revealed a little of his past that he kept so well guarded and that made her warm a little inside.

"In case you wonder why it took me so long to get to town, I got held up because of a low tire and then a cattle drive," he said. "I wish you had waited for me."

Darby nodded. "I felt bad about asking you and I just wanted to get it over with." She met his gaze. "Thank you. I don't know what I would have done without you. I thought I could handle him myself…"

"No problem. I'm sorry if I disappointed you." Their gazes held for a long moment.

"You could never do that," she said, her voice breaking. "I just didn't want you to kill him and go to prison on my account."

He smiled and broke eye contact first. "I was hungrier than I thought." He took a bite of his meal, which looked a whole lot like hers. They ate in silence for a few minutes. "Maybe you should get a restraining order on him."

She shook her head. "You should know that they aren't worth the paper they're printed on. He said he was leaving town in the morning and that will be the end of it."

"Are you sure about that?"

She heard the worry in his voice. She wasn't sure and she could see that he knew it. "I told him I bought a gun and learned how to use it."

"Is that true?" he asked, looking worried.

"I have a gun and I do know how to use it…"

"But you couldn't kill him."

Darby shook her head. "A part of me feels sorry for him. He's not a happy person. I think he hates himself and that's why he takes it out on other people."

"You're cutting him a whole lot more slack than I would. I think he's an arrogant, privileged, overindulgent asshole who's used to getting his way." He looked down at his plate and she saw him hesitate, but only for a moment before he put down his fork and said, "I also think you should stay in my guest room out at the ranch at least for tonight." She started to argue, but he stopped her. "That wasn't a suggestion. Neither of us will be able to sleep otherwise and I need my sleep."

As he pushed his nearly empty plate away, the waitress came with their cake. Four pieces, one for each of them to eat now and two to go.

Jasper grinned over at her, looking as happy as a kid on Christmas morning. "Bessie makes the best red velvet cake."

"I couldn't agree more," Darby said and took a bite. "By the way, thank you." He didn't ask for what exactly. He flashed her a smile, but she could see worry in his gray eyes. Jasper thought that they hadn't seen the last of Aiden. She feared he was right.

AIDEN FELT IN SHOCK. He couldn't believe that Darby could brush him off that easily. Did she really think she could just tell him to get lost and he would? He considered waiting for her outside of the café. But the spring night was cold and anyway, he couldn't get to her with the ex-cop around. No, he had to bide his time.

He walked away from the café through the darkness that had dropped like a blanket over the town. He could feel the ring box in his pocket. Had he really offered it to her only to have her turn him down? Who did the bitch think she was? Didn't she realize he could do better?

His head ached. He felt as if he might explode if he didn't release some of this tension. He couldn't remember ever being this furious. He'd come all this way to try to get her back. Now he couldn't imagine why. What was wrong with him?

Ahead, he could see the light of the gas station he'd passed on the way into town. This wasn't the way to the motel. He'd gone the wrong direction. Looking behind him, he could see the Sleepy Pine Motel sign on the other side of the highway and clear at the other end of town with nothing but darkness beyond it. He thought the cold spring night air might calm him, but like his walk in the wrong direction, it only seemed to fuel his wrath.

If he could get his hands on Darby he could make her change her mind. He told himself that he wouldn't hurt her. He'd just talk to her. Once she realized how much he needed her right now...

Still filled with blind fury, he saw a cat hunkered in the shadows at the mouth of an alley. He kicked at it, but the damned thing leaped in the air, a claw catching his good pants. He felt the pants tear even as he tried to kick it again. But the cat was too quick. As it scurried down the alley, he almost went after it, determined to punch out the last of its nine lives.

Instead, he kicked an empty metal garbage can sitting at the mouth of the alley. His boot put a satisfying dent in the side of it. He kicked again and again, pretending it was the cat, Darby, Jasper the cop, until the can was nothing but a heap of cheap metal and he was breathing hard.

"Excuse me." The voice coming out of the darkness startled him. He swung around, at first not seeing where the sound had come from.

"I'll pay for the garbage can," Aiden said, thinking destroying it had been worth most any amount. Not that it had completely satisfied the need inside him.

"That won't be necessary," said the low male voice.

He looked down the short alley to a building hunkering there. It appeared to be an old carriage house. But someone had put black paper over the windows. A faint light glowed behind it. He couldn't quite make out the sign in the window. Gossip? That couldn't be right.

At the sound of boots on gravel, Aiden looked quickly to his right as a small man dressed all in black stepped forward. He was much closer than Aiden had thought—and much older too. The man was holding a cat. Aiden had a bad feeling it was the one he'd tried to kick.

"I didn't mean to startle you," the man said in a low, almost hypnotic voice.

If the man planned to give him shit for kicking at his cat, he'd picked the wrong night and the wrong man. The old man looked decrepit and puny. "You didn't startle me," Aiden lied.

The man smiled, exposing a row of tiny corn kernel–like teeth. "That's good. Then you don't mind giving me a hand."

His first impulse was to simply pay for the man's garbage can, apologize for kicking at his cat and be on his way. He reached for his wallet.

"No, please," the man said with a chuckle. "I don't need your money. I could use just a few moments of your time, though. I'll make it worth your while."

That made him laugh. "If you're offering me money—"

"I wouldn't insult you like that. No," the man said. "I've found information is often worth much more than money, don't you agree?"

Aiden had had enough of this. After the way this day had gone, he just wanted to get back to his motel room, turn on the TV, have a drink from the bottle he'd brought for the trip and try to forget all of it. He'd actually thought he'd be sharing his bed with Darby. What a fool he'd been.

"I'm not sure what you're selling, but I'm not interested. I've had a bad day and the night hasn't been that good either."

He started to take a step away when the man said, "Oh, I think I can fix that. Unless you aren't interested in what I could tell you about Darby Fulton—and her friend, former homicide detective Jasper Cole." That stopped him. "I thought that might interest you. I do need help carrying something out to my truck, but then I'll give you something that will make up for the day and night you've had. I promise. It will make you much happier than kicking a garbage can. Or even a cat," he said as he lowered the feline to the ground. It immediately took off at a run up the street.

"I take it that wasn't your cat," Aiden said, thankful for that.

The man started down the alley toward the shop. "By the way, the name is Leviathan Nash, proprietor of my shop, Gossip. Catchy name, don't you think?"

Aiden watched him go, telling himself it was time to put Darby behind him even as he ached to get more than even. "How heavy is this something you need carried?"

"Don't worry, you can handle it easily with my help," Leviathan Nash said.

If this man had something on Darby and the cop... Aiden hesitated only a moment before he followed the odd little man down the alley.

As they reached the building, the door to Gossip opened as if by magic. Leviathan Nash stepped through, Aiden right behind him before the door closed and locked.

In the middle of the floor sat a large wooden box several feet wide and high and a good six feet long. Aiden felt a little unease as he joked, "I hope that doesn't have a body in it."

JASPER NOTICED THAT Darby was quiet as they left the café and walked down the street through the pockets of darkness between the streetlamps to his pickup. He'd half expected Aiden to be lying in wait and was a little surprised—and maybe a little disappointed—when the man didn't leap out from somewhere by the time they'd reached his truck.

If Aiden had plans to ambush Darby again tonight, Jasper wanted to be there. He also would feel justified to subdue him until Marshal Leroy Baggins could be there. The man thought his jaw hurt now... Try to hurt Darby again and Jasper swore he would show Aiden real pain.

At his pickup, he spotted Ruby sitting in the front seat, wagging her tail enthusiastically. He'd left her to guard the pickup and it appeared that it hadn't been tampered with. He'd half expected Aiden to at least put a knife through one of his tires or take a rock to the windshield. He seemed that kind of guy.

He checked the tire that had been going flat before he'd driven into town. It was still fine.

Darby appeared surprised too that there had been no sign of Aiden or any damage to his truck as she joined Ruby. "If that puppy crowds you, just push her over," he said as he slid behind the wheel. Darby had her arm around Ruby and had pulled her over onto her lap. Ruby was licking her face, making Darby laugh and Jasper smile. He did love a woman who loved his dog, he thought.

As he drove out of town, he passed the motel. There was only one car parked in front of any of the rooms. He figured the gray SUV belonged to Aiden, but he didn't see him anywhere. Nor was there a light on in the motel room where the SUV was parked.

"That his rig?" he asked Darby, who nodded and was also looking in that direction. He wondered if like him, she'd hoped that the man had just left town and not looked back. No such luck.

He was glad he'd invited her out to the ranch for the night. He feared it would be just like Aiden to be waiting for her down near her office and the apartment over it where she lived.

Neither said much on the drive out to the ranch. The night was dark except for the rim of gold peeking over the peaks to the east. By the time he pulled into the yard, the moon had scaled the mountains.

He parked and they climbed out into the moonlight splashed across the landscape. The smell of pines and the creek drifted on the slight breeze. Standing in the moon's warm glow out here away from everything, Jasper felt as if he could finally breathe. He looked over at Darby who'd joined him. She had turned her face up to the moonlight. He was struck by the peaceful expression on her face. Maybe they weren't all that different after all.

The stir of the boughs of the nearby pines played a lullaby. It teased at her hair. As she lifted a hand to brush a lock back from her eyes, he reached out for her, wanting to touch her more than he wanted his next breath. The last time he'd kissed her, he'd been a different man. They'd both been so young, so inexperienced. But still he found it hard to believe that she could have forgotten especially when he'd later realized that it had been her first time. He'd never forgotten that night. Or her.

He hadn't realized how badly he'd wanted to kiss her again until he pulled her to him. Her gaze locked with his as he slowly lowered his mouth to hers. Her lips parted, opening to him. She tasted of cream cheese frosting. He heard her emit a small pleased sigh as he deepened the kiss, and she leaned into him. Wrapping his arms around her, he pulled her close. His pulse quickened as her full breasts pressed against his chest.

Need made his knees weak. His heart was a hammer in his chest, his pulse throbbing hard just beneath his skin.

But it was the fire in his belly that surprised him. He hadn't wanted a woman in so long. He'd told himself that he didn't want this, didn't need it. And he hadn't. Until Darby. Even then, he'd tried as hard as he could not to want or need her. But it had been a lie. He'd never wanted or needed anything more in his life.

And that terrified him. Especially after what had happened earlier tonight.

He pulled back, holding her at arm's length. Her eyes were wide and honey filled in the moonlight. "Darby." Her name was on his lips and now in the night spring air. He let go of her and took a step back as if he didn't trust himself while he was touching her. "This is not why I invited you out here."

She nodded, looking as shaken as he felt.

Ruby came running up, jumped against him and began barking for her dinner, then did the same with Darby. She reached down to pet the pup, but her gaze was on him. Her look said that she didn't appreciate the diversion as much as he did.

"We should get inside," he said, his voice filled with emotion. He wanted to say so much more, but was afraid that if he tried he would only make things more uncomfortable than they already were.

He turned toward the house, his heart beating hard at even the thought of how close he'd come to sweeping her up into his arms and taking her to his bed—if they made it that far before he stripped off her clothes.

It would have been impulsive on both of their parts. She'd just had a run-in with her ex. Both of them would have regretted it tomorrow, he told himself. He hated to think how awkward even the kiss might make things. And yet, all this rational thought did little to cool the desire that burned through him.

He glanced at her, telling himself that Darby wasn't ready for a relationship any more than he was. As he pointed her in the direction of the guest room, he said, "Let me know if you need anything."

"If you had an old T-shirt I could sleep in." Her voice sounded hoarse as if she too was filled with emotions after the kiss. What the hell had he been thinking kissing her? She'd looked so good in the moonlight, so pretty, so downright delectable.

"I think I can scare up a T-shirt," he said. In his bedroom, he opened a bureau drawer and pulled out a soft old one he thought she might like. Back at the door to the guest room, he saw her standing silhouetted against the moonlight pouring in through the large window. What had he been thinking inviting her to stay with him out here? Had it really been to keep her safe? Or was it to keep her close?

"The view is amazing," she said without turning around.

He put the T-shirt on the bed. He could hear Ruby throwing her food bowl into the air and chasing it around the kitchen. "I need to feed the dog."

Darby turned to look at him and for a moment it was all he could do not to close the distance between them again and take her in his arms once more. But he knew if he did, it wouldn't end there. Nor was Ruby going to let him forget it was dinnertime. Bessie didn't know how right she was about him needing that pup.

Jasper took a step back and then another one. He wasn't ready for this. He hadn't thought he'd ever be again. Darby Fulton was a surprise. And not a welcome one at the moment. He told himself that no other woman could have broken down his barriers, annihilated his defenses. Another step back and he was in the hallway. She'd turned from the window and had been watching him, seeming amused.

"I—" He felt as if he needed to explain his actions, all of them tonight, but she stopped him.

"I know," she said, smiling. "It's been quite the night." She spotted his T-shirt on the end of the bed. He'd also left her a new toothbrush still in the package. "Thanks." Her gaze returned to him. "For everything."

All he could do was nod and say, "Sleep tight." With that he headed into the kitchen to feed his dog. By the time he had Ruby fed and in her kennel where she could come and go inside a portion of the garage, he was relieved to see that the guest room door was closed.

DARBY THOUGHT SHE'D never be able to sleep—not after everything that had happened tonight. She felt as if she were floating after that kiss. She'd been half-afraid the magic wouldn't still be there, that she'd blown their last encounter out of proportion, that it had only been her inexperience all those years ago that had made her think she and Jasper had such amazing chemistry.

But tonight, she'd felt it down to her toes and seeing the expression on Jasper's face… He'd felt it too. She'd seen desire burning in those gray eyes of his. He'd wanted her as much as she'd wanted him. So, what had scared him?

She suspected it was whatever had been holding him back since they'd crossed paths again. Until she knew why he'd quit being a homicide detective and moved back to Buckhorn to ranch and to become practically a recluse, she wouldn't have all the pieces of the puzzle. Not unless he told her, which she knew was a really long shot.

But she'd been right about that strong, urgent something still being there between them, she thought as she hugged herself. The last time a man had made her feel like this was years ago the night she and Jasper had met at that party. Aiden certainly had never made her feel like this, she thought with a jolt as she remembered his threat before leaving the café.

Aiden. A shudder moved through her. She looked toward the window. She was safe here with Jasper. That thought still had her going to the window and closing the curtains. Aiden hadn't followed them out here, had he?

She went back to bed, determined to put Aiden behind her. Hopefully, he would be gone in the morning. She couldn't imagine him sticking around. She'd been as direct as she could possibly be. Maybe even going to the café with him had been a mistake since she'd already ended it. But she'd thought that once he had his say, he would accept that there was no going back.

Now she wasn't so sure that Aiden would finally give up, which made her nervous. Worse, she'd dragged Jasper into her problems and that was the last thing she wanted to do.

After undressing, she pulled the too-large T-shirt over her head and let the soft worn fabric drop over her body. It felt so good that she hugged herself again, remembering being in Jasper's arms. Remembering what had begun all those years ago with just one kiss. As she crawled between the sheets, she told herself that she'd never get to sleep.

CHAPTER FIFTEEN

DARBY WOKE TO sunlight with a start. For a moment, she didn't know where she was. She'd been having this dream… She sat up and looked around the room. Jasper's guest room.

With a sigh of relief, she lay back down. The dream, though, still hung on the edge of her consciousness. She couldn't remember what it had been about—just the scared feeling she'd awakened with.

Seeing the time on her phone next to the bed, she was surprised that she'd slept better than she thought she would in Jasper's guest room. She'd had such an emotional day yesterday that she'd been convinced that even the comfortable bed, adjoining bath and wonderfully soft T-shirt weren't going to help her relax enough to sleep.

But sleep had come like a dark cloak dropped over her even as high as her emotions had been running. She hadn't planned on going home with Jasper. She hadn't planned on going home with anyone. Aiden showing up had surprised her more than she wanted to admit. She'd thought she would never see him again—and that had been more than fine with her.

That he'd come so far and was intent on them talking… Had he really tried to give her back the engagement ring? The man had to be delusional. She'd known better than to meet him alone, but calling Jasper had been impulsive— and desperate. Actually, she'd been surprised when he'd agreed since they both knew he'd been determined to hold her at arm's length. She'd been even more surprised when he'd insisted she stay with him.

The kiss though, now that was really the surprise. She smiled to herself. She'd bet that Jasper regretted it this morning. And he thought she didn't know him.

With a sigh, she climbed out of bed, ready to take on another day. Aiden frightened her before last night. Now she had no intention of letting him get near her again. She would start carrying her gun. She would keep her office locked. She would watch her back—just as he'd warned her.

Moving to the window, she opened the curtains and let the sun pour in. There was a fresh layer of snow on the mountain peaks, the sky behind them a brilliant blue, no clouds. She loved spring. It seemed to fill the air with excitement and…possibilities.

Darby stretched, feeling as if everything was going to be all right. Nothing like a sunny day to make her feel as if she could conquer anything. Also waking to the smell of coffee in Jasper's ranch house didn't hurt either, she realized, and hurried to shower and dress.

"Good morning," Jasper said as she walked into the kitchen.

"Morning." She felt almost shy remembering being in his arms last night.

He handed her a glass of orange juice and motioned to a stool at the breakfast bar. She sat, drank some of the orange juice and happily took the cup of coffee he offered her. "I know you take cream and sugar," he said. "Help yourself to more if I didn't get it right."

"It's delicious," she said, surprised that he knew how she took her coffee. "Just like I like it." She cocked her head at him in question.

He laughed. "I've been at the café when you've called in an order for coffee to go." He shrugged and leaned against the counter as he sipped his apparently plain black coffee. "Couldn't help overhearing."

She *was* particular about her coffee. Real cream. Real sugar. And just the right amount. When she was really busy at the office she called the café and they were kind enough to run her down a cup—made to her specifications. She realized that she must have sounded like one of those demanding people everyone hated.

"How did you sleep?" he asked, changing the subject to her relief.

"Wonderful."

"No nightmares?"

She hesitated for a moment, still feeling that darkness at the corner of her mind, but shook it off. "None that I can remember." She glanced toward the window and the mountains beyond. A memory surfaced. She frowned. "Did I hear you leave last night?" She shifted her gaze to him.

"Sorry if I woke you. I couldn't sleep. I remembered I hadn't checked some fence that had been down. I was about to do that when I got your call to come to town. Sorry that it woke you."

"No, it's fine. I went right back to sleep apparently. I feel bad about keeping you from your work."

"There's always plenty of work on a ranch."

She nodded, hating that as a reporter she had trouble taking anything anyone told her at face value, even from Jasper, one of the few people she trusted. Middle of the night was an odd time to check a downed fence. She suspected he couldn't sleep and had been busy mentally kicking himself for kissing her and decided to go for a ride.

Darby glanced toward the window and the view of the creek. "It's so quiet out here."

"Bet you missed the semi trucks shifting down on the way through town. Or Lars Olson in that old truck picking up garbage first thing in the morning," he said, smiling. He had a really nice smile, though he seemed...a little uneasy around her. Like that was anything new. It must feel weird for him having her in his house. She bet he was anxious to get her back to town and off his hands.

"I've gotten used to the town noises," she said and laughed, hoping yesterday's events—including that kiss—wouldn't ruin their budding friendship. "But I have to admit, out here I fell asleep the minute my head hit the pillow. Thank you again. For everything."

"My pleasure." He pushed off the counter. "I have your breakfast. You left it in the pickup." He took two to-go containers from the refrigerator. "Red velvet cake. The breakfast of champions."

She couldn't help but smile even though eating was the last thing she could do right now. "I'm still full from that dinner last night." She saw that Ruby was waiting by the door. "And you normally go into town to have breakfast with Bessie at the café." Cocking her head, she eyed him. "You didn't go in for quite a few days last week. I thought you were probably avoiding me."

He chuckled at that, but didn't meet her eyes. "I've been busy."

"Is that so?"

JASPER HAD BEEN worried that things would be awkward between them after everything that had happened—especially the kiss.

But when she quickly changed into reporter mode at

even the hint of suspicion when it came to him changing his routine, he knew they were going to be all right. She was back to her default mode even though he was sure she had been suspicious of why he'd backed off after the kiss last night. Nothing got past this woman. It was her nature as well as her occupation to question everything and then go looking for answers.

He quickly changed the subject. "I thought we'd check to make sure your former fiancé isn't still lurking around town."

"I appreciate you being there last night, but I'm fine."

He nodded. "Just the same, I'll see you to your office." He wasn't going to let this go.

"Such a gentleman."

"Aren't I, though?" he said in a self-deprecating tone.

She smiled and shook her head. He couldn't tell if she was pleased or not. But at least he'd gotten her mind off his change of routine. He wished he could get his mind off the feel of her in his arms, the taste of her on his lips as quickly. "Hopefully, Aiden is long gone."

"Hopefully." He heard the worry in her voice. Just like he'd heard what Aiden had said to her before he'd left the café last night.

Darby finished her coffee and stood. "I'm going to take my cake with me. Rudy is clearly anxious to go for a ride and Bessie will be wondering if you aren't going to make it in to the café again. She'll be sending out the cavalry, if she hasn't already."

"What if he hasn't left town?" Jasper asked, not letting her change the subject. He could see that she didn't have an answer for that. He, on the other hand, did. If the man was still around? He'd personally see him out of Buckhorn.

"I'm sorry I involved you. I don't want you worrying about me," she said as she turned toward the door.

"Anyone who knows you is worried about you," he joked, but didn't get the lighthearted response he usually did from her. He finished his coffee, and grabbing his Stetson and coat, headed out the door to his pickup.

On the short ride into town, Darby talked mostly to Ruby as she petted the pup and laughed at the wet, sloppy kisses she got in answer. Jasper was content to watch the two of them out of the corner of his eye. The dog had taken to her. He suspected all animals liked her. There was just something about her.

As JASPER DROVE past the motel, Darby saw that Aiden's car was gone. She looked for it as they drove through town and was relieved when she didn't see it. Jasper turned around out past the filling station before going back through as if he too was looking for the man's car—or the man himself.

"Didn't see any sign of him, did you?" he asked as he parked across the street from her office and apartment.

She shook her head and gave him her it's-all-good smile. He didn't look relieved. Actually, he looked more worried.

"Call me if you see him," he said and held her gaze. "Don't try to reason with him yourself. Promise me."

She promised, making an X with her finger over her heart. He hadn't looked like he trusted even that. The man was as skeptical as she was. She liked that about him, she realized. He questioned things, never taking one person's opinion for fact. He would have made a good reporter. It was probably why he'd made a good homicide detective. Until he didn't.

One of these days maybe he would tell her what happened. Or not. Maybe he would also tell her why he was so afraid of the chemistry that had caught fire between them last night in the moonlight. It had been sparking between them for weeks now. She'd thought that maybe he hadn't felt it. Until that kiss.

"Thanks again," she said as she gave Ruby one last hug and climbed out of his pickup. She headed for her office, all her senses on alert. It wasn't like Aiden to give up so easily. She didn't trust it.

She could feel Jasper's gaze on her as she dug her keys out of her purse and unlocked the door to her office and apartment. Out of the corner of her eye, she watched the street. No sign of Aiden. The door opened and she hesitated a moment to wave to Jasper before she stepped in and closed and locked the door behind her.

For a moment, she stood with her back to the door, listening. Was she afraid Aiden would have broken into her office? She glanced up the stairs to her apartment where she'd left her gun and ammunition.

She took a breath and started up the stairs. It only took a moment to check the studio apartment. No sign of Aiden. No sign that anyone had been there. She went to the locked cabinet, opened it and took out her gun and a box of cartridges. After loading the gun, she dropped it into her large purse.

As she went back downstairs with it, she knew she couldn't stay locked away from the world. She was a reporter and she had another newspaper to put out next week. She needed copy, which meant she would have to hit the streets.

Unless she heard something on the hair she'd taken from Leviathan Nash's hairbrush and any fingerprints that could be obtained from his cup, she had nothing new on Gossip. Time was running out. His lease would be up in just over a week and she feared he would be gone before she got to the bottom of the mystery.

As she moved to sit down behind her desk, she looked across the street in the direction of Gossip in time to see Earl Ray Caulfield go through the front door and disappear inside.

CHAPTER SIXTEEN

JASPER LEFT HIS pickup parked across the street from Darby's office where he could see it and walked down to the café. Darby was safe—at least for the moment. He knew he couldn't keep her safe without staying with her 24/7 and there was no way she'd put up with that. Not to mention that he didn't trust himself to be with her and not do more than kiss her.

He'd been worried about her digging into Leviathan Nash's past. He'd thought that was where the danger would come from. He hadn't known about an abusive ex-fiancé. But he did now. He'd seen enough of Aiden that he didn't need to check for a rap sheet to know he was a violent offender. He'd been in law enforcement long enough to spot his kind. Once they got obsessed with someone, it usually ended badly for the woman. Now that woman in the spotlight was Darby.

The moment Jasper entered the café, he saw Bessie standing at the front window. The café was empty except for a couple of ranchers sitting at the counter. Neither had seemed to notice Bessie. She stood with the lower part of her apron bunched in her fists. She was so still...too still.

Jasper looked past her. She was staring at Gossip. As he approached her, he could see that something was horribly wrong.

"Bessie?" She started, then turned slowly to look at him, her eyes wide, her face a mask of shock—and alarm.

"Earl Ray," she said in a whisper. "He just went inside that shop. He must have gotten an invitation. Wouldn't he have told me?"

Looking across the street, Jasper could see no one, but he didn't doubt that she'd seen her husband go inside. That meant that like him, Earl Ray had gotten an invitation. But unlike Jasper, Earl Ray had decided to go to his "special showing."

"I'm sure he's fine," he said, even though he wasn't at all. He touched her arm and she nodded, tears in her eyes.

"Why would he do this?" she whispered, clearly not wanting to draw the attention of the customers.

Jasper led her over to a table and into a booth. He went past the ranchers behind the counter to get the coffeepot. Filling both ranchers' cups first, he returned to the table with the pot and two cups. As he filled each cup, Bessie hardly noticed as she sat staring through the window across the highway at Gossip, her hands clasped together, her look filled with both dread and fear.

After taking the pot back, he leaned through the pass-through to order them both breakfast since they had the same thing every morning he came in. He knew Bessie wouldn't be hungry, but he'd try to get her to eat while they waited for Earl Ray to exit Gossip.

Back at the table he sat down, then reached across and covered her hands with his two large ones. "It's probably my fault," he said. Her gaze shot to his. "Darby has been digging into Leviathan Nash's past." He could see that this didn't come as a surprise to her. "She's discovered that he is probably using a false name. She came by some hair of his and a cup he drank from. I asked Earl Ray to see if there was anything in the databanks."

None of this seemed to surprise her.

"I'm sure he's just doing a little reconnaissance on his own." Even as Jasper said it, he hoped that was all it was.

EARL RAY HAD known how dangerous it would be once he pushed open the door to Gossip. He told himself he had to accept the invitation. He couldn't protect the town and the people unless he looked into Leviathan Nash and Gossip. Nor could he stop now out of fear of what the man might have in store for him. Whatever it was, he told himself it wouldn't break him. He wouldn't let it.

But as the door closed behind him and he spotted the small gray-haired man sitting behind the antique desk, he felt his stomach churn. He hadn't been this afraid since Bessie had been shot in an altercation at the café. He'd thought he was going to lose her before he could tell her how much he loved her.

But he'd gotten a second chance and had not only gotten to tell her, he'd made her his wife. He was remodeling the home of her dreams. He had sworn to dedicate the rest of his life to her.

That was why this man had better not tell him anything bad about Bessie. Earl Ray might snap the little man's neck. Even as he thought it, he knew the emotion was driven by fear. He had no doubt that whatever vile thing Leviathan Nash had to tell him, it would be devastating. He told himself that he couldn't imagine anything about Bessie that would be so horrific that it would destroy him. But then again, if he had learned anything in his more than half a century of life, it was that people kept secrets. Especially from the ones they loved the most.

Look what he'd done himself, keeping the invitation to Gossip from her. She would have tried to stop him, of that he was sure. He'd seen the worry in her face every time someone came out of the shop looking shaken only to later fall completely apart. He thought of Nancy Green. No business card was found next to her body. Only during the autopsy had it been found partially chewed-up in her stomach. Whatever her secret, she'd taken it to her grave.

"So glad you could make it," Leviathan Nash said, now rising to his feet. He was definitely diminutive. But Earl Ray feared that people often underestimated him because of it. He didn't plan to make that mistake as he looked around the shop, surprised by how few wares the man had.

But then again, trinkets weren't what the man was really selling, were they.

"I have something I thought you might like," the man said as he headed across the room to the wall of shelves.

Earl Ray saw that a single light shone on one object centered there. He recognized it at once and felt a shock rattle through him. That was when he knew that this wasn't about Bessie at all. He should have felt relieved. Instead, he felt a new bone-rattling terror building.

BESSIE HAD TAKEN the news with little reaction after hearing where Darby's investigation had taken her—and how the two of them had involved her husband. Jasper was surprised, though, that she wasn't upset. But then again, she knew Earl Ray probably better than most after all these years.

"I just wish he'd told me," she said. "So you're telling me that we don't know who Leviathan Nash really is. No surprise there, I guess. I just wonder why he sent my husband an invitation."

Jasper shook his head. He had no idea, but if he had put any money on it, he'd bet it wasn't good. He sensed that Bessie felt the same way.

"You think he's doing his own investigating right now over at the shop," she said. He heard the disbelief in her voice. Her eyes filled with tears as she met Jasper's gaze. "But for Earl Ray to get an invitation, that means…" Her voice broke. "Leviathan Nash has something on my husband."

"Not necessarily," Jasper said quickly.

"You're right. That isn't how the evil man works. He has something on someone close to Earl Ray. News that will break my husband's heart." She pulled her hand free from Jasper's to cover her mouth as tears cascaded down her cheeks. "What if it's something about me?"

"Bessie, no. You're jumping to conclusions. Until Earl Ray comes out of the shop, we won't know."

"Will we even know then?" she demanded, making the ranchers glance over their shoulders for a moment before returning to their breakfasts. She lowered her voice. "You know Earl Ray. He'll keep it to himself." She shook her head. "I could kill that man, whoever he is, myself."

"I know how you feel, but he's only rented the building for a month. In a matter of days, he'll be gone. If we get a hit on the man's DNA, he could be gone even sooner. I'm sure the marshal would be happy to send him packing if he proves to have a criminal record, especially as a con man."

"Not soon enough," Bessie said as the cook brought out their breakfasts. She started to push hers away.

"Please eat something. Usually whoever goes into Gossip comes out within thirty minutes."

She glanced across the street at the shop. He could see

how anxious she was. "Switch sides with me. You can tell me when he comes out."

Jasper nodded and traded places with her, taking his usual seat after also switching their meals. "How are your pancakes?"

Bessie took a bite, clearly just to appease him. "Who was that man in the café with Darby who everyone in town is talking about?"

"Darby's former fiancé. You haven't seen him this morning, have you?" She shook her head. "He didn't come in early for breakfast?"

She frowned. "No, I got here at four to start baking, and my new cook came in shortly after that. He said the man's car was gone when he walked to work. The man must have left sometime last night."

Maybe, Jasper thought. Or maybe not.

He'd dutifully eaten in an attempt to get Bessie to do the same. He was almost done when he looked up and saw Earl Ray come out of Gossip. The older man was holding a white bag. He didn't look in the direction of the café, but hurried down the street a few yards before he opened the bag and pulled out what looked like a business card.

A moment later, he stumbled into the side of the building next to him as if someone had kicked his legs out from under him.

"WAIT HERE," JASPER said as he sprang from the booth and rushed for the door. He quickly checked to make sure no traffic was coming and ran across the highway to where Earl Ray was still leaning against the side of the building.

As he approached, he saw the business card flutter to the ground followed by the Gossip bag the man had been carrying. He heard something break from inside the bag as it hit the concrete. He scooped up the business card and stuffed it into his pocket, instinctively knowing that Earl Ray wouldn't want his wife to see whatever was written on it.

"Let me help you," Jasper said as he took Earl Ray's arm.

The man stared at him for a moment unseeing before he blinked. Jasper felt the strength come back into the older man. He straightened and cleared his voice. No one was stronger than Earl Ray Caulfield. Jasper couldn't imagine what Leviathan Nash could have told him to cause such distress.

"I'm all right." But Earl Ray didn't sound all right. All the color had leeched from his face and Jasper could see that he was still shaking. From across the street, they heard Bessie come out of the café.

"I don't want her to see me like this," Earl Ray said and began to look around for what he'd dropped. "She can't see it. No one can." Jasper nodded as he picked up the bag from the ground. "Please get rid of that for me?"

"I will," Jasper assured him as Bessie hurried across the highway to them.

"Earl Ray?" she cried, and he held out his arms to her.

Jasper stepped away, taking the bag and the business card in his pocket with him. The last he saw of them, they were headed down the street arm in arm toward the house Earl Ray was getting ready for them.

As he headed for his pickup, anxious to get rid of whatever was in this bag, he could hear the broken pieces banging together as if in protest inside the bag. He didn't even want to think about the card in his pocket. Given Earl Ray's reaction, he told himself he didn't want to know.

DARBY HAD BURIED herself in work this morning so she didn't think about Aiden. Or Jasper. But now she looked up from her computer, drawn away from what she'd been typing on her computer by movement outside her front window. People were hurrying down the street toward the west part of town. *Something had happened.*

As the marshal's patrol SUV whizzed past, lights flashing, she quickly rose from her chair and grabbed her jacket and bag with her notebook and pen—and her loaded gun inside. Aiden be damned, she was going to cover the news.

"What's going on?" she asked as Vi Mullen came rushing from the general store. Vi shook her head and kept going. Darby hurried along as well. Ahead, she saw that the marshal's patrol SUV had stopped in the empty lot next to the motel. The coroner van drove past to pull in next to the marshal's rig.

Darby couldn't help the sinking feeling in her stomach as she began to run toward the crowd gathered at the edge of the lot. She could hear the marshal ordering people back. The coroner pulled a rolling stretcher from his van and was pushing his way through the crowd.

"Who is it?" she asked the moment she reached the people gawking there.

"Some man," Mabel Aldrich said. "I was walking my dog when…" Her voice broke. "It's awful what someone did to him."

Darby knew. She didn't know how, she just knew. She pushed her way past everyone, ignoring the marshal's orders to stay back. She rushed toward the center of the lot where the marshal had squatted down next to the body. She could hear more officers arriving. One with a camera rushed past her.

She still wasn't close enough to see much of the body on

the ground. But as the marshal stood, she saw the bloody pulp of what had once been a face. The marshal turned toward her, raising a hand as if stopping traffic. She could see his lips moving, but she couldn't hear what he was saying over the ringing in her ears as she looked beyond the mutilated face to the man's feet. One foot was covered with only a brown sock. The other a single dress shoe.

She recognized the shoe. Aiden had always prided himself on his expensive Italian leather.

CHAPTER SEVENTEEN

JASPER DIDN'T REMEMBER the drive home with Ruby. He'd been too shaken. Earl Ray was one of the toughest, most capable and resilient men he knew. The man had clearly been through a lot while in the service—not even to mention what he'd been through recently when three killers had taken everyone hostage in the café—and Bessie had been shot. And yet, whatever he'd learned from Leviathan Nash had gutted him.

After parking in the yard, he climbed out, Ruby right behind him. He'd tossed the bag on the passenger-side floor before he'd left town. Now he hesitated before reaching in for it. He told himself he didn't want to know even as he knew he had to.

But as he opened the bag, all he saw was a broken ceramic ballerina and what appeared to have been a small glass jewelry box. As he reached for the ballerina who was now missing her legs, the jewelry box she'd been perched on began to play a song. He didn't recognize it, but the sound sent a chill rippling through him.

He tossed the bag back onto the floorboard and slammed the door. Once inside the house, he headed for the kitchen where he poured himself a shot of bourbon. It was way too early to be drinking, something he hardly ever did anytime of the day. The bottle had dust on it he'd had it so long.

But right now, he needed a drink. The alcohol burned all

the way down. Within a few moments he felt a little calmer. He wondered what memories the ballerina jewelry box and its tinny music had unearthed in Earl Ray to cause such a devastating reaction.

He stood for a moment, letting the bourbon work, before he reached into his pocket for the business card. The writing was small and neat, the ink black as Leviathan's heart. For a moment, he hesitated. Once he read the words, he knew he would regret it. He would never be able to unsee them.

AT FIRST EARL RAY could only shake his head and fight the tears welling in his eyes. He knew he had to pull himself together for his wife. Just as he knew that she was the one person he couldn't keep this from—as much as he wanted to.

"Talk to me," Bessie pleaded once they'd reached her house and she'd gotten him into his favorite chair. She'd brought him a glass of water and then seeing that it wasn't going to do the trick, she'd brought him a shot of peppermint schnapps that they only drank around Christmas.

He took the glass, threw back the burning liquid and swallowed as she kneeled on the floor in front of the chair, putting her head in his lap. He stroked her hair and felt some of the strength come back into his limbs. After a few minutes, she raised her head to look into his eyes.

She smiled as if she could see him coming out of it, coming back to her.

"Thank God I have you," he whispered.

"Tell me," she said, offering him her incredible strength, something that he desperately needed right now. "Together we are strong against anything. Everything—isn't that what you told me the day we married?"

He smiled and nodded. He could tell she wanted to yell

at him for going to Gossip. For not telling her he'd gotten an invitation. For taking whatever that horrible Leviathan Nash had told him seriously.

But she held her tongue because she knew that he regretted it more than he could ever say and her chastising him would only add to the pain he'd suffered.

"If it's something about me—"

He shook his head. "No, Bessie, it wasn't about you." His voice broke as he said, "It was Tory."

She frowned at the pain in his voice as if a blade had sliced into his heart. It had. "Tory?" The woman had been dead for years. Bessie had to be wondering what Leviathan could have possibly said to cause such pain.

He cleared his voice, needing to just get this out as quickly as possible. "I don't know if you're aware of this, but for years Tory and I tried to have a child," he said slowly, his voice breaking with regret and the ache of never having a child of his own. Tory had refused his suggestion they adopt. "She knew how badly I wanted children. I thought we had so much to offer."

He swallowed and looked away. This was so much harder than he thought it would be. "What I hadn't known was that she'd gotten pregnant when I was home on leave from the military." He felt his gaze cloud over for a moment before he blinked and looked to his wife for strength. "She didn't want it, tried to get rid of it on her own and without success, gave birth to a daughter I never knew about."

Bessie stared at him. "How is that possible?"

"Apparently it was during the time she'd said she'd gone back to Indiana to take care of her sick grandmother. That too was a lie."

Bessie stared at him, hearing something in his voice. "Surely, you don't think that she was responsible for the fire. I mean, how do you know anything he told you is the truth?"

He felt a fist grip his heart, remembering what the small man in black had told him and how he'd wanted to argue that it couldn't be true. But Leviathan Nash—or whoever he really was—had dates and times and even a copy of a newspaper story to back up his claims.

Worse, all of it had a ring of truth that Earl Ray hadn't been able to deny. "Tory was suspected of setting the fire. She was on the run that day she stepped off the bus and into my life." His voice had dropped as the pain of his words dug deeper into his wounded heart. "All these years..." His voice broke again and he didn't finish.

He'd idolized Tory—even long after her death. To find out that she wasn't the woman he'd thought she was, that everything had been a lie, was bad enough. But then to find out that they'd had a child and she had kept his daughter from him.

Fighting to breathe, he couldn't imagine a worse betrayal. He'd put Tory on a pedestal and kept her there. For years he hadn't let Bessie into his heart because he'd felt he would be betraying Tory. Now to find out that she was the one who'd betrayed him—and in the worst possible way.

"I'm so sorry."

Earl Ray reached down and drew her up onto the large recliner with him. She nestled against his chest. He could feel the steady beat of her heart. He would recover from this with Bessie by his side. He was strong and determined. It was a terrible blow, but he would be the man Bessie believed she'd married.

"I'm here for you," she whispered, and he held her tighter. It wasn't until later that the weight of the news would drop on her. He had a daughter who would be about thirty now. Bessie had to know that he would move heaven and earth to find her.

IT HAD BEEN one of those days, Jasper thought as he wandered around his house too upset to sit. He hadn't been able to get what was written on Earl Ray's Gossip card out of his mind. He felt as if nothing could shock him after that. Earl Ray had a daughter. His late wife had hidden it from him, the pregnancy, the birth and whatever had happened to the child while Earl Ray had been overseas fighting for their country.

Everyone in town had known how much he'd idolized his first wife, Victoria "Tory" Crenshaw Caulfield. The man kept flowers on her grave and had spent years denying his feelings for Bessie because of it. No wonder the shock had knocked Earl Ray for a loop, Jasper thought.

The ballerina jewelry box. Had Earl Ray given it to Tory? He would have recognized the music. Hell, the song alone would have been a gut punch and taken him back to that other life, only to have it ripped to shreds.

Jasper hated to think what the man must be going through. To have a child he'd known nothing about. A grown daughter? At least he had Bessie. She would get him through this. No one was stronger than that woman.

Jasper was on his second shot of bourbon when Ruby barked to let him know that they were no longer alone. He wandered to the front window in time to see the marshal drive up. What now? he wondered as he opened the door and stepped out on the porch.

Leroy cut his engine and climbed out of his patrol SUV. He had on his lawman face, Jasper saw and felt his pulse spike. His first thought was Earl Ray.

"Need to ask you a few questions," Leroy said as he removed his Stetson. "Mind if we step inside, Mr. Cole?"

"It's Jasper, just like it was a few days ago when you stopped by to ask for my help." The seriousness of the marshal's tone set Jasper's nerves on end. "What's this about?" he asked, but got no answer as he let the marshal into the house. "Let me put my guard dog in the kennel." He whistled and Ruby grudgingly followed him to the kennel instead of jumping all over, wagging her tail and ultimately licking the marshal in the face.

Leroy didn't speak until he came back and they were seated in the living room, the marshal perched on the edge of the couch turning his Stetson's brim in his fingers. "There's been a murder."

Jasper hadn't been ready for that. Was it possible after he'd left that Earl Ray had gone back to Gossip and killed Leviathan Nash? "A murder?" he repeated nonsensically and wished he hadn't indulged in the second helping of bourbon.

"A man was found bludgeoned to death in that empty lot near the motel this morning," Leroy said. "He's been identified as Aiden Moss."

Jasper swore as he'd been given yet another shock today. Darby's former fiancé? "Does Darby know?"

The marshal nodded and seemed to hesitate for a moment before he said, "We have a witness who saw an altercation between you and the victim earlier in the evening yesterday."

"What? No," Jasper said shaking his head. "I didn't kill anyone."

"I'm going to need to get a statement from you."

He sighed. "I'm happy to give you a statement. You want to do it here or—"

"Here's fine," the marshal said and pulled out his phone and hit Record. He went through the preliminaries: date, time and name and place where he was interviewing a suspect. "Start at the beginning please, Mr. Cole."

He took a breath, let it out, warning himself to be careful, and began. "If you've talked to Darby, then you already know that she called me. She was scared of her former fiancé—and with good reason—and asked me to come to town and make sure she got to the café safely where she'd agreed to meet him at his insistence. Her ex was an abusive jerk. Not to speak ill of the dead," he added quickly. "I was driving into town when I saw him step out of a dark alley and grab her. I jumped out of my pickup. When he refused to let go of her, I hit him."

"The witness said you knocked him to the ground then jumped on him and had to be pulled off by Darby," the marshal said.

Jasper groaned. "It wasn't quite that dramatic."

"Darby's name and address were found in the deceased's pocket along with a switchblade knife," Leroy said.

A knife? The bastard had a switchblade knife. Jasper felt his pulse bump up. What was the man planning to do with a knife? He remembered the way Aiden had been trying to reach for something from his pocket when Jasper had him down on the ground. But what had his heart pounding was the thought of what the man had been planning to do when he'd pulled Darby back into the alley.

"Now that I think about it," he said to the marshal. "At one point Aiden reached toward his pocket as if to pull out a weapon. I thought the fool was bluffing. Apparently not. But it just proves what I'm telling you. I jumped him because he was trying to drag Darby back into the alley and she was fighting to get away from him." He sighed and continued with what he'd overheard at the café. "He threatened her before he left."

"What happened after Aiden Moss stormed out of the café?"

"I was worried about Darby so I insisted she stay in my guest room out at the ranch, which she did. I gave her a ride into town this morning, saw Aiden's car wasn't at the motel and figured she would be all right in broad daylight since hopefully he'd left town. End of story."

"Not quite. Miss Fulton substantiates your story. But she said after she went to bed, she heard you leave the house last night."

Jasper groaned again and ran a hand through his hair. He didn't want to tell the marshal about the kiss. "I couldn't sleep. I went to check on a fence that had been down to make sure none of the cattle had gotten out. That's where I'd been headed when she called needing my help. I wasn't gone long."

"You didn't go back to town?"

"No, I did not. Look, I was happy to do this for Darby, but it isn't like that between us. Aiden Moss was an incredible jackass and apparently even more dangerous than I thought, but I had no reason to want him dead—let alone any reason to kill him. With guys like him, karma is the best reckoning. Or at least we hope it is."

"You didn't see Mr. Moss again?"

"No. Like I said, I thought he'd left town." Jasper frowned. "Where's his car? It wasn't at the motel when we drove by this morning."

The marshal shut off his phone, thanked him and pocketed it. "We haven't found his car yet. You wouldn't mind if I had a look around your ranch, would you?"

He felt a sliver of fear slice up his spine. If someone was

setting him up... He hadn't experienced that kind of paranoia since leaving his job in homicide. He'd thought he'd put it behind him. "You're welcome to look around." But even as he said it, his stomach dropped at the thought of the car turning up out here. But who in Buckhorn would want to frame him?

"You do realize that I can't drive two vehicles at the same time, right?" he asked as the marshal stood to leave.

Leroy's smile never reached his eyes. "Miss Fulton would have had to have driven one of them." Before Jasper could reiterate that she'd been sound asleep when he'd gotten back from checking the fence, the marshal raised a hand to stop him. "You aren't planning to leave town anytime soon, are you?"

CHAPTER EIGHTEEN

Darby sat at her desk, too shocked to move after the marshal's visit earlier. At her office, she'd given him her statement, but she'd sensed that he hadn't believed her. He kept asking about Jasper and their relationship. What a laugh. There was no relationship. That too the marshal hadn't seemed to believe.

"Why would you call him to help you, then?"

How could she explain the way she felt about Jasper? She knew she was a pain in his neck. He'd been pretty clear that he hadn't appreciated any of her visits. Last night he'd only been nice to her because he realized why she was so scared of Aiden. It had been the cop in him coming out, nothing more.

"He's just a nice guy who I knew I could depend on." She thought about saying that they had met in college. But it had been so much more than that. Her feelings for him were so much more as well. Any hint of that, and it would only make the two of them look guiltier.

Leroy had been particularly interested in Jasper driving away from the house last night. "He went to check some fence."

"That late at night?"

She had thought the same thing. "He'd been about to do that when he got my call."

"When did he return?"

She hated to admit the truth. "I don't know. I fell asleep."

The marshal had stared at her for an unnervingly long moment. "After seeing your ex-fiancé again, being so afraid of him that you called Jasper Cole to go with you to meet him at the café and what happened after that, you simply went to sleep?"

"It was emotionally exhausting and the bed was so soft and it was so quiet out there at the ranch…"

"Had you stayed out there before?"

"No, I told you, Jasper and I don't have the kind of relationship you're insinuating."

"But he was the one you called when you needed help. Did you call anyone else first?"

She shuddered again at the memory of the interrogation— not to mention what the marshal had showed her at the end of it.

"Would you recognize Mr. Moss's handwriting?"

She had said that she would.

He'd pulled out a plastic bag with a sheet of paper covered with Aiden's writing. She saw that the pages were from a Sleepy Pine Motel notepad. It was impossible to read all of what he'd written. Words were jammed together, some of the writing almost too small to read, other words large and bold and underlined so many times that the pen had cut through the paper.

But she didn't have to read much of it to realize what it was. Hatred. Threats. All the things Aiden planned to do to her if she didn't come back to him. Just a few lines in, she'd pushed the bag away with a shudder, her hand going to her mouth to keep from throwing up.

"It would appear that your ex-fiancé was obsessed with you and wanting revenge for you breaking up with him," the marshal had said.

All she'd been able to do was shake her head and keep this morning's cake down. "I had no idea. I knew he was angry but…"

"Really? He hadn't contacted you before this?"

Another shake of her head. "I left right after the breakup. I didn't tell anyone where I'd gone. The last time I saw him, he'd scared me. His temper… I wanted nothing more to do with him."

"So why did you agree to meet him at the café?"

"I thought he needed closure. He told me when he stopped by my office that he hadn't gotten to have his say. I figured once he had, he would leave me alone."

"But after your meeting at the café you knew he wasn't going to let you go that easily." The marshal had checked his notepad. Clearly, he'd talked to the residents who'd been in the café and had heard Aiden threaten her. "What were his last words to you as he left the café?"

"I don't remember."

"Well, the other people in the café *do* remember," Leroy said. "He said it wasn't over, that you were going to be see-ing him again, that he was going to make you sorry. Isn't that why you went home with Jasper Cole? Isn't that why he invited you? You both had to know that Aiden Moss could be dangerous. Whoever killed him took their anger out on him."

She'd felt shocked that he thought she might have… "I didn't kill him."

"No. It was someone who didn't like him and since Mr. Moss had just arrived in town, you and Jasper were the only ones with a motive to want him dead… Who do you think did this?"

The memory of the marshal's last words still vibrated

through her. Leroy Baggins thought Jasper had done this. That he hadn't been checking his fence in the dark last night. That instead, he'd been killing Aiden—for her.

And when she'd thought it couldn't get any worse, the marshal had said, "But if Jasper drove his pickup into town and killed your ex-fiancé to protect you, someone would have had to drive Mr. Moss's car since it wasn't in front of the motel this morning. Now who would that have been, Ms. Fulton?"

VI MULLEN COULDN'T believe after everything that had happened recently that someone was calling with good news. She carefully disconnected. She stood ramrod straight, her head up, chin out—just like her mother had always nagged her to do. She'd felt beaten down for too long, then add this latest thing with Karla Parson—

She shook her head and took a deep breath, letting it out slowly. The call had been from the prosecutor. Karla had dropped the assault charges against her. There would be no trial. No more jail time. It was over.

Vi knew she'd gotten off easily, that she should look at this as a change in her luck. But what about justice? Karla had broken that vase on purpose! She'd admitted it. Instead, it had been Vi who'd been arrested and made a fool of in public. Probably most everyone in town agreed with Karla, who'd said it was an ugly cheap vase and no big deal.

Well, it was still a very big deal to Vi. She pursed her lips in thought. Karla thought it was over. Not by a long shot. Vi would bide her time, but she would get even.

In the meantime she had a celebration to finish planning. Buckhorn would be celebrating its 125th birthday this fall and darned if she would let anything keep her from making it happen. She'd been working on the event for the past eighteen months.

Unfortunately, there'd been a few bumps in the road on her end. Fortunately, she'd gotten more of the residents involved including Melissa Herbert who'd just moved to town. According to the scuttlebutt, Melissa had been seeing Dave Tanner who owned the bar on the edge of town. Vi was pleased and had gotten both of them onboard to help with the celebration.

She'd sent out invitations to everyone she could find who'd ever lived in Buckhorn. There would be fireworks, guest speakers and dances during the four-day event. Vendors would be coming to sell their wares in the new fairgrounds where the Crenshaw Hotel had once stood, along with a huge carnival with lots of rides for both kids and adults.

For a moment, she thought of the beautiful old hotel, long gone now, and the painful memories it evoked, but she quickly pushed such thoughts away. This celebration would be a new beginning for all of them—a rebirth of Buckhorn, and she was the one who could make it happen.

But even as she thought it, she was already thinking about how dangerous something like that could be. All those people in town, the craziness of the rides and the fireworks… Karla should be careful. Accidents happened all the time, but especially in the middle of all that excitement, noise and confusion. A woman who would probably be already half-drunk could end up dead so easily.

Or at the very least…broken.

DARBY WASN'T HUNGRY, but she couldn't stand just sitting in her office any longer. She headed down the street to the café, knowing that everyone would be talking about the murder. She took a seat in one of the empty booths since the place wasn't as busy as she'd expected.

From where she sat she could see the crime scene tape down the street in the empty lot next to the motel. That appeared to be where everyone was since there was a line of gawkers down there. She shuddered at the memory of what she'd seen out in that field earlier.

"Are you all right?" Bessie startled her as she slid into the booth across from her. The older woman reached across the table, took Darby's hand and squeezed it.

"I'm still in shock," Darby whispered. "I just got through being interrogated by the marshal. Leroy acted like he thought I had something to do with it."

"That's just crazy," Bessie said. "Anyway, your ex-fiancé wasn't the only one who was attacked last night."

"What?" She sat up straighter in the booth.

"Didn't Leroy tell you? I suppose not." Bessie sighed. "Another man staying at the motel was attacked and robbed."

"Do you know who?" Darby asked, pulling out her notebook and pen.

"I didn't catch his name, but I'm sure if you check at the motel..."

She was already out of the booth and headed for the door. "Thank you," she called over her shoulder.

An hour later, Darby finished writing the story on the man who'd been attacked last night near the motel. A robber had come up from behind him, stuck what he assumed was a gun in his back and demanded his wallet. He said he'd hurriedly handed it over without turning around and was struck in the head, knocking him unconscious. When he came to after a few minutes, his wallet and the man were gone.

In an attached story, she wrote about Aiden's murder.

While Marshal Leroy Baggins said there was no evidence that the two incidents were connected, he did say that Aiden Moss's wallet was also missing. According to Baggins, it appeared Moss had put up a fight and had been bludgeoned to death. The marshal said both incidents were under investigation.

It seemed pretty clear to Darby that the two incidents were connected. So why was the marshal so sure she and Jasper were involved?

Her phone rang, startling her out of her thoughts. She checked her cell phone screen. Jasper? It rang again. She hesitated, feeling as if she were adding fuel to the marshal's fire by even talking to Jasper. Leroy already thought they were romantically involved and had killed Aiden together. As the phone rang again, Darby reminded herself that she was the one who'd involved Jasper in this. Also, he wasn't a murderer. Of that she was sure.

On the fourth ring, she picked up. "Hello?"

"We need to talk." He didn't sound happy, which meant the marshal had already shared his theory with Jasper.

"I know you didn't do anything to Aiden."

"Thanks for that vote of confidence. Nice of you to mention that you heard me leave the ranch house last night."

"I had to tell the truth. The marshal asked me if we were both at your house from the time you took me to your place until morning."

He sighed. "I know. Sorry. There would have been no reason for you to lie. Or for me to either. But someone killed Aiden. I'm hoping you have some thoughts on that. Can you come out here?"

"I don't think that's a good idea. Maybe it would be better if you came in here. We could talk at the office so it looks like business. Anything else might make it look as if we are trying to get our stories straight."

He swore. "I'm coming to town. Let's meet for lunch. What's the special today?"

"You didn't read the newspaper I sent you?"

"Darby." He sounded as if he was on his last nerve.

"Sorry. French dip and fries. The soup's vegetable beef. If you get to the café before I do, order me a cheeseburger and fries." She disconnected and sat for a moment, heart pounding. Just the sound of his voice did that to her. Not to mention the tingling sensation she'd had all over her body when he'd kissed her or that shot of heat that had raced straight to her center when he'd pulled her close.

She fanned herself, laughing at the trail her mind had taken. Jasper was right. They hadn't done anything wrong. Once the marshal found the robber, he'd find the killer…

And if it hadn't been the robber? It wasn't like anyone in this town had reason to kill Aiden. Unless someone had followed him to town. Maybe that new girlfriend he'd dumped. That seemed unlikely, she had to admit, and shuddered at the memory of what someone had done to Aiden's face.

Had the robber done that? Or was there a murderer in Buckhorn? She'd like to think it would have been unheard of; unfortunately it wasn't the first murder. She just feared it wouldn't be the last since the killer might still be in town.

EARL RAY PRIDED himself on always knowing whom he could call for help. He'd just never used his contacts to help himself before. That was why he hesitated on doing so now even though he had to know about his daughter. If she was still alive. Tory had given birth, but then what had happened to the baby? If Leviathan Nash knew, he was keeping it to himself.

He assured Bessie that he was fine and sent her back to the café, feeling as if he'd made enough of a scene earlier. He wanted things back to normal, even though he knew the past never would be the same again for him.

Tory had betrayed him in an unimaginable way. She'd taken from him the one thing he'd wanted so desperately and she'd known it. That she'd tried to kill their child and failing that had given the baby away was deplorable.

How could she have kept something like this from him all those years before she died?

At loose ends, he went back to work on the house and tried not to think about what he'd learned. He hadn't questioned anything the man had told him. Why was that?

It was that damned musical jewelry box with the ballerina that made him so malleable. He'd been ready to demand proof of anything that Leviathan tried to tell him. But when the man had wound up the music box and played that song… It reminded him so much of Tory that it had transported him back to that other life before her death, the one he'd cherished for so long.

Then Leviathan had dropped the bomb. Earl Ray hadn't wanted to believe it, but seeing a music box exactly like the one Tory'd had since childhood that played the same song… He hadn't questioned anything after that. He'd known that all of it was true.

The shock of it still made him sick inside. He'd thought Leviathan was going to try to tell him something bad about Bessie. He'd never imagined it would be about Tory.

His cell phone rang. Bessie was probably calling to check on him. He didn't mind. He loved hearing her voice. He was so glad she'd been there for him earlier. Bessie and Jasper. By now Jasper would have read the writing on the card—not that he could blame him. He wished that no one else knew because he felt such shame for how he'd put Tory on that damned pedestal like that ballerina on the music box. She must have had a good laugh at his expense all these years.

The phone rang again. It wasn't Bessie.

"Caulfield here," he said without preamble.

"I'm calling about the DNA test you requested."

He'd completely forgotten about it until this moment. But now more than ever he wanted to know who the hell Leviathan Nash was. "You got a match?"

"Sorry. No DNA or fingerprint results. You were that sure we would find something?"

He was. Pulling out a chair, he dropped into it. He'd been so sure that Leviathan Nash's DNA would uncover a criminal record. After meeting the man and discovering what Gossip was peddling—a hell of a lot more than idle gossip—he had to know where the man got his information, why he was dispensing it and what his endgame was.

He thought of the small wiry gray-haired old man at the shop. "If he doesn't have a record maybe someone in the family does. I need to know who this man is and as soon as possible."

"I could do a familial DNA search," Barry said. "Could get a hit on a parent, sibling or even a distant relative."

"Please run more tests," Earl Ray said. "I have to know his connection to Buckhorn." Now more than ever, Earl Ray needed to know everything there was to know about

Leviathan Nash. The man's lease on the shop would be up at the end of the week. Time was running out.

He was convinced that when that happened, the man would disappear as abruptly as he'd appeared. Like a puff of smoke, he'd be gone—leaving behind heartache and pain, and taking all his secrets with him.

CHAPTER NINETEEN

AS JASPER ENTERED the café, he spotted Bessie and gave her a hug. Neither of them mentioned what had happened with Earl Ray before he took a seat in a booth to wait for Darby. He could feel the tension buzzing in town. The gruesome murder had everyone talking as the café was fairly busy with the lunch crowd. He saw several people look in his direction. Someone had seen him slug Aiden so of course the story had spread.

Maybe this hadn't been a good idea for him and Darby to have lunch together. But damned if he was going to hide out at home.

Fortunately, he saw that most of the patrons had already eaten and would be on their way soon. He hoped to have a little privacy. Glancing out the window, he could see that the crime scene tape had been removed down at the empty lot, but he knew for a fact that the marshal hadn't left town.

He'd seen his patrol SUV parked down the street and he'd passed a cruiser on the way into town. He'd wondered if the cruiser was headed for his ranch. He'd thought about driving around the ranch to make sure Aiden Moss's car wasn't there. But he thought that might make him look even more guilty if caught. Anyway, the car wasn't on his ranch. Why would it be?

"Hi." Darby slid into the seat across from him and laid

her notebook and pen on the table before she reached for her menu. "Are you okay?" she asked from behind it.

He reached over and took the menu from her. "You already know what you want and you look ridiculous hiding behind the menu." He smiled at her. "How are you doing?"

She dropped her voice to a whisper. "Great, my ex-fiancé was murdered, the marshal thinks you and I did it, why wouldn't I be just dandy?"

"I guess we feel about the same, then."

The waitress came up to the table and they ordered cheeseburgers and fries and colas. "Who would want him dead?" he asked quietly after the waitress left to put in their order.

"Anyone who met him," she suggested.

He gave her a not-helpful look.

"I think it's the robber," Darby said. "If you'd read my latest release, you'd know that another man from the motel was attacked and robbed last night. He handed over his wallet. Knowing Aiden, he wouldn't have, which would explain why the other man only got a knot on his head and Aiden…" Her voice broke.

"So why is the marshal acting like we had something to do with it?" Jasper asked.

She shrugged. "Maybe he knows something we don't. Maybe it was someone else. In the mood Aiden was in when he left the café, he could have gotten into a fight with someone in town. If not the robber, then what else could have happened?"

Jasper wished he knew.

"Maybe someone followed him to Buckhorn. A girlfriend? Or older brother?"

That was an even longer shot and a thought he'd had as well. She was just spitballing ideas. As she fell silent, she turned pensive. Was she thinking about a time when she'd loved this man? When she'd agreed to marry him? He felt an emotion that was unwelcome. Jealousy.

"The marshal showed me the things Aiden had written about me at the motel before we were to meet here at the café," she said and shuddered visibly. "He really hated me. The things he wrote that he wanted to do to me…" She bit her lip and looked away, tears filling her brown eyes. She made a swipe at them. "I had no idea."

"I'm sorry." At least now he knew what she'd been thinking about. "Your instincts about him were right on, though. If you hadn't called me…" He saw her swallow and nod. "Did he tell you that Aiden had a switchblade knife? No? Well, apparently he did."

She shuddered. "He would have killed me if he'd gotten me into that alley. He was so obsessed… I suspect he lied about breaking up with his latest girlfriend."

"What about past girlfriends with really mean brothers?" Jasper asked, only half joking. They desperately needed a murder suspect other than the two of them.

She shrugged. "I never asked, and Aiden never mentioned any. You're thinking he was like this with other relationships he had."

"More than likely. No offense. I've always thought you were unforgettable, so I'm not surprised someone else did too."

SHE COULD TELL that Jasper had meant it as a joke, but the "I've always thought you were unforgettable" comment made her wonder if he was referring to that night in college. Had he remembered her? Remembered everything they'd shared? Then why would he pretend not to? Probably for the same reason she had.

Darby studied him, trying to decide. She shouldn't have let him believe that she didn't remember him from college. She'd been afraid that he wouldn't remember her. That it hadn't meant anything to him. That what she thought they'd had had only been like any other encounter he'd had with a woman.

"Cheeseburger deluxe with fries," the waitress said as she put down the heaping plate in front of her and the moment was lost. She placed a similar plate in front of Jasper.

"Good choice," he said and reached for the ketchup the same time she did. Their fingers brushed. She jerked hers back as if burned, the electrical shock running from her fingertips straight to her heart.

"Ladies first," he said and handed her the ketchup bottle, his eyes locked with hers. The look in his smoky gray eyes made her tingle all over. She quickly dropped her gaze to her burger. The last thing they needed was some helpful local telling the marshal that they'd been making eyes at each other over lunch.

"So, what is it that we have to talk about?" she asked, hating that little catch in her voice.

"The marshal thinks you and I are an item."

"You told him that wasn't true," she said, wondering exactly how Jasper might have put it. Words did matter. She knew that well enough as a reporter.

"He couldn't understand why you would call me."

She looked up. "What did you tell him?"

"That you're a pain in the ass reporter who's been bugging me for a story, so you probably have me on speed dial."

She saw that he was kidding. "I'm sorry I involved you in my mess."

He shook his head as he picked up his burger and took a bite, chewed, swallowed and finally said, "I'm just glad that you did call me. After all, what are we?" He seemed to be looking for a word to describe what they were. "Friends?"

The way he'd said the last almost sounded as if he was waiting for her to argue differently. "Friends, huh?" She picked up her burger and smiled across the table at him. He smiled back, but he looked a little uneasy.

She got the feeling that he hadn't been honest with her. If he remembered what they'd shared all those years ago, then he would have known from the get-go that they were destined to be more than friends. At least she hoped that were true.

Add to it that kiss in the moonlight last night...

"What?" he finally said to her because he must have seen that she had more to say.

She smiled, unable to contain her amusement at his discomfort. "Jasper, you and I could never be just friends and I think you know it." She chuckled and met his gaze again. She could tell. He remembered the two of them his final night of college. Oh yes, he remembered. No wonder he'd tried to keep his distance from her.

JASPER RETURNED FROM his lunch with Darby to find Marshal Leroy Baggins waiting for him. A bad sign, for sure, he thought. He already felt off balance. Darby sometimes made him feel as if she knew something he didn't. Was it obvious that he liked the hell out of her? That he often found himself wanting to kiss her? That he'd never been able to forget their night together all those years ago? He'd tried to find her the next day, but she was already gone and he had to get ready for graduation. He'd told himself it was for the best. They'd been too young.

Not too young to make love, but too young to take it any further. But he'd known that if he had found her the next day, it wouldn't have ended there. How different their lives might have been.

Over the years, he'd often thought about her, wondered how her life had turned out, wondered if she would even remember him. As it turned out, she hadn't apparently. Or had she? She'd settled in Buckhorn. Not just that, since coming to town she'd managed to do serious damage to the walls he'd carefully constructed around himself. She'd come barging through, heading straight for his heart the way she barged into his house, his life, his defenses. Worse, most of the time, he was secretly glad of it.

But at the sight of the marshal waiting for him, his thoughts turned to murder and jail. "Now what?" he asked Ruby who was also studying the lawman intently as they pulled in and parked next to the patrol SUV.

As Jasper climbed out with Ruby, the marshal stepped from his rig. Jasper had heard women remark on how handsome Leroy was, especially when he smiled. He wasn't smiling today. Today he was all lawman again.

Ruby ran over to Leroy, wagging her tail. "Great guard dog I have here," Jasper said under his breath as he approached the two.

Leroy was petting Ruby, but looked up and squinted into the sun at his approach. "Going to have to ask you a few more questions, Mr. Cole."

"It's still Jasper."

"Unfortunately, as you know there's been a murder. Aiden Moss is dead. That kind of changes things," the marshal said. "We found Mr. Moss's car." He seemed to be waiting for him to say something.

The knot that had formed in his stomach when he'd seen the marshal waiting for him rose to his throat. He waited, knowing he wasn't going to want to hear where the car had been found.

Leroy scratched the back of his neck. "It wasn't on your property, but it's real close by. The crime lab is processing it right now. Were you ever in Mr. Moss's car?"

"No." He knew that when faced with the law short answers were the best. But he also knew that he should be calling an attorney about now.

"But you knew he was staying at the Sleepy Pine Motel?"

Jasper gave him a come-on-marshal-you-know-it's-the-only-place-open-this-time-of-year look.

"I'm assuming you knew which car was his at the motel since you said you didn't see it when you drove Miss Fulton into town the next morning."

Leroy had him there. "It was the only car at the motel the night before when Ms. Fulton and I left town."

"Depending on what we find in Mr. Moss's car, I'll want the team to take a look inside your pickup."

Jasper smiled. "You won't find anything but dog hair and cow shit, but be sure to bring a warrant. That's if you can get a judge to approve a warrant on such flimsy evidence."

The marshal smiled and nodded. "I'll keep that in mind." They both knew that Darby's DNA and prints could be found in his pickup since he'd given her a ride out to his ranch.

Jasper watched as Leroy tipped his Stetson and started toward his patrol SUV, but then stopped and turned. He looked as if he was going to warn Jasper not to leave town, but apparently changed his mind as he kept going to climb into his patrol SUV and leave.

Angry and upset to find himself on this side of the law, Jasper headed for his front door where Ruby was waiting patiently for her lunch. That was when he saw the small white bag hanging on his doorknob and swore.

"This day just keeps getting better," he said as he angrily ripped the bag from the door. He didn't need to look inside, but something warned him that he should.

Pulling out the invitation, he saw the date and time of his "special showing" was tomorrow at eight in the morning. But this time, Leviathan Nash had added a handwritten note in small, carefully printed black letters.

Please don't turn down my invitation. I'd hate to see your luck get any worse.

CHAPTER TWENTY

FOR MONTHS THE only thing on Earl Ray's agenda was getting the house renovation done so they could move in. But after his visit to Gossip, as hard as he tried he couldn't concentrate on the work that needed to be done. His thoughts kept straying back to what Leviathan Nash had told him. Tory wasn't the woman he'd thought she was, and he had a daughter that his wife had kept from him.

Not just kept from him. Tory had tried to kill their child. Failing that, she'd gotten rid of her. Who had this woman he'd loved all those years really been?

If Leviathan could be believed, then Tory might have murdered her parents by burning down her childhood home with them in it.

He had to know the truth even if it would be next to impossible to live with. He'd always taken one step at a time both in the military and in life. Now was no different. He needed to find out everything about Tory, starting with her childhood.

It took only a moment to get high-level access using his passcode. He started to type in Victoria Anne Crenshaw. But that hadn't been who she was, according to Leviathan Nash.

Instead, he typed in Althea Sue Drayton, Beans Creek, Tennessee. He didn't have to wait long. The case was still open. He read the file that included a photo of the house on fire. According to the story, the thirteen-year-old daughter had escaped without injury from a second-story window by climbing down a tree. Both parents perished in the fire that was started in the girl's room.

He looked for a follow-up, but didn't find one. The *Manchester Times* had run a paragraph on the fire saying the family had been renting the farmhouse outside of Beans Creek at the time of the tragedy. Nothing more about Althea Sue Drayton.

The *Tennessean* in Murfreesboro had a longer article because the daughter was now missing. She was wanted for questioning by officials investigating the cause of the fire. The article about the fire and the missing girl included a photograph. He stared at the photo that had been taken the night of the fire.

Althea had looked directly at the photographer, her big blue eyes wide and dry, her red hair blowing back in the breeze as behind her flames roared.

For a moment he could only stare at the screen, remembering the first time he'd laid eyes on the woman he'd known as Victoria Anne Crenshaw. His Tory.

Why had he never done a background check on her? In all those years, he'd never questioned anything she'd told him. Even her name. Crenshaw. He'd just assumed that she was related to the Crenshaws who'd originally built the hotel in Buckhorn. She said they must have been shirttail relatives and hadn't seemed interested in learning about the connection.

Tory had painted an idyllic picture of her childhood in Washington State until the loss of her parents in a fire. She'd told him that she felt guilty because she was sleeping over at a friend's the night it had happened. Maybe if she'd been there...

He knew he'd never questioned any of it because he'd been in love with this beautiful beguiling waiflike woman. She'd been a vision from the first time he saw her with her long curly red hair and a red-and-white polka-dotted sundress. Those eyes, the deepest blue he'd ever seen, and her smile... Even her voice with its slight southern accent...

Earl Ray shook his head. How had he missed all the signs? He'd asked her once about the accent. It was most noticeable when she was tired. She'd said that as a girl, she'd spent a lot of time with her grandmother from Alabama during summer visits. The grandmother she said had died a few years ago. She'd laughed and said she couldn't help picking up other people's accents. Mostly she told him that meeting him was like starting her life anew. Now he understood why.

The day they'd met on the main street of Buckhorn, Victoria Crenshaw hadn't existed. Had she merely come up with the name on the spot? Seen the Crenshaw Hotel with its Victorian architecture?

She'd covered her trail well, though, slipping into that woman as easily as changing her dress. She'd been so young that he'd never questioned her lack of identification. She'd only just gotten off the bus, literally. She wasn't even eighteen like she'd said.

He swore as he realized that he'd helped her fabricate the lie that was Victoria Crenshaw. He'd aided and abetted by teaching her to drive so she could get her license. Somehow, though, she'd come up with a birth certificate that said she'd been born in Seattle, just like the story she'd told him. That meant that she'd known someone who could get the false documents for her.

The thought turned his stomach that as young as she was, she'd known who to go to for a fake birth certificate.

Back then, admittedly it had been easier to fake a birth certificate than it would have been now, he knew. Also, he himself hadn't gotten a social security card until his first job at sixteen.

Still it bothered him that Tory had known someone outside the law. Possibly someone in Buckhorn. Maybe even someone Earl Ray knew. She'd taken a chance. He chuckled bitterly to himself. Or maybe she hadn't. She wasn't worried that he would find out—even later when she had to have some idea of the kind of power he had at his fingertips because of his military background. She hadn't worried, because he was putty in her hands from the moment he'd laid eyes on her and she knew it.

He found no more information on Althea Sue Drayton from Beans Creek, Tennessee. Just as there was little information about Victoria other than what she'd made up and he'd added to. But she was still the main suspect in the unsolved arson that had killed her parents.

As he pocketed his phone, he thought how ironic it was that Leviathan Nash had so much in common with Tory. He was hiding behind a false name as well.

Earl Ray still didn't want to believe any of it. But the photograph taken in front of the burning house, the young girl looking at the camera… It was his Tory. There was no doubt about it. He checked the date of the fire.

She'd shown up in Buckhorn a year and a half later, which would have made her sixteen—not eighteen. He'd been twenty-two. He didn't even want to think about how she'd managed to survive those eighteen months after the fire.

With a sinking feeling, he realized that he had no reason not to believe everything Leviathan Nash had told him. The man hadn't had to lie. He had enough truth that he didn't need to. But how had Gossip's owner known any of it? And what did he get out of passing along this horrendous news? What had happened to the man that he went to all this trouble to disrupt and ruin other people's lives?

Earl Ray wouldn't know until he found out who Leviathan Nash really was.

Unfortunately, time was running out. With Nash's lease up in a matter of days... His fear was that the man had saved the worst for last. Or maybe he'd already done all the damage he had planned. What if he left before his lease was up?

At a knock at his door, he looked up to see Jasper Cole standing there. "Come on in," he called as he got to his feet. He still felt shaken, his world tilted off balance.

Jasper must not have heard him because he hadn't moved from where he stood on the porch. When Earl Ray opened the door, Jasper seemed startled as if lost in his own thoughts.

"I was going to call you," Earl Ray said, realizing that he hadn't told him yet about the DNA lack of findings. "The lab is running more DNA tests since the first ones didn't bring up anything on the databases."

Jasper nodded, but didn't seem all that interested as he held out something he'd been holding in his hand.

Earl Ray took it, surprised to see that it was an invitation to a special showing at Gossip. He recognized the card at once. It made his stomach turn at just the sight of it. Then he saw what was written on the card. His gaze shot up to Jasper's in question.

"Maybe I'm delusional, but that sounds like a threat to me. As you know, it's not the first invitation I've gotten— and ignored. This is the first one with a note on it."

Frowning, Earl Ray said, "What kind of threat?"

"I would imagine you've heard about Darby Fulton's

former fiancé being murdered? Well, his car was found near my ranch. I've had several visits now from Marshal Leroy Baggins. Right now there isn't sufficient evidence to arrest me." Jasper took a deep breath and blew it out. "I know this is going to sound as if I've lost my mind, but I think Leviathan Nash is trying to frame me for murder and if I don't go tomorrow..."

"I think you'd better come in and sit down," Earl Ray said.

MARSHAL LEROY BAGGINS hadn't expected any evidence to turn up in Aiden Moss's abandoned car found near Jasper's ranch—especially almost a week after the murder. Jasper was a former homicide detective. He would know how to cover his tracks.

Which made finding the car in a gully so near the man's ranch one of those head scratchers Leroy hated. Why not take the car farther from Buckhorn? Why move it at all?

He could think of only one reason. If Jasper and Darby had done this, she would have been following him in his pickup or Moss's car. Either or both could have been seen. It would have been smarter to dump Aiden's car close to home in a spot that didn't get traffic and yet wasn't far from town. Maybe they planned to move it farther the next day.

Jasper would also know that there was little chance of him being arrested without more evidence. He wouldn't have left any evidence in Aiden Moss's car. Nor would there be any in Jasper's pickup—if Leroy could get a warrant to check.

What the marshal needed was the murder weapon. The coroner had speculated that something like a baseball bat had been used. Smooth edges. Not like the old two-by-fours that they'd found in the empty lot near the body.

There'd been no splinters in the wounds. But if the killer had used a bat, then the attack would have most likely been premeditated—something else that pointed to Jasper Cole.

Jasper could say what he wanted about there not being anything between him and Darby Fulton. Leroy didn't buy that just from the witnesses he'd interviewed about the pair. Also, Jasper was the protective type.

By Jasper's own admission, he'd driven into town simply to walk Darby down to the café for this meeting with her former fiancé that she had reason to fear. Not just that. He'd asked her to stay at his house after Aiden had threatened Darby and left the café. And she'd taken him up on it. That certainly looked as if the two were…close, no matter how much they both denied it.

On top of that, he had no other suspects. No one else in town even knew about an ex-fiancé let alone had ever laid eyes on him. The residents who'd been in the café and overheard a lot of the conversation between Aiden and Darby had stated they were glad that Jasper had been there. They'd feared for Darby.

Leroy thought he was a pretty good judge of character, but the anonymous witness who'd seen the fight before the three had gone to the café said that Jasper had jumped out of his truck and attacked the man. Darby had had to pull Jasper off her former fiancé.

Leroy didn't want to believe that Jasper had later murdered the man. But it bothered him that he was unable to find out anything about why Jasper had left his job in homicide. The file was sealed. That told him there was more to Jasper Cole than met the eye.

"LET'S TAKE A step back and look at this," Earl Ray said once he'd invited Jasper in and they'd both sat down. "Why would Leviathan Nash—or whatever his name is—want to frame you for murder?"

The younger man shook his head. "That's just it, I have no idea. I don't want to know. But if I had to guess, there's something he is itching to tell me about my family that quite frankly I don't need to hear. If anyone would understand that, I suspect it would be you. I've lived this long in the dark, I'm fine with it."

"I don't blame you," Earl Ray said. "A part of me wishes I'd never gone through that door." And yet he would never have known that he had a daughter. But if she was alive, then just the thought of all those years he'd lost broke his heart not to mention how he now felt about Tory.

He considered his friend. Earl Ray had moved to town while in the service, seeing it as a great place to live when he decided to settle down. He wondered what had brought Jasper here. "Your family is from Buckhorn, right?"

"My grandparents lived their whole lives here. My parents moved to a house on their property after they got married. They had me and eight years later my father packed us up and we left."

"You think this has something to do with your grandparents?"

Jasper shook his head. "I don't know. Maybe. Or my parents. I've always wondered why we left the way we did. My father could have had an argument with his old man and just decided it was time to leave. Or it could be some dark secret."

"But you don't want to know or you would have gone to Gossip the first time you got an invitation," Earl said with a sigh. "I understand completely. I shouldn't have gone and yet if I hadn't…" He shook his head, unable not to keep thinking those same thoughts over and over.

"Grandpa was a rancher. Grandma was a county health nurse," Jasper said. "They loved this community and were active in it."

Earl Ray nodded. "I remember. Your grandmother worked with the other county health nurse, Thelma Rose. Leviathan told me that Thelma Rose delivered my daughter. But that he didn't know what happened to the infant after that."

"I wonder if my grandmother would have known?" Jasper asked. "This was around thirty years ago? About the time my grandmother died in a fall down the stairs."

Earl Ray felt his stomach turn as he had an awful thought. He told Jasper about what he'd found out about his deceased wife. "Tory was still wanted for questioning in the fire."

"What are you saying?"

He shook his head. "I know this sounds crazy but if your grandmother knew about the pregnancy, it just seems odd that she would die so soon after my daughter was born."

"You can't think Tory…"

"That a woman who killed her own family in a fire she set and tried to kill our child would kill your grandmother if she threatened to talk?" Earl Ray let out a bitter laugh. "I suspect my deceased wife was capable of about anything."

Jasper looked as horrified as Earl Ray felt.

"You're determined not to go to this appointment tomorrow morning, right?" he asked. "What is it you fear Leviathan will do if you don't?"

"The only reason I'm not in jail right now is a lack of evidence. If the murder weapon should turn up, though…"

"You're assuming that either Leviathan Nash killed this man or knows who did and is now in possession of the murder weapon."

Jasper nodded before dropping his head into his hands.

"Tell me I'm delusional." He looked up when Earl Ray didn't. "What would you do?"

"I can't advise you. Even if you were to go in the morning to your special showing and you're right about Leviathan framing you for murder, he could still make sure the murder weapon turned up on your ranch."

"So if I'm right, I'm screwed either way."

They sat in silence for a few minutes. "What about you?" Jasper asked. "What are you going to do with what you know?"

"Find my daughter, if she exists, if she lived. What did you do with…everything I gave you?"

"I have it out at the ranch," Jasper said. "I was going to destroy it, but felt it wasn't my place. I have a fine old dump out there. I could bury it deep."

Earl Ray shook his head. "It's evidence. I can't tell you to destroy it yet. Do you mind hanging on to it for now?"

"No problem. It just reminds me of all the reasons I want nothing to do with Leviathan Nash. Who the hell is he? Where does he get this stuff?"

"I'd say he's been planning this for some time. As to where he gets his information…" Earl Ray shook his head. "I hope the more extensive DNA tests will give us some idea who he is. In the meantime, I'm worried about you."

"Me too. I'm just waiting for the other shoe to drop." Jasper met his gaze. "I hope you know a good criminal lawyer."

"Let's hope it doesn't get that far."

Vi Mullen took Aiden Moss's death as a personal attack on her and Buckhorn's 125th birthday celebration. Another murder in Buckhorn? This was not the kind of news she wanted or needed when putting together a huge celebration for the town.

Her first thought was to throw up her hands in defeat and cancel the whole thing. She was in tears, ranting and raving about this awful year she'd had, when her daughter came in with granddaughter Chloe.

"Don't be silly, Mother." Tina actually laughed. "If something like a murder kept people away, they wouldn't go anywhere. We have less crime in Montana than probably anywhere else in the country. It will be completely forgotten by this fall and your celebration."

"It's not *my* celebration," Vi corrected her. "It's for the town."

"Sure it is," Tina said, still smiling.

Vi held her tongue. She and Tina were often at loggerheads. Lately, they'd been getting along better. She didn't want to disrupt that with an argument.

"Maw Maw," her granddaughter said and held out her arms to Vi.

As Tina handed the toddler over, Vi hugged Chloe and felt herself smile. Her granddaughter always had that effect on her. She felt her heart fill with love as she looked into that adorable little face. The toddler snuggled against her, bringing her so much joy that sometimes she felt as if she would burst wide-open with it.

Vi often wondered how her husband, Axel, could have left her—let alone his daughter and granddaughter. He was missing out on so much. Served him right, she thought uncharitably. She hugged her granddaughter closer.

"See? It's all going to be fine," Tina said as she stood back, watching the two of them as if surprised at the effect Chloe had on her mother.

Vi considered her daughter for a moment. "You look happy."

"I am," she said with a laugh. "I have everything I've ever wanted."

Vi didn't point out that Tina had never wanted very much in her estimation, her husband being a prime example. Grudgingly, she had to admit that Lars *had* finally managed to marry Tina and her daughter did seem happy. Wasn't that what mattered, not the fact the Vi still had her problems with the man?

At least he did love Chloe, even though she wasn't his biological child. Did it really matter how the three of them had become a family? Vi supposed not, thinking of how shocked her own mother would have been. Thank goodness Vera was no longer around to see how much times had changed.

"You should let yourself be happy," her daughter said.

"You're right," Vi agreed, making Tina laugh.

"I never thought I'd hear that," Tina joked as she reached for Chloe. "We're going to Billings. Can I bring you anything?"

Vi shook her head. She had everything she needed right here in Buckhorn. She hated going to the big city. The traffic. All the people. It gave her a headache just thinking about it. She glanced out the window down the street to where crime scene tape no longer flapped in the breeze.

"Don't forget," Vi said. "You're covering the store the day after tomorrow. I'm going to need all the help I can get with summer coming."

"I won't forget," Tina said patiently. "I've been working the store since I was old enough to make change. I know what my hours are."

"I know," Vi said and swallowed the lump that had

formed in her throat. "Have a safe trip," she said and gave her granddaughter a kiss on the top of her head. "Bring Maw Maw back something sweet."

"Can Dee!" Chloe cried excitedly.

"It's no wonder that her first word was *candy*," Tina said shaking her head. "You're an awful grandmother," she said, but she was smiling.

DARBY CLOSED THE door behind the marshal as he left and tried to breathe. He'd asked the same questions over and over. There was no doubt that he thought Jasper had killed Aiden—and that she'd helped him hide the car to cover up the whole thing.

"I've answered all your questions," she'd said finally. "I'm not talking to you again without an attorney present." She'd stood, the interrogation over.

"I'm sorry you feel that way," Leroy had said. "Darby, I think you got caught up in something. You were scared of Aiden and with good reason, from what I've heard. If it hadn't been for Jasper, the man might have hurt you, even killed you. A judge will take all that under consideration."

She had shaken her head and pointed to the door.

The marshal had slowly risen from his chair. "You saw what was done to your former fiancé. That kind of anger…" He met her gaze. "If Jasper did this, then he just might be more dangerous than even Aiden."

Her body now vibrated with the tremors that rattled through it. She couldn't quit thinking about Jasper when Aiden had grabbed her and wouldn't let go. Jasper had gone for Aiden's throat. But he'd quit when she'd asked him to. Except that she'd seen how badly he wanted to pummel Aiden. It seemed to take all of his strength to let the man up.

Pacing her small office, the marshal's words resonated

with thoughts that had kept her from working all day. Jasper's controlled anger had been more frightening than Aiden's blustery, male ego–filled fury. Jasper had always been so calm, so laid-back, appearing so indifferent. She'd really thought that nothing could ruffle those feathers of his.

But seeing his expression when he leaped from his pickup and attacked Aiden... And later when he was clearly fighting to control his anger...

She hugged herself. What if the marshal was right? She shook her head. He couldn't be. She thought of being in Jasper's arms, the gentle loving way he'd held her so many years ago and again in the moonlight at the ranch.

Like a bucket of ice water poured over her, she was reminded that she still didn't know why Jasper was no longer a homicide detective. Something had happened. Something she needed to be worried about?

That aside, it made no sense that Jasper would go back into town to confront Aiden. How could he have gotten rid of Aiden's car by himself? He would have had to walk back into town for his pickup. She shook her head. If only she had gotten up when she heard Jasper leave. If only she'd gone with him wherever he was going.

Darby stopped pacing. The Jasper Cole she knew wouldn't have done this. She believed that in her heart. Her experience with Aiden had left her questioning her instincts. It had also left her afraid of a man's anger. Jasper wasn't a killer. He might have wanted to beat Aiden senseless, but he wouldn't have killed him. Jasper would have stopped on his own. She had to believe that.

No, this was all her fault. She'd gotten Jasper into this. She would get him out. After all, she'd once been a damned good investigative reporter, hadn't she? She reminded herself that she'd given up her last job because of Aiden.

Aiden. She'd always been skeptical about most things, but not love. When she'd met him, he'd seemed so nice and sweet. She shook her head now, realizing how much he'd hidden that dark side of himself.

Now she could admit that he was the reason she'd left her good-paying newspaper job. She'd always played with the idea of starting her own newspaper, but Aiden had been the catalyst. She'd never dreamed he'd come after her.

But she should have.

Jasper was nothing like Aiden. She'd turned to Jasper because she trusted him with her life. She still did. Now it was up to her to find out who'd really killed Aiden before the marshal came for her and Jasper.

CHAPTER TWENTY-ONE

AFTER JASPER LEFT, Earl Ray knew he couldn't put it off any longer. He walked down to the café. It was midafternoon so the place was nearly empty. He took a booth. Just as they had done for years, Bessie brought him a cup of coffee and whatever she'd baked that day. Today it was an apricot fried pie, his favorite.

He'd eat it, because it would please her even though he had no appetite at all and hadn't since his trip to Gossip.

She brought her own cup of coffee and slid into the booth across from him. Her expression said he was doing a lousy job of pretending he was all right. She knew him too well. She could see how shaken he was no matter how hard he tried to hide it.

"I have to look for her," he said as he wrapped his hands around the coffee cup, needing the warmth more than ever right now. "If she's alive, I have to find her."

She smiled even as she seemed to fight the tears that shone in her blue eyes. "Of course you do. I know how hard this has been for you. But if anyone can find her, it's you."

He felt relief fill his heart to overflowing. He reached across the table and took her hand, squeezing it since right now he couldn't speak.

"I'll do anything I can to help," she said, as he knew she would. The woman's heart was so much bigger than that of anyone he'd ever known. He tried not to think of Tory or how broken she'd been. Why hadn't he seen that?

Because he hadn't wanted to. She'd been his precious little doll. Maybe that was why he'd felt so protective. A part of him had seen fragility that he'd mistaken for tenderness.

"I boxed up a lot of Tory's things a long time ago," he said. "I'm glad now that I didn't get rid of them. I'm hoping to find a clue as to where she took the baby." He squeezed her hand again. "But it will take time away from the house."

"Earl Ray, this is more important than the house right now." She held his gaze so gently that he had to swallow the lump in his throat. "We're fine."

He nodded and let go of her hand to take a sip of his coffee.

"Find your daughter."

As he put down the cup, he thought of all the years he and Bessie had sat across a table in this very café. "I don't know what I would do without you."

"Isn't that true," she said and laughed, though it wasn't one of her usual hearty ones. "If I have a say in it, you're never going to find out." Bessie would know that finding his daughter was only the beginning. Like her, he had no idea what he would find—or what an offspring of his and Tory's might do to their lives.

Bessie believed that their bond was strong enough to withstand whatever this discovery might bring. He loved that about her, even as he feared she might be wrong.

JASPER DROVE BACK to the ranch. As he neared the house, he saw the crows and felt his stomach clench. A shiny black row of them were strung across the power line. He slowed the pickup. Whether they were a sign of death or just bad luck or nothing at all, right now they were the last thing he wanted to see. He recalled them perched outside his kitchen window the day Leviathan Nash came to town.

Why were they here again? For a funeral? To let all the other crows know where they could find food? Or to warn them that this was a dangerous place? He thought about what Earl Ray had said. The danger, that Jasper knew, just might be in stubbornly flying solo.

Ruby began to bark, front feet on the dash, as he pulled into the yard.

His gaze went to the front door, half expecting to see another small white bag hanging there. But it was bare. Something told him that the most recent invitation would be the last. Whatever the man had planned, there was no stopping it now.

As he parked, he recalled the concern he'd seen on Earl Ray's face earlier. Like him, the man was worried the invitation and note were a threat. If Jasper didn't go in the morning, Leviathan would make him wish he had.

He climbed out of the pickup, Ruby rushing out after him, still barking. The crows shifted on the wire, feathers ruffled, but settled in again as if they weren't going anywhere.

Sighing, he headed for the house. His cell phone rang. He saw it was Darby and picked up. Like it or not, they were in this together.

"Hello," he said into the phone before it could ring again.

"We have to find out who killed Aiden," she said without preamble. "I was once a pretty good investigative reporter. You were once a pretty good homicide detective. We can do this."

He laughed. He couldn't help himself. "Are you drunk?"

"Sober as a judge. Leroy was just here."

Jasper knew what that meant. "Yeah, he stopped by here earlier too."

"So?"

He looked toward the crows all huddled together against whatever was coming. "I'm listening."

"The marshal said someone saw you attack Aiden."

"Not my proudest moment," he said through gritted teeth. "When I saw him trying to drag you into the alley..."

"I know. But it's why the marshal is convinced that you killed him and that I helped you," she said. "I'm wondering who made that call? Did you see anyone on the street?"

He started to say no, but then he remembered a door opening and closing across the street at Gossip. "It could have been Leviathan Nash."

She sighed loudly. "We need to go talk to him. Seriously. We know he's lying about his name. He might be lying about—"

"I just heard on the DNA test and the fingerprints from the cup."

Darby went quiet, something unique for her, before she said excitedly, "Who is he?"

"Nothing came up. He wasn't in any databases. More extensive tests are being run, but at this point, the man isn't in the system so there's nothing criminal in his background to be found."

"That can't be right. I think if we got over there inside his—"

He heard her stop on a surprised breath. He froze. "What's wrong?" No answer. *"Darby, what's wrong?"* He was ready to head into town when she finally spoke.

"Leviathan," she said in a whisper. "He was just at my door. I was so surprised that I couldn't move. He tried the knob. I have it locked. I know he saw me, but he didn't knock. I think he left something on my door."

"Darby, don't go after him."

"I'm going to see what he left," she said.

He heard her move to the door, unlock it and open it. "Darby? Did he leave something? *Darby?*"

"I just got an invitation for a special showing," she said as he heard her close and lock the door again. "It's for Saturday morning—the day his lease is up at midnight."

CHAPTER TWENTY-TWO

"Listen to me," Jasper was saying in the phone. "Darby, are you listening to me?" His voice sounded miles away. There was a buzzing in her ears. She stepped back to her desk and dropped into her chair.

Since opening the small white bag, she'd been staring at the invitation. This was her ticket inside the shop. This was her chance to break this story. So why was her hand holding the invitation shaking so hard?

"I'm listening," she said and swallowed the lump that had crawled up her throat.

"I'm on my way to your place. Stay there, keep the door locked. You hear me? I'm on my way."

She started to tell him that there was no reason for him to come into town to what? Hold her hand? But instead she said, "I hear you." In truth she didn't want to be alone. Also she was grateful for someone she could talk to about this.

Eight o'clock Saturday morning. She'd seen enough people step through Gossip's door—and come out devastated—that only a fool wouldn't realize how dangerous this was. She wasn't from here. All the others had lived here most of their lives. So why her? Why now? And if he planned to invite her all along, why had he waited so long to do it?

GOOD TO HIS WORD, Jasper arrived not ten minutes later. She realized that he must have sped the entire way as she opened the door for him.

"Are you all right?" he asked the moment he stepped in.

She nodded and then shook her head as tears stung her eyes. "You think it has something to do with Aiden's death?"

"I don't know, but I don't like it." He glanced toward the stairs up to her studio apartment. "Do you have anything to drink up there?"

"Beer."

"That'll do," he said and glanced toward the front window. She followed his gaze down the street. Light shone behind the black paper covering the windows at Gossip. She knew that Jasper was wondering the same thing she was. Had Leviathan Nash been watching her office all this time? Or just since he'd dropped off the invitation. She figured the man was always watching and shuddered that now she hadn't just drawn his scrutiny—Jasper had too.

"I've dragged you into this," she said, emotion making her voice rough. "First with Aiden and now this." He started to object, but she cut him off. "He drops off an invitation and ten minutes later, here you are. This will only make it look like you and I are…more than friends. If he's the one framing you for Aiden's murder—"

"Darby, I was involved long before this. You aren't the only one to get an invitation," Jasper said without looking at her.

"Did you—"

"Go? Not a chance in hell," he said and finally looked at her. "But it seems Leviathan isn't taking no for an answer. His last invitation made it clear that if I didn't come for my special showing tomorrow, I'd be sorry. I'm not going."

She stared at him. He'd gotten more than one invitation and ignored them only to have Leviathan threaten him? "Threaten you how?"

"I think he's about to frame me for Aiden's murder and involve you as well."

"We should definitely go upstairs for that beer," she said and led the way upstairs on wobbly legs. The apartment wasn't much larger than her office. There was a kitchenette with a refrigerator, sink and stove that she'd never used. A couch that converted into a bed, a small television and a bathroom with a shower.

She went straight to the refrigerator and took out two beers. She handed one to Jasper. Opening her own, she took a drink before she said, "I checked with the marshal's office. The call from the person who said they saw you attack Aiden? It was anonymous, but the dispatcher told me off the record that it had been an elderly man, she was pretty sure. The voice, she said, sounded old and low. He refused to give his name, but he said that if the woman with you hadn't pulled you off the man, he was sure you would have killed him."

Darby could see that the news didn't come as a shock to him. "If it was Leviathan, then I'd say he is definitely framing you for the murder. But that would mean that sometime that night he either stumbled across Aiden after he was attacked by the robber or he killed him in that empty lot not far from the motel."

"If he was the one who made the call to the marshal's office, then he had been watching us—watching Aiden," Jasper said.

As she took a seat at the other end of the couch, her mind was racing. "If he doesn't have a criminal record, then I don't believe he killed Aiden. Why would he commit murder just to try to make you come to Gossip so he can tell you something horrible you don't want to hear?"

Jasper shook his head as he dropped down on the other end of the couch. "All I know is that I can't let you go to Gossip. It's too dangerous."

"But what if I don't go?" she asked, her voice breaking. "What will he do?"

He looked over at her and shook his head again. "I think you should get out of town for a while."

DARBY COULDN'T BELIEVE that she was actually tempted to run. But wasn't that what she'd done because of Aiden? And look how that had turned out. Some things you couldn't run from.

"Are you thinking what I am?" she asked.

"I hope not," Jasper said with a groan.

"We need something on Leviathan Nash."

He shook his head. "I thought that's what we've been trying to get with the DNA?"

The answer came to her in a flash. "We need to find out where he goes at night," she said and took a drink of her beer. She was calmer now, feeling stronger, more determined. She always was once she had a plan. She wasn't letting some old man with his secrets run her out of town. She had fallen for Buckhorn—and a certain cowboy rancher, she thought, meeting his gaze. "We stake out his cabin and when he leaves, we follow him."

"What?"

Maybe she was calmer, but clearly Jasper was not.

"I just told you that I believe he's trying to frame me for murder and you as my accomplice. Did I not mention that you're in almost as deep because Leroy believes you drove Aiden's car that night—or my pickup?" He waved a hand through the air, clearly exasperated. "Now that creepy old man has invited you into his lair? He is coming for us, you realize that, right?"

"Which is why we have to do something other than just wait to be arrested or worse… run." She leaned toward him, warming to her idea. "I realized the night when I got into his cabin, that I've heard his old truck leave town other late nights. Where does he go?"

Jasper shook his head. "Maybe for a ride, for all we know."

"Exactly, we don't know. But he seems to know all about us. Doesn't seem quite fair." She watched him take a long drink of his beer. She could tell that he was at least giving it some thought.

"What are you suggesting?" he finally asked.

Darby glanced at her phone to check the time. "He left later than this the other night. Come on, let's go stake out the place and when he leaves, we follow him."

JASPER THOUGHT OF several good reasons this was a bad idea. Leviathan was determined to tell him whatever it was he knew about him and probably his family. The man had warned him. But would he go so far as letting him go to prison for murder? What the hell did Leviathan have to tell him that was so damned important? Or was the whole thing a trap?

He had a bad feeling that all the things Leviathan Nash had done so far were leading up to some grand finale—as if the man were saving the really bad stuff for last.

But Darby was right about one thing. They were already in this too deep. The marshal could be coming to arrest them any day now. If Leviathan was framing the two of them—which Jasper was damned sure he was although he had no evidence to prove it—then they could just wait for it to happen or they could fight back. Just as Darby had been saying, they needed to know who they were dealing with now.

He finished his beer, got up and walked the can over to the recycling bin in her small kitchenette. "Okay," he said, turning to face her.

She was already reaching for her coat. "There's an old empty building next to Gossip. It shouldn't be that hard to get into it. We can see the alley and his cabin from there."

Breaking and entering. "Why not? He knows both of our vehicles. So, we stake out the place. If and when he moves, we'll come back for my pickup."

Darby smiled and reached into her purse and brought out her penlight. When he saw her check her gun and ammunition before swinging her purse over her shoulder, he felt even more worried that this was a bad idea—and one of the many reasons he hadn't wanted to get involved with any of it—especially with this woman.

"We aren't shooting anyone," he said.

"Of course not." She shrugged. "It's only for protection."

"Right. You weren't kidding about knowing how to use the gun, right?"

Her smile widened. "Guess you'll have to wait and see."

He nodded. "Great."

She moved to the front window of her apartment, drew back the edge of the curtain only a fraction of an inch and turned to him. "The light is still on at Gossip. I think we can assume he's in there."

Jasper didn't want to assume anything when it came to Leviathan Nash and that shop of his. He checked to make sure he had his phone. He had a pistol in the pickup and a shotgun behind the seat. He didn't plan to use either, but he knew he would if it came to protecting Darby. "Let's go. I need to stop by my pickup and then I'm ready."

"Not getting involved, huh?" she said.

"Against my better judgment." But he knew she was right. He couldn't stand back and just let this happen. If he was right about the man framing him for murder, then it was high time he did something about it—especially since the man had now involved Darby.

ENTERING THE EMPTY building next to Gossip turned out to be even easier than Darby had suspected. The old door into the place with its crystal doorknob didn't lock. It was just a matter of prying one side of the plywood free that had been nailed over the door, slipping past it and into the pitch-black space.

Because of the hour, there was little to no traffic. Jasper had insisted on doing the breaking and entering part while she stood back as lookout.

"Never thought you'd be doing this as a civilian," she whispered, unable to hide her excitement.

"Never. Now I feel like a criminal," he whispered back, shaking his head as he held the plywood away so she could slip in. "And you're enjoying every minute of it."

She was, since breaking into an empty building was way down on her list of criminal behavior. Once inside, they both stopped to listen. With Gossip right next door and sharing a wall, they had good reason to worry that they might have been heard.

But she could hear nothing coming through the wall and assumed that Jasper didn't either as he turned on his flashlight and shone it around the room. It appeared that someone had started to renovate the building, but stopped in the middle of the process. "Watch out for nails," Jasper warned as they began to step over boards filled with nails that had been torn from the walls.

As if nails were the most dangerous thing they had to worry about, Darby thought as she headed for the stairs to the second floor. If she was right, there was a window up there that overlooked the cabin. They would be able to see and hear the truck leave.

When she reached the top of the stairs, she moved toward the south-facing room, but stopped before she reached the closed door. Jasper, as if already thinking a step ahead of her, turned off his flashlight. They stood there for a moment, neither of them moving, before he stepped past her and pushed open the door into the room.

Just enough light came in through the dust-covered windows that they could see where to step. Darby followed him to the window facing Gossip and the cabin and peered out. She could see light coming from the back of the shop. Which she hoped meant that Leviathan Nash was still inside.

"Might as well settle in," she said, holding her phone away from the window to check the time. "If I'm right, he's a creature of habit."

"I guess we'll see," Jasper said as he dragged up two small wooden crates and offered her one. "A seat, my lady?"

She gave him a slight bow and took it. "Thank you. We should have brought some beer. Chips would have been nice."

He shook his head as he sat down on his crate, making it groan under his weight. Sometimes she forgot just how intimidating a figure he made. Over those broad shoulders, slim hips and long legs was a lot of muscle. She'd gotten a look at how strong and powerful he was when he'd gone after Aiden.

"Tell me why you left law enforcement." Darby surprised herself. But once the words were out, she turned toward him. In the faint light coming through the dirty window from the starry moonlit night, she saw his surprise—and the way his face immediately closed up.

"I have to know," she said quietly, needing an answer, and looked away to the scene below her. The golden light that bled from the back of Gossip fell over the stone walkway and the front of the old truck. She concentrated on it and waited, thinking that if there was a time or place that he might tell her, this would be it.

JASPER RECOGNIZED THE stubborn set of her jaw. He knew he shouldn't have been surprised by the question. Hell, she was a reporter. But he also knew that it wasn't the reason she was asking.

Given the way he'd kissed her the other night at his ranch, she had every right to ask. Add to that they were both probably about to be arrested for Aiden's murder and her alleged part in the cover-up. He knew he did owe her something.

He looked out the window, chewed at the side of his cheek for a moment before he sighed. "I lost my objectivity. I got too involved in a case. I almost killed a suspect." He knew that was just the tip of the iceberg, so to speak.

"Bessie and I think a woman was involved," she said flatly without looking at him.

Jasper let out a chuckle. "You and Bessie, huh? You have a long conversation about me?"

"Long enough." She turned then and leveled those brown eyes on him.

He felt himself weaken. This damned woman had that effect on him in a way that stole his strength of will. She'd been hell on his barriers, worse on his heartstrings. He'd known it was only a matter of time before he opened his heart to her. But that would mean telling her the truth, opening up that private, most painful part of his life to her. She was asking if she could trust him. Or if she should fear him.

"I got a woman killed. I promised to protect her, and I failed. Worse, the man who killed her did so because of me."

"He's the man you tried to kill?"

He felt the full weight of his past settle on his shoulders. "I failed at that too. Now because of who he is, he's sitting in some country club–type private prison cell watching cable TV at the taxpayers' expense."

"Did they fire you?" she asked.

He shook his head. "After that it was clear to me and my bosses that I could no longer do the job I was hired to do. I had to walk away."

Darby nodded. "Were you in love with her?"

"I was, but maybe for all the wrong reasons since she was with the man I was investigating for murder," he said after a moment.

"I figured it was something like that. I take it that the man was someone with influence."

His chuckle held all the bitterness he still felt. "He was a US senator and one of the most dangerous and crooked men I've ever met. The good news is that he'll never be able to hold office again."

Darby knew she shouldn't ask, but she had to, even though she feared the answer. "What happens when he gets out of prison?"

A cold, dark silence filled the room for too long. She

met Jasper's gaze and held it as she waited, now desperate to know the answer.

"He'll take his millions and live a life of luxury," Jasper finally said. "He'll find another woman he'll abuse, and he'll get involved with people who will do his dirty deeds. He won't change."

"You can live with that?" she asked quietly.

He chuckled. "I have to since I want a life away from all that."

"Which explains why you didn't want to get involved in this," she said, feeling regret that she'd dragged him into it. "I'm sorry."

He shook his head. "While I no longer want to be in law enforcement, you've made me realize that I can't just stick my head in the sand when it comes to trouble. I didn't ask for any of this and yet here I am because of Leviathan Nash—not you. You were right. I can't hide out at my ranch. I can't stand back and let this man destroy my life and yours. He needs to be stopped, should have been stopped, before it's too late."

The light inside Gossip went out. They both froze, their conversation forgotten for the moment. Seconds later, Leviathan came out the back of the shop and headed for his cabin—just as he had done the other night when she'd been hiding behind the cabin. Only this time, he was carrying something. Flowers?

He disappeared inside the cabin, the door closed, a light came on.

"Was that a bouquet of flowers?" she whispered, realizing that she'd been holding her breath. She looked over at Jasper.

He looked as surprised as she felt. "I guess we wait to see if he comes back out."

She settled onto her crate again to wait. "Thank you for telling me what happened. Do you think Marshal Baggins knows about your past?"

"I'm sure he does." Jasper didn't sound happy about that.

Of course. It would only give credence to Jasper losing his cool with Aiden. Only this time, nothing stopped him from killing the man who was threatening a woman he cared about.

"I didn't kill Aiden," he said quietly.

"I know that." She felt his gaze swing to her.

"You sure?"

Darby turned to look at him. "Positive. You're not a killer. I suspect that's why the senator is still alive."

He shook his head. "I wanted him dead. I live with that every day."

The door of the cabin opened, the light inside went out and Leviathan emerged. He now wore a coat. Darby watched him carry the flowers to the truck and slide behind the wheel.

A moment later, the truck's engine rumbled to life.

CHAPTER TWENTY-THREE

JASPER WAS ON his feet with Darby heading for the door. He turned on his flashlight, and they moved swiftly through the building, slipping back out onto the sidewalk. A semi roared past before they could cross the highway in its wake to climb into his pickup.

Once behind the wheel, Darby riding shotgun, he started the engine and went after Leviathan.

"Last night, he went straight down the back street, then turned onto that old road out of town," she said. "Do you think he's taking the flowers to someone? Is it possible he has a lady friend?"

"Anything is possible," Jasper said as he took the first street off the highway and then the next right. There was no sign of the truck's taillights, but Jasper turned right again and raced down the back street. He hoped they hadn't miscalculated how much of a head start the man had.

The back street ended at the county road. He glanced over at Darby.

"Left," she said with enough conviction that he turned and headed away from the lights of town. Clouds moved across the moon, pitching the road into darkness beyond the pickup's headlights. The mountains rose to their left, towering over the county road.

"I don't think anyone lives out here," he said, voicing his thoughts. "It's the road to the dump." He was beginning to wonder if they should have turned right back at the T when he saw the flash of brake lights ahead off to his right.

"I know where's he going," Darby cried as the lights they'd seen went out. "I drove out past here the other day to interview Karla Parson. He just pulled into the old part of the cemetery."

Jasper felt his stomach knot. If the man was taking flowers to the old cemetery then he had had kin here. He kept going up the road until the land fell away and he could stop without being seen from the cemetery. He pulled over, feeling a little sick. If Leviathan had had kin from here, then that could explain how he knew so much about Buckhorn and its residents.

"I think we need to walk from here," he said as the moon broke free of all but a veil of clouds, throwing a thin yellow sheen over the landscape. "If I try to drive closer, he'll hear us."

"It will be hard enough to keep him from seeing us," Darby agreed. She opened her door quietly and climbed out.

The cemetery was a half mile back up the road. "Let's cut through the old Miller place," he suggested as he joined her behind the pickup. "It's abandoned. We might have to go through a couple of barbed wire fences, but it should bring us out close to where we saw him stop."

DARBY'S MIND RACED as they walked back up the road to the barbed wire gate going into the old Miller place. Jasper held two strands of wire wide apart to let her slip through. She did the same for him. Their gazes met for a moment.

She'd taken her now loaded gun from her purse along with her penlight back at the car. She'd tucked both into her coat pockets. The spring night air had a bite to it. Still early in the year in Montana, the nights often dropped down close to freezing. She could see her breath as she walked, but she hardly noticed the cold.

What was Leviathan doing at the local cemetery in the middle of the night?

A dozen thoughts whizzed past, only one worthwhile. He knew someone who was buried out here. That would explain the flowers.

She stumbled in a gopher hole as they crossed a stretch of pasture. Jasper caught her arm, preventing her from falling headlong in the dirt. She'd been deep in thought. Not about Leviathan at that moment, but Jasper and what he'd told her. She hadn't been surprised. It made her sad. She suspected he'd been good at his job.

But it also explained why he appeared gun-shy at getting involved with anything—especially her. So why had he opened up to her? He had to be aware of the strength of the chemistry between them. How could he not feel it after that kiss the other night? Even if he didn't remember the other time.

They angled past the old farmhouse toward the pines that stood along the older cemetery fence. A newer cemetery was at the other end, closer to town. As they reached the trees, they both grew even more quiet. They crossed another barbed wire fence and then stepped over a low wrought iron one.

Headstones began to appear from out of the darkness with pines here and there. They wound their way through them, Darby being careful not to step on any more graves than she had to. They hadn't gone far when Leviathan's truck suddenly took shape at the edge of the only road into this section of the cemetery.

Jasper touched her arm to get her attention, then leaned closer to whisper in her ear. His breath tickled her neck and sent goose bumps running all over her skin. "I think he's just on the other side of the truck."

She nodded and let him lead the way. As long as Leviathan stayed on the other side of his vehicle, they should be able to get closer without him seeing them. Another cloud shrouded the moon. Dark shadows spread across the tombstones and turned the hulking truck black.

At the edge of the road, Jasper stopped. She did as well. She could tell he was listening. It took her a moment, though, before she heard it. Singing. It was low, barely audible with only a few words coming to her on the slight breeze.

She felt her eyes widen as she locked gazes with Jasper. Leviathan was singing. Cautiously, they crossed the narrow dirt road to the truck. Jasper moved toward the back of it. She was right behind him as he peered around the tail end. She couldn't see anything and figured he couldn't either because he moved slowly forward until he was at the far edge of the covered back.

She edged closer until her body was pressed against his. He shifted a little so she could see.

Leviathan sat in front of a small gravestone some distance away. He rocked slowly back and forth as he sang. His voice was so low she couldn't make out the words. It almost sounded as if the song were in another language.

The song stopped and he got to his feet with an ease that surprised her. Maybe he wasn't as old as they'd all thought. She realized that if he'd killed Aiden he could be a lot stronger than he seemed as well.

He stood over the grave for a few moments longer, his

head bowed and then he began to make his way back to the truck where they were hiding.

WITH DARBY'S BODY pressed against his, Jasper had been distracted for a moment. Being this close to her was playing hell with his libido. He'd been remembering the feel of her in his arms.

Then Leviathan had suddenly stopped singing and rose and Jasper had realized that they would be sitting ducks if they stayed where they were.

He eased Darby back, putting a finger to his lips before motioning that they should go back across the narrow dirt road to the other cluster of gravestones. None of them were very large, not large enough to hide behind. Their best bet, he realized, was to get to a large old pine with a thick trunk and sweeping low boughs.

But they would have to move quickly—and quietly. Leviathan was making his way back to the truck. A part of Jasper wanted to confront the man, demand to know who he was, who he was visiting and what the hell he was up to.

The only thing that held him back was the feeling that showing his hand right now would be a mistake. Better to wait. Once they checked out the tombstone of the grave where he'd left the flowers, they might have all their answers.

They'd just reached the large pine when Jasper heard the truck door open and then slam close. He pulled Darby close behind the pine tree. If the clouds stayed over the moon and if they huddled close enough, they might not be seen should the man look in their direction. He held his breath, waiting for Leviathan to leave.

It took a few moments before they heard the sound of

the engine rumble to life, let alone for Leviathan to shift it into gear and start to drive away.

Still, Jasper didn't move. He had Darby backed up against the tree, his body against hers, his head resting on top of her hers. As the sound of the truck died away in the distance, he pulled back to look into her face.

The moment seemed to hang in the cold spring air. He could *not* have kissed her any more than he could have *not* taken his next breath. He slowly lowered his mouth to hers, brushing his lips across her bow-shaped mouth, the tip of his tongue teasing at one corner.

He felt her shiver before he drew back to meet her gaze. Then he slowly lowered his mouth to hers again, her lips parted on a sweet sigh. He felt her hands grip the sides of his coat at his waist and draw him even more tightly against her as he parted her lips even wider with his tongue.

When her tongue met his, he groaned with a need he'd kept checked for too long. He deepened the kiss, taking possession even as he surrendered to the taste and feel of her. He cupped her head in his hands, the kiss taking on a power of its own. He'd never wanted a woman like he did this one. Desire burned so hot inside him that he thought he would catch flame.

He dropped one hand to the front of her jacket and jerked the zipper down, desperate to caress her naked flesh. His fingers found the top button of her blouse, slipped it loose and dug deeper until he could cup the warm naked breast in his palm. The moan that came from his mouth was purely primal, the sound Darby made matching his own.

His thumb flicked the hard nub of her nipple and he felt her knees buckle under her. Any moment they would both be on the ground—

The thought wormed its way through the hot, slick desire that roared in his veins and he drew back, fighting to catch his breath. She groaned as he abandoned her mouth and took his hand from her breast. As he tried to pull himself together, he fumbled the zipper of her coat back up.

"Not here, not the first time," he said, his voice sounding hoarse with emotion and lust and regret. He shook his head as if telling himself no again. She looked so damned beautiful. Her lips dewy and still parted, her honey-brown eyes dark with a desire that threatened to take him to his knees.

He stepped back from her, the night air suddenly feeling colder. Darby slowly pushed off the tree and looked around as if, like him, she'd gotten lost and was just now finding her way back.

"Let's take a look at that grave," he said, his voice sounding a little more normal while his need for this woman made him ache.

DARBY TOOK A clumsy step away from the base of the pine. He grabbed her arm to steady her and for a moment she thought he would pull her to him and kiss her again. She knew exactly what would happen if he did. All his best intentions would fly on the breeze and they would make love.

The need inside her made her weak, but she straightened, bit down on her lower lip with the taste of him still in her mouth and met his gaze in the semidarkness under the pine. She could see the battle going on inside him mirrored in the gray of his eyes.

He quickly let go of her arm and took a step back, then another as if he didn't trust himself. She followed, but awkwardly. It was like learning to walk again. She felt a dampness between her legs and an ache of regret that made her chest hurt. She feared that Jasper would never let himself go that far with her again.

As they worked their way back across the road and into another section of the old cemetery, the breeze picked up. Her cheeks began to sting from the cold. She reached up to brush away an errant tear.

"I think it's over here," she said, surprised that her voice sounded fine even though she was far from it. She headed through the gravestones discolored with age. The moon peeked out, then ducked back again behind a bank of clouds. Shadows moved across the graves, leaving behind a feeling of melancholy that hung over the place.

The moon appeared again, throwing the cemetery into a pale light. "There!" Jasper said a few seconds before she saw the small gravestone—and what Leviathan had carried from his shop out here to leave in front of the marker.

As she moved closer, she saw that the bouquet of flowers was made from tissue paper like a child might have made. Something about that made her heart hurt as she pulled out her penlight and shone it on the letters and numbers carved into the headstone.

CHAPTER TWENTY-FOUR

EARL RAY STARTED at the sound of his cell phone's ring—and not just because of the hour. He wondered if he would be startled each time it rang from now until he got the call about his daughter. He'd put out some feelers with people he knew could help. All he had to go on was that a baby girl had been born to a woman who might have called herself by one of two names or made up a new one—about thirty years ago between the dates he'd been gone. He wasn't even sure the birth had taken place in Montana.

It was so little information that all he could do was hope. That was what he'd been doing as he waited for the phone to ring.

His cell rang again. He quickly found it and hit Accept without noticing who was calling. All he'd seen was that it wasn't a local number. If it was another person trying to sell him warranty insurance for his pickup—

"Earl Ray," the man said on the other end of the line. It took him a moment to recognize the voice and by then he'd heard the words *DNA tests*. He felt a wave of disappointment. It wasn't anything about his daughter.

"I'm sorry. Would you repeat that?"

"I know it's late, but you said you needed this right away," his friend said. "We ran more extensive tests on the DNA that you sent us, and we got a hit on a close relative who is set to be executed in Texas the first of next month."

"How close a relative?" he asked, suddenly more interested. He felt as if he owed the man calling himself Leviathan Nash. Not revenge exactly. But at the very least, he wanted to know exactly who he was dealing with.

"Probably his son. The man in the Texas pen is forty-two."

Earl Ray did the math. "It's hard to know this man's age." A stray thought struck him. "You say he's going to be executed the first of next month?" Right after Leviathan's lease was up in Buckhorn. Right after he finished what he'd come here to do.

"It was a brutal murder of a woman that shocked the state. He got the chair four years ago."

He took a breath. If this man in prison was Leviathan's son, then having his son facing execution could have been the catalyst for what had been happening in Buckhorn. Having his son looking at the chair could have pushed Leviathan Nash to hurt others he felt had wronged him.

"What is the man's name?"

"Everett Ford."

DARBY MOVED CLOSER and shone the penlight on the faint letters now barely visible from the years the weather had damaged the stone. "Can you make out the name?" she asked Jasper.

"Thelma," he said, a catch in his voice. "Thelma Rose."

She stared at the stone, wondering how he was able to make it out. Turning, she saw his expression in the ambient glow of her penlight. His gray eyes were wide in the moonlight, his face washed of all color. Goose bumps rippled over her skin. "What?" she said on a breath. "You knew her?"

He nodded, looking as if a ghost had just risen from the grave. "My grandmother...worked with her. They were... county nurses together. I remember the name."

She swung the beam of light back on the headstone. "It looks like her last name was Lee?"

"I never knew her last name. It was always just Thelma Rose."

Darby checked to see when the woman had died. A little over thirty years ago. "When did you say you left Buckhorn with your parents?"

"When I was eight. About thirty years ago," he said.

"So you weren't here when she died. She was forty-five when she died. So that would make her seventy-five if she had lived. Do you remember anything about her family?"

He shook his head. "I just remember her name. My grandmother used to talk about her all the time. They were good friends." He frowned. "Thelma Rose had lost her husband, I think in the war. I'm sure Bessie or Earl Ray will remember her. I don't know if she had any kids."

"She obviously has some connection to Leviathan. I suppose he could be a son if she had him when she was really young, but that would mean he isn't as old as we thought." She shook her head. "He must have some connection to her. But if he is her son, why didn't anyone from Buckhorn know about him?"

Darby glanced at Jasper, wondering if he was listening. He appeared to be lost in his own thoughts. "You don't remember her having a son?"

He shook his head. "I'm pretty sure she didn't have any kids, or I would have seen them."

"That's odd," she said as she noticed what appeared to

be an unmarked grave next to Thelma Rose's. "I wonder who's buried there?"

When Jasper said nothing, she turned to see him looking down the row of headstones and felt a chill.

"Are your grandparents buried here?" she asked. She saw him swallow.

"They are."

She had the feeling that he'd never come out here. Jasper and his parents had left suddenly when he was five. Everyone just assumed there'd been an argument between his parents and grandparents. Most everyone was surprised that he came back and bought a ranch just miles down the road from the place his grandparents had owned.

"Are your parents—"

He shook his head. "They're buried in Nebraska." He had his hands shoved down in his coat pockets. He looked cold. Or maybe he felt like her. Like someone had just walked over his grave. "You ready?"

She nodded, her gaze skittering past him to look in the distance. Mist rose from between the pines. The night had turned even colder, and they weren't going to learn anything else out here.

Nor was Jasper going to tell her what had him looking so locked down again. Was it what they'd learned or what they'd almost done out here? She bit her lower lip, sorry that just when she thought the two of them were making their way to each other, she felt Jasper pulling away again.

She pushed to her feet. "I'm cold," she said, which was true enough. She was more than ready to leave, and she could see how badly Jasper wanted to get far away from here. Thelma Rose Lee had worked with Jasper's grandmother. Was this what Leviathan was so desperate to tell him? Even if the woman was Leviathan's mother, Darby couldn't see how any of this fit together. Or why Jasper was so determined not to find out what Leviathan knew about him.

They took the road back to where they'd left the pickup, both silent. The night air hurt her cheeks and stole her breath, but that wasn't why she was shaking.

Seeing that grave had scared Jasper. Darby wasn't sure why. But it had to have something to do with Thelma Rose and his grandmother. He'd said he'd gotten an invitation to go to Gossip. But he hadn't gone. Was there something more that Leviathan had uncovered about the Cole family just as he'd suspected? Whatever it was, clearly Jasper hadn't wanted to know.

Now she wondered if tonight had changed that.

ONCE IN THE PICKUP, Jasper started the engine and got the heater going. He knew the chill that had settled in his bones had nothing to do with the cold spring night. When he'd recognized the name—Thelma Rose—he'd known. Whatever Leviathan had to tell him had something to do with his grandmother.

He remembered her as small, almost delicate with the face of an angel. She used to bake him cookies and make a fuss over him. In his memory, she was sweet, generous and often busy. She would get called out in the middle of the night to see to someone who was sick or having a baby. He recalled the exhaustion on her face in the morning when he got up and yet she would still make him pancakes.

As they neared town, he looked over at Darby. "If you want to come out to the ranch—"

"No, I'm fine. You're welcome to stay with me at the apartment."

He shook his head. "I need to get home to the cattle and Ruby." He thought about telling her again that he didn't want her going to Gossip. But her special showing wasn't until Saturday. There was time.

Still, he didn't like leaving her. But he needed to be alone right now. He thought she might have realized that since she'd been so quiet on the ride back into town.

As he made a U-turn in the middle of the highway and pulled up in front of her office and apartment, she opened her door to get out, but hesitated.

"Are you going to be all right?" she asked.

He had to smile. "I'll be fine. I'm more worried about you."

She returned his smile. "Don't be. We're going to figure this out. Everything's going to be all right."

He loved her optimism. For a moment, he thought about going inside with her, climbing into her converted couch bed, snuggling together for the rest of the night. Just the thought made him ache. "Be careful," he said, not sure if he was warning her or himself.

She nodded and closed the door. He waited until she was inside, the door locked behind her. Climbing out, he stared up at the apartment, waiting for the light to come on. A few moments after it did, she moved to the window and parted the curtain. He waved and she waved back before the curtain fell into place and he climbed again behind the wheel.

He didn't remember driving home. Ruby barked from her kennel beside the house, her tone definitely angry at being left behind, as he parked. He went to her first. She instantly forgave him, jumping up excitedly until he crouched down and hugged her.

It wasn't until he headed for the house that he saw what was hanging on his front door.

CHAPTER TWENTY-FIVE

AFTER A RESTLESS NIGHT—what had been left of it—Jasper showered, dressed and drove into town. It was Friday and he wanted to catch Bessie before the café began filling up. She was in the kitchen when he came in, finishing up her strawberry tarts. The café smelled of strawberries and rich buttery pastry. Normally that scent would have made his stomach growl.

Instead, he felt a little sick as he stuck his head into the kitchen. "I need to talk to you."

Bessie looked worried as she wiped her hands on her apron and checked her tarts in the oven. "Get us a couple cups of coffee. I'll be right out."

He was sitting in his usual spot looking across the highway at Gossip. It was still dark inside the shop. He thought about the man they'd seen singing over Thelma Rose's grave last night and had to look away. His latest special showing was at eight this morning. He wondered what Leviathan Nash would do when he didn't show up this time.

The café was nearly empty except for a long-haul trucker sitting at the counter. Jasper had seen him in here before. A couple of the local ranchers would be along soon as well as the cook and the waitress for the early shift. But for a while, they pretty much had the place to themselves.

Bessie slid in opposite him in the booth and seemed to brace herself for the worst.

"You've lived all your life here. I need to ask you about my family," he said before she could even reach for her coffee cup. "Do you know why my parents left Buckhorn?"

She looked surprised. "No, I just remember your grandmother being upset."

"How well did you know my grandmother?"

"Edith? Everyone knew her. She was such a sweet thing. I think about all the people she helped, all the babies she brought into the world." Bessie shook her head. "It was so horrible when she died. Everyone loved her."

"My grandmother worked with another woman."

"Thelma Rose." Bessie smiled. "If those two weren't a pair. I haven't thought about them in years." Her smile waned. "Why are you asking about them? Thelma's been gone for…gad…what, almost thirty years now? I remember how hard your grandmother took her death. You and your parents hadn't been gone long. Your grandmother wasn't the same after that. She quit, you know."

"As a county nurse?"

Bessie nodded and took a sip of her coffee. "With Thelma Rose dead and your grandmother quitting… That was back when the town depended on the county nurses since we didn't have a doctor in town. Nowadays they send an ambulance or if an emergency is really critical, a helicopter. Back then, especially in the winter when the roads were bad, it was up to one or both of those two women to keep people in Buckhorn alive."

Jasper fell silent for a long moment. He'd never realized how important his grandmother and Thelma Rose had been to Buckhorn. Suddenly remembering the photo Darby had sent him, he pulled out his phone. He called it up. "Do you recognize any of these people?"

Bessie took the phone, still looking worried, and glanced

at the photo for a moment before shaking her head. "Who are they?"

"I don't know." He pocketed the phone. "Maybe the people who raised Leviathan Nash."

"Him! What do Thelma Rose and your grandmother have to do with that awful man?"

"I'm not completely sure. Did Thelma Rose have any children?" He saw the change in Bessie's expression at once and knew why there was an unmarked grave next to Thelma Rose's.

"She died in childbirth," Bessie said. "Your grandmother did all she could including calling for an ambulance and sending for a doctor. But with a hundred miles of bad roads that spring, the ambulance and doctor didn't get here in time. Not that there was much they could have done."

She stared down into her coffee for a few moments before she spoke. "I'm sure your grandmother blamed herself and that was part of the reason she just couldn't do it anymore and quit. But there was nothing anyone could have done outside of a hospital, the doctor said. Thelma Rose was at high risk already and then being almost forty-five… The doctor said she should have never let the pregnancy go that far given those circumstances." Bessie pulled a napkin out of the dispenser and wiped her eyes. "The whole county turned out for Thelma Rose and her daughter's funeral and then your grandmother's funeral a month later. That was one horrible spring."

He felt a jolt, even though he wasn't sure it meant anything. "It was about this time of year?"

She nodded. "But unlike this spring, the weather was so much worse. We thought winter was never going to end. What are all these questions about?"

He quickly told her about following Leviathan Nash to the cemetery. "He has some connection to Thelma Rose."

Her hand went to her mouth as tears filled her eyes. "That he might be her son…" The two usual ranchers who ate breakfast this time of the morning came in with the young waitress, the three of them laughing. Bessie blew her nose and stuffing the napkin into her pocket, got up to check her tarts.

"You want me to order you something?" she asked.

He shook his head and finished his coffee.

Bessie hesitated. "If Thelma Rose had a child before she came to Buckhorn, she might have told someone. You might ask Earl Ray. There is little he doesn't know about Buckhorn and its residents. He might have heard something."

"I'll do that," Jasper said, getting to his feet.

"*We'll* just do that," Darby said as she slid into the spot Bessie left and gave him a bright big smile.

"Good morning to you too," Jasper said, actually glad to see her. He'd given it a lot of thought last night when he couldn't sleep and he'd realized she was right. They were in this together whether he liked it or not.

ON THE WAY to see Earl Ray, Darby and Jasper shared pleasantries that had nothing to do with anything but the pretty spring day or how they'd both slept. They were wary of each other. Last night at the cemetery had surprised and scared at least one of them. They could have been strangers except for the chemistry that arced between them, Darby thought.

They found Earl Ray polishing the tile he'd recently grouted in one of the bathrooms. "Don't let us stop you," Jasper said. "I just have a couple of quick questions."

If Earl Ray was surprised to see them together, Darby noted that he didn't show it. He ushered them into the kitchen and poured three cups of coffee. Once they were settled around the table, Jasper said, "I need to know about Thelma Rose Lee. Bessie told me she died in childbirth. Is it possible she'd had a son before she came to Buckhorn?"

The older man frowned. "Not that I know of. Why are you interested in Thelma Rose?"

"We followed Leviathan out to the old cemetery last night," Jasper said. He quickly told Earl Ray what they'd discovered.

"I would have never guessed Leviathan Nash might be related to Thelma Rose," he said. "She was the sweetest woman. What she and Edith did for this community. But I do recall your grandmother being worried about her friend's pregnancy. She came to me because she'd hoped I might intercede. I knew both women well and I had some medical experience in the military." He made a surprised sound. "Now that you mention it, at the time, Edith mentioned that Thelma Rose had problems with her first pregnancy when she was fourteen. The infant came early. Thelma Rose had almost died from complications. I just assumed the baby died. It was long before Thelma Rose moved to Buckhorn. I didn't know what the complications were."

"Do you know if she went by any other name before she came here?" Darby asked. "I assumed she'd been married or was Lee her maiden name?"

Earl Ray rose, left the room and returned with his laptop. It took him only a few moments. "Lee was her married name. Her maiden name was Ford. Thelma Rose Ford." He let out a curse. "This is all starting to make sense. Late last night, I finally heard back on the more extensive DNA tests. We got a hit on a relative. His name is Everett Ford and he's in a prison in Texas for murder. He's due to be executed in a matter of days."

"Ford?" Darby said. "He's a relative of Thelma Rose's— *and* Leviathan Nash?"

"Given his age and matching DNA, it appears Everett Ford is Leviathan's son," Earl Ray said as he pulled his laptop over and began to type. "I just found Thelma Rose's son she gave birth to who almost died. His name is Ethan Ford, age sixty-one. Leviathan Nash looks much older, but if he was born early and had medical problems, it could have aged him—not to mention whatever kind of life he's led. It would explain his small stature."

"But if he was her son..." Darby said, frowning. "How old was she when she came to Buckhorn? She didn't have him with her? And why didn't anyone know about him?"

Earl Ray shook his head. "If she gave birth at fourteen, I would assume that someone else raised the child. Maybe a parent or grandparent. Thelma Rose had her nursing degree. She would have had to help make that happen if she'd gotten pregnant at such a young age."

Darby pulled out her phone. "I copied a photo I found in Leviathan's cabin." She handed it to Earl Ray. "I wonder if these weren't the people who raised him."

"Could very well be," he agreed.

"I kept wondering why this man waited until now to open Gossip and terrorize Buckhorn," Jasper said. "Do you think it might be connected with what is about to happen to his son?"

Earl Ray nodded. "That and maybe his age. Now or never."

"But it doesn't explain how he came into possession of all the information he's been dispensing," Darby said.

"I think it might," Jasper continued. "I remember how my grandmother knew almost everyone in the county. She had a journal that she kept track of births and deaths and medical information on her patients in. But it also had personal information on them like their favorite food, allergies, whether they had pets. It was kind of a history of the people she'd come to know."

"I see where you're headed with this," Earl Ray said. "If Thelma Rose kept such a journal, which I'm sure she did, it might have had a lot of information about her patients. They both spent a lot of time in people's houses. They probably knew the county residents better than anyone—especially their secrets. Amazing what people tell a health care worker on their death or sick beds. I heard more than my share in my time in the military."

"If Thelma Rose's son, Ethan Ford, came into possession of her journal…" Darby said. "You don't think he blames Jasper's grandmother for the death of his mother and sibling, do you?"

"I suppose it's possible," Earl Ray said.

"Wait a minute." Darby was on her feet, her face feeling flushed with excitement. "Do you know what Thelma Rose was going to name her daughter?"

"Levi," Earl Ray said as if he just saw it as well. "Levi as in Leviathan."

"So there's a good chance he has the journal," she said. "Who knows what all is in it."

Earl Ray made a wounded sound. "It could contain information about my daughter."

"But why didn't he share that information with you when he told you the rest after your visit to Gossip?" Jasper asked.

"Because he blames this town for taking his mother away from him all those years ago, for letting her die, for who knows what all," Earl Ray said. "Clearly, he wants someone to blame. I'm worried just how far he's going to take it before this is over."

"He sent me an invitation to a special showing," Darby said and saw the older man's surprise. "Saturday morning at eight."

"Tell me you aren't going," Earl Ray said.

"She's not going," Jasper said and met her gaze. "If I have to hog-tie her, she's not stepping foot in that place."

Darby had to clamp her lips shut. If Jasper noticed, he didn't say anything. If he knew her at all by now, he'd know that he would have to do more than hog-tie her to keep her from going Saturday morning.

She noticed that Earl Ray looked close to tears and realized why. "Thelma Rose had to have brought your daughter into the world," she said. "That's how Leviathan knew."

Earl Ray nodded. "If true, Tory wouldn't have had her baby here unless she had to for some reason. Probably because she knew she could trust them to make it all go away. I was in the military far from here. It's the only way Leviathan—Ethan Ford could have known. Thelma Rose delivered my daughter. She had to know what happened to her. Unless the whole thing is a horrible lie."

CHAPTER TWENTY-SIX

JASPER FELT BOTH relief and anguish as he and Darby left Earl Ray's house and headed back toward her office. The pieces of the puzzle were finally coming together. While that relieved him, it also worried and angered him. He had seen the torment Earl Ray was now going through. Just like a lot of the other residents who'd paid a visit to Gossip.

He now could understand why Leviathan Nash, better known as Ethan Ford, would try to frame him for a murder. Maybe it was true that the man blamed Jasper's grandmother for the death of his mother and baby sister.

"At least now we know what we're up against," he said to Darby as they reached her office and she dug for her keys. Not finding them in her purse, she reached into her pocket and pulled them out with a flurry and a grin. He could only shake his head as she unlocked the door. "As impossible as you are, you were right. Ethan Ford came to Buckhorn for revenge."

When she didn't answer, he glanced over at her. He could tell she'd been mulling it all over in that reporter mind of hers and wasn't surprised when she let out a cry and rushed over to her computer.

"Nash!" she said and began to laugh. "Of course. Ford. Don't you see? That's how he came up with the last name Nash. Leviathan for his sister, Levi, and Nash as a play on his real name, Ford."

He watched her clacking on the computer keys furiously. "There was a car by that name, right? Nash Rambler? Here it is. The car company ran from 1937 to like 1957? Get this," she said excitedly. "Nash debuted the heating and ventilation system in *1938* that is still used today. Apparently, his company also came up with unibody construction in 1941 *and* seat belts in 1950. How cool is that? It looks like they even came up with the compact car in 1950 and muscle cars in 1957. Who knew?"

He laughed. "Fascinating, but I doubt Ethan Ford is connected to car manufacturing."

Darby wasn't listening. He saw her freeze and when she looked up, her eyes were wide. "Leviathan was being cute when he came up with the name," she said, "but listen to this. Charles Nash's slogan was '*Give the customer more than he has paid for.*'" She shivered as if feeling a chill in the air. "Doesn't that sound like what Leviathan does at his shop?"

Jasper felt the same chill circle his neck. "He chose the name, playing off his last name, Ford, and his deceased sister's name, Levi."

Darby nodded and swallowed. "You said you thought the name meant something to him."

"You've been right from the beginning. Leviathan Nash is Ethan Ford and Ethan Ford is dangerous."

"He must have his mother's journal," she said, her voice a whisper. "That's how he knows so much about Buckhorn and its residents." She looked up at him. "I have to go to Gossip Saturday morning. It's our last chance to find out the truth about all of this. What happened to Earl Ray's daughter might be in that journal. I have to go."

Jasper pulled back. "Have you been listening to anything I've said?" Resentment made his words come out too sharp. "It's too dangerous. This is about him getting even with me because of my grandmother and he's planning to use you to do it."

Darby stopping pacing to stare at him. "You don't know that."

"Darby, you aren't from here so we know he doesn't have anything to tell you about you or your family. What possible other reason could he have to involve you?"

She felt even more flabbergasted he would say that. "I'm more than just your alleged girlfriend. *I'm a journalist.* I believe in printing the truth. The real story because readers have the right to know."

"You can climb down off your soapbox now," Jasper said.

If he was trying to lighten the moment, he wasn't succeeding. "Did it ever cross your mind that he might want to tell me why he's doing this?" she asked, digging in her heels. They'd gotten this far. They now knew who he was and possibly why he had targeted Buckhorn and some of its residents. But there was more to the story or he would be gone by now.

"What if you're wrong?" Jasper demanded.

She shook her head. "This elaborate plan of his had to take months, maybe years to put together. He'll want to tell someone. He'll be too proud of himself not to share it. I think he sent me an invitation to Gossip because his lease is up Saturday night at midnight and it's his last chance to tell his story to the whole world."

Jasper shook his head. "The man's dangerous."

"Only to people with secrets to be exposed. Like you said, he doesn't have anything on me and by your own admission, he hasn't done anything illegal."

"Have you forgotten that he might have killed your former fiancé?"

"We don't know that," she said, pacing in the small room.

"He's trying to *frame* me."

She turned to look at him. "Maybe someone else is trying to frame you." He stared at her until she said, "Okay, you probably don't have *that* many enemies. But maybe Leviathan came upon Aiden after he'd been robbed and murdered in that empty lot and decided to use it to his advantage. There was that other assault and robbery that night."

"I don't think the marshal is buying that it was the same man," he said. "Or he thinks I robbed the man to cover up my real crime."

"That's ridiculous. If you read the article in my newspaper, you'd know that the robber came up behind the man, demanded his wallet, and he handed it over, feeling it was too dangerous not to. He was then hit with something and knocked out for a while. He never saw the man's face. Aiden, in the mood he was in after leaving the café that night, wouldn't have simply handed over his wallet and it would have gotten him killed."

"I *read* the story in your paper," he said with a groan. "Isn't it just as possible that Leviathan did all of it to shift the focus off him and what he's doing at Gossip? Don't you get the feeling that his son going to the chair has the man desperate and feeling he has nothing more to lose?"

"But how are we going to *ever* know the truth if I don't go? When his lease is up Saturday night, he'll leave. Worse, he'll leave with Aiden's death hanging over both of us."

"Better than being dead. Darby, you can't go to Gossip. Who knows what kind of trap he's setting for you?" He moved to her, taking her shoulders in his hands. "I can't let you go. Damn it, woman, I'm crazy about you. Don't you get it?" His voice broke. "As hard as I've tried not to, I've fallen in love with you."

She felt the shock of his words reverberate through her an instant before his mouth dropped to hers. He pulled her to him. As angry as she'd been just moments before, she felt herself melt into his arms, lost in the taste and feel of him. He'd said he'd fallen for her. Hadn't she known that it was only a matter of time before he accepted the chemistry between them?

He pulled back to look at her. "I think I've been in love with you since the first time I saw you. Why do you think I kissed you that night back in college?"

"You remember that?" she asked in surprise.

"Are you kidding? I've never been able to forget you or the kiss or making love together—unlike you. Apparently, I didn't make much of an impression."

Darby laughed. "I pretended I didn't remember because I thought *you* didn't remember." She looked into his gray eyes, drowning in them. "That night changed my life. But then I left for my summer job, you graduated and I didn't see you again. I just assumed you hadn't felt anything since I never heard from you."

Jasper shook his head as he pulled her close. "I did try to find you. Would have helped if we hadn't been going our separate ways the next day. All I can say is that it's a good thing you made your way to Buckhorn." He drew back again to look at her. "It was fate, right?"

She laughed. "*You* can't even believe you just said that. I saw you and Buckhorn looked as good a place as any. I've been trying to get you to notice me ever since."

His chuckle was deep and low. It sent vibrations rippling

through her. "How could anyone not notice you, Darby Fulton?" She saw the desire in his eyes mirrored in her own. "It's all I can do not to carry you upstairs."

She grinned at him and stepped from his arms to lock the office door. Turning, she looked at him. She knew this man, maybe a little too well. "You think you can get me into bed and change my mind about going to Gossip on Saturday, don't you," she said with a shake of her head.

He grinned. "I'm damned sure going to try."

AS THEY REACHED the top of the stairs, Jasper grabbed Darby, swung her into his arms. He kissed her, parting her lips with the tip of his tongue and delving deeper as she opened to him. Passion burned along his veins like a dynamite fuse.

He'd denied his feelings for so long. But he could no longer. He wanted her. Darby broke away long enough to toss the couch cushions aside and pull out the bed. Jasper grabbed her from behind, turned her and kissed her. He kept his mouth on hers as he slowly lowered her to the mattress. He only broke away to look down into that face of hers as he knelt over her.

Jasper had to smile—she'd grabbed his attention the first time he saw her. Was it those honey-brown eyes fringed with dark lashes? Or that incredible mouth? Or that trail of freckles across that perfect nose?

Maybe at first, he thought. But once he'd gotten closer, he'd seen the intelligence in those eyes, the determined set of that jaw, the honesty that came out of those lips. He'd fallen for the whole package.

"What?" she whispered, looking worried.

"I like looking at you," he whispered back and began to trail kisses slowly down her slim throat to the V of her blouse, until he reached rounded flesh at the top of her bra where he rooted out a nipple.

She let out a moan of pleasure as he sucked it into his mouth and laved the hard tip with his tongue. Darby pressed her breast harder against his mouth. His fingers freed the buttons of her blouse and pushed aside the fabric, taking in her white lacy bra.

"I would have taken you for black," he said of the bra, one eyebrow cocked humorously.

"It would have been black if I'd known you'd be in my bed."

He chuckled and unhooked the front of the bra, letting her full breasts spill out and into his hands. His thumbs flicked over her nipples as he dipped down to kiss her again. He felt her shudder, her lips trembling against his as she arched against him. He could feel her need ramping up like his own.

This had been coming for a long time. Why the hell had he fought it?

Darby unsnapped his Western shirt in one swift movement, pulling the fabric apart and drawing him down to meld their bodies together. His hot flesh pressed against her own, making her breasts ache, nipples so hard that they hurt with a need for release.

Jasper rolled to the side, taking her with him as his hand snaked into the top of her jeans. She felt his fingers part her to get at what he was searching for. She held her breath as he found her most sensitive skin. She threw back her head with a groan of pleasure as his fingers began to slowly move.

She'd wanted this for so long that his fingers barely stroked her before she felt herself climax. She shuddered again and again, crying out as he pulled her close, holding her as the tremors slowed.

Then he kissed her lips, her hair, his lips a whisper at her ear as he helped her wriggle out of jeans and panties—also white. Goose bumps covered her body as she was freed from all of her clothing. She'd never felt more naked or more vulnerable or more of a woman. Nor had she ever wanted Jasper more than she did at this moment.

She helped him out of his clothing before he pulled her into his arms again. She could feel him against her belly and ached for him to enter her, to take her to a place that she knew only he could. This chemistry they felt, it was unique to the two of them. They were in this completely together.

Her body was quivering by the time he rolled over on top of her, parted her legs and just as slowly filled her. He did it carefully and with such care that she thought she would burst with the need to feel him move inside her. They both lay perfectly still for a moment.

When he began to move, it was with slow, sure strokes that inflamed the passion that had been arcing between them for months. She wrapped her legs around him, bit down on her lower lip to keep from crying out as he lifted her higher and higher until she thought she wouldn't be able to breathe and then he fulfilled her. She clung to him, riding it out, their bodies molded together as wave after wave of pleasure surged through her.

Later she lay in his arms, trying to catch her breath. She felt empowered as if she could do anything, be anything. She looked over at Jasper, wondering if it had made him feel the same way. He looked as happy and content as she was.

"I'm a writer and I can't even begin to tell you how you make me feel," she said.

He smiled, leaned to her and brushed a kiss over her

forehead before he swept another one over her lips. "You really *are* going to be the death of me," he said with a chuckle as he lay back again.

"Really? Why do you say that?" she asked, rolling up onto one elbow to look into his handsome face.

"Because all I can think about is doing that again with you," he said and clutched her, pulling her down on him.

It wasn't until much later that Darby's brain had another cohesive thought.

When the thought did come, she suddenly pushed herself up on one elbow to look over at him. "Thelma Rose wasn't married, right? So who was the father of her baby girl, Levi?"

CHAPTER TWENTY-SEVEN

JASPER WISHED HE could stop time. They stayed holed up in her apartment, ordering in food from the café and exploring each other's bodies. The chemistry between them was electric. He could feel the sparks in his fingers and toes. It radiated through him—straight to his heart like an arrow. Everything he'd feared had come true. He'd fallen in love with this woman.

He couldn't live without Darby now. Nor could he stand the thought of being away from her even when he had cattle and a dog to feed and care for and she had a newspaper to get out. He always found his way back to her bed.

But tomorrow was Saturday. He didn't have to ask Darby if what they shared would change her mind about going to Gossip for her 8:00 a.m. appointment. He knew her too well. She would go.

Unless he did something. Ethan Ford aka Leviathan Nash wanted him—not Darby. The last time he'd returned to his house to see to Ruby, he'd found a small white bag on his front door. Written inside on the invitation were two words: Time's Up.

Jasper didn't have to wonder what it meant. The threat was obvious. Not that he didn't think Darby might be right. Maybe Ethan wasn't just using her to get to him. Maybe he did want to tell someone how he'd done all of it.

But unfortunately, all his instincts told him that bragging on himself wasn't all the man wanted to do.

Look how much they already knew about Ethan Ford. Darby had gotten more of those who'd been inside Gossip to talk to her off the record. Each had gone and been surprised to find that the man calling himself Leviathan Nash had a special gift for them. It was often something they had valued in the past or a trinket that reminded them of another time. Like the ballerina that Earl Ray had given his first wife. Bessie had confided that the original was packed away—after spending years on the table on Tory's side of the bed.

It must have taken Ethan Ford months if not years to find those replicas—items that made residents believe without question the next thing that Leviathan had given them— bad news.

But Darby's learning the man's story was a moot point. Jasper wasn't going to let her get near the man. The question was how to convince her to let the snake oil salesman slink out of town with his secrets. There was only one way. Jasper had to give Ethan Ford what he really wanted. He had to let the man tell him what was so important that he couldn't leave town without sharing it.

"Can you stay?" Darby asked Friday night after they'd had dinner down at the café together.

"Ruby's out in my pickup. I have to take her home. Come home with me." He pulled her into a kiss, the promise of what he had in mind later. He could feel her surrender to the passion between them. Would it always be like this? He suspected it would as he nibbled at her ear and felt her tremble in his arms. "I love you," he whispered against her throat, making her quiver and press closer for a moment, before pulling back.

Darby cocked her head at him. "This isn't about keeping me from going to Gossip in the morning, is it?"

"Seriously? I confess my love for you, show you how badly I want to get you into my bed to ravage you and you think it's just to stop you from doing something...reckless? Are you always so suspicious?"

"Always," she said, her gaze holding his with an intimacy that made him weak inside. "You can't change me."

"I don't want to."

She nodded. "I'm telling you upfront, I'm going to the shop in the morning." She waited for him to protest.

He held up both hands and took a step back. "One of the things I love about you is that you're your own woman. I've told you all the reasons I don't want you to go." He shook his head. "Ultimately, what can I really do to stop you?"

She quickly stepped to him to cup his face in her hands. "I can't wait until this is over." She kissed him gently on the lips, knowing that he knew she wasn't talking about the two of them.

He pulled her closer. "Me too."

"I'll come with you, but I'm taking my own car." She could see that he knew what that meant. Nothing could stop her from leaving in the morning so she could reach Gossip at eight.

Jasper nodded slowly. "Okay," he agreed.

Maybe a little too quickly, she thought, but she put it out of her mind as he kissed her again.

JASPER LAY AWAKE in the darkness, sated, but unable not to think about tomorrow. He had no intentions of letting Darby go to Gossip alone in the morning. He was convinced that Ethan Ford wanted him and was merely using Darby to try to get to him. Jasper mentally kicked himself for letting this go so far. If he had responded the first time he'd received one of those invitations…

He looked over at the beautiful naked woman lying in his bed and felt such an overwhelming surge of love. Darby Fulton. He smiled, thinking of all the times she'd driven him crazy and all the times he'd denied his growing feelings for her.

They'd driven separate vehicles out to the ranch, made love and then gone for a walk with Ruby around the ranch. For a while, they'd sat down by the creek. The evening had felt warmer. Summer wasn't that far off. He'd been thinking about the future. Damned if he wasn't going to ask this woman to marry him by the Fourth of July—if not sooner.

Back at the house, he'd barbecued chicken outside on the patio and they'd sipped wine until the stars had come out. When the temperature had dropped, they'd moved inside to make love yet again in his big bed.

Looking at her now, he felt overwhelmed by the love he felt for her. That was why he couldn't let her put herself in more danger tomorrow, he told himself now. He'd already made up his mind that he was going to confront Ethan Ford. He just hadn't told Darby. He was the one Ethan Ford was trying to frame. It was time he faced whatever it was the man had to tell him. He wasn't letting Darby go. He couldn't. He'd deal with the fallout when he got back from town.

She would be furious. For a while, he might not be her favorite person—not even close. But they'd get through it. He figured once Ethan Ford told him what he needed to tell him, that would be the end of it. But just in case, he was taking a gun. He didn't trust the man and figured Earl Ray was right about the timing. It was quite possible that

Ethan, believing he had nothing to lose at this point might do something dangerous—like try to kill him.

Darby had left her purse on the floor by the bed. It took him only a minute to find the keys to her vehicle. He padded into his spare room to his gun safe. He took out what he thought he'd need and put it aside. Darby would be furious with him, but if he was right, she wasn't the one Ethan Ford wanted—he was. He put her keys into the safe and closed and locked the door.

Closing the guest room door behind him, he went back to his bedroom and Darby. He saw his wineglass next to the bed and picked it up, going over to the window and looking out on the beautiful spring night. A breeze came in the partially opened sash. He breathed it in, feeling as if he'd come back to life after being in a coma for several years. Darby, he thought. She'd awakened in him joy after thinking he would never feel it again.

He glanced back at the bed, finished his wine and put down the empty glass. Tomorrow he would face whatever ghosts Leviathan Nash had dug up from his past. He was through hiding from life. Back at the bed, he climbed in beside Darby. She sighed in her sleep as her body seemed to find his unconsciously. He pulled her close, breathing in her scent, and closed his eyes.

SUN STREAMED IN the window, splashing across the sheets. Darby had heard Jasper slip from the bed. A few moments later she heard the sound of the shower in the principal suite's adjoining bathroom. She quickly slipped from bed and pulled on her clothing.

She'd warned him that she was going to Gossip this morning. But still she felt guilty slipping out while he was in the shower. She just wasn't up to an argument. Last night had been too wonderful. She didn't want to have words with him. She knew his feelings; he knew hers.

Still, she hated to think what he would do when he came out of the shower and found her gone. She pushed that from her mind. She knew this man. He'd given in too easily last night. He had something up his sleeve and she had a pretty good idea what it was.

He was planning to go in her place to Gossip. She couldn't let him do that. She figured she would be safe since she wasn't the person Ethan Ford really wanted. But if Jasper went... It was too dangerous.

Ruby watched her from the kennel as she went to Jasper's pickup. It took a few minutes to let the air out of one of his tires that was already low. Moving to her own rig, she reached into her purse and felt around for her keys. It dawned on her what he'd done. She had to laugh. It appeared both of them were trying to protect the other with dirty deeds.

She glanced back at the house before she reached under the bumper of her SUV for her spare key. Jasper knew how she was always misplacing her keys. He should have known she'd have spares.

As she left the ranch as quietly as possible before he came out of the bathroom and found her gone, she hoped this went the way she had planned. She knew the chance she was taking and not just with Ethan Ford. She didn't want there to be anything between her and Jasper that could ruin what they had started.

She could understand why he was worried about her going to Gossip. Was she just being naive in believing that Ethan Ford's reason for inviting her had to do with the fact that she was a newspaper reporter and not involved with Jasper Cole? Probably.

But she had to get to the truth to save them both. If Ethan Ford's ultimate plan was revenge against Jasper's family, she needed to get the man to tell her—on the record—or at least on a recording on her phone. She had an opportunity to clear Jasper of murder and she had to take it.

She checked her rearview mirror before turning onto the highway toward town. She felt a tug of guilt. He'd know where she'd gone. What was to stop him from putting air in the tire and coming into town? She glanced at her phone. He couldn't get there in time, she hoped.

Her thoughts had been at war since she'd awakened. Last night and again this morning had been so amazing. Her skin tingled at the memory of their lovemaking. But if she didn't do this, she would regret it. They both would, especially if Ethan Ford's plan was to frame them.

Her heart aching at how upset Jasper would be, she was relieved to see Buckhorn appear on the horizon. She told herself it had to be done. She would never know the truth unless she went to the shop for her special showing. But was she really willing to jeopardize what she had with Jasper just to know the truth about Gossip and the man behind it?

Darby told herself that it wouldn't come to that. The thought made her ache, though. There was a reason she'd chosen this career—or it had chosen her. He said he'd fallen in love with her—the newspaper woman she was. Then he had to understand her need to get to the truth. But even more important was protecting the man she loved. She couldn't let Ethan Ford skip town and disappear as she suspected he would, leaving a cloud over Jasper. She and Jasper could be arrested. Any proof otherwise would be gone. Proof that might also lead Earl Ray to his daughter.

She was almost to town when she spotted the first patrol SUV headed toward her. As Marshal Leroy Baggins raced past, she saw there were two more patrol SUVs behind him and a cruiser, all headed in the direction from which she'd just come. Maybe they were on their way to some horrendous traffic accident. But they didn't have their lights and sirens on, she thought, frowning.

Wherever they were headed, she didn't have time to speculate, she thought as she drove into town and parked across from Gossip. She dug her extra office key out of the glove box.

She had just enough time to shower and change before her appointment.

CHAPTER TWENTY-EIGHT

IT WAS PLENTY EARLY. Jasper was drying off, thinking about catching Darby still in bed naked, when he heard the pounding. He cracked open the bathroom door. Had Darby gone outside and locked herself out? Why would she do that?

He thought of their night of lovemaking. No wonder he was still having trouble making sense of what was going on, he thought as he wrapped the towel around his waist and stepped out of the bathroom. His gaze went to the bed. Empty.

Chuckling, he thought he must be right about her getting locked out. He wondered how disrobed he would find her. The thought sent pleasure through him as he headed for the front door.

"Darby?" He moved quickly through the house. "Darby?" But he hadn't gone far when he heard Ruby barking and felt his first inkling of unease. Something wasn't right. His heart was pounding by the time he reached the front door and threw it open.

Marshal Leroy Baggins stood framed in his doorway. "I have a warrant to search your property." He thrust it at Jasper.

He took the order without looking at it. Leroy had his cop face on, which alone should have warned him how serious this was.

"The warrant includes your house and outbuildings," the marshal was saying. "You might want to get dressed."

Past Leroy, he could see other officers of the law getting out of their rigs. Why so many? Because they knew what they were looking for. His stomach dropped and he felt sick as Leroy and several other lawmen pushed past him into the house.

But right now, he had bigger problems. As he looked past the marshal's patrol SUV parked in front of his house, he saw that Darby's car was gone. When had she left? He had no idea. But he had a bad feeling that he knew where she was off to as he checked the time—7:20 a.m.

He went back to the bedroom, one of the law officers following him. After pulling on his jeans, boots and a shirt, he headed outside to get Ruby fed. She'd spent the night in her kennel and was already excited by all the visitors swarming the ranch. One of the officers went with him, making him shake his head in frustration and annoyance. He didn't have time for this. He had to get to town.

He could see officers going through his shed and barn while others were tearing his house apart. He knew what they were looking for. He wondered where they would find it. Wherever Leviathan Nash aka Ethan Ford had left it.

"I need to go into town," Jasper told the marshal after putting Ruby back in the kennel.

"I can't let you do that," Leroy said.

"I'm not under arrest and until I am—" They were interrupted by a shout coming from the barn. A moment later, an officer came out carrying a baseball bat in his gloved hand. Even from where Jasper stood, he could see the blood and tissue still on it. *Nice touch, Leviathan*, he thought.

"Another anonymous phone call?" Jasper said to the marshal. "Look, Leviathan Nash is behind this. His real name is Ethan Ford. And Darby Fulton is probably going into his shop right now. I can't let that happen. I have to—"

The marshal pulled his handcuffs and reached for him. "Jasper Cole, you're under arrest for the murder of Aiden Moss. You have the right to remain silent—"

Jasper stepped back, hands held up out in front of him. "You have to listen to me, Leroy. Darby's life is in danger! She's going to Gossip right now."

"Don't make this any harder," the marshal said, and grabbed him and spun him around, snapping the cuffs on him.

"Then arrest Darby too, right?" Jasper said as the marshal pushed him into the back of the patrol SUV. "Pick her up now. You know if I killed Aiden, then she had to have helped me move his vehicle. She's at Gossip. Go pick her up."

Leroy said nothing. "I'll have someone take care of your dog and see that your cattle get feed until you can make arrangements." With that, he slammed the patrol SUV back door.

DARBY TRIED NOT to think about Jasper as she hurriedly finished dressing for her appointment in jeans, boots and a Western shirt and jean jacket. Her phone would be in a pocket of her jacket, on Record.

She took a deep breath and tried to relax. But all she kept thinking about was Jasper and how he would feel when he found her gone, especially after the night they'd had together. Jasper had been so loving and tender. She shivered at the memory of their bodies molded together in passion. It was everything she'd ever imagined it could be.

And while she understood why he was so worried about her meeting Leviathan Nash this morning, she knew she was as ready as she could get. Her gun was in reach inside her purse.

She checked her phone again assuring herself that Ethan Ford wanted to tell her about what he'd done. She'd been a journalist for too long not to know his type. He couldn't leave town without telling someone. For a newsperson at heart, she had to hear it. But she also needed for him to admit that he was framing Jasper for Aiden's murder. She tucked her cell phone back into her pocket and practiced hitting Record. She would get proof.

Darby checked herself one last time in the mirror. All morning, she'd been telling herself that she wasn't afraid of visiting the shop in broad daylight. Jasper would know where she'd gone in case she didn't come back out, so it wasn't all that dangerous. She only hoped she could get what she needed before Jasper showed up.

She met her gaze in the mirror. Wasn't she afraid that Ethan might tell her something that would destroy her like he had some of the others? What if he knew why Jasper had quit his job with homicide and there was more to the story? Was there anything that could make her think less of the man she loved? No. She knew his heart. She trusted him with her life.

Assuring herself that she could do this, she told herself that most of the "special showings" at Gossip hadn't taken more than half an hour. She figured this would take a little longer, but still she'd drive back out to the ranch when she was finished. Jasper would be upset that she went to Gossip for her appointment, but once he saw that she was all right, he'd be fine.

She'd have proof that the two of them had nothing to do with Aiden's murder. She'd also have her page-one story.

Maybe she'd print it right away. She knew she wouldn't be able to hold it until her usual press date.

That was if Ethan told her what she needed to know. She realized she was getting ahead of herself. Maybe he wouldn't tell her why he'd come to Buckhorn, what he'd hoped to accomplish, how his story would end or admit his part in Aiden's murder.

Her stomach fluttered at the thought that Jasper might be right. What if she was walking into a trap? Of course she was nervous. She had no idea what Ethan Ford was going to tell her or if she could get the evidence she needed. But she'd been here before.

She checked the time. She had to go. She headed for the door. It was eight on the dot when she stopped in front of Gossip. Reaching into her pocket, she hit Record and tried the knob. It turned. Taking a breath, she pushed the door open and stepped in.

CHAPTER TWENTY-NINE

As Darby stepped in, the door closed behind her. She heard a click as it locked, the sound loud in the empty room. The only thing louder was the pounding of her heart.

For weeks, she'd been curious and not just about Leviathan Nash. She'd wondered what he'd lured his victims in with and what he might have for her. The inside of the shop was an immediate disappointment. There was nothing on the shelves and with the black paper still on the windows, the place had a depressing, deserted feel to it.

Had he already packed up for his exit tonight at midnight? Was he finished here in Buckhorn and there was nothing left to sell—or any more bad news to dispense? Why invite her here?

Her gaze went from the empty shelves to the small desk in the shadowy corner and the man dressed in all black sitting behind it. Maybe she was right after all. Maybe he wanted to gloat, which meant she was here because he needed to tell her his story. As he rose, he took a small bow. "Miss Darby Fulton, what a pleasure it is to meet you," he said as he walked toward her.

He wasn't any taller than she was. He'd been so much larger in her mind because of the havoc he'd unleashed on this town. Staring at the small gray-haired elderly man, she felt almost disappointed now that they were face-to-face.

Jasper's and her own fear of what might happen if she came to the shop seemed silly now. This man looked harmless.

"I've been looking forward to meeting you, too, Mr. Ethan Ford," she said.

He broke into a smile, exposing small childlike teeth. "Bravo! I'd heard that you were not just bright and talented, but a very impressive investigative reporter." He gave her another slight bow.

"You have nothing to sell me?" she asked, glancing around.

He chuckled. "Was there something in particular you wanted?"

Her gaze returned to him. "Just the truth."

"Ah, of course. That I do think I can provide you. But first there is something I want to show you, something I saved just for you. If you would be so kind as to join me out back."

"Said the spider to the fly," she quipped. "I've been waiting to see the inside of your shop for weeks and now you want us to leave it to go where?"

He smiled. "Not to my cabin, if that's what you're worried about since you've already been there...haven't you?" He laughed at her surprise. "Did you enjoy your trip to the cemetery? I've always loved cemeteries. How about you?"

She couldn't help the feeling of unease that washed over her at his words. He knew that she'd been in his cabin, just as he knew that they'd followed him to the cemetery. She had the sudden fear that he'd been feeding her bits and pieces. Leaving her a trail of breadcrumbs as he cleverly led her up to this point in time.

"Why don't you tell me why you invited me here." She hated that her voice sounded strained.

He cocked his head, seeming amused by her discomfort. "You already know why I came to Buckhorn."

"I'd love to hear it from you."

"I'm sure you would, but aren't you more interested in the part you play in all this?"

"What part might that be?"

He merely smiled and held out an arm as if to point the way out the back door. Those dark eyes seemed to bore into her as he said, "If you really want to know, I'd be happy to show you. Just step outside."

She didn't move. All her senses were on alert. She glanced toward the back door. His truck was parked just outside the door next to his cabin. He was right. She'd been there before and had no desire to go inside again.

But it was just after eight in the morning. Broad daylight outside. And Jasper knew where she was. All that aside, why did she feel that leaving the shop would be a huge mistake? She tried to tell herself that the man wasn't much larger than her and she had youth on her side. Still, she didn't trust him.

His smile was gone, and his eyes had darkened almost black. "We both know what you came here for. To save your lover. But the journalist in you would really like this." He stepped over to the desk and picked up a weathered journal, the edges worn and bent with age and use. He held it up. "Do you know what this is?"

She was through being coy. "Your mother's journal she kept as a county health nurse."

"Well, well," he said, his voice low and deep. "You're as smart as I suspected you were. Of course, you've had help. Jasper Cole and Earl Ray Caulfield." He looked over at the journal he was still holding up. "My mother was invited into every home in this county. She helped so many people, kept them alive, held their hands when they were dying, brought their new life into the world with every baby she pulled from their wombs. But when she needed help, where was everyone?"

"She almost died when you were born," Darby said. "As I understand it, you almost killed her."

His face morphed into a mask of fury. "Who told you that?" he demanded.

"Do you blame the town for her death? She knew the risks. She'd been told that she should never get pregnant again," she said, hoping that her phone was recording all of this conversation. "She knew it would probably kill her—and her child."

He shook his gray head. She could see that he was trying to contain his anger. "I don't blame the entire town. I blame Jasper Cole's family."

"Everyone knows that his grandmother did everything she could to save your mother."

"No one could save her after she fell in love," he said bitterly. "You of all people should know how love can make a person do rash, senseless things. Like you coming here today. You love what you do. Jasper didn't want you to, did he? And yet here you are."

"I came because he believes you're trying to frame him for my ex-fiancé's murder."

Ethan raised a brow. "You're that sure he didn't kill your former fiancé?" His thin laugh echoed in the empty room, giving her a chill. "It wouldn't be the first time Jasper lost his temper when it came to someone who hurt his lady love. I'm sure he's told you all about his first love, the woman he got killed and how his actions got him not only thrown off the force, but also almost thrown in prison."

She could see that he was trying to rattle her. "I don't

care about that," she lied. "I want to hear how you did it. I don't think you killed Aiden yourself. It's not your style." He rewarded her with a grudging nod of his head. "You must have found him dead and realized you would use Aiden's death to your advantage." He smiled and she continued. "You would have taken his car keys. The mugger turned killer only wanted his money, but Aiden wouldn't have given it up without a fight. You left the car near Jasper's ranch." She cocked her head at him, remembering how Jasper had been waiting for the other shoe to drop. "You would have taken the murder weapon as well. But how did you get back into town?"

"I walked. It was a beautiful spring night. I'm glad to see that I wasn't wrong about you."

"But why? Why frame Jasper for murder?" She felt even more uneasy as she asked it. But she had him talking and she now knew that she'd been right about Aiden's death. If the recorder on her phone had caught it, she could clear Jasper.

"What has Jasper told you about his parents?" She said nothing since he'd told her very little. "Did he tell you they packed up and left town eight months before my mother gave birth and died, taking my little sister with her?" She waited, heart pounding, for him to drop his bomb. She could already see it coming. Was this what Ethan had wanted to tell Jasper, the big reveal?

"A smart woman like yourself, a journalist, I would have thought you'd have figured it out by now. Didn't you ask yourself who the father of that baby might have been?" She felt a hard knot form in her stomach from the way he was looking at her—as if he were about to spring something on her that she didn't want to hear.

"It's a story as old as time. Jasper must pay for the sins of his father." His voice broke with an anger she suspected had been building for years. "The father of her baby was William Cole, Jasper's father," Ethan said with a wave of the journal. "It's all in here. My mother's confession."

EARL RAY GOT the call shortly after Bessie had gone to the café to get her famous cinnamon rolls started. He'd made her promise to save him one. Today, he was determined to finish the last-minute things that had to be done before they moved into the house.

Heart lodged in his throat, he took the call. For weeks, he'd waited and hoped that one of his contacts would be calling with good news about his daughter. He didn't doubt that Tory had covered her tracks. But he was now fairly certain that the baby had been born here in Buckhorn—delivered by Thelma Rose—because of what her son had told him.

What had happened to the infant after that, though, was anyone's guess. Thelma Rose would have detailed the pregnancy in her county home nurse's journal that she kept. But had she told anyone about the birth? Had Ethan Ford just kept that part from him out of meanness? Or hadn't the man known?

Then yesterday, he'd gotten a call from the private investigator he'd hired.

"I have a lead," PI Edmond Voss had told him. "It's tentative so I hate to get your hopes up. I'm traveling to Houston today. I'll call you tomorrow once I know something more."

"Did you find her?" Earl Ray asked into the phone now, his pulse racing. Somewhere, he had a daughter who would be about thirty years old. She could be married with children of her own. He'd used all his available resources and come up with nothing. Desperate, he'd hired a private investigator he'd used before.

"I'm sorry, Mr. Caulfield," a woman said on the other end. "I'm Edmond's secretary Margaret Brewer. I'm afraid I'm calling with some bad news." She explained that Edmond has been killed in a hit-and-run accident in Houston Heights.

"No," Earl Ray said in shock. "Is that all the information you have?"

"There was an eyewitness who saw the vehicle and man who ran him down," she said, stopping to blow her nose. "I'm sorry. It's just so upsetting. Apparently, the driver stopped after running him down and took Edmond's briefcase before speeding away. The police are investigating it."

"You know he was working on a case for me."

"I do, but when I spoke with him after he reached Houston, he hadn't learned anything new. He was only then following up the lead. I'm so sorry. I'm sure any information would have been in his briefcase."

"I'm the one who's sorry. Edmond was a fine man. My condolences."

Earl Ray felt an icy chill at the news. The killer now had what information Edmond had gathered on the case—and Earl Ray's and Tory's DNA that he'd provided for the PI. This had been no accident. Someone was determined to keep him from finding his daughter.

"Tory, my God, what have you done?" he cried as he hung up the phone. "What kind of people did you get involved with?" The kind of people who didn't want their past exposed even after all these years. He shuddered at the thought. "Who did you give our daughter to?"

DARBY FELT THE stale air stir as Ethan waved the journal angrily at her, an unpleasant scent coming with it.

"That's right," Ethan cried. "It was Jasper's father! He and my mother!"

She wanted to argue that it couldn't be true. But from what little she knew of Jasper's parents, they had unexpectedly taken him away when he was five. Had he known why?

"Your mother wrote about it in her journal?" she asked, trying not to show her disbelief. Ethan had only one side of the story.

"She wrote down *everything*. She was obsessive that way. Every secret. Every dirty little detail this town had ever had because my mother was the kind of woman people confided in. When they were in pain. When they were filled with gratitude. They repaid her with truths about themselves and others. They confessed their sins. And she put it all in her book as if it could save their souls."

"Including about her own life? Did she write down how she felt about William?" She could see from his expression that she had. "She was in love with him."

"He bewitched her into thinking it was love," Ethan cried. "She would never have gone with a married man. They were going to run away together."

"Why didn't they?" she asked, the words almost on a whisper.

He shook his head. "She pretended that she was fine. That her heart wasn't broken, but I could tell by her writing…" He seemed overwhelmed with emotion. "She could have let me die. The doctors said I would never survive at such a low birth weight. But she fed me with an eyedropper, determined that I would live."

Darby knew that Ethan hadn't been with his mother

when she'd come to Buckhorn. He must have seen the question in her expression.

"It was only when I needed surgery for my heart defect that she had to let me go. She didn't have the money and the hospital wouldn't do the surgery unless...unless..." He looked away. "She left me on the hospital doorstep with a note. She never forgave herself. It's all in her journal. She swore she would never have another child that she might lose. And then William Cole came along."

"So, she made a choice to have his child even though she knew it would probably kill her."

"He was married!" Ethan screamed the words at her. *"He found out about the pregnancy and left her to die with his child!"*

DARBY STARED AT ETHAN. "Your mother detailed in her journal why he left?" she asked and saw his expression change. Thelma Rose had, but still Ethan blamed the Cole family—including Jasper. "Was she the one who broke it off?"

"Because she knew this baby was going to kill her because of him!"

She remembered what Earl Ray had told him about Ethan's son facing the death penalty in Texas. "You must have been planning this for years. But why now? Is it because of your son's death sentence?"

His face contorted into raw pain for a moment. "You really have done your homework, haven't you? It would be a shame if you didn't have the whole story now, wouldn't it?"

Darby could feel the phone in her pocket. She'd gotten what she'd come for. He'd admitted that he had framed Jasper for Aiden's murder. But she realized she didn't have everything as she looked at the journal in the man's hand. "Is what happened to Earl Ray's baby in there?"

Ethan smiled. "The only record of his precious daughter. If I were to destroy this journal, he would never know. He'd never be able to find her. Ever." His smile vanished in an instant. "The journal is yours. But first there is something I need to show you. Unless you've changed your mind about getting the whole story from me. In that case, you're welcome to leave. I'll be happy to unlock the door and let you walk out. But you won't be taking the journal. I will destroy it the moment you walk out that door."

She swallowed and hesitated. She needed that journal and not just for the marshal to prove what Ethan Ford had done, but for Earl Ray so he could find his daughter. She'd come here to get to the truth. Was she willing to walk away now? Ethan would be gone after midnight and the journal with him—if he didn't destroy it as he'd threatened.

"You promise to give me the journal after I see whatever it is you need me to see?" she asked, even as her instincts told her that she couldn't trust him. Shouldn't.

"I promise," he said. He again motioned for her to lead the way out the back door. She stepped past him, telling herself that nothing was going to happen to her. Any number of people could have seen her come inside the shop. Jasper would come looking for her soon if he wasn't already on his way.

As she stepped through the door, she thought she heard him unlock the front door of the shop. Because he was finished there and never coming back? Or because he wanted to make it easy for Jasper to get in. She realized Ethan Ford was planning on Jasper showing up.

The truck was parked directly behind the shop like it always was. She started walking along the side of it when she saw something that made her stumble. There was a large wooden box behind the truck. She told herself that he had probably packed items from the shop in it. The box sat at the rear of the vehicle on what appeared to be a hoist to load it up onto the truck bed.

But as she drew closer, she saw with surprise that it was empty. What struck her like an arrow to her chest was the size of the box. Coffin-sized.

Darby felt the hair on the back of her neck rise. Goose bumps rippled over her skin. She was starting to turn to look back at Ethan when she realized he was right behind her. He was so close that he hardly had to move to hit her.

The blow made her stagger. She crashed into the side of the truck, careening off to fall to her knees on the ground just inches from the wooden box. Her vision blurred and then darkened. She fought not to pass out as she tried to stagger to her feet.

Ethan moved swiftly to her, surprising her with his speed as well as his strength. He swept her up in his arms and carried her the few steps to lay her down in the box. Still fighting to stay conscious, she grabbed hold of the black coat he wore and tried to pull herself up. He tore her fingers away and took her purse with her gun and cell phone inside.

She hadn't realized that she was screaming until the sound stopped when he punched her again. Her head fell back, hitting the wood hard. Gasping, she tried to rise, but he was already sliding the lid onto the top of the box. Not a box. A coffin—just as she'd feared.

Suddenly, she was in total darkness. She tried to push the lid off even as she heard him hammering in the first nail. But the lid wouldn't budge and she realized he was crawling around on top of it, driving in nails. Her screams were more like muffled gasps that echoed back at her.

"No one can hear you," he said in that low voice of his.

She felt her flesh crawl. It was as if he had his lips next to her ear. "No please," she whispered. "Please."

"I'm disappointed. I'd hoped Jasper would be stopping by. Odd. Maybe he doesn't love you as much as you thought. Too bad. I hate for you to die alone, especially now that you know almost everything. I guess you'll never know about Earl Ray's daughter. Don't worry, I'll keep my word. I'll give you my mother's journal. I'm finished with it. Unfortunately, I'm not sure you'll be able to read it in there before I start to shovel dirt on top."

"No!" she cried, terrified as she imagined the sound of dirt falling on the wood over her head.

She heard him hammer in the last nail. A motor whirred to life, and she was being lifted into the back of the truck.

CHAPTER THIRTY

"WHAT TIME IS IT?" Jasper asked from the back of the SUV patrol car as the marshal started the engine and headed away from the ranch.

"Eight thirty-five." The marshal had left him in the back of the patrol car while he talked to his deputies and took a couple of calls.

Jasper swore now and began to talk quickly, desperately. "Darby has gone to Gossip to confront Leviathan Nash, who we now know is really Ethan Ford. The man blames this town for his mother's death. He blames my grandmother. Ethan only invited Darby to the shop to get even with me. She's in terrible trouble."

"Take it easy," the marshal warned him as Jasper moved closer to the partition between them.

"Come on, Leroy, you know I didn't kill Aiden Moss. I'm being set up for this," Jasper cried. "You really think I'd keep a baseball bat I used to kill someone in my barn? A bat still covered with the blood of my victim?"

The marshal sighed. "You know I have to take you in. The car was found near your ranch, the murder weapon in your barn. I don't think you should say anything more until you talk to an attorney."

"I don't care about me. Darby's walking into a trap. At least stop at Gossip and make sure she's all right. If you really believe I'm guilty of the murder, then arrest her. She had to have helped me, right? Leroy, do it before something horrible happens to her. You know Ethan Ford is behind everything that's been going on in Buckhorn. His lease is up tonight at midnight. This is his last chance to get even."

The marshal turned onto the highway and started toward Buckhorn. He glanced back at Jasper. "I'll stop at Gossip, okay?"

Jasper couldn't believe the relief that flooded him. He sat back and tried to breathe. "Thank you. Please hurry."

The marshal glanced in the rearview mirror at Jasper again before he turned on his lights and siren.

Praying it wasn't too late, Jasper fought the fear that wanted to overtake him as they sped the rest of the way into town. If they could just get there in time. He'd never been so happy to see Buckhorn come into view.

As THE ENGINE started up and the truck began to move, Darby felt her fear escalate. Her head ached, the skin around her eye burning from where he'd hit her. She blinked back tears and tried to pull herself together.

She had no idea how much air she had left before she would suffocate. Just the thought had her gasping for oxygen. "Calm down," she said to herself in the darkness and was slammed against the side of the box as the truck hit a bump in the road. "Think. Stop panicking."

Easy to say, but so hard to do. Still, she managed to breathe more naturally. She had no idea where he was taking her. But she had a pretty good idea what would happen when they got there. That thought sent her pulse climbing even higher. "Stop," she warned herself. "Panicking is doing you no good at all."

She thought about the construction of the box. She'd already tried to push the top off. How many nails had he put in it? Not that many. Did that mean he planned to open it at some point? To let her go?

Doubtful. No, she would have to get away on her own. She tried to get her feet up to kick at the lid of the box but there wasn't enough room to get leverage.

Sliding down some, she bent her knees as much as she could and kicked hard. She tried again and again and felt it give a little, bringing a flood of hope.

The truck slowed. She stopped kicking to listen as he turned onto what felt like a gravel road. The rough road made her bounce around more inside the box. She wedged herself in as best as she could to make the most impact on the end of the box at her feet—and kept kicking. She heard the wood rend as it tore away from a nail.

Her heart soared. She kicked even harder, feeling the bottom left side give a little. She put all her effort into the top left corner and kicked. Darby realized that she was breathing hard from the exertion. Too hard. She felt a little dizzy, as if she were suffocating.

But she couldn't stop. If she could kick the end free, she'd have air. If she could push her way out of the box…

The truck slowed and turned again. Her pulse pounded in her ears as her stomach dropped. They must be getting close to where he was taking her. She kicked harder, more desperate as she felt not just her air running out— but time itself.

More wood splintered as she put every ounce of strength she had into kicking the end panel free. She could feel air leaking in through the narrow opening she'd made. Only a few more kicks—

The truck stopped. The engine died. The driver's-side door groaned open. Time was up.

THE MARSHAL CAME to a stop in front of the old carriage house and climbed out to head toward Gossip. Jasper could only watch from the back of the patrol car as the marshal reached the front door, turned the knob and the door opened. Even from where Jasper sat, he could see that the place had already been cleaned out and was empty.

"Darby? Leviathan?" He could hear Leroy calling the names as he moved through the shop and opened the back door. Jasper could see that the old truck was gone—just as he'd feared. He closed his eyes, the pain like a spike drilling into his skull. Darby was gone. They both were gone. He and the marshal were too late.

Leroy came back to the patrol SUV only to walk past it to head across the street to Darby's office. He returned almost at once and climbed behind the wheel. He reached for his radio and put a BOLO out on Leviathan Nash, his truck and Darby Fulton.

Jasper fought to breathe. Leroy's radio squawked. Jasper listened, his heart in his throat, praying for news on Darby—and yet terrified to hear it because on the marshal's radio it would have to be bad.

But the news wasn't about Darby. A homeless man had been arrested for an attempted mugging at a truck stop not far from Buckhorn. The man had several wallets on him, including Aiden Moss's. Also, he was wearing bloody clothing.

"That's your man," Jasper said, even though he knew that until the clothing could be analyzed and the man questioned, he was still under arrest. "I need you to let me go, Leroy. I need to find Darby before it's too late."

The marshal looked at him as if he thought it might already be too late. "I have a BOLO out on them both.

There's only one highway out of town. It's just a matter of time before—"

"She doesn't have time," Jasper cried. "Please, Leroy. I'm begging you."

"Aiden Moss's murder is still under investigation. A homeless man didn't move Aiden's car or leave that bat in your barn."

"No, Ethan Ford did. Please. You know you can trust me."

The marshal seemed to be making up his mind. Sighing, he climbed out, opened the back door and pulled Jasper out to uncuff him. "Don't make me sorry about this."

The moment he was free, Jasper took off toward Earl Ray's house. He ran, telling himself that somehow he would find Darby. He would get there in time. He had to.

"I need to borrow your pickup," he called the minute he saw the older man working on the outside of his house.

It was so like Earl Ray not to ask questions. "Keys are in it."

Behind the wheel, Jasper started the engine and pulled out. Where would Ethan take her? It hit him the moment he turned onto the highway.

CHAPTER THIRTY-ONE

DARBY FROZE AS she heard Ethan get out of the truck. A moment later, she heard the whir of a motor. The box shuddered, then began to rise. She held her breath. Where were they? She thought she smelled pine trees, which didn't much help with her whereabouts since Buckhorn was surrounded by them. All she knew for sure was that she had to get out of this box—no matter what she had to do.

She felt herself being lowered. A moment later, the box hit the ground. She felt it give a little and looked down toward her feet. She could see daylight. It wouldn't take much pressure against the end panel of the box for her to free herself. Then it would just be a matter of scooting out. She didn't want to think past that. As long as Ethan was out there—

To her surprise, she heard a sound that startled her. He was pulling out the nails on the lid of the box. Was he going to let her go free? That she knew was beyond doubtful. Especially since he'd taken her phone. He had to know that she'd recorded their conversation, which would clear Jasper—the last thing Ethan wanted.

The lid suddenly came off. She blinked at the sudden brightness and breathed in the fresh air in ragged gasps as she started to sit up. Ethan handed her the journal.

"As promised," he said as she took it in surprise.

Darby was telling herself he'd done all this to scare her,

when she realized where he'd taken her. The cemetery? That was when she saw the hole that had been dug only feet away from the box she was in, the dark earth piled to one side.

"Sorry, but you won't have much time to read it." He hit her, knocking her back down and slamming the lid. Stars danced before her eyes, darkness threatening at the edges, but she didn't pass out from the blow. Dizzy and weak, she tried to shove the lid off, but heard him climb on top of the box again as he began to nail it shut. With more than a few nails this time.

JASPER DROVE OUT of town headed for the cemetery. He told himself that Ethan would stop by for one last visit with his mother before he left town. Unless he'd already gone to her grave. But right now, it was all Jasper had.

He felt as if he were reliving a horror. He had. The race to save Camille. Driving terrified, running on adrenaline and hope to save a woman he believed he was in love with. He could feel the same cold hard fear that settled around his heart like a frozen fist. He'd made deals with God, just as he was doing now.

Like then, he'd thought he'd known where the killer had taken her. The drive had seemed interminable—just like now. Every second was one closer to either saving her or losing her. He blamed himself then—just as he did now. He should have stopped Camille. He should have stopped Darby.

He kept seeing the last time. He'd come around the bend in the road and spotted the bridge ahead. That was when he'd seen her. Too late. His foot had come off the gas for just an instant before he'd hit the brakes. Jumping out, he screamed her name as he'd run toward her, telling himself that once he cut her down from the noose around her neck, once he had her in his arms...

The cemetery came into view ahead. Jasper felt that same sense of bottomless despair mixed with unrealistic hope. Hope was the killer, he'd already learned. Only this time, it was Darby and he loved her, wanted to spend the rest of his life with her, wanted her more desperately than his next breath. This time, he had everything to lose.

He saw Ethan Ford's old truck near the pines and his mother's gravesite.

What he didn't see was Darby.

BESSIE HUGGED HER HUSBAND, seeing how all of this was weighing on him. She knew that he'd made inquiries about his daughter. She'd hoped with all of his connections, he would have found something.

When she'd walked in the house, though, and saw the slump of his shoulders, she knew he hadn't gotten good news. She felt her heart sink. What if he found out it was all a lie? Or worse that Tory had injured the infant after it was born, and Earl Ray was looking for a daughter who never survived?

Her throat went dry as she looked at her husband. "The news..." She couldn't bring herself to say anymore.

"There's no paper trail," Earl Ray said. "I'm sure Tory planned it that way."

"How is that possible?" she asked, not sure what it meant. No paper trail because there was no longer an infant? Or because Tory had covered her tracks.

"Tory probably had an adoptive family lined up. One where there would have been no record."

"Or if Thelma Rose delivered the baby and knew that Tory didn't want it maybe she found her a home," Bessie said, terrified of what Tory would have done if she'd been alone with that infant. "Maybe Thelma Rose already had someone in mind who was planning to take the baby."

Earl Ray nodded. "That's possible, I suppose. We know that she didn't keep it. If she gave my daughter to someone, the adoptive mother could have passed the infant off as her own, saying it was born at home. Thirty years ago no one would have questioned the mother, especially if she'd been confined at home with a pretend pregnancy awaiting the birth. No one was doing DNA tests back then so it would have been hard to prove the infant wasn't hers."

Bessie felt ill. What if he was never able to find his daughter? She could see that his heart was breaking. "There must be another way to find out the truth."

Earl Ray looked up at her, hope in his eyes.

Bessie had no doubt that either Thelma Rose or Edith Cole would have protected that innocent infant from her mother. She said as much to him.

He nodded. "I suspect Ethan Ford gave me just enough information to destroy me. If the truth is in his mother's journal, he'll make sure that I never see it." Her husband must have anticipated her next question. "I already went to Gossip. He's gone. The old carriage house is empty. So is the cabin and his truck is no longer parked out back. Whatever he knew, he took it with him. I suspect that's the way he planned it. Apparently he came here to get his revenge on this town the only way he knew how. I suppose he sees me, because I've tried to protect Buckhorn, as being responsible."

"That horrible, horrible little man," Bessie said.

"Ethan Ford has me questioning everything including my instincts," Earl Ray said. "I hired a private investigator to find her. He was killed in a hit-and-run in Houston, his briefcase stolen by the driver of the car before speeding away."

Her eyes widened in alarm. "What are you saying? That he was purposely run down?"

He shook his head. "I had suspected as much, but I just heard from the police. The driver was picked up. Just some teenager. He and his friend had pried open the briefcase no doubt hoping it had something valuable in it. But finding only papers, had thrown them away. I thought for sure it was Tory's doing—even from the grave."

"How is that possible?" Bessie hugged her to shake off the chill that now moved through the room. She hated seeing her husband doubting himself.

"I figured she had friends in low places who helped her when she was on the run—and maybe after. Tory produced a false birth certificate before we were married. She had to know someone who could get it for her. I suspect she was mixed up with some very bad people who are still trying to bury some truth either about her or them." Earl Ray shook his head before dropping it into his hands. "How could I have not known?" he mumbled into his hands. "How could I have loved that woman for so long and not had a clue that I was living with a monster?"

FOOT FLATTENING THE gas pedal, Jasper headed for the truck. He could see the front of the truck parked under some pines inside the cemetery some distance from where he'd been the other night. The sun shone off the windshield, making it impossible to tell if anyone was behind the wheel as he roared straight for it. He saw no one around and that sent his pulse drumming.

What if he was too late? What if Ethan was gone and so was Darby?

He slammed on the brakes just inches from the front of the large old truck. He'd half expected gunfire to splinter the pickup's windshield into a million pieces. Instead, nothing happened. Because they were gone.

Killing the engine, he threw open his door and, gun in hand, he stepped out.

The moment he did, he heard pounding. It was coming from the rear of the truck. Brandishing Earl Ray's pistol, which he'd found in the pickup's glove box, he moved cautiously toward the sound.

The closer he got he could hear something else in between the sound of a hammer driving nails. Singing. The same song they'd heard the other night not far from here. Ethan Ford was singing—and hammering. Beneath the banging and the singing was yet another sound. This one tore at his heart. Muffled screaming.

As he moved closer, he realized that over all the noise, Ethan hadn't heard him approach. Either that or he was pretending to have not heard.

The moment Jasper came around the back of the truck, he saw the wooden coffin and knew. He felt his eyes widen in horror. The gun in his hand trembled and he thought his head might explode with both fury and terror.

"Stop!" he yelled as the man started to pound down another nail. Ethan didn't seem to hear. He drove another nail into the wood. *"Stop or I'll shoot you in the back."*

Ethan turned slowly, a nail in one hand and the hammer in the other. He didn't seem surprised to see Jasper—nor the gun in his hand.

"I thought you weren't coming," the man said. "Darby, I'm sure was holding out hope, but I didn't think you had the guts."

"Put down the nail and the hammer and step away with

your hands up. Now!" Jasper ordered as he stared at what he now knew was pure evil.

"I made the hole plenty wide and deep so the two of you could be together forever," Ethan said, smiling. "You really shouldn't have ignored my invitation. Look what it's going to cost you."

Jasper told himself the man was mad. Didn't he see the gun pointed at him? He barely had time for the thought before the hammer came flying at him. He ducked, but when he looked again, Ethan was gone like a puff of smoke.

He rushed around the end of the truck. "Darby?" he yelled. He heard a groan from inside the box. "I'm going to get you out. Just hold on." He looked around for the hammer wanting desperately to get her out of there, but he knew that he couldn't trust what Ethan would do now. He couldn't see him in the pines, but he knew he couldn't have gone far.

Backtracking, he found the hammer where it had landed and hurried back to the box. He began to pry at the lid, keeping the gun within reach and keeping an eye out for Ethan. The man had put so many nails in the top that it was taking far too long. "Darby, are you okay in there?" he yelled. He heard a muffled sound in answer at the same time he heard the old truck's engine turn over.

Jasper thought Ethan was making a run for it—until the truck came roaring backward. It caught him in the shoulder, sending the hammer in his hand flying and knocking him over the box and into the open grave. His head struck something solid.

He saw stars until he saw nothing at all.

"JASPER?" DARBY DIDN'T know what had happened. She'd heard him make a strangled sound before something struck the box. Now all she could hear was the sound of the truck engine. *"Jasper?"*

Fear had her hyperventilating. She'd been so surprised when she'd heard Jasper's voice. Of course, he'd come. He would have gone by Gossip. He would have seen it empty and been terrified. But he would have figured out where Ethan would take her.

She'd heard him trying to pry the lid off the top of the box. Then the truck engine had started... No! She couldn't bear the thought of what had happened. This was all her fault. All of it. She should never have gone to Gossip. She should never have—

Suddenly, she heard the truck engine rev. The box began to move. No! She'd seen the open grave only a few feet away. She'd heard Ethan telling Jasper that he'd dug it deep and wide enough for the two of them.

The box moved a few inches. *He was going to push it into the hole he'd dug!* "Jasper!" Something had happened to him. Something that was keeping him from stopping Ethan. She kicked at the panel on the end of the box. It gave a little more. She hadn't tried to dislodge it after the truck had stopped and she'd heard Ethan nearby. He would only have put more nails in it to make sure she didn't get out if he'd known that she'd managed to kick it partially open.

But now he was in the cab of the truck. She had to bust out of this coffin or... She couldn't let her mind go there. Ethan had done something to Jasper. She kicked harder, putting all of her waning strength into it. Her oxygen supply was running low. She didn't know how much more time she had.

The truck motor roared louder. The box moved a few more inches. No! She kicked harder and saw more daylight at the bottom of the panel she'd loosened. She kicked, feeling her air supply dwindling along with her strength. The truck struck the box again, rocking it, making her lose her balance. She kicked out as hard as she could and saw through the opening evergreen trees nearby. She kicked again and made a bigger gap, the nails screaming in protest as she gave it one last kick.

The box moved a few more inches and teetered as if on the edge of the grave. If she didn't get out now... She pushed with her hands and feet, crab crawling as best she could in the confined space. She got one leg out and was able to turn on her side to get more purchase. She managed to get her lower body out as the box began to tip.

She scrambled the rest of the way out, cutting herself on the sharp nails. She had to find Jasper. She had to stop this. As she spilled out onto the upturned earth, she looked into the dark cavern of the grave—and saw Jasper lying in the bottom.

Ethan was pulling the truck forward. She knew it was to make one final push of the casket into the grave. The tires on the truck spun in the loose earth. Ethan put the truck into Drive and pulled up a few feet forward. As he shifted back into Reverse, he revved the engine. One more push and the wooden casket would fall into the hole and crush Jasper.

CHAPTER THIRTY-TWO

"JASPER!" DARBY SCREAMED, but got no reaction. Her first thought was to jump down into the hole and pull Jasper out. Unfortunately, she knew there wasn't time, even if she could manage to get them both back out.

She had to keep the casket from tumbling into the grave and crushing him. The truck was large enough and she was short enough that if she stayed down, Ethan wouldn't be able to see her in his rearview mirror. She glanced toward the pine trees, saw a log lying on the ground. She had to take the chance that he wouldn't be watching in his side mirror. Rushing over to the limb, she grabbed hold of the end and tried to drag it over.

Because of the girth of the log and its length, it didn't want to move. But she was desperate. It moved a few inches, then a few feet. She dragged it back over, staying out of Ethan's view in his driver's-side mirror. Hurriedly, she shoved one end under the now empty box and dragged the other end over to the opposite side of the open grave before being forced to jump back.

The truck hit the casket, rocked it, but the log kept the box from falling. Dirt from the edge though cascaded down on Jasper.

"Jasper!" she called down into the hole. "Jasper!" She could hear Ethan pulling up again before revving the truck engine and coming back. "Jasper!"

She saw him open his eyes, brush dirt off his face as he started to sit up.

The back of the truck hit the casket hard—hard enough that it shoved it back onto the log—but off to one side. One end of the box was on the side of the grave. The other end hung in the air as it balanced on the log.

"Go hide in the trees!" Jasper yelled at her as he had before, but there was no way she was leaving him down there. She lay down on her stomach and reached for him. He was on his feet now trying to climb up the side of the open grave, but she couldn't pull him up and the sides of the grave only kept crumbling away.

He let go of her hand, grabbed hold of the log and was about to pull himself up when he cried out and had to let go as his hand went to his shoulder. She could see his shirt was red with blood from where he'd been injured.

Ethan had pulled the truck up. *Just drive away*, she willed him. Instead, he threw the truck into Reverse and backed up again, coming faster this time.

"Jasper!" He'd already heard the roar of the engine. Grimacing in pain, he grabbed the log again. She grabbed hold of his shirt and helped pull him up the side of the grave. He'd barely gotten over the edge as the truck crashed into the casket, splintering the side.

The log slipped and both the end of the log and what was left of the wooden box fell into the grave with a crash.

The truck engine died. The door opened. She saw Jasper looking around. "My gun," he said. The ground was torn up from where the truck tires had chewed into the soft earth. She didn't see it anywhere. "Go!" he said. "Go! Please!"

She heard the truck door open with a groan. Jasper shoved her and she stumbled back. He reached down and picked up a rock, motioning for her to go. She quickly moved along the passenger side of the truck, staying low. She couldn't leave him, wouldn't. Ethan Ford was right about one thing—she and Jasper would go down together if that was what it took. She moved stealthily along the side of the truck and across the front.

As she reached it, she saw Ethan. His back was to her as he headed toward the grave. She also saw the gun dangling from the fingers of his right hand.

CHAPTER THIRTY-THREE

JASPER HELD THE rock he'd picked up in his left hand. He had little strength in his right with his shoulder injured from being hit by the truck and thrown into the grave. He was unsteady on his feet, his eyes a little unfocused from the blow to his head. It had taken everything in him to get out of the grave. He would have never made it without Darby's help.

Now the bottom of the hole contained the broken casket. The log stuck up out of it, the other end buried—buried in the grave intended for him and Darby.

But Ethan Ford was still here determined to kill them both and Jasper knew even if it were a fair fight, he didn't have much to bring to it.

"Well, well," Ethan said as he reached the back of the truck, stopping on the opposite edge of the grave. "Where is our girl?"

"She's gone," Jasper said, hoping she kept going and didn't look back. All he had was a rock. Ethan had a gun. But he'd been in no shape to run—not that he thought this man wouldn't come after them and track them down and kill them. Ethan was obsessed with seeing this end the way he'd planned it. He had to know he wouldn't get away with it. Instead, it appeared he was ready to die—and take them with him.

"I'm sorry she left, but not to worry, I'll find her and bring her back. I want the two of you to be together. Unless

she goes too far and then I'll just have to bury her somewhere else all alone—after I make her pay for putting me
to the trouble."

"Why take it out on her," Jasper said. "I'm the one you
want. This is about my grandmother, right?"

Ethan chuckled. "I have no quarrel with Edith Cole. Although she was threatening to tell everyone the truth about
Tory Caulfield's baby. My mother was warning her not to
for her own safety. Did I hear your grandmother had a fall
down the stairs?" He smiled. "Sounds like she should have
listened to my mother."

Jasper felt a chill at what the man was implying. "If you
didn't blame my grandmother, then I don't understand why
you're doing this."

"Had you accepted my invitations to my shop you would
have found out. I had something special planned for you.
But you didn't want to come, did you? Haven't you asked
yourself what it was you were so afraid to hear from me?"

Jasper still didn't want to hear it. Worse, he feared what
the man was going to say even more than the gun in the
man's hand. Since all of this had begun, there'd been a
memory at the edge of his consciousness—something he'd
hidden away and was determined not to let out.

"Did you suspect the truth that you're responsible for
your parents leaving Buckhorn, for the destruction of your
precious little family?"

"I was five. I was just a child." But even as he said the
words, he felt a chill as a partial memory flashed before
him. Him in his mother's arms, her screaming as he tried
to get her to stop.

Jasper slowly dropped the rock as Ethan laughed.

"That's right, you're the one who spilled the beans, Jasper. You're the one who saw your father with another woman

and told. You're the one who destroyed your mother's life along with my mother's. Just like I am going to do to you."

DARBY REALIZED THAT her purse might be in the truck—with her gun in it. Or was the gun in Ethan's hand her own? She couldn't take the time to open the truck and search for her purse, even if she could do it quietly enough.

She looked around for something she could use as a weapon. She spotted the hammer lying only a short distance to the side, not far from Ethan. Could she sneak up behind him, get the hammer? She began to ease her way along the side of the truck toward his back. She could hear the two men talking. She knew what Ethan was telling Jasper and her heart broke for him.

She just didn't know how he would take the news. He hadn't wanted to hear it as if somehow he'd known. Or guessed? It didn't matter now. All of that was history. The only thing that mattered now was keeping Ethan from killing the man she loved.

Moving as quickly and quietly as she could, she was almost to the hammer when suddenly Ethan stopped talking and shifted on his feet. Had he heard her coming up behind? She froze, holding her breath. The moment he began speaking again, she let out the breath caught in her throat and inched closer to the hammer. Just a few more feet.

"You blame a child for telling something he saw but didn't really understand?" Jasper said, sounding resigned. "My father and your mother made the choice. Not me."

"Yes, your father. And now you will pay for his sins. Who better? And just when you've found your true love. Darby Fulton is your true love, isn't she? After all, she risked her life to save yours by getting me to confess to framing you for murder—for all the good it does now. But what a sign of commitment to a man who's been living like a hermit after getting the last woman in his life killed."

Now just a little to the right and behind Ethan, Darby bent down and, closing her fingers around the hammer, she lifted it from the ground, surprised by its weight. She realized it wasn't a standard hammer. As she straightened again, she heard Ethan start to say something and stop in midsentence. As she looked up, she saw him starting to turn as if he'd caught the movement out of the corner of his eye.

As he spun around, he led with the gun in his hand. She felt her heart stop as she saw the dark round hole of the barrel swing to her. Tightening her grip on the hammer, she swung the weapon. But she missed Ethan's head and only grazed his shoulder. As he let out a cry, he pulled the trigger.

For a moment she thought she'd been shot. But she didn't feel any pain. She was charging the man again when he caught her on the side of the head with his fist holding the gun and slammed her to the ground.

Pain radiated through her skull. The fall had knocked the air from her lungs, but that wasn't what was keeping her down. As she tried to get to her feet, her vision blurred, making her unsteady. As her eyes focused for a moment, darkness hovering at the edge of her sight, she saw something that chilled her to her soul. Ethan was turning the gun on Jasper.

From the other side of the grave, Jasper had watched Darby sneak up behind Ethan with growing fear that the man would sense her behind him even if he didn't hear her approach. Jasper told himself that he should have known she wouldn't go into the woods and save herself. Ethan was right about one thing. Darby had risked her life for him. Again.

He'd watched in horror as Ethan turned, pointing the gun in her direction. Jasper had no doubt that the man would fire the weapon clutched in his hand. Having already gauged the distance across the grave, Jasper lunged the moment Ethan had started to turn toward Darby.

Stepping onto the broken casket just long enough to vault himself to the other side of the freshly dug hole, he lunged for Ethan. The splintered wood of the casket gave way under him, just as he knew it would. Unfortunately, as it fell away, it threw him off balance. If he hadn't been able to push himself off the back of the truck to catch himself, he would have fallen backward into the grave and onto the splintered casket.

He ricocheted off the back of the truck, pointing all that momentum toward Ethan's outstretched arm and the gun at the end of it. Jasper heard the gunshot an instant after he'd thrown himself at the man. He heard Ethan scream even before Jasper grabbed the man's wrist, twisting it with all his strength until he heard a loud snap. The gun flew through the air, cascading down into the grave. Ethan howled in pain even as he reached down with his left hand and pulled something from his boot.

While small, Ethan was also quick and agile and eerily strong. As he turned toward him, Jasper saw the knife in the man's left hand. The long, lethal-looking blade caught the light as Ethan closed the distance between them. He saw the wild, take-no-prisoners look in the man's eyes as he lashed out at him.

Jasper tried to shift his weight, but the grave was behind him, the back of the truck next to him. Without any room to maneuver, all he could do was try to hold the man off. As Ethan swung the blade in an arc at him, Jasper went for the man's arm. But Ethan was stronger than he would have thought, tearing his arm free as the blade continued its arc.

He felt the tip of the knife blade cut through his shirt to graze his ribs. Before he felt the pain, he heard the sound of the hammer connecting with the back of the man's head.

For a moment, all three of them were suspended in time. Jasper teetered on the edge of the grave. Ethan stood, his eyes wide as blood began to pour down over his weathered face, his gray hair quickly matted with it. Darby still held the hammer high, ready to strike again if she had to even as a look of horror twisted her beautiful face.

Ethan took a step toward him, the knife still clutched in the man's hand. He stumbled, stepping onto the soft earth next to the grave. Jasper watched as the man lost his balance. He windmilled with his one good arm, the other hanging at his side, the knife blade flashing. And then Ethan fell, crashing into the splintered remains of the casket.

A hushed quiet fell over the cemetery. Jasper heard the birds before he saw them. The crows flew in, one after another, to line up along the fence. As if on cue, they began to caw. Closer, a breeze sighed in the pines.

It wasn't until Jasper heard the sound of sirens approaching that the birds took flight in a flurry of black wings. The spell broken, Jasper limped over to Darby. She released a sob and dropping the hammer, let him pull her to him.

CHAPTER THIRTY-FOUR

THERE WAS NOTHING like a Montana spring, everyone said as the foothills turned green, the big sky turned a deep blue, and the sun finally began to feel truly warm. But nothing about the days following the incident at the old cemetery felt spring-like.

An evil darkness had come to Buckhorn in the form of Leviathan Nash. He'd spread his poison at Gossip and even his death didn't lift that black cloud from over the town. He'd exposed their closely guarded secrets. They felt exposed and now knew how easily their lives could be turned upside down. They weren't ready to trust that something as dark wouldn't happen again.

It wasn't until the story came out in the *Buckhorn Independent Press* that residents realized how Leviathan Nash had known what he had. There was no mention of the journal being found. Everyone just assumed either Leviathan Nash had destroyed it—or it was missing. That news swept through town like a nasty squall.

Knowing where Leviathan had gotten his information didn't come as a relief as long as someone had possession of that journal. Many residents feared what else was in there and worried about how long it would take for even more secrets to surface.

In truth the journal wasn't missing. Jasper had retrieved it. As a former law officer, he knew that the journal was evidence and would be held possibly for months if not longer while the investigation into Ethan Ford's death was ongoing. So he'd hidden it, believing that at least one person in Buckhorn needed what was in that journal more than the law.

Both he and Darby couldn't bear the thought that Earl Ray wouldn't know about his daughter for that length of time. So by the time Leroy reached the cemetery, sirens blaring, the journal was simply gone. The marshal no longer needed it to convict Ethan Ford because the man was dead. Jasper and Darby had decided that the best thing that could happen to the journal was for it to never turn up.

It took a few days for Jasper to recover from his injuries. Fortunately, the knife hadn't cut deep. A few stitches and he would be good as new. What was much harder was living with the realization that both he and Darby had almost died at that man's hands.

Jasper was more worried about Darby. She'd taken risks with her job, but she'd never come so close to death. Jasper had. It was one reason he was no longer a homicide detective. She was shaken, but a strong woman. She'd been through an ordeal. She'd killed a man. He knew it would take time.

Being the woman she was, Darby had thrown herself into her work. She had a story to tell and being a journalist, that was the way she coped. She told the story of the man residents had known as Leviathan Nash.

Because of Thelma Rose's young age and Ethan being a sickly baby and young adult, she'd left a note behind with the infant. He'd been raised by his grandparents. The plan had been for him to join his mother once he was well, but that had never happened. Before she died, Thelma Rose sent her journals to him to let him know how important the work she did was and prove that she had always been thinking about him.

His mother mentioned him often in the journal Jasper had rescued. It spanned an eighteen-month period in the lives of area residents. Thelma Rose often wrote how much she loved him and missed her son.

There were secrets about residents woven into the stories the county nurse wrote in the journal. It was clear that she had worried about the people she treated and hadn't documented the stories out of malice, but out of concern for them.

The story of what had happened to Buckhorn was picked up by the wire and went national. Darby's newspaper's subscribers soared in numbers. She was offered numerous jobs with large papers across the country. She turned them all down.

Writing about what had happened had given her a form of release that Jasper didn't have for himself. He kept seeing that damned casket in his nightmares, hearing Darby calling from inside it.

The only bright spot, other than having Ethan Ford gone forever, was knowing the truth about the past. The true story was there—just not the one Ethan had told them.

After the dust had settled, they planned to visit Earl Ray. Jasper had marked the pages in the journal that dealt with Victoria "Tory" Caulfield's pregnancy. They'd decided they would give the journal to Earl Ray, figuring he was the person who should have it to do with it as he saw fit.

Not that Jasper hadn't read what Thelma Rose had written about his own family. It was true that she'd been in love with his father and had been for some time. But in the end, she'd let him go, sending him away. When William Cole had left Buckhorn with his family, it was over.

Once Thelma Rose knew she was pregnant, she'd known they had no future because she anticipated that the pregnancy would kill her. She hadn't told him about the baby. She'd hoped he would again be happy with his wife. When Jasper thought of his parents, he thought of the little things he saw his father do to make up for his betrayal. In the end, he thought his parents had been happy again.

DARBY WAS WAITING anxiously as Jasper drove up in front of her office—just as he'd known she would be. She locked the office door behind her and hurried out to his pickup. The day was warm, all blue sky and sunshine. They both couldn't help being excited about giving Earl Ray the news.

She had to push an excited Ruby over to climb in, laughing as the dog licked her face and tried to sit on her lap.

"Ruby," Jasper warned.

Ruby wagged her tail and turned to whip her tongue across his cheek before he pushed her away laughing. "Someone needs to train this dog," he said and smiled over at Darby.

He could tell that they were both nervous about today. Jasper figured the marshal suspected that they'd at least read the journal—if they didn't have it or know where it was. He and Darby had debated turning it over to the marshal, but feared too much of it might leak out since it would become public now that the investigation was over.

But they were also worried about how Earl Ray would take the news they were bringing him. Pulling up in front of the new house where Earl Ray and Bessie now lived, Jasper shut off the engine and looked over at this woman who'd saved his life in so many ways. Her cheeks were flushed, her eyes even brighter than normal. They hadn't told Earl Ray anything, not wanting to drag him into their misdeeds until the investigation was final.

"Ready?" Jasper asked.

Darby nodded and opened her door. They walked up the sidewalk hand in hand, the journal tight against Jasper's healing chest. They'd waited until Bessie had gone down to the café, not wanting to involve her as well.

Earl Ray answered the door. The moment he saw them he seemed to instinctively know why they were there. He quickly ushered them in and closed the door. "Coffee?"

"Only if it is already made," Darby said and nodded to Jasper, who pulled the journal from under his shirt.

Earl Ray froze, his gaze going to the journal. Jasper held it out to him, but the older man didn't reach for it. Instead, his eyes lifted to Jasper's in question. Jasper smiled and nodded. What had happened to Earl Ray's daughter was in the journal—just as they had hoped.

"Come into the kitchen," Earl Ray said, his voice filled with emotion. "Darby, would you do the honors? The cups are in that cabinet. Coffee first. Then whiskey as needed?"

Jasper nodded and again held out the journal.

This time, the older man took it. Earl Ray's fingers trembled as he held it as if it were breakable. He dropped into a chair at the table. "It's in there?" he asked, his voice breaking.

"I marked the page," Jasper said. "It's toward the back."

Earl Ray held the journal against his chest for a moment before opening it. Slowly, he began to turn the pages until he found the one with the bookmark. The room fell silent as they watched him read what Thelma Rose had written.

CHAPTER THIRTY-FIVE

DARBY JOINED THE two men at the table with the cups of coffee. The room was so quiet she really thought she could hear a pin drop. She already knew the story. The journal had been the first thing she'd read with Jasper.

She and Jasper had both agreed that they would see what was inside the journal before they decided what to do with it.

Now as she watched Earl Ray read what Thelma Rose had written, she felt good about their decision. The story was a sad one. Tory Caulfield had realized that she was pregnant after Earl Ray had been home on leave. She'd panicked because as much as she knew her husband wanted a child, she didn't. She told Thelma Rose that she just wasn't good mother material. Tory was intent on having an abortion, but feared that with Earl Ray's connections, he might find out somehow. Tory came to Thelma Rose, who refused to abort the baby and told her horror stories of illegal abortions done by untrained clinicians. She offered an alternative. She knew of a place Tory could stay outside of town, she would bring her food and anything else she needed. When the baby was born, well, they would cross that bridge when they got there.

Thelma Rose wrote that she was sure Tory would change her mind once she saw her baby. She'd known other pregnant women who were afraid they'd make bad mothers.

But that was before Thelma Rose knew about Tory's background.

Sworn to secrecy, Thelma Rose brought her food and checked on her. Tory paid her, something that Thelma Rose had written that she felt guilty about. But she needed the money. She sent most of what she made home to her parents for Ethan's medical bills.

Ethan had obviously preferred to believe she took the money so she could meet up with the man she loved, William Cole. But apparently that had never been the plan. If anything, Thelma Rose might have been thinking that the baby she carried of William's might survive and need expensive medical help for months to come. As it was, the money was probably used to bury her and buy the headstone.

In the journal, Thelma Rose said there was already another woman in labor the night she got the call from Tory. She let Edith Cole take the other delivery because she was worried about Tory's state of mind and wanted to make sure nothing happened to the baby once it was delivered.

Thelma Rose had gone to Tory, who gave birth to a baby girl. Tory hadn't wanted to even see the child or hold it. She'd told Thelma Rose she didn't care what she did with it just as long as no one ever knew that she'd had the baby. Thelma Rose had written that she assumed that the father wasn't Earl Ray and that was why Tory said no one could ever know that she'd been pregnant, let alone given birth. Thelma Rose said she just did her job and didn't ask questions.

She'd written, *I needed the money and that is my shame. What I did later, I believe was saving this precious baby's life and I stand by that.*

Thelma Rose had taken the infant away, fearing Tory

would harm it. As she left, Edith called. She needed help with the delivery of the other woman's baby. It wasn't going well. She'd called the doctor and an ambulance, but feared they wouldn't arrive in time.

When Thelma Rose reached Vivian "Vi" Mullen's house, she left the infant in another room to go help Edith. Vi's baby was born minutes later, stillborn. Vi was exhausted and had fallen asleep—until she heard the sound of a baby crying.

It was the infant in the next room. Thelma Rose wrote: *The decision was made in an instant. I looked at Edith and she looked questioningly at me. I said to Vi, "Let me get her cleaned up and you can hold her." I took the stillborn baby and went into the next room. I returned with Tory Caulfield's baby. At the time, it seemed the right thing to do. The baby needed a home and Vi needed a baby. It was clear from the problems during Vi's delivery that it would be the only child she would ever have. God forgive me.*

Earl Ray looked up from the journal. His hand went to his mouth for a moment as his eyes filled with tears. "Tina Mullen is my daughter." He let out a strangled sound. "I have a granddaughter, too. Chloe."

CHAPTER THIRTY-SIX

DAYS LATER AT the café, Darby looked across the table at Jasper. She wasn't sure how she felt. She'd written her last story about Gossip, a follow-up about the closing of the investigation. As promised, she'd put the photocopied pages Jasper had made her of the journal through the shredder after weeks of poring over them. Thelma Rose had documented the life of the county and Buckhorn for years in her journals. The journal that Earl Ray now had was filled with stories, while sometimes sad, they were the fabric of this small, isolated town in the middle of Montana. They were real life, the good, bad and ugly.

Ethan Ford had focused on the ugly out of anger. But he was gone. So was his son, who'd been put to death in Texas.

In the wake of the pain that had been caused, the closing of the investigation seemed to lift the dark veil that had been hanging over the town. For her and Jasper and of course Earl Ray, the good news from the journal had given them renewed hope.

Christina "Tina" Mullen was Earl Ray's daughter. Darby had wondered about the pretty redhead when she'd first come to town. With her red hair, Tina looked nothing like dark-haired Vi nor were their dispositions anything alike. No one scowled quite like Vi, who anyone could see even on sight was a bitter, unhappy woman.

Tina always had a smile and anyone who saw her with

her daughter could tell that the sun rose and set with Chloe. It seemed strange now to Darby that no one had questioned why mother and daughter were so different. She remembered asking someone where that red hair had come from that both Tina and Chloe shared.

Bessie had told her that she believed Axel's grandmother had red hair. Or at least reddish hair. Darby hadn't given it any more thought. She'd never met Axel, the husband who'd left Vi last year.

Vi had thrown herself into the upcoming Buckhorn birthday celebration. To everyone's surprise, there was talk of someone building another motel at the opposite end of town from the Sleepy Pine. Darby didn't recognize the names, but apparently everyone else in town did.

Finnegan and Casey James had already donated land to the town across the highway from the Sleepy Pine for a park. According to Vi, it would be made into a fairgrounds and that was where the carnival and a lot of the celebratory events would be taking place.

But Vi had told them that what Buckhorn also really needed were more accommodations. Finn and Casey were breaking ground in the coming week on a hotel complex. It would have a convention-type center for weddings and funerals and other events that had always been held at Dave's bar. The hotel wouldn't be as grand as the old Crenshaw Hotel that Darby had only seen photos of and heard stories about. But it would be a huge boost to Buckhorn's economy.

Meanwhile, Dave was adding on to the bar and putting in a steakhouse that he and his future bride, Melissa Herbert, were working on together. There were other projects in the works, all of them surprising Darby. The town of Buckhorn was growing.

As spring approached summer, Darby could see a return of hope in Buckhorn and the rest of the county. Summer was coming and so were the tourists. Soon the streets would fill with people who appreciated the state and had come to have some fun—and spend their money.

The changes the season brought to Buckhorn were everywhere. Businesses were opening, new ones were breaking ground, even the old carriage house had been leased for the next five months.

Not surprising, people in town were excited to see what would be coming into the space. Maybe they hoped it would be something that would take away the bad taste Leviathan Nash/Ethan Ford had left behind. Or maybe they worried it could be something worse.

"It'd better be something good," Mabel Aldrich said. She'd once owned that building and the cabin behind it. "The town owes it to Jon Harper that the space is used for something good." Darby had learned that Jon Harper was a carpenter who'd rented the space from Mabel. He seemed to be a town legend and used to spend long hours working on furniture he sold to tourists in the summer and toys he gave away to kids. Jon, she was told, was now buried in the new section of cemetery outside of town.

She'd asked Bessie about the man only to be told, "That's a long story that will have to wait for another time."

"You all right?" Jasper asked now as he reached across the table to take her hand.

She nodded and smiled. She would be. Under all this optimism and good news in town, including for her newspaper, was the memory of what had almost happened to the two of them.

"I guess it's finally started to sink in how close we came to dying." He squeezed her hand. "I know Marshal Baggins feels bad that he didn't listen to you."

"It wasn't his fault," Jasper said. "I shouldn't have let it go on as long as I did."

"I think he still suspects that we weren't completely honest with him," she said.

Jasper shook his head. "Leroy's smart, but fortunately, he's also a good guy." Darby agreed. She liked the marshal. She wondered why some woman hadn't latched on to him. He was certainly good-looking.

"I recognize that smile," Jasper said as the waitress brought their breakfasts and he had to take his hand back. "I hope you're thinking about me," he said after the waitress left.

She laughed. "Honestly? I was thinking about Leroy Baggins and how handsome he is and wondering who we could hook him up with."

Jasper swore and shook his head. "I'm not playing matchmaker. Wait, you think he's handsome?"

"Who's handsome?" Bessie asked as she came up to the table, carrying her cup of coffee. It was early, the café almost empty except for the three of them.

Darby moved to let her slide in beside her. "Marshal Baggins. Don't you think he's handsome? We need to find him a good woman."

"We need to stay out of his life and maybe he'll stay out of ours," Jasper said and took a bite of his breakfast. He'd gone back to his usual, ham, eggs, hash browns and toast, Darby saw.

"I love your new house," she said, changing the subject as she looked over at Bessie. "Are you all moved in?"

"I am," the older woman said and smiled, her eyes lighting up. She took a sip of her coffee. "You'll be getting an invitation for the housewarming party we're throwing."

"It's certainly cause for celebration," Jasper agreed.

"Earl Ray has worked so hard on it." Bessie seemed to lose herself in thought for a moment. Darby wondered how much Earl Ray had shared with her.

"How's he doing?" Jasper asked, even though Darby knew that the two had talked recently.

"Good, really good. I'm just so glad that he's found his daughter," she said, lowering her voice even though there was no one to hear. "And granddaughter. He hasn't done anything about it yet. In time, maybe he will, but for now he's just happy keeping an eye on Tina and Chloe."

"Did I hear that Tina and Lars are expecting?" Darby asked, unable not to grin. She did love happy endings. "There might be another grandbaby on the way soon?"

Bessie nodded, smiling as well, a faraway look in her eye. "I never thought I'd have grandchildren." She shook her head. "But I feel for Vi. I doubt she'll take the news well. I think that's what is holding Earl Ray back. He doesn't want to hurt her. Hopefully, Tina will let him into their lives at some point."

"I'm sure she'll let you both in. She couldn't ask for better grandparents for her children," Darby said. "From what I've seen of her, she's a smart, lovely young woman." She didn't say, *much nicer than her mother*, but she was sure that the other two heard the statement echo in their own thoughts. "Tina clearly idolizes Chloe—and has always loved Lars, from what I've heard. Have you seen him with Chloe? He's amazing. What a good father."

Bessie nodded. "They make a nice family."

"Looks like someone is moving into the old carriage house," Jasper said, looking past them to the street.

"Didn't you tell me that it used to be a woodworking shop?" Darby asked, turning to see a U-Haul pull up across the highway. "I've always loved that building."

"I told Darby that Jon Harper used to make furniture in there," Bessie said. "I have a rocker he made for me. I think Tina has the last one he made before he died. Jon made it for her when she was pregnant with Chloe."

"I love small towns," Darby said with a sigh. "You all know each other's history. I really want to be part of it."

Bessie chuckled. "Oh, you are. But it also means that everyone knows your business. And now we all know each other's deepest darkest secrets thanks to Leviathan Nash or whatever his name really was." She sighed. "At least now we know where the man got his information. Thelma Rose was such a sweet, loving woman. She never meant for any of that to be used against local people."

"That reminds me," Jasper said. "I still have that photo Darby gave me on my phone." He found the photo and handed his phone to Bessie. "It has to be the grandparents, don't you think?"

Bessie studied the photo on his phone for a moment before she laughed. "I didn't even notice that little face almost completely lost in the photo. Thelma Rose was so young that I didn't recognize her. I bet these are her family. Just imagine having a baby at fourteen, almost dying, almost losing her baby and her own life. I wonder if that's why she became a nurse?" She handed the phone to Darby. "See that child trying to hide behind that woman's skirt? That young girl is Thelma Rose all right. I don't know why I missed it. I guess I was looking for her all grown, the way I knew her. That had to be taken years before she came to Buckhorn."

"I can see why Ethan kept this photo. It's the last of his family and the ones who raised him," Darby said. She handed the phone to Jasper and he pocketed it.

Lost in their own thoughts, Darby and Jasper ate in silence, Bessie absently sipping her coffee. Darby found herself stealing looks at Jasper. She knew he'd been struggling with what he'd learned about his father. She hoped that one day he could forgive the man—and forgive himself.

"I like to think of that journal as a love story about her work—and love, right or wrong," Bessie said.

Jasper shook his head. "That's a romantic way to see it. My father was married. My mother was happy. I thought he was too."

"Who says he wasn't?" Bessie asked. "He stood by your mother and you, by packing you all up and leaving here."

"Sometimes people fall in love even when they're trying not to." Darby looked at him meaningfully, making him groan. "My point is they fell in love against their wills. Thelma Rose paid a high price for that love."

"I've never understood why Thelma Rose went ahead with the pregnancy," Bessie said. "She must have loved that child right to the end, praying that like Ethan, baby Levi would make it."

"I wonder if your father ever heard what happened to her," Darby said. Jasper shook his head. "It's such a tragic story. I'm sure your father loved both women. Thelma Rose cut him loose when she realized she was pregnant and probably wouldn't survive the birth. She must have really loved him to do that. I wonder if he knew she was pregnant."

"I doubt it, given when your parents left Buckhorn," Bessie said. "She wouldn't have been far along. It's clear from her writings that life was too precious to her to do that."

"Some things will always be a mystery," Darby said with a sigh.

Jasper shook his head. "I knew something was wrong with my parents. I didn't know what had happened, but that they were different. Not bad. Just not like they'd been at my grandparents' place here." He rubbed a hand over his face. "I hate that I was the one who told my mother that I'd seen my father with Thelma Rose."

"You were *five*," Darby reminded him. "You weren't to blame."

"No, my father was." He shook his head. "I think on some level I've been angry with him my whole life. It's definitely colored my feelings about marriage and commitment without me even realizing it." He met Darby's gaze and held it. "I have to admit, I'm glad I now know what happened. My parents were close at the end, I know that. My father did love my mother and she him."

"It's possible to love more than one woman," Bessie said quietly. "It took Earl Ray years to realize that it doesn't take away from the feelings you had for the other one."

Darby wondered how Earl Ray felt about his late wife now, though.

Bessie sighed again and rose from the booth. "As my mother used to say, all's well that end's well. But now I have to go to work. I have fried pies baking back there. Apricot, Earl Ray's favorite."

"Wait a minute," Darby cried. "It's not fried pies day."

"I decided to shake things up a little," Bessie said, grinning.

"No! Buckhorn citizens know what day of the week it is by what you're baking," Darby said. "This is going to throw a wrench into the works."

Bessie laughed. "Well, they'd better get used to it. Maybe it's the weather, but I'm feeling my oats, so to speak." The three of them laughed.

"You have no idea what you might be stirring up," Jasper said.

As she watched Bessie head for the kitchen, Darby said more to herself than Jasper, "I have a feeling this is just the beginning." She felt a shiver of worry and wondered what would happen when Earl Ray told his daughter—let alone Vi Mullen.

VI MULLEN COULDN'T contain her excitement. Her plans for Buckhorn's 125th birthday were coming along better than even she'd expected. She'd reached out to the governor and a lot of former residents. Reservations at the local bed-and-breakfasts were filling up fast.

She was especially delighted that the town was getting the tourist accommodations it so needed to grow. She'd called wealthy investor Finnegan James and his wife, Casey Crenshaw James. Both were planning to come to the birthday celebration as it was. Casey just happened to be the granddaughter of Anna Crenshaw who'd owned the Crenshaw Hotel in town before her death.

Finnegan had loved Vi's hotel idea. It wouldn't be anywhere near as grand as the Crenshaw had been. But now with the Crenshaw Hotel gone...

Vi tried not to think about that as she worked to put the past year behind her. Onward and upward, she kept saying to herself. Good times were coming. She had to believe that because she'd gone through some awful times the past year, including the divorce papers she'd gotten from her husband, Axel, which she had no intention of signing. It shouldn't have been a surprise. They'd been separated for months, and he'd made his intentions fairly clear when he'd left her.

Still, it hurt. She thought of herself as Mrs. Mullen. Well, she wasn't taking her maiden name back—not after all these years. But now Axel wanted half of everything. Over her dead body.

Vi just hoped he wasn't foolish enough to come back to Buckhorn making his demands. It would take so little for her to do harm to the man. Some days she felt as if she was already right on the edge after everything she'd been through. Anything could set her off. She tried to put that thought back where it had come from.

But it was true, she realized as she tore up the divorce papers. She couldn't be responsible for what she might do if she got any more bad news.

JASPER HAD SPENT as much time with Darby as was humanly possible since what they now referred to as "the incident." They'd gotten closer after what had happened to them. But still, he worried about her.

Coming back from fixing fence, he found Darby curled up on the porch swing with Ruby in her lap. He stopped to take in the scene, feeling his heart lift. She'd been so quiet since writing the last story about Gossip. He knew that writing was the way she had been able to deal with her ordeal. With that part over, he feared that she was reliving what had happened. He worried that it would change her, make her fearful, make her want to hide out like he had done.

"Hey," he said as he approached. "Can just anyone join this party?" Both Darby and Ruby looked up at him for a moment before he moved Ruby over to make room for himself on the swing. "How are you two doing?"

Ruby wagged her tail, but his attention was on Darby's face. The sun shone on her cheeks, making her freckles pop out and warming her brown eyes. She turned her face up to the rays and closing her eyes, took a deep breath. As she released it, she opened her eyes and looked at him. Her smile felt warmer than the sun and filled him with more joy than he'd felt for days. Maybe she was going to be all right.

"I'm doing...okay," Darby said and petted Ruby for a

moment. "I'm going to be all right." She raised her gaze to his. "I know you've been worried about me."

He nodded. "I just don't want it to...change you."

She shook her head. "Everyone changes from their experiences. Some more than others."

"No kidding, look at me," he said with a chuckle. "I thought I could never give my heart to anyone again. Then Bessie gave me that darned dog..." He chuckled again, his eyes locking with hers. "Then you came back into my life. I never believed I could love like this."

Darby nodded. "I know what you mean."

"I just don't want you to be...afraid of life," he said.

"Ethan scared me, but what terrified me more was how arrogant and foolish I'd been—something that led to you almost being killed. I really thought I could take care of myself, that I would be safe simply because I was doing what was right. I won't make that mistake again." Seeing his frown, she quickly added, "I'm still going after stories I think are important and need to be told. I'll just make sure I have backup on the dangerous ones." She reached over and covered his hand with hers on Ruby's warm back.

"I can live with that," he said, smiling as he leaned over Ruby to give Darby a kiss. Of course Ruby had to get involved, which left them laughing and abandoning the swing for the bedroom sans Ruby.

SHIRLEY LANGER READ about Buckhorn's 125th birthday celebration in the newspaper one of the guests had left behind at the motel where she worked. After it became clear to her that Lars belonged with Tina and the baby, she'd left Buckhorn, but hadn't gotten far. Low on money, she'd gotten a job in Billings at one of the motels near the interstate. She'd told herself that she'd put Buckhorn behind her.

Until she heard from Linsey Adams who used to waitress at the Buckhorn Café. Shirley hadn't had many friends before she'd left. Jennifer Mullen had been her best and really only friend, but now she was locked up in the state psychiatric ward. If she ever got out, she'd probably go straight to prison after what she'd done.

After months of having an affair with Lars Olson, Shirley had felt like a pariah. Everyone in town had sided with Tina Mullen, who'd been living with Lars at the time.

So, Shirley had been surprised when Linsey called. They'd never been that close, but clearly at some point she'd given the young woman her number.

"I thought you'd want to know." She'd figured Linsey was calling about Buckhorn's birthday celebrations. Everyone who'd ever lived there was invited according to the article she'd seen in the *Billings Gazette*.

"Tina is pregnant with another baby," Linsey had said. "This time it's Lars's baby. At least we think it is."

Shirley hadn't been able to speak for a moment. "Why would you think I'd want to know?"

"Because Cheri said that day at the café you'd wished them well when you left town," Linsey said. "You should probably know that Vi told everyone that you got run out of town."

"Vi." She said the word like a curse. Shirley had left town right after that horrible incident at the café. At the time, she'd told herself that Lars belonged with Tina and the baby. It didn't matter that Chloe wasn't his biological child. Now they were having a baby of their own? Great.

She'd regretted leaving Buckhorn since it had always been her home. She also regretted giving up Lars so easily. It wasn't like her life had changed for the better. She'd taken all her problems with her while Lars had stayed and

B.J. DANIELS

was now married and happy and having a baby with Tina. It seemed unfair that she was being portrayed as the town jezebel while he was as equally responsible for his actions as she was.

"I'm happy for them," she said, the words nearly sticking to the roof of her mouth like peanut butter.

After she hung up, she cried, then dried her eyes and told herself that she'd never really loved Lars. For years she'd run the Sleepy Pine Motel because her mother's boyfriend had offered her the job. After two divorces, she'd stayed in Buckhorn because she didn't have anywhere else to go. Like the job, Lars had been convenient.

Now, looking around the lobby of yet another dead-end job, she thought maybe she would go back to Buckhorn for its birthday. She had as much right to be there as anyone. She couldn't let people think that she'd been run out of town. True, she'd left with her tail between her legs, but she wouldn't be going back that way.

She checked the date on the newspaper, thinking about how happy Vi Mullen would be to see her and smiled.

Why not go back and stir up things? Her old friend Jennifer Mullen would have cheered her on—if she'd been able to. Jennifer had always been up for just about anything—especially making trouble.

Yes, she would go to the celebration. There was time to drop a few pounds, pick up some new clothes, maybe even do something different with her hair. Shirley let the fantasy go for a while longer before she realized she couldn't go back. She couldn't bear seeing Lars and Tina so happy.

She'd balled up the newspaper story and thrown it away. There was no going back to Buckhorn.

Then she'd gotten the collect call from her friend Jennifer from the psychiatric ward for the criminally insane. She always took Jen's calls. She would have felt guilty if she hadn't—and maybe a little afraid not to accept the charges.

But she'd wished she hadn't taken this one.

JASPER SETTLED INTO his usual booth, then got up and moved to one closer to the café's front window. The sun shone in a cloudless blue spring Montana sky, making the pine-covered mountains beyond town glisten. It felt like a day for new beginnings, he thought as he looked across the street.

The black paper had long ago been removed from the old carriage house windows. He could see two young women hard at work as they readied their craft shop. He watched them laughing and talking excitedly as they wiped away all sign of Leviathan Nash from the building.

He remembered when it had been a wood shop and couldn't help but think about Jon Harper and the woman who'd come to town believing he was her long-deceased husband. Kate Jackson. He hoped Kate was doing well now. The whole town was talking about the upcoming town's birthday celebration. He hoped Kate would return. Maybe she'd met someone and would bring him. It would be good for the town and maybe for Kate too, since everyone had fallen in love with her.

Bessie brought out two cups and the coffeepot. She looked confused for a moment. "You changed booths?"

"Some people have said I was getting too set in my ways. So this morning I'm going to have *bacon*, eggs and toast."

She laughed. "Anything special causing this change in you?"

Smiling, he said, "Spring in Montana."

"I'm sure that's it," Bessie said, returning his smile as she poured them both a cup of coffee and returned the pot to the kitchen along with his order.

He figured everyone in town knew what had buoyed his mood and brought about a change in him. Just the thought of Darby had him smiling to himself. He couldn't remember ever being this happy. He pulled out his phone and sent her a text.

Five minutes later, she came through the door and slid into his booth. She dropped her notebook and pen on the table. "I can't stay long. I have a newspaper to get out and still two new business owners to interview." She took a moment to catch her breath. "What are you grinning about?"

"You. I love seeing you in your realm."

Bessie brought out his breakfast and put it in front of him. "Darby?"

She shook her head. "I can't stay, but thanks." She looked at his plate as Bessie went back to the kitchen.

Jasper could smell cinnamon rolls baking and was thinking he'd take some home for later when Darby got off work. She'd been spending most of her nights curled up with him in his bed.

"What is that?" she said as she took a half slice of his toast. *"Bacon?"*

"I'm a new man."

She grinned at that and locked eyes with him, making his heart pound. "I liked the old one just fine." She reached over and took a piece of his bacon, still grinning as she did it.

Jasper had been contemplating for weeks how to ask her to marry him. He'd been carrying the ring around the whole time, waiting for that perfect moment. It wasn't until she left to interview one of the new business owners that he knew what he was going to do.

"You look like the cat who ate the canary," Bessie said as she slid into the booth across from him with her cup of coffee.

"I need you to do me a favor."

She eyed him warily. "Am I going to like this?"

He nodded. "I think you and the rest of the town will."

TWO DAYS LATER, Darby was surprised to get Jasper's text to meet her at the café immediately. It was high noon. He normally avoided the café when it was busy. She texted back. What's up?

No answer. Getting up from her computer, she grabbed her purse, locked her office behind her and headed for the café. Town had been getting increasingly busier with the beginning of the tourist season just around the corner. She'd been occupied writing about the changes in town—and selling more ads to new businesses.

Buckhorn was booming, but as she walked down the main drag to the café, she noticed that there weren't a lot of people on the street. Had something happened? She was wondering if she should have brought her camera, when she saw Jasper waiting for her in front of the café.

"What's going on?" she asked, worried. "Jasper?"

He was smiling from ear to ear as she approached. When she was within feet of him, she watched him drop to one knee. She felt her eyes widen. About the same time she noticed all the people pressed to the front windows of the café.

"I've been wanting to ask you to marry me for weeks," Jasper said. "It just never felt like the right time. But then I got to thinking about what Earl Ray said about the crows…"

"Crows?" she asked, feeling as if she was in some kind of weird dream. Was this really happening?

"This town," Jasper said. "We're a like a murder of crows."

"I'm afraid to even ask where this is going if murder is part of it," she said.

"Buckhorn? We're a family. So I decided asking you to marry me in front of our family was the only thing to do," Jasper said as he reached for her hand.

She could hear tittering and voices inside the café and Bessie telling them all to be quiet.

"Darby Fulton, I'm asking for your hand in marriage."

Her eyes filled with tears as she looked into his handsome face. "This part I understand," she said and bit her lower lip to keep from crying.

"Will you be my wife?"

"Say yes," someone yelled from inside the café.

She turned to look at all the happy faces of people she'd only known for a few months, but had come to love. Bessie was dabbing her eyes and so were some of the others. She smiled at them before she turned back to the man still down on one knee in front of her.

"Yes!"

A cheer came up from inside the café and cell phone cameras flashed as Jasper opened the small velvet box, took out a beautiful diamond engagement ring and slipped it on her trembling finger. "It was my mother's," he said.

The tears came then as if a floodgate had opened. Was this the same Jasper Cole from a few months ago? She couldn't believe this was happening. "It's beautiful," she said as Jasper rose and took her in his arms and everyone came spilling out of the café onto the sidewalk with well wishes.

Carried along with the crowd, they all ended up back in the café. Bessie had made a special lunch for the town— and the newly engaged couple.

"This is exactly what this town needed," Bessie said, still dabbing at her tears. "When are you getting married? I'll bake the cake."

Another woman said she and a friend would see to the flowers. Dave and Melissa said they would take care of the music and a few kegs of beer from the bar. Tina Mullen shyly offered to take the wedding photos. Vi said she could probably come up with an antique altar, if they were interested, for a price.

"Mother," Tina said, and Vi swore she'd only been joking about charging them.

"You're welcome to get married in our backyard," Earl Ray said. "I think it is plenty big enough for the whole town. Unless you'd preferred to get married out at your ranch."

Darby looked to her soon-to-be husband, her head spinning. This was all moving so quickly. She still didn't know what crows had to do with it, but Jasper was right. Buckhorn was family. They often had their disagreements, but when push came to shove, they came together.

"Thank you all so much," Jasper said and met her gaze. "We haven't really had a chance to talk about the wedding yet."

"I love everyone's ideas and offers," Darby said. "It sounds like it will be the perfect wedding."

Her future groom gave her a nod and a smile. She'd never felt so blessed as he pulled her close for a kiss and the crowd went wild.

Darby loved it all. It wasn't until later back at the ranch that she got to admire the beautiful ring he'd put on her finger—and her soon-to-be husband. She felt blinded by both—not to mention their future that lay ahead of them.

She'd fallen in love with this man not once, but twice, years apart. They'd already been through so much and yet here they were, sitting on the swing with Ruby between them.

The sun had set, leaving behind the cool twilight. She

could smell the pines and hear the creek rushing over the rocks. This was home. The thought made her heart swell.

"A penny for your thoughts," Jasper asked.

"I was just thinking how lucky I am," she said as he reached across the dozing dog to take her hand. "What about you?"

"I was enjoying the evening and wondering if we were always going to have this dog between us every time we sat out here," he said.

She laughed and Ruby raised her head as if she knew they were talking about her. "I wouldn't have it any other way. You both stole my heart."

A FEW DAYS LATER, Jasper fought the bad memories as he drove out to the cemetery. It was a beautiful spring day, the blue sky seeming endless overhead as the sun shone bright and warm over the mountains.

He'd thought a lot about his father and what had happened all those years ago that had changed the trajectory of their lives. He'd known love twice now, although what he'd had with Camille couldn't hold a candle to what he had with Darby. But he felt he understood how a person would love two people.

He was even learning to forgive. When he thought of his father, he felt more compassion for him and the impossible situation he'd found himself in. Forgiveness didn't come easy. Someday, he thought, he might even forgive himself for Camille's death and telling his mother what he'd seen.

As he neared the old cemetery, he slowed his pickup. The pine trees gleamed in the sun. The place looked so different than it had the last time he was here that it surprised him. He realized that his perception had changed because the evil that had shrouded the place was now gone.

He pulled in and parked near Thelma Rose's grave. After getting out, he walked through the peaceful sunlit cemetery. He'd never visited his grandparents' graves. He felt guilty that as much as he'd loved them, he hadn't wanted to think of them dead and buried. But now that he was here, he knew he would start visiting them. Next time, he thought Darby might want to come with him.

Nearing Thelma Rose's grave, he saw the new smaller headstone next to it. The stone caught the light, making him stop, a lump forming in his throat. When he'd ordered it, he hadn't been sure if he would come out to see it. He'd still had mixed feelings then.

Now he was glad that he had. It read Levi Lee Cole and her date of birth and death. Under that was one word. *Loved.* His baby half sister.

Leaning down, he placed the flowers he'd brought on her grave.

CHAPTER THIRTY-SEVEN

DARBY COULDN'T BELIEVE she and Jasper were getting married. She stared at the woman in the full-length mirror and broke into a huge smile. All her dreams had come true. She wanted to pinch herself, afraid she might wake up.

"That dress is beautiful," Bessie said next to her.

"It was my mother's," Darby told her. It was a simple knee-length A-line in white with a scoop neck. "I was so happy when it fit—especially after all your cooking."

The older woman chuckled and smiled at her in the mirror. "You make a beautiful bride. Jasper's a good man. The two of you are perfect for each other," Bessie said as if putting her stamp of approval on their union.

"You think?" She had no doubts about her connection to Jasper, but she knew they would butt heads in the future—probably over her job. She couldn't imagine giving it up, and the one thing they hadn't discussed, she realized, was children.

She and Bessie had both almost forgotten about Tina Mullen, but as Darby reached for Bessie's hand to give it a squeeze, Tina snapped a photo. She was just starting to show, her stomach a little rounded, but her face glowed whenever anyone asked about her pregnancy. Darby loved to see how happy Tina was. She'd never spent much time around her until recently, but she liked her and realized that they might become good friends after this. From what she'd seen of Tina's work, the woman was quite the photographer. She might hire her if the newspaper kept growing like it was.

Since coming to town, she had been so busy getting her newspaper up and running that she hadn't had much time to make friends. But she liked the idea of spending more time with some of them she'd met, including Melissa Herbert soon to be Mrs. Dave Tanner. She missed her female friends from her last job.

Even as she thought it, she knew it hadn't only been because she was busy that she hadn't even tried to make friends. Aiden had made her afraid in so many ways. She doubted her judgment after him. It had made her leery of everyone. Everyone but Jasper and of course Bessie and Earl Ray.

But looking in the mirror at the woman in the wedding dress, she knew she was ready to open up to life again. The future stretched out before her, full of possibilities she couldn't wait to explore with Jasper and her new family here in Buckhorn.

A door opened. Melissa stuck her head in. "Ready?" she called, all smiles. "Wait until you see your groom. I've never seen him in anything but Wranglers and boots. He is gorgeous in a tux."

Darby laughed. "I can't wait." She'd never been more ready for anything in her life. She took one last look in the mirror. Bessie had given her a necklace that had belonged to her mother on her wedding day for something old. Melissa had provided a pair of blue earrings for something blue.

She picked up her bouquet and took a deep breath. Letting it out slowly, she smiled in the mirror at the single Darby Fulton and said goodbye.

ON THIS BEAUTIFUL summer evening, Jasper held his breath as he watched the back door of Bessie and Earl Ray's house for his bride.

He'd thought he'd never marry after Camille was killed. So he'd certainly never imagined the perfect wedding setting, but that was what this was. The huge backyard was ringed with white twinkle lights. Vi had found not just a beautiful antique altar but provided the seating as well from her antique barn with old church pews.

Lights were strung everywhere, giving the whole scene a festive atmosphere. Dave had used his carpenter skills to build a bandstand and had gotten some friends to play the music. There was a dance floor and everyone had brought food, so much so that it appeared the tables would collapse under the weight.

"This is exactly what this town needed," Earl Ray said. He would be marrying them in a short and sweet ceremony. Jasper couldn't wait to see his bride, let alone kiss her before the party began. The whole town of Buckhorn had turned out. Marshal Leroy Baggins had shown up to the delight of some of the single young women.

Tina had been taking photos all afternoon as the wedding venue had come together. At one point, he saw Earl Ray watching his daughter with pride in his eyes. Her hair, red like her birth mother's, shone in the twinkling lights. But from what Jasper could tell from photos he'd once seen of Tory, that was the only resemblance. It appeared that Chloe had taken after her mother and would be a red-head as well.

The back door opened. Everyone in the backyard rose and fell silent as the wedding march began to play. Jasper only had eyes for Darby. His heart drummed in his chest at just the sight of her. He couldn't believe that this woman was about to become his bride.

As she came toward him, he felt the whole town around them holding its breath in anticipation. He barely remembered anything that Earl Ray said before he was kissing his bride, lifting her in the air and swinging her around to the cheers of the crowd.

When he put her down, he looked into her brown eyes and felt such a sense of awe. It couldn't get any better than this, could it? He took her out on the dance floor for their first dance, holding her close. "You are the most beautiful woman I've ever seen."

Darby laughed. "Have you already gotten into the champagne?"

He shook his head. "I'm drunk on you."

The song finished and the party began in full force around them with one after another of the town's people congratulating them.

"Your wedding is just the beginning," Vi told him later. "Wait until Buckhorn's birthday celebration this fall."

Jasper had to admit that there was an excitement in the air that he knew wasn't just about this wedding. The town had lived through some bad times recently, but soon Buckhorn would be one hundred and twenty-five. That definitely was cause for celebration. Everyone seemed to be looking forward to all the events that were planned and appreciated Vi for planning it.

Later, as the festivities were winding down, he found his bride visiting with some young women near the bar area. "Mind if I steal her?"

"How are you doing, my beautiful bride?" he asked as he pulled Darby out on the dance floor for another slow song. He'd missed having her in his arms. Her cheeks were flushed and those honey-brown eyes gleamed. She'd never looked more beautiful. He told himself he would remember this moment always. It would be imprinted on his heart and he could call it up anytime he needed it.

"I've never been more happy. How about you?"

He nodded and glanced around. "Isn't this amazing?"

"It is. We brought half the county together and there hasn't even been a fistfight yet," she said with a laugh.

"I realize that I never asked you how you felt about children," Jasper said.

She grinned. "I was thinking the same thing earlier. Children? I'm for them."

"A couple, maybe three or four. After all, we have a ranch, we could use some good hands," he joked.

"As long as it isn't a baseball team, count me in."

He grinned, his gaze locking with hers. "I was thinking—"

"That we should start right away," she finished for him, grinning as well. "I'm way ahead of you." She put her head on his shoulder as they continued to dance.

"Wait a minute, how far ahead?" he asked. "Darby, are you telling me what I think you are?"

JENNIFER MULLEN USED the dull children's scissors to cut out the article from the *Billings Gazette* about Buckhorn, her hometown's 125th birthday celebration. She'd started keeping a scrapbook of articles about Buckhorn after she'd been committed to the state psych ward for the criminally insane.

She was told that she'd killed at least three men. If that were true, then the men had it coming. Her doctor here said that wasn't a good excuse. She told him that she figured there were more men just asking for it as well. He told her they would discuss that during their next session.

Jennifer had smiled and thanked him. Dr. Hanson was another reason she needed to get out of this place. He thought he could "fix" her like she was a broken doll. Even if she did need fixing, she didn't think it was possible. But thanks, Doc.

The main reason she had to get out of here, though, was that she'd left a few things undone back in Buckhorn. People back there might have forgotten about her, but she hadn't forgotten about them.

Like her Aunt Vivian Mullen. Was she worried about her favorite niece being in a place like this? There wasn't any reason for concern. Most everyone here left her alone, which made her laugh. They all seemed a little afraid of her.

Using the glue with the attendant watching to make sure she didn't eat it, she pasted the article in her scrapbook. It gave her a sense of pride to see that her aunt was the organizer of the celebration, according to the article. That was so like Vi.

She tried not to let it bother her that her aunt hadn't come to visit. It wasn't like she wanted anyone from Buckhorn to see her here. A place like this would scare them.

She did, however, miss her friend Shirley Langer and her cousin Tina Mullen. Tina always had such nice clothes and had been a good sport about letting her borrow them. The last she saw her cousin, Tina had been so pregnant, she'd looked like she might pop.

For the first six months, Jen hadn't been allowed to have any phone calls from even a relative. That was so no one upset her, apparently. After the six months was over, the only person who'd taken her collect calls was Shirley. Her friend had left Buckhorn and was now working at a motel in Billings—after getting her heart broken.

"Didn't I tell you to dump Lars?" Jennifer had said. "I always said you could do better."

Shirley was the one who'd told her that her cousin Tina had given birth to a baby girl she'd named Chloe. "Lars and Tina got married. They're expecting a baby."

"What is it with my cousin and babies," Jennifer had said, unable to hide her jealousy. She'd never had any luck with men—unlike Tina. Maybe if she'd been born a redhead like Tina… "Are you still blond?" The last she'd heard, Shirley had gotten her hair cut and gone blond. "Do you have more fun?"

"You're not missing anything, trust me," her friend had said, and they'd run out of things to say even before their time on the phone was up.

Jen finished gluing the last of the article about Buckhorn's birthday into her scrapbook. The attendant took the scissors and glue, probably afraid of what she'd do with them if left to her own devices.

She reread the celebration article before the attendant came back to take her scrapbook for safekeeping. Jen figured Buckhorn's birthday party would draw a lot of people she knew with the carnival and the dance. There were some men she wouldn't mind seeing again. She thought of Marshal Leroy Baggins, the man who'd arrested her for the murders. Good-looking, but a little uptight. Not really her type. Still, she wouldn't mind seeing him again as long as he wasn't thinking he was going to haul her back here.

No, once she escaped from here she wouldn't be coming back, one way or the other. As she pretended to read the article yet again, she watched the comings and goings in the large social room. She'd been so well-behaved here that they let her hang out in the main lounge without an attendant standing over her. She'd been watching the way things worked around here for months as she'd planned her escape. Until now, she hadn't had a definite plan.

But thanks to her aunt Vi, she had a date and a destination. The 125th birthday celebration in Buckhorn was the perfect time to make her break and return home. She smiled as she thought of how people in her hometown would react if they knew that she'd be attending without guards or a straitjacket. There would be so much going on, she figured they wouldn't see her unless she wanted them to.

The attendant came back to take her scrapbook. A moment later, a guard stuck his head in and motioned that it was time to take her back to her cell. In the shatterproof mirror on the wall, she caught her reflection as she rose and headed for the door. She'd changed during her months in here thanks to the drugs they'd been giving her and the time she'd had for reflection—at least that was what she let the doctor think. Dr. Hanson liked the idea that he had been doing something to rehabilitate her.

"You're so young," he'd said. "This isn't the end of your story. We just need to get to the source of why you've done the things you have."

"Maybe I'm just evil."

He'd put on his serious face. "No, that's not true. Something triggered this behavior. I suspect it's something in your past. Once we know what that was..." He'd smiled and she'd smiled back at him, thinking he had no idea what he was talking about. "You're doing so well. So we'll keep digging, yes?" She'd nodded yes, even as she thought the man was a quack. But she liked making him happy because then he gave her more freedom.

With the Buckhorn celebration coming up, Jen thought of her image she'd seen reflected in the mirror. The hair that she'd sawed off with the dull children's scissors when she'd first arrived here had grown out. But it wouldn't hurt to change her appearance even more after she left here. She wanted to look her best when she saw some of her old friends—and enemies.

It was all she could do not to break into a little dance. Look out, Buckhorn. Surprise! *I'm coming home.*

* * * * *

OUT OF THE BLUE

OUT OF THE BLUE

CHAPTER ONE

IF NOT FOR bad luck, Tanya Owens wouldn't have had any luck at all, she thought as smoke began rolling out from under the hood of her car. She had enough trouble without this. Now in the middle of Montana, she was on her way to Vegas to make her fortune at the first roulette wheel she saw. Until her car engine began making odd noises a few miles back, she'd thought maybe her luck was changing for the better.

Ahead, she could see nothing but more of the same. Trees, rocks, mountains and a narrow black strip of two-lane highway. It wasn't like there was anywhere she could stop and have the engine looked at out here in the middle of nowhere.

The noise under the hood began to grow louder, the smoke thicker and darker. Were those buildings ahead on the horizon? The car began to jerk as something under the hood began to clank. As she limped toward what might or might not have been a town, she saw an old-timey gas station and garage ahead and pulled in. As she did, the car died. She tried to restart it, but the motor refused.

Disgusted, she climbed out, scuffing her best pumps as she did. She was bent over trying to rub out the spot on her shoe when she heard someone approach.

"You can't park there." The voice was rough and gravelly. "I said you can't park there." A shadow fell over her.

Straightening, Tanya saw that the voice belonged to a large older woman, somewhere between fifty and eighty. Under her trucker's cap, her hair stuck out in a cloud of wiry gray. She wore baggy green overalls and stood over her, wiping her dirty hands on a rag. The name stitched on the overalls read Gertrude.

Tanya looked into small dark eyes set in the lined broad face. From the depth of the frown, she assumed it must be perpetual. She didn't have time for nonsense nor did she have the patience to put up with this woman.

"There's something wrong with my car." She looked past Gertrude to see if there was anyone back in the garage who might be able to fix it. "Is there a mechanic on duty?" she inquired.

"What do I look like? Chopped liver?" Gertrude asked.

"I've never understood that expression," Tanya said with a shake of her head. "Can you fix my car?"

Gertrude eyed the vehicle for a moment. "Hard to say without looking under the hood."

"Perhaps you could do that then." This woman was trying her patience.

"Perhaps I could," Gertrude said in a way that made it obvious she was mocking Tanya's finishing-school pattern of speech.

"Wonderful." She held out her keys. When the woman finally extended a palm, she dropped them into it. "Where am I anyway?" she asked, looking around.

"Buckhorn, Montana."

This was a town? From what Tanya could see, it wasn't much more than a wide spot in the road. The gas station and garage were on the edge of the place. Past it she could make out a few more buildings. From where she stood, she could see signs for what might be a store and a café.

Was that a motel at the other end? Beyond that, there was the same nothingness that she'd been driving through for hours. Had her car not died, she could have blinked and missed Buckhorn completely.

She glanced across the two-lane highway that cut through this burg. "Is that a tavern by any chance?" she asked.

"Isn't that what the sign says?" Gertrude asked rhetorically.

The sign looked as if it used to be larger, as if the bar once had a name that had been removed. Now all that was left was one small word: *Bar*. If it wasn't for the neon beer sign in the window, Tanya wouldn't have even noticed the place. The log structure looked rustic enough that she wasn't sure the establishment was even open.

"Well," Tanya said, "if it's open, that's where I'll be. I don't have a cell phone. I…lost it."

"Oh, darn," the woman said, making it clear she had no interest in any hard luck stories as she walked over to the sedan and popped the hood.

A semi passed, kicking up a cloud of dust. Tanya let it blow by before she crossed the two-lane highway. She just hoped the bar was open. There weren't any vehicles parked out front. But there was a pickup sitting along the side, next to a stairway that went to an upper floor over the bar. Maybe whoever owned the place lived up there and would open up if she asked sweetly, because right now she really could use a drink.

The front door was thick planks of wood covered with flyers and hand-printed notes from people looking for jobs or used cars and appliances. Tanya was having her doubts about going in—even if it was open. If she hadn't needed a drink so badly…

THE DOOR SWUNG open and all her apprehension dissolved as she breathed in the familiar scent of stale beer and floor cleaner. It was a saloon, by the looks of it, and saloons were a second home to her.

A small television droned at the far end of the bar where a couple of older, no-doubt regulars were propped up on stools. She relaxed a little as she took in the mirrored back wall and the illuminated liquor bottles that ran the length of it. After climbing up a stool a good distance from the two old men, she checked her hair and makeup in the mirror. The dim light was forgivingly kind to her. She told herself that she could pass for thirty instead of almost forty-five. Fluffing up her long, dark curly do, she put her purse on the stool next to her and looked impatiently for the barkeep to take her order.

When she'd come in, he'd been visiting with the two old guys. Now he finished setting fresh glasses of tap beer in front of them and headed her way, smiling. She reminded herself just how little cash she had left. She'd already decided she would flirt with the bartender for a free drink or two, and then she recognized him.

Tanya blinked. It couldn't be. He was partway down the bar, headed for her when he seemed to realize that he knew her as well.

"Davey?" she said, unable to hide her surprise and delight on several levels. Could she really have gotten this lucky? Not only did she know him, she *knew* him intimately. She and Davey had history. She was betting he remembered the two of them that time under the bleachers, the first time she let him get to third base.

Added to her initial surprise was the fact that Davey looked good. *Really good.* She'd heard that he'd let himself go after his football injury his senior year in high school and the loss of his scholarship to play ball in college. She would never have thought he could look this buff at forty-five.

"Davey, is it really you?"

CHAPTER TWO

"TANYA?" DAVE TANNER couldn't believe it. He'd never thought he would see her again, and now here she was.

She let out a laugh, jumped off the bar stool and cried, "Come around here and give me a hug!"

Like he had to be asked twice. He stepped around the counter, and she literally jumped into his arms. She was still petite and slim. In shock, he spun her around, laughing. He'd never thought that he'd ever see her again after high school, let alone have her in his arms. It was like no time had gone by.

He set her down and drew back to look at her, still refusing to believe his eyes. Tanya Owens. She'd aged—just as he had. He could see tiny lines around her eyes, but she was still the beautiful head cheerleader that he'd fallen so hard for all those years ago. His hair had thinned, and recently, he'd shaved his head, which was now tanned. He hardly recognized himself in the mirror after all these months working construction when he wasn't working here at his saloon.

"What are you doing in Buckhorn?" he asked, his mind crazily wondering if she could have come here looking for him.

"I was on my way to Vegas and my car…it just quit." She waved a hand through the air and laughed again. "What's that line from that old movie? With all the gin joints in the world, I just happen to walk into yours."

She'd murdered the line, but he didn't care. He couldn't take his eyes off her. "You look just the same."

She pretended to blush, sweeping her hair back with a shy smile and shake of her head that was so familiar. It was what he'd called her come-hither look, and it still had the same effect on him that it had all those years ago.

"You don't look so bad yourself," she said. "You going to buy a girl a drink?" she asked coyly as she took her seat again.

He laughed and hurried behind the counter. "What can I get you?"

She seemed to think it over, biting at her lower lip for a moment, making him remember kissing her that first time behind the bleachers. "How about a gin and tonic. The *top-shelf* gin," she added with a grin. "This is cause for celebration, don't you think?"

Dave did. His heart was lodged in his throat as he moved down to the speed well to make her drink. He'd forgotten all about Ralph and Wilbur. He'd left them at the end of the bar, arguing over the ball game on the television.

But they'd apparently lost interest in the contest. All eyes and ears were on Tanya. They had the look of men who hadn't seen anything like her.

"You *know* her?" Wilbur asked, sounding skeptical as he watched Dave make her drink.

"We dated my senior year of high school," Dave said, embarrassed and yet pleased that he'd surprised the two men. Like a lot of people in town, they probably thought that he had always been a loser when it came to women.

"You *dated* her?" Ralph said.

Dave wasn't sure *dated* was the right word for it. "Three

months and nine days." He stopped making her drink for a moment to look back down the bar. He'd been so surprised to see her that he hadn't really noticed what she was wearing. A leopard-patterned top hugged her ample breasts and slim waist. A short black skirt did homage to her shapely legs, which ended in a pair of tan pumps.

She had a bar napkin and was rubbing at the top of one of her shoes, giving the three men an enticing view of her sensational thighs, not to mention a fair amount of cleavage.

"Tend to your ball game," he said to Ralph and Wilbur as he finished Tanya's drink and carried it to her. Behind him, he heard the two men discussing Tanya loudly as they talked above the noise coming from the television.

"That woman is trouble," Ralph said.

"Uh-huh," Wilbur agreed. "I bet she's the one that got away."

"What the hell is that?" Ralph demanded.

"The one he never got over," his friend said. "Uh-huh. Trouble."

MELISSA HERBERT PUSHED her way into the back door of the saloon, humming to herself. She'd been listening to a song on the radio down at the café before she left, and now she couldn't get it out of her head.

"There's a breath of fresh air," Wilbur said when he saw her come in the door. It was what he always said.

And like always, Melissa laughed and patted his shoulder as she passed. "Hi, Ralph," she said, giving him a pat as well before drawing up a stool next to him.

"What do you have today?" Ralph asked as she put the two small brown paper sacks she'd been carrying on the bar. "Smells good."

She'd gotten into the habit of sharing her lunch with

Dave. It had started last spring when she'd hired him to remodel one of the buildings she'd bought in town from Mabel Aldrich.

Mabel had finally parted with the old carriage house that had last been used as a carpenter's workshop. Melissa thought it would be a great space for a shop and planned to lease it come summer. Dave had worked so hard on it, and she loved watching the space being transformed. So she'd started bringing her lunch to watch the progress, adding extra so the two of them could visit while they ate. Dave had understood her vision for the place, while some people in town hadn't been as friendly or as supportive.

It took her a moment, with that darned song still playing in her head, to realize that Wilbur and Ralph were acting stranger than usual. She looked around for Dave. Usually this early in the season, the two older men were the only ones here at lunchtime, so she was surprised to see that Dave had another customer.

The song in her head died as she watched him lean toward the woman at the bar as if hanging on her every word. The two looked…intimate.

"Her name's Tanya. They used to date in high school," Wilbur blurted. "She was the one who got away."

Melissa blinked. A woman Dave had dated in high school? She cleared her voice. "Well, that's nice that she stopped in to see him on her way through town."

Ralph coughed. "Her car broke down so she might be staying for a while."

"Even better," she said, the words like sawdust in her mouth. "I'm sure Dave was glad to see her."

"You could say that," Wilbur muttered, and Ralph kicked him. "Ouch!"

"Well," she said, sliding off her stool. "I can't stay today. You're both welcome to share the lunches I brought." Dave had yet to notice her. He probably hadn't even realized it was midday. "I have a lot of work to do, so I'm going to get moving."

"Want us to tell Dave anything?" Ralph asked.

"Nope," she said, pretending that seeing him with the woman hadn't upset her. There was no reason it should. She and Dave were just friends. They worked together, and while they'd gotten close, she had no right to feel hurt, let alone jealous. She'd hoped for more with Dave, but...

"Just give him his meal," she said over her shoulder. "Or if he isn't hungry, you two can split that one too." She smiled, even though it was forced and hurt her face as she hurried out. She thought she heard Dave call after her, but she couldn't be sure. Either way, she couldn't go back in there right now, not with her eyes stinging with tears.

Dave was the first person she'd met when she'd come to Buckhorn months ago. She'd been looking for a small town in Montana to invest in after her grandmother left her what she called her "stake." She'd had a blowout just outside town, and Dave had happened to come by in his pickup. He'd stopped and changed her tire for her. They'd got to talking. He'd been so helpful in telling her what buildings might be available in town to buy and remodel.

When she'd found out that he had some skills in the carpentry department, she'd talked him into doing the remodel work for her. They'd become good friends, often working late at night, either on one of her projects or at the bar where she filled in when he needed her help.

In all the hours they'd spent together, they'd both opened up, talking about their pasts and their plans for the future.

But she couldn't remember Dave ever mentioning an old
girlfriend by the name of Tanya.

What had Wilbur called her? The one that got away.

CHAPTER THREE

"MEL!" DAVE CALLED after her as he saw her leaving the bar, but too late. She hadn't heard him. He felt a stab of guilt when he realized the time. He'd forgotten all about lunch and the fact that she would be stopping by. He would have introduced her to Tanya if she'd stuck around.

Down the bar, Ralph picked up the sack of food that Melissa had left for him and wagged it as if trying to make him feel worse. It appeared Ralph and Wilbur had split whatever was in the other bag—Melissa's meal?

"So," Tanya said, dragging his attention back. "I have no idea how long I'm going to be in town. What is there to do here?"

"Probably nothing that would interest you," he said with an embarrassed laugh.

"Davey, you used to know what I liked," she said, lowering her voice as she put her hand over his. He felt his pulse jump. "Something tells me you haven't forgotten." The look she gave him brought it all back. The nights parked in the woods, steamed-over windows and uncomfortable sex on the bench seat of his old Ford pickup. And he'd never forget their first time behind the bleachers. It was every high school boy's dream—especially for a teenager as shy as he'd been around girls.

The front door of the bar banged open, bringing a gust of spring air. A shaft of bright light shone in, silhouetting

Gertrude Durham in the doorway for a moment before the door slammed shut behind her. Gertrude made a beeline for Tanya. She slapped a set of keys down on the bar and started to leave.

"Wait, you fixed it that fast?" Tanya cried. She sounded both surprised and relieved, and Dave felt his heart drop. Once her car was ready, she'd be leaving.

Wilbur was right. Tanya was the one that had gotten away. The woman he'd dreamed about. The one he'd put on a pedestal all these years—and with good reason. Just look at her. Now she was here, sitting at his bar in Buckhorn. He didn't want to let her go. Not again.

"Fixed it?" Gertrude scoffed. "Even if I had the parts, I'm not sure I could fix everything that car needs. I'd be better off to take it out in the woods and shoot it." The woman turned to leave again, the way she'd come in.

"What? You aren't going to repair my vehicle?" Tanya slid off her bar stool to go after her. "You have to."

Gertrude stopped to look back at her, clearly about to disagree.

"If anyone can fix your car, it's Gertrude," Dave interceded quickly. "She can fix anything."

Gertrude snorted, giving him a look that said she knew what he was about. "If—and I'm not saying I am—if I were to order the parts for that expensive foreign piece of junk out there, I would have to have the money up front."

"How much money are we talking?" Tanya asked.

"Parts and labor? I'd say about three grand."

"What…?" She turned to look at him. "I never dreamed… I'm so embarrassed. My purse was stolen at the last gas station where I stopped. Almost all of my cash and my credit cards were taken. I've called the credit card companies and they're sending me new cards, but I'm having them posted to the resort where I'm staying in Vegas. Same with my bank."

"That's what I thought," Gertrude said and started for the door again.

"Wait," Dave said. "Go ahead and order the parts. I'll pay so you can order the parts until Tanya can have money wired here instead of Vegas. Same with the credit cards."

Tanya gave him a smile so bright it half blinded him. "Oh, Davey, are you serious? You are such a lifesaver, but I hate to ask you to do that."

"You didn't ask. I offered. It's really no big deal, right, Gertrude?" he said.

The older woman grunted and shook her head at him as if he'd lost his mind. "Fine. It's your funeral." With that she left, slamming the door on her way out.

"Is she always so…dramatic?" Tanya asked as she took her place again on the stool.

Dave chuckled. "No, usually she's much ruder. You caught her on a good day. Are you hungry? A friend of mine just dropped off some lunch. I'd be happy to share."

Tanya smiled and covered his hand again, her blue eyes locking with his. "I've missed you, Davey."

"I've missed you too," he said around the lump in his throat. Was this really happening? Maybe in a movie or a book, but not in real life.

Ralph called down the bar to say that they could use a couple more beers—if he wasn't too busy. "I'll be right back," he said to Tanya and headed toward the two men.

"Are you an idiot?" Ralph asked too loudly the moment Dave reached him.

"I'm hoping that's a rhetorical question," he said.

"The parts alone could cost you a small fortune."

"It's fine," Dave said, trying hard not to tell him that it

was none of his business. "Tanya's good for it." She was born into a wealthy family. He wasn't surprised that she drove an expensive, foreign-made car. Look at the way she dressed. He poured them two beers and then reached for the sack that Melissa had brought.

Ralph grabbed it and held it out of his reach. "You're going to share the lunch that Melissa brought you with... *that* woman?"

Dave sighed and snatched the bag from the man's hand. "Mel wouldn't mind. I know her."

"You are a bigger fool than even I thought," Ralph said, shaking his head.

Dave ignored him as he went back down the bar and opened the bag to see what Melissa had made for him today. He was just sorry he hadn't seen her so he could have thanked her.

TANYA COULD NOT believe her luck. It was about time that it changed for the better, she told herself as she looked at Dave. He really did look good, and apparently, he owned a bar. Which wasn't much as far as appearances went.

"You really own this place," she said, glancing around as he returned with something in a greasy brown paper sack.

He nodded. He would, that is—once he finally got the place paid off.

"Is it usually busier?" she asked.

"It's early in the season," Dave told her. "You should see it in the summer. I have about five months when it is packed almost every night. I have a band play on Saturday nights, a disc jockey on Fridays and karaoke, which is really popular with tourists. They love putting on cowboy hats and singing the old Western songs."

"Sounds like fun," she said. "You must make a lot of money."

"I do okay," he said, and she swore that he flushed.

Which meant he did better than okay. It was so like Davey to play it down.

"What about you?" he asked.

She flipped her hair back. "What about me?"

"Do you have a career, a job?"

Tanya laughed. "A job?" She shook her head. "I'm too much of a free spirit to let myself get tied down to a job. I'm kind of a—" she gave it some thought "—consultant." She laughed. "I advise people on what to do with their money."

"Really?"

Before he could ask for more details, she said, "What's in the bag?"

Later, after being forced to split a tuna salad sandwich— apparently, his favorite since meeting someone named Melissa—she regretted saying she was hungry.

"Where are you staying?" Dave asked.

She thought about her lack of money. Fortunately, Davey had been supplying her with drinks and that awful lunch. She really hadn't thought about what she was going to do. Once she got to Vegas… "Where do people stay in Buckhorn?"

"There's the Sleepy Pine Motel."

"You're joking," she said with a laugh. She'd had just enough to drink that she couldn't help herself. "Anywhere else?"

"It's the only motel in town. Most of the bed-and-breakfasts haven't opened yet, since tourist season doesn't start for a few more weeks, but I could probably make some calls." He finally picked up on her expression. "Oh, that's right. You lost your purse. I'm sorry. How foolish of me."

She saw him glance at the shoulder bag sitting on the stool next to her and felt her pulse jump.

"They took my phone and my wallet out of my purse," she said quickly and mugged what she hoped was a sad face as she picked up her bag from the stool and held it to her. "I don't know where I'm going to stay or what I'm going to do until the parts come in and I get my car fixed." She looked up at him. "How long will that be?"

He shrugged. "Gertrude's good, but she isn't fast. I'll tell you what. If you don't mind staying in my place upstairs… It isn't fancy by any means, but it's comfortable. At least I think so."

"Oh, Davey, that is so sweet." She couldn't wait to see what he thought was comfortable. He looked good, but he lived over his bar. "With the place doing so well I would have thought you'd have built yourself a house somewhere around here. Didn't you used to work for your father? He built homes, right?"

He nodded. "I can definitely do the work, but truthfully, living upstairs is so handy, and I really haven't needed anything more."

Tanya was beginning to remember why it had been so easy to break up with Davey after his accident cost him his football career. She put a smile on her face. "I'd love to stay with you if you're sure it isn't an imposition."

"Not at all," he said and smiled. "I'll run across the highway and get your suitcase." From down the bar, he heard Ralph groan.

DAVE ASKED RALPH to watch the bar for a minute while he went over to the gas station to collect Tanya's bags. She insisted on coming along. "Beautiful afternoon," he said as they crossed the highway. He never got tired of the view of snowcapped mountains against the huge blue sky this time of year.

He'd started to point out one of the mountain ranges when she said, "It's seventy-eight degrees in Las Vegas right now." She shivered. "How can you live in such a cold, isolated place?"

He quickly took off his jean jacket and put it around her shoulders. "Better?"

She nodded and smiled. "Much." At the sound of a semi horn, they quickly hurried out of the middle of the highway as the truck roared past. Traffic was supposed to slow down to thirty-five miles per hour once in Buckhorn proper, but often didn't. It wasn't like there was anyone in town to arrest the drivers. The nearest law was a good hour away in either direction.

From the trunk of her car, Dave pulled out two large suitcases. He didn't know much about luggage, since he'd never really had the need for any. But he could tell that these were expensive valises. Also well used, he noticed as he lifted them out and saw how worn they were. Knowing Tanya, these cases had probably already been around the world a couple of times. He couldn't imagine the life she'd lived and tried not to compare it to his own.

"I've been meaning to get new suitcases," she said as she ran her hand over one of the worn spots on the larger of the two.

"They look fine to me," Dave said and felt her slide a glance at him before smiling.

"You've always asked for so little in life," she said.

Her words made him bristle. "I don't think that's true." It surprised him that, from her, judgment could still hurt. Seeing her again had made it slip his mind how she'd dumped him after his accident so many years ago.

"No, that came out wrong," she quickly corrected. "You appreciate what you have. Some of us are always wanting more, when if we could just stop and enjoy what we have, we'd be much happier. You're content and that's a good thing, Davey."

"It's Dave now," he said as they crossed the highway again. He'd always felt a sense of pride when he saw his place from a distance. He was surprised that it looked shabbier than he'd realized.

"Tell me, what brought you to Buckhorn?" she asked, clearly trying to smooth over things with him.

He wasn't one to hold a grudge or stay upset long. Anyway, he got the feeling that Tanya wasn't as happy as she pretended to be. He doubted she could ever be content, but it made him wonder where life had taken her in the years since high school.

"A friend of mine owned the bar here," he said as he carried the suitcases up the stairs to his apartment. "I stopped by to see him and ended up staying and buying the place." He opened the unlocked door and pushed it open for her to enter.

Dave had never been a slob, so he wasn't worried about the place being a mess. But as he pushed open the door, he saw it through her eyes.

"It isn't much," he said apologetically.

"It's adorable." He looked at her to be sure she was serious. "Did you decorate it yourself?"

"My friend Melissa." He chuckled. "She's good at making something ordinary beautiful."

MELISSA, TANYA THOUGHT with a silent groan. The friend who brings lunch, who can make something ordinary beautiful. It was enough to make her grind her teeth.

"You'll have to tell me more about her," Tanya said.

"You can have the bedroom," he said, carrying her bags in. "I just changed the sheets this morning. It's almost like I knew you'd be dropping by." He turned to smile at her, everything forgiven. He reminded himself that Tanya had always been out of his league. He couldn't hold it against her that they were so different.

"I don't want to toss you out of your bedroom."

"It's fine. I'll sleep on the couch."

"You were going to tell me more about your friend. How long have you known Melanie?"

"Melissa?"

"Sorry. Melissa."

"She arrived in town about six months ago, looking for some property to invest in."

Tanya raised an eyebrow. "She has money?"

He laughed. "Not like your family. Her grandmother left her what she calls her stake. She wanted to invest it wisely."

Wisely? "In Buckhorn?" Her tone must have given away her disbelief.

"You'd be surprised. For some reason, the place is starting to grow. I think more people are anxious to get out of the big cities and are looking for open spaces and a more laid-back lifestyle."

Couldn't get more laid-back than this town, she thought. "You've never married?"

He shook his head. "Didn't I hear that you got married not long after high school to some tycoon?"

She laughed. Tycoon? What he meant was some older man with money. "I can't imagine where you could have heard that." She turned away and quickly changed the subject. "Well, can I at least buy you dinner for letting me stay with you?" He started to say something, no doubt remind her that she had no money. "Silly me. I keep forgetting that I don't have my credit cards or any cash. It's such a nuisance."

"I thought we'd get dinner from the café," he said. "I'll just call and get tonight's special delivered for the two of us. We can eat it in the bar."

She couldn't hide her disappointment. "I thought for sure you'd have a steakhouse in town. I'm really craving a nice, thick juicy steak."

"Funny you should mention steakhouses. I've been thinking about opening one. Mel—Melissa—thinks I should add on a kitchen for the busy season." He shrugged. "I'm thinking about it."

She noticed how his face lit up when he talked about Melissa. If this was going to work, Melissa was going to have to go. She looped her arm through his and squeezed his biceps. "Nice muscles."

"It's all the construction work I've been doing for Mel. You'll have to see the project we're working on. In fact, I need to be there first thing in the morning. The bar is closed tomorrow until two, so I can get more done on the remodel. I have to get it completed before the tourist season starts. She wants it available for lease by May."

"I could tend bar so you don't have to be closed," she said with a burst of inspiration. "I'd love to do that for you."

He hesitated. "Have you tended bar before?"

"At my father's parties, silly. I can handle it with one hand tied behind me, trust me."

"Well, then, thanks, but I still want you to see the old carriage house I'm remodeling. The bar doesn't open until ten, normally, so we'll have plenty of time in the morning."

"I can't wait," she said as they headed back downstairs. She felt her stomach growl. The half a tuna fish sandwich was all she'd had to eat all day. "What is the daily special at the café tonight?"

Dave shrugged. "I have no idea. But I promise that it will be good." She pretended to pout. "Come on, you used to like surprises," he added with a laugh.

Did she used to like surprises? She tried to remember the girl she'd been in high school. She had only vague recollections of those days. They were a blur of clothes shopping, parties and boys. She'd had it all. That was probably why she'd never given any thought to the future.

She cut a look at Dave as he stepped behind the bar and she took a stool. Was he the answer to at least some of her problems?

CHAPTER FOUR

THE AFTERNOON AND evening passed quickly as the bar got busy. Tanya seemed to enjoy herself, playing pool with the locals, even dancing with a few of them. He kept her in fresh drinks, a little surprised how much liquor she could put away.

He liked watching her. It was as if she could sense his eyes on her, because she would look in his direction and smile or wink. He still couldn't believe that she'd walked back into his life. Not that she would be here long. He was no fool. She was on her way to Vegas. Buckhorn wasn't her kind of place. He wasn't her kind of man.

But a few times when she'd looked at him, he wondered if things would have turned out differently if he hadn't gotten hurt and lost his football scholarship. She didn't seem happy now, as if she were looking for something. He remembered that, for a while in high school, he'd made her happy.

"Davey," Tanya said as she collapsed on the countertop, laughing. "I can't remember the last time I've had this much fun. Dance with me."

He looked around the bar. Things were slowing down as patrons wandered home—usually after getting calls from their mothers, girlfriends or wives, reminding them of the time.

Reaching into the till, he took out some money and handed it to her. "Play us some music."

Her blue eyes lit up as she took the money and twirled away. A few minutes later, a slow song came on and she reached for him. He could tell she was feeling the booze she'd been drinking all afternoon as she snuggled into him and stepped on his boot. He realized, in the few months that they had gone steady in high school, they'd never danced together. It surprised him how awkward it felt. He told himself it was due to the alcohol Tanya had consumed and all the years since he'd danced with a beautiful woman.

"I'm so glad my car broke down here," she whispered as she nuzzled his neck. She'd been flirting with him all afternoon and into the night. "What time do you close the bar?"

By the time Dave closed, he had to help a staggering Tanya up the stairs to the apartment. He got her into the bedroom where she sprawled on his bed. The moment her head touched the pillow, she was out. He took off her shoes and closed the door.

He was tired as he lay down on the couch. What a day! He still couldn't believe that Tanya Owens was sleeping in his bed. He smiled at irony. And he was sleeping on his couch.

MELISSA WAS DETERMINED to keep her mind on what had to be done at the remodeling site. She would be all business when Dave showed up. She wouldn't mention his old flame from high school. The last thing she would do was act jealous and make a fool of herself.

But when Dave walked in—with that woman—she felt her heart break all over again. She'd been hoping his ex-girlfriend was just passing through and had left town.

Dave made a beeline for her. "Hey, Mel, thank you so much for bringing me lunch yesterday. I suppose Ralph and

Wilbur told you…" He stopped talking as the woman in question came up beside him and looped her arm through his.

"…that his old girlfriend was in town?" Tanya said with a laugh.

"Tanya and I knew each other back in high school," he said.

"Oh, Davey, it was much more than that," Tanya said and laughed again.

"This is my good friend Melissa and this," he said as he retrieved his arm to motion to the inside of the carriage house and all the work they'd been doing, "is our project." He sounded so proud, Melissa couldn't be mad at him.

"It's nice to meet an old friend of Dave's," she said to Tanya. "Isn't this a great building?"

The woman glanced around. "So, what is it going to be?"

"Whatever someone wants it to," she said as she pointed out the built-in shelves along one wall. "It could be a candy store, a clothing emporium or gift shop." She couldn't help her enthusiasm. "Dave has done such a good job, I almost want to open my own shop, but we have other buildings that need to be remodeled." She looked to Dave and saw that he was holding his back as if in pain. "Are you all right?"

"It's nothing," he said quickly. Tanya had walked over to the window to look out on the street. "It's my old couch," he whispered. "Tanya's staying with me for a few days until her car is repaired."

"I'm on my way to Vegas," Tanya said, turning to smile. "But I'm not going to make Davey stay on that couch the whole time."

"Well, I'd better get to work," Melissa said as she saw the woman give Dave a very pointed look. "I have a lot of varnishing to do if these shelves are going to get dry before my renter gets here."

"You already have someone interested in it?" Dave asked, sounding excited and happy for her.

"I got a call last night. He'll be coming through town next week. I described the place to him and he sounded really interested. He said he was looking for a spot exactly like Buckhorn."

"Amazing," Tanya said and brushed dust off her trousers.

"That's great, Mel. I better get busy too." He turned to Tanya. "You sure you don't want to just spend the day taking it easy?"

"I'd be bored to death." She held out her hand. "Just give me the key. I'll man the bar for you. See you later?"

"It was nice meeting you," Melissa said, but Tanya was already out the door. She looked over at Dave, who was watching her go. "So she was the one who got away."

Dave looked as if he wanted to dig a hole and climb into it. "Ralph and Wilbur." He sighed, but he didn't deny it. "It's so weird that her car broke down here after all these years."

She could see where he was headed with this. "Almost like fate, huh?"

"Yeah, maybe. You must think I'm silly."

"No," she quickly assured him. "I think you're sweet. I have one of those. The one I still recall fondly."

He looked surprised. "What would you do if he showed up here out of the blue?"

"Truthfully? I don't know. What are *you* going to do?"

"Do? You mean like what?" Dave asked. "It's not like I can wine and dine her and try to get her to stay."

"If that's what you want, why not?" Melissa asked, even though it broke her heart. "Isn't this your chance to see if there is something still there?"

He laughed. "I wouldn't even know how to begin. It's been so long…"

"I'll help you," she said and wanted to smack herself. But if this woman was his true love, then he needed to find out. Otherwise, even if Tanya left, he'd be mooning over her and she'd always be the one who got away.

"Tonight, I'll tend bar. You can get the cook at the café to give you a couple of steaks, two potatoes and some asparagus. You said you're a pretty good cook, right?"

"I said I was a *great* cook," he corrected and laughed. "You're serious."

"I'll drop by a couple of candles. You have wine and everything else you need. Just one thing," she added. "Don't wear that one green shirt of yours."

"What? That's my favorite shirt."

She nodded. "Wear that blue one with the stripes. It brings out the blue in your eyes." She could see him warming to the idea and felt another chunk of her heart break.

"Thank you. You're the best, Mel," he said.

Not the best, she thought as they went to work. She wanted Tanya gone, instantly disliking her. She hadn't even given the woman a chance, and that wasn't like her.

TANYA USED THE key to open the bar, stepped in and locked the door behind her. For a moment, she simply stood breathing in the familiar scents and looking at the place with a critical eye. She could have this establishment if she wanted it. The thought sent a little thrill through her. She tried to imagine it packed in the summer and could almost hear the *cha-ching* of the till as it filled with money. Davey wanted to add a steakhouse. *Cha-ching, cha-ching*.

Frowning, she reminded herself of the downsides— staying in this town in the middle of nowhere—with Davey. She couldn't see herself tied down to him, living in that apartment over the bar for the rest of her life. She could nag him into building them a really nice house, she supposed.

But it came down to the question of how desperate was she?

Her cell phone rang. She dug it out of her purse, cursing herself for forgetting to turn it off again. She'd have to be more careful since she'd told Davey that her phone had been stolen along with her wallet.

She recognized the number and considered not answering. But she also couldn't keep putting off the inevitable. The man was already furious enough that he wanted to kill her. Antagonizing him would only make it worse. "Steven," she said as she accepted the call. Crossing the room, she stepped behind the bar to pour herself a drink. She was going to need one after this.

"Where the hell are you?" he demanded at the top of his lungs. The sound of his voice was like a screwdriver plunged between her eyes, making her hangover even worse.

She dropped ice cubes into her glass and covered them with some of Davey's good bourbon. She took a long drink. It slid down her throat, warming her and giving her courage. She kept her voice calm. "Nice to hear your voice too."

"You're a dead woman, you know that, right?" As she lifted her drink to her lips, the ice cubes rattled in the glass. "Are you already drinking this morning?"

"What would you expect of a dead woman?"

He growled and broke something. She heard it shatter and smiled. At least she wasn't there to take the brunt of that anger. "You do realize that I have my men looking for you. When they find you——"

"I told you I'll get you your money. I have a couple of options," she said, looking around the bar.

"You expect me to believe anything that comes out of that mouth of yours? You don't think I know that your family cut you off? You've strung me along far too long. We are through negotiating."

"Seriously, I can come up with it." She opened the till. Bless Davey, he'd gotten it ready for her this morning. She counted out what was in there and then put it back. It wasn't even enough to tempt Steven with. Even if she took the bills, she had no way of leaving town until her car was fixed. "I just need a little time."

"It's too late," Steven said.

"Come on, you kill me and you'll never see a dime."

"Sometimes a person has to cut his losses. You'll be seeing one of my associates very soon. Goodbye, Tanya."

She stood holding the phone, her heart pounding. She downed the rest of her drink, considered taking the cash from the till and borrowing Davey's pickup to try to get as far away as possible before she was found.

Pouring herself another drink, she tried not to panic. Davey had money. He'd give her whatever she needed. Or how about Melissa? Apparently, she had her "stake." Between the two of them...

She downed the drink, her mind whirling. She'd figure this out. She regretted ripping Steven off. That had been a mistake, but she'd been desperate. She'd thought that she could double the money in the first Montana casino she hit. She'd thought she could pay him back everything she owed him, but unfortunately, she'd hit a string of bad luck. How was she to know that Steven was connected and that he owed that money to some bad guys? Apparently, they were both having some bad luck, but once she got to Vegas she knew a guy there who could hook her up. The problem was getting there before one of Steven's goons found her.

Opening the till, she took out fifty bucks. Tonight, she'd pocket whatever she could by not ringing up the drinks. She'd try to get more out of Davey, and then she'd take his truck and go to Vegas.

She told herself that her luck was improving. Look where she'd broken down. Buckhorn, the home of her old boyfriend Davey—and talk about luck! The man owned a bar. Once she got to Vegas, she'd make back what she owed Steven.

After another drink, she was feeling better. She'd get herself out of this with Davey's help. She'd seen the way he was looking at her last night. He still wanted her. He'd do anything she asked—just like he had when they were teenagers. The old man at the bar yesterday had said that she was the one who got away. Which meant that he realized Davey had never gotten over her. Davey would be putty in her hands—if she could keep him away from Melissa.

Davey's best friend, huh? *We'll see about that.*

MELISSA COULD TELL that Tanya was drunk when she showed up to take over the bar. Earlier, from their work project, Dave had called and told Tanya that he was making her a steak dinner tonight. From the rest of what Melissa had heard of the conversation, Tanya had been all over the idea.

"You like Davey, huh," Tanya said now as Melissa stepped behind the counter and began washing up the dirty glasses that the woman had left in the sink.

"He's a nice guy," she said noncommittally.

Tanya's laugh had a bite to it. "Dull as dirt, you mean, but still a catch if you live in Buckhorn, huh?" Melissa shot her an annoyed look, but Tanya waved it off, saying, "Can't you take a joke? Davey's great. I just hate to see you wasting your time. Sorry, but he only sees you as his *good friend.*

Get a clue. He calls you *Mel*." She laughed and gave Melissa a pitying smile. "Davey's never gotten over me, you know. He never will."

"Dave's waiting for you upstairs," she said, trying hard to understand what Dave saw in this woman.

"You are so right." Tanya ran her hands over her hips as if dusting off her slacks. "I shouldn't keep him waiting. We have big plans tonight." She winked, turned and stumbled out.

"Maybe she'll fall down the stairs and break her neck," Ralph suggested.

For a man who swore he was hard of hearing, he didn't miss much. "She's just had a little too much to drink."

"Uh-huh," he said. "She spent the entire day stealing from Dave."

"What? I don't like her either, but to accuse her—"

"I can prove it," Ralph said, lowering his voice. "I marked my bills I gave her with the word *THIEF*. There were seven of them. You won't find them in the till."

Melissa was too shocked to speak. Ralph had seen Tanya stealing money from Dave's business? She couldn't believe what he was saying. He had to be mistaken, but she didn't have time to prove him wrong as the bar got busy.

Worrying, though, did help a little to keep her mind off what was happening upstairs. She hoped that Dave's dinner went well. She wanted him to be happy. If that meant Tanya... Unless Ralph was right and the woman was a thief.

Once she closed, she took the cash from the till and began to count it—watching for the seven bills that Ralph had said he'd marked. They weren't there. Worse, the till was short by about seventy dollars.

She felt sick to her stomach. She counted again, looking around to see if there was more money that Tanya had just forgotten to put where it went. She glanced at the tip jar. Empty except for what Melissa herself had put in it tonight.

"Is there a problem?" Ralph asked. He always waited if Dave wasn't around to walk her back to her apartment. Everyone else was gone for the night.

She turned to look at him. When she'd come in to relieve Tanya, the place had been busy and yet the take was lower than normal, even without the missing seventy dollars. She realized she should have counted the money before she started work. It was too late now.

"Told you so," Ralph said, nodding. "She was pocketing the bucks. Hardly any of it went into the till." Melissa closed her eyes for a moment. When she opened them, Ralph was on his feet, ready to walk her home.

"I can't tell Dave," she said. "It will break his heart."

"Break his heart or break his business," Ralph said. "Tough choice. I'm not going to be the one to tell him. But someone needs to before it's too late."

CHAPTER FIVE

AFTER A RESTLESS NIGHT, Melissa woke on a mission. Her first stop was a visit to Gertrude at the garage. She hardly noticed the beautiful Montana day. The sky was cloudless and a blue that normally would have had her smiling. The spring air was so fresh, with just enough bite to it that she'd worn a jacket, and there was fresh snow on the mountain peaks.

She could hear Gertrude under Tanya's car, working. Every clank of metal was punctuated by a curse. "How's it coming?" she called down. All she could see were Gertrude's boots sticking out.

A moment later the mechanic rolled out. "Piece of junk," Gertrude spat. "She send you over to find out how it's going?"

Melissa quickly shook her head. Now that she was here, she wasn't so sure what it was she was looking for. "Just curious."

The older woman eyed her for a moment. "You have heard what curiosity does to cats, right?"

"Have the parts already came in?" she asked hopefully.

"Nope. I was just dismantling the components, so when the new stuff comes in, I can get this hunk of junk running and Tanya can be on her way." She cocked a brow at Melissa. "I suspect I'm not the only one wanting her out of town." With that, Gertrude slid back under the car and proceeded to cuss and clank.

After peering in the car windows, Melissa left, even more convinced that Tanya wasn't who Dave thought she was. Not that she had any proof. But the more she thought about it, the more convinced she became. Tanya had said that her purse was stolen, but she'd still had one when Melissa had seen her at the bar.

That she had no money, though, seemed true.

She thought of the outfit Tanya had been wearing. Her shoes were expensive, but the heels were run-down. Her clothes also looked as if they sported name brands but were beginning to fray around the edges. Even her car fit the picture Tanya painted of a successful woman on vacation, unless you looked inside and saw the worn upholstery. Dave had told her that Tanya came from money, but from what Melissa could see, apparently, the money had run out.

She was dreading what she had to do next. By now, Dave would be down in the bar, making coffee for the regulars who would be stopping by the moment the doors opened. She hoped to get there before them to talk to Dave alone.

When she walked in the back door, she saw Dave behind the bar and smelled freshly brewed coffee. He looked up and smiled, and she remembered the special dinner he'd had last night with Tanya, the dinner she'd suggested and helped him with. She tried to read his expression to see how it had gone.

She'd planned to get right into the missing money, but instead said, "How was the meal?"

"Good," he said. "The steak was great. Thanks for suggesting it."

It was what he wasn't saying that made her ask, "How did Tanya like it?"

"She liked it, I think." He shrugged. "She wasn't all that hungry. She said the bar was busy yesterday. She was pretty tired." He picked up a clean cup and poured her a cup of coffee.

Melissa took it, studying him. The date hadn't gone well. "You didn't wear that green shirt, did you?" she joked.

"No, I took your advice and wore the blue one."

He picked up the bank bag. She hadn't seen it lying on the counter by the till. So, he'd already gone to the safe. Had he counted it yet?

"The till was short last night by seventy dollars," she said.

Dave didn't look surprised. "What do you think happened?" It was pretty obvious, given what Ralph had told her. But she didn't want to be the one to tell him.

But before she could say anything, Dave responded with, "I shouldn't have let Tanya open up by herself. All she had to do was get busy and someone could have taken the money."

Melissa couldn't speak for fear of what would come out of her mouth. The chances of anyone going behind the bar and stealing the cash was next to impossible with Ralph and Wilbur glued to their stools right in front of it. She bit her tongue and said nothing as the two elderly men came through the door.

They took their usual stools, and Dave set a cup of coffee in front of each of them before excusing himself to go meet the beer truck that had just pulled up out back. As Dave walked away, he got a call on his cell. She heard him say, "Hello, Marshal, what can I do for you?" before he disappeared outside.

"I'm guessing the date didn't go all that well," Wilbur said. "Even with your help, Melissa."

Ralph swore and turned on his stool to face her. "What is wrong with you?" he demanded. "You're helping him win back that woman, especially now that you know what I told you?" He shook his head. "When are you going to tell him?"

"I'm not." She picked up her coffee cup.

"That wasn't what I was asking," Ralph snapped. "When are you going to explain to him how you feel about him?"

"I don't know what you're talking about," she said as she took a sip of her coffee. She wanted to simply leave, but Dave would think she was upset if she didn't drink at least some of her coffee.

Ralph swore. "The stealing aside, she ain't the woman Dave thinks she is, and we all know it."

"How is it you know so much about women?" Wilbur asked. "Bet you can't even remember the last time you were with one. So don't be giving this young gal advice." He winked at Melissa.

"Ralph's just looking out for me," she said, smiling at the older man.

Ralph smiled back. "Melissa knows what I'm saying is true and I *am* looking out for her." He nodded. "The problem is getting Dave to see it. That's why I marked my bills last night. I saw her pocketing the money. All you have to do is find the ones I wrote on in that purse of hers, and you'll have your proof."

Dave returned and they all fell silent. He eyed them suspiciously as if he thought they might have been talking about him.

Melissa did her best to act normal, but there was nothing normal about this situation. Even if she could find the bills Ralph had marked in Tanya's purse... "Thanks for the coffee, but I need to get going." She quickly drank what she could as fast as possible, scalding her mouth. "We'll talk later." And she was out the door.

Once outside, she let herself breathe. *There are none so blind as those who cannot see.* Where had that thought come from? she wondered. Shaking her head, she hadn't gone far when she saw Tanya sitting on the steps next to the bar, smoking a cigarette. The woman hurriedly put it out and rose to her feet, dropping her lighter and cigarettes into her open purse. Like everything else, the designer shoulder bag had seen better days, Melissa noticed.

Tanya looked hungover. "Where can I get a latte in this town?"

"The coffee kiosk is closed for another few weeks, but you can get a cup of coffee in the bar or down at the café."

Tanya mugged a disapproving face. "How can you stand this place? I mean, don't you miss civilization?"

She shook her head. "I love Buckhorn. It suits me. Anything you can't get here, you can order online and have it delivered. It's the best of both worlds."

"Huh," Tanya said and eyed her more closely. "Is it Buckhorn that suits you or Davey?" Tanya asked. "I've seen the way you look at him."

Melissa shook her head. She was not having this conversation. "Sorry, I'd love to visit, but I'm running late for work." She'd taken only a few steps away when she heard a cell phone buzzing. She turned to see Tanya grab her purse up from the step where she'd left it and quickly silence the phone inside. As she hurried away, she could feel Tanya staring after her. Hadn't Dave told her that Tanya had lost her wallet and cell phone? Was the woman worried that Melissa had caught her in a lie? She wanted to laugh. Tanya had no idea. If those marked bills were in her purse along with that cell phone, she would be caught out in something even worse.

But if she'd lied about having her wallet and cell phone stolen, what else was Tanya lying about?

TANYA HUGGED HER shoulder bag to her for a moment. That had been too close. She had to be more careful—especially around Melissa. She'd forgotten to turn off her phone again. She'd left it on vibrate. Melissa had heard it buzzing inside the purse on the wooden step. Would she tell Davey?

Already in hot water with him, she hoped Mel kept her trap shut. Last night hadn't gone well. Davey had planned a romantic dinner. She blamed all the booze she'd guzzled while tending bar. She hadn't been hungry. She'd pushed her food around, spilled her wine and almost passed out in her plate.

At the memory of her failed attempt at seducing Davey when he carried her to bed, she felt her face heat. She hoped she hadn't blown it with him. She had a good thing going here. A bar where she could drink all she wanted, a man who would do anything for her, a place to hide out and all the money she could steal—if she could get more chances. She couldn't mess this up.

She looked into her open purse and saw the wad of money she'd taken last night. Looking around to make sure she was alone, she took it out, hoping there would be more than the four hundred dollars she'd estimated without counting this morning. She needed enough for a fresh start if things went south with Davey.

She'd begun to quickly tally what she'd gotten away with when she spotted a crumpled bill with writing on it. The word jumped out at her. *THIEF.* She stared at it for a full minute before she assured herself that it didn't mean anything. But as she began to thumb through the rest of the money, she found more with the same word penned on them. Her heart began to pound.

Maybe it was someone's idea of a joke. She wanted that to be the case, but it wasn't funny. She thought of the two old men at the bar. They'd both been watching her like hawks. She realized they must have seen what she was doing. She'd thought they were just ogling her butt in those tight pants she'd been wearing.

Going through the money quickly, she pulled out all the bills with *THIEF* written on them in the same handwriting. There were seven total. She stared at them, considering. Throw them away? She couldn't bring herself to do that. Even seven dollars in Vegas could make the difference between winning and losing.

Then an idea came to her. A surefire way to get rid of Melissa for good.

CHAPTER SIX

TANYA ROSE AND headed for the front door of the bar. But as she stepped in, she saw Davey counting last night's receipts and feared she'd already screwed herself. Why had she pocketed so much money last night—let alone taken that fifty from the till? What would she do if he threw her out now? Her car wasn't fixed. If he didn't pay for the parts...

"Good morning," she said as she climbed up onto a stool in front of him.

"Morning," he said and closed the bag, put it into a drawer and turned to look at her. "Coffee?"

She nodded. She could tell he was upset, and yet he was still being that gentle, polite man he'd always been. Maybe she could talk her way out of this. After all, she wasn't the last one in that till. His sweet Melissa had closed last night.

"Mmm," she said, taking a sip of the plain black coffee he placed in front of her. "This is delicious." The lie came easily; they always had. "Thank you so much for dinner last night. I don't feel I did it justice." She'd told him she was craving a steak, and then she hadn't eaten but a few bites. "I hope you aren't upset with me."

He shook his head. "I do need to ask you about the till though. It was over seventy dollars short."

"Oh no," she said, giving him her most appalled look. "Did I mess up or did someone take it?" She thought about the bills in her purse, but realized Dave would never ask to see what was inside it. But what if whoever had written *THIEF* on those seven bills planned to tell Dave?

She knew that she should have rung up more of the sales instead of pocketing the cash last night. Of course Dave was suspicious. What if he never let her run the bar alone again? A few more nights like that, and she would have her own stake, as Melissa called it.

Just the thought of Melissa… "You don't think Melissa… No," she said as she saw his expression. "She wouldn't."

"No, she wouldn't," he said quickly. Too quickly. "I should have warned you about leaving the till open at any time. All you have to do is step away for a minute."

"I'm so sorry. I'm sure that's exactly what happened. I'm good at making drinks, but money…" She shrugged and gave him a coy smile. "You know, speaking of Melissa, I was just thinking that I'd like to go help her today. Do you think she'd mind?"

Davey got a call on his cell phone before he could respond. He motioned that he had to take it in his office. He grabbed the money bag from the drawer as he went and mouthed, "See you later."

She could tell that he wanted her to be friends with Melissa. Like that was ever going to happen. But at least she could support the illusion. At the same time, she could do what she could to get Mel out of his life—and her own.

TANYA WAS THE last person Melissa had expected to see again today. When the door opened, she'd turned, hoping it would be Dave. But he was working the bar today, she reminded herself. Most of his labor was completed on the old carriage house. Once she finished with her part, it would be ready. She was excited to hear what kind of business her prospective renter would open in Buckhorn.

So she was surprised to see Tanya walk in dressed in jeans and an old shirt that she recognized as one of Dave's. She was even more surprised when Tanya announced, "I've come to help."

"I appreciate the offer, but there's not much left to do," Melissa said, trying to hide her distaste for the woman.

"What are you doing? That doesn't look hard," Tanya said, coming over to where Melissa had been removing the masking tape from around the windows. Practically pushing her aside, Tanya began pulling off the tape. "Tell me about Davey."

Well, Melissa thought, at least now she knew what the woman was doing here. "You know more about Dave than I do."

Tanya laughed. "Not this new Davey. Has he been dating anyone?"

This conversation made her uncomfortable, but she busied herself by climbing up the ladder to remove the tape off the high arched windows in the front. "Not since I've been in town, but that's only for a few months."

"He said you were encouraging him to open a steakhouse. That steak he made us last night was delicious. You really think it would do well in a town like this? Buckhorn is so small."

"It's growing and the steakhouse would be open just the busiest months from May through September," Melissa said. "A lot of businesses are seasonal in Montana."

"But the bar would be open all year, right?"

Why the interest in Dave's business? she wondered. The woman was a thief and a liar and who knew what else. But she couldn't be thinking about staying, could she?

"I heard you're on your way to Vegas. You have plans once you get there?" Melissa asked her.

"If I ever get there, gamble," Tanya said. "Davey said your grandmother left you a stake. Isn't that what you called it?"

Melissa wasn't sure she liked Dave telling this woman so much about her. "I can't imagine how I came up in your conversations. I'm sure you have a lot more important things to catch up on after all these years."

Tanya waved that off. "I like the idea of a stake. Fresh starts and all that. Your grandmother must have left you a lot if you could start buying buildings and afford to hire Davey to remodel them."

Subtle, Melissa thought, but she didn't bite. "I'm surprised you and Dave didn't get married after high school. Didn't you date his senior year?"

"He got hurt playing football and was laid up a few months," she said. "We...grew apart, and by the time he came back to school, I was dating someone else."

Melissa stopped to look at the woman. Did she have any idea how telling that was? "But the two of you must not have gotten over each other to pick things up where you left off way back in high school."

"I suppose you could say that." Tanya wadded up a ball of tape and dropped it on the floor. "He talks about you a lot."

"We're friends." She realized that Tanya had stopped working and moved to another spot in the room, behind her. At the sound of something hitting the floor, Melissa turned on the ladder to see her purse had fallen from the shelf where she'd put it, the contents scattered across the floor.

"Oh, I'm so clumsy," Tanya cried. Melissa started down the ladder, but Tanya waved her away. "I've got it."

She watched the woman pick up everything and stuff it back into the handbag before setting it back again.

"The thing is," Tanya said, continuing the earlier conversation as if nothing had happened. "I might be staying here in Buckhorn."

"Really? I got the impression earlier that it was too small for you," Melissa said and reached up high to peel off a strip of tape.

"If I stay," Tanya said, surprising Melanie at how close she suddenly was, "I wouldn't want you to come between Davey and me."

"I'm not the problem," she said, unable to hold back her dislike for the woman any longer. "If you keep stealing from him, he's going to find out."

Melissa had her arm extended, reaching for the tape when she felt the ladder begin to shake. She shot a look down and saw Tanya's expression. It sent a spike of fear straight to her heart. She started to grab hold, but Tanya was quicker, clutching the ladder and shaking it violently.

Clinging to it, Melissa hung on. Tanya rattled it harder, but then seemed to realize that her efforts weren't working. Melissa saw the knowledge cross the woman's face just an instant before Tanya gave the ladder a violent shove.

The ladder tipped, Melissa's weight near the top throwing both her and the device off balance. She felt herself falling at the same time she heard the door to the shop open. She didn't see Dave—not until he caught her.

The ladder thundered to the floor at his feet as he held Melissa in his arms. Her heart threatened to pound out of her chest. If he hadn't come in the door when he had... Her gaze shot to Tanya. Had he seen her push the ladder over?

"I tried to catch her when I saw it going!" Tanya cried. She pretended to be horror-struck.

But it was Melissa who was both shocked and terrified. The woman had tried to kill her. She was shaking so hard that Dave seemed not to want to put her down. He kept saying, "You're okay. I've got you." Even when he lowered her to her feet, she wobbled, her legs weak with reaction.

"You're my hero!" Tanya cried and rushed at Dave, throwing her arms around his neck and kissing him. Melissa could only stare as the woman turned toward her. "Isn't he amazing? I was helping take down the tape around the window when I saw her ladder start to go. I just wasn't strong enough to stop it from happening. I'm such a weakling, all hundred and fifteen pounds of me soaking wet."

Melissa wondered how long it would take for Tanya to make the comparison between the two of them. While Tanya was slim, stacked and beautiful with her curly long dark hair and big blue eyes, Melissa was average in just about every way, from her brown eyes to her brown hair and her face and figure.

Now she could only watch as Tanya made the whole ordeal about her, telling Dave that she was so upset she really needed a drink. It was all Melissa could do to watch. The worst part was that Dave seemed to be buying Tanya's account of it as she leaned against him for support.

What if she spoke up and said that the woman had tried to kill her? Would Dave even believe her? Tanya was such a perfected liar. Add to that, Dave was infatuated with this woman, to the point that he didn't see Melissa—at least not the way Melissa wanted him to see her.

Dave shot her a look. "Are you sure you're all right?" The concern in his voice made her want to cry. They'd been so close before Tanya arrived in town with her broken-down car. She'd actually started thinking that there might be something happening between them.

"I'm fine. I was just…scared." Tanya was staring at her,

daring her to speak up. They both knew how that would go if she did. "Really, I'm fine. Who's taking care of the bar?"

"I decided to take the day off. I came to see if Tanya wanted to go for a ride." He turned to her then. "Thought you might like to see the area."

Tanya clapped excitedly. "I'd love to." She shot Melissa a mocking smile. "You don't mind if I quit helping, do you?"

What a laugh, Melissa thought. Her kind of help she definitely didn't need. Tanya had tried to kill her. Or had she been trying to only warn her off? Would she have caught the ladder before Melissa hit the floor? Either way, she'd gotten the message. Dave was Tanya's.

"No," she managed to say. "Thanks for your...help."

"Great, then I guess we'll see you later," she said and snuggled against Dave.

He turned, hesitating for a moment. "If you need me, call." She met his gaze and held it, trying to warn him telepathically. But clearly her powers weren't working as he said, "See you later, then."

She could only nod as the two left. Tanya looked back before the door closed and smiled her winning smile.

CHAPTER SEVEN

THE TOUR OF the area was the most boring thing Tanya had ever seen, she thought as she feigned a headache and got Davey to take her back to the apartment. "Maybe I'll lie down for a nap," she said.

"Why don't you do that. I need to go check on Melissa. I'll order us dinner from the café later."

Oh joy, she thought. "Or you could join me for a nap," she suggested. "Not that we need to sleep." The last thing she wanted him to do was go check on Melissa. The stupid woman might tell him about the missing money before Tanya could spring her trap. Or Mel might try to convince him that she'd pushed her over on the ladder. It had been impulsive. She'd seen a chance to be rid of her. Unfortunately, Davey had ruined that plan.

Why was she having such a hard time getting him into her bed? Well, his bed actually, but with her. She was beginning to think that she'd lost her touch.

She knew that wasn't true. She still looked good. She'd spent enough money improving her body that she should. Back when she had money, that was, she thought dismally.

She assured herself that once they made love, he would be hers. She wouldn't even have to worry about that simpering Melissa. Nothing the woman could say would tear them apart. Davey would be hers—and everything he owned—if she played her cards right.

"You just get over your headache," he said as he headed to the door, obviously in a hurry to check on Melissa. "I won't be long."

"Wait," she said quickly. "I've been worrying about the missing money." He started to wave that off, but she continued, "Last night, I noticed that several of the bills had something written on them." She looked at him. "The word *THIEF*. I didn't think anything of it until earlier at the shop, with Melissa. I'm so clumsy, I knocked her purse off the shelf when I was helping her and..." She hesitated, holding his gaze. "I saw one of the bills with *THIEF* written on it."

As expected, Dave immediately said there had to be a mistake.

"I would think that you'd at least want to ask her where she'd gotten the bills, since when I left, they were in the till," Tanya said. "Otherwise, it makes it look like I did something wrong, and I really can't live with that. I feel I'd have to move out. Maybe try to get a ride on to Vegas and have my car brought to me when it's fixed."

She saw that her words had hit their mark. He didn't want her to leave. In fact, he'd do almost anything to make her stay. She tried not to smile as he said, "I don't want that. I'll talk to Melissa."

"Wouldn't it be best if you had her come over to the bar?" Tanya asked. "That way we can all be there and get this sorted out."

DAVE COULD FEEL Tanya's gaze on him as they waited for Mel to join them in the bar. With it closed until tonight, they were alone when Mel walked in. He hated this sort of thing under normal circumstances. And this situation was far from normal. Melissa was his best friend. He trusted her with his life. He would have sworn on a bible that she would never steal from anyone—especially him.

But he found himself between a rock and a hard place. He glanced at Tanya. She gave him an impatient nod. She wasn't going to let this go. He had to let this play out.

"Mel," he said and had to clear his throat. "I could use some extra singles. You don't happen to have any, do you?"

If she was surprised by the request, she didn't show it. "Let me see," she said as she quickly opened her purse. When he'd called and asked her to come over to the bar, she hadn't hesitated. Now, as she looked inside her bag, she seemed to hesitate. He saw her eyes widen in alarm. She froze, her gaze going from her purse to him and back to what was inside.

"Is there a problem?" Tanya asked as she got off her stool and came around so she could see. "That's odd," she said, snatching the bills from Melissa's bag. "Those are the same ones I saw when I bartended yesterday. I put them on the bottom of the ones slot because I noticed that someone had written on them. I mentioned them to Davey, but he said they weren't in the money bag this morning."

Dave watched tears flood Melissa's big brown eyes as she looked up at him. Her lips parted, but nothing came out. Tanya made a satisfied sound as she took her stool again. He could tell she was waiting for him to say something.

"We can talk about this later," Dave said, seeing how miserable Melissa was and feeling even worse that he'd put her through this. He couldn't bear it.

She clutched her purse and shot a look at Tanya before she stormed out of the bar.

"That's all you had to say, Davey?" Tanya cried as the back door slammed. "The woman is a *thief*."

He held up his hand to silence her. "I can't talk about this right now." With that, he turned and went after Melissa.

MELISSA COULDN'T BELIEVE THIS. Ralph's plan with the bills had backfired big-time. When had Tanya put the bills in her purse? It came to her in a flash. At the shop earlier. Tanya had knocked the purse to the floor and insisted on picking everything up since Melissa was up on the ladder. That must have been when she'd put the marked singles into her purse. Of course, spilling the contents of her bag hadn't been an accident, any more than trying to knock her off the ladder.

Why hadn't she told Dave what Ralph had done to try to trap Tanya? Because he'd seemed so happy. It had been on the tip of her tongue, but then she'd looked at him and just couldn't do it. She cared too much about him to break his heart.

When Tanya counted her take, she must have seen the word *THIEF* written on the bills and figured it out. Of course she would implicate her since she was jealous of the relationship Melissa had with Dave.

"Mel!" she heard Dave behind her. "Wait up."

She stopped and turned, refusing to run away like a true thief.

"Hey, I know there's an explanation for this," he said. She could hear how badly he wanted to believe that. "When I realized that money was missing and Tanya told me about the bills she'd seen in the till... How do you think this happened?"

She shook her head. "That's what I was just trying to understand. I guess I could have put in a ten and taken ten ones when I closed out last night. I really wasn't paying attention." No, she'd been thinking about Dave and Tanya upstairs in his apartment, having an intimate dinner date.

"Of course." Dave let out a relieved laugh. "I've seen you do that every week before wash day!" He shook his head. "I'm just sorry I upset you. It's the last thing I ever wanted to do."

She nodded. "I was so surprised to see the bills in my purse. I didn't know how they got there. I'd forgotten and I couldn't stand the thought that you might think—"

"I knew you would never steal," he said quickly. "I knew there had to be an explanation." His gaze locked with hers for a moment. He looked as miserable as she felt. "I better get back to the bar." *Back to Tanya*, she thought, before the woman did any more damage. "Again, I'm sorry. No hard feelings?"

Melissa shook her head. "Of course not. Better to get to the bottom of it."

He nodded and sighed. "Thank you." He held her gaze a little longer. "See you in the morning at the shop?" She nodded and smiled, even as her heart broke. Dave had no idea who Tanya was, but Melissa now knew only too well. The woman was determined to get her out of Dave's life.

What was she going to do? She could tell Dave and break his heart. But what if he didn't believe her? There was always that chance, because of the web Tanya had already spun. Surely once the woman's car was fixed, she would leave. Dave would be hurt, but not as hurt as he would be if he knew the truth.

But what if she didn't leave?

TANYA COULDN'T BELIEVE how well her plan had worked—up to a point. Davey's reaction, though, had been all wrong.

What was the matter with him? She couldn't believe it when he'd gone after the woman.

Disgusted with him, she'd gotten up and stepped behind the bar to make herself a drink. She was on her second by the time he returned.

"I hope you went easy on her," she said as she gave him a sympathetic look. "We just won't let her bartend again."

To her shock, Davey shook his head. "It was just a misunderstanding. That's what I thought. You don't know Melissa like I do. She would never steal." He seemed satisfied with whatever story the woman had cooked up.

"I'm sorry, but how was it a misunderstanding?" she asked, unable to let it go. What kind of fool was this man? "It seemed pretty clear-cut to me."

She listened to him explain something about washday ones and tried not to gag. She needed to be the fill-in bartender—not Melissa. She'd be more careful about pocketing the money next time and make sure that the till came out right. Her car could be fixed at any time. How was she supposed to have a stake before she hit Vegas if she didn't have access to money?

She could rob the place.

The thought came out of nowhere. But she tucked it away as a last resort.

First, she would try to get closer to Davey. There had been a time when she could get the man to do anything she asked. Her feminine wiles weren't working quite as well, but she wasn't giving up. She blamed Melissa. She thought that once she got the woman out of the way, there would be no more problems. But Melissa was proving to be a powerful opponent. Tanya realized she would have to up her game.

"Davey, I feel like I've done nothing but cause you trouble," she said and made her pouty lips. "Maybe I should go stay down at the motel until my car is fixed."

"Don't be silly," he said, but didn't look at her as he began setting up the bar that would open at two. That meant he would be working and she'd have no chance at the till. That definitely wasn't going to work. "I'm glad you mentioned the bills. We got it all cleared up. Melissa understood." Of course she did, Tanya thought. He finally stopped what he'd been doing to look at her. "I'm just glad your car broke down here rather than somewhere else."

"I'm so glad you feel that way," she said, leaning over the bar a little just in case he wanted to steal a kiss. Apparently he didn't. "Would you mind refreshing my drink? I can't tell you what it means to me to be here with you."

"I feel the same way," he said as he refilled her glass. "Also, I meant to ask you... When I stopped by the post office and checked my box, there was nothing from your credit card companies or your bank. If you had them sent by express mail, they should have been here by now. You might want to check on them."

"You're right. I'll check, but I would imagine things take a while getting to Buckhorn. I mean, it is in the middle of nowhere." She laughed, but he didn't join her.

"Buckhorn's on a main highway through the middle of Montana," he said. "We get mail service pretty much like anywhere else."

Tanya figured they probably did. How long could she pretend that she called to have credit cards sent to her here? The ones in her purse were maxed out and worthless, since her accounts had probably been closed by now. What little money she'd had was gone. There was no bank account. Not anymore.

She was in a desperate situation. But was she reckless

enough to tell Davey the truth? She'd rather rob him at gun-point, she realized, and took a sip of her drink. Tonight, she had to get him in her bed—no matter what she had to do. But she would be drunk by the time the bar closed. Un-less... Fortunately a plan came to mind.

MELISSA WAS STILL shaken when Dave called and asked if she would work at the bar tonight after she'd been accused of stealing earlier. "You're sure you still want me to?"

"Of course, Mel," Dave said. "Tanya has something spe-cial planned. You sure you don't mind?"

"Not at all," she said, even though she would have pre-ferred to stay as far away from Tanya and the bar as pos-sible. She knew the woman wasn't through with her.

"I still feel bad about earlier," Dave said.

"Please don't. Seriously. It was just a misunderstanding. I'm fine. I'm sorry I made you doubt me."

"You could never make me doubt you. Not ever. You know how much your friendship means to me."

She felt her heart break a little more. "I feel the same way."

"See you about five?" he asked.

"I'll be there."

Now, as she walked into the bar, she saw Wilbur and Ralph on their usual stools. There was a couple down at the other end of the counter and two young men playing pool. What she didn't see was Tanya and was glad of it.

"I made you a new till," Dave said. "I never want there to be a problem between us." She nodded and smiled. "I better get busy then."

The moment he left, Ralph said, "Well?"

She turned to look at him. "It backfired. She found the bills with *THIEF* written on them and put them in *my* purse, and then she told Dave." Ralph looked appalled. "I explained it away. Dave is fine."

"Dave is not fine," he cried. "This woman has to be stopped. What if this special night she has planned leads to a quickie marriage? You can't let that happen."

"Excuse me? Dave is a grown man. He makes his own decisions. If he wants to marry her..." Even saying the words hurt her heart. "Then there is nothing I can do about it."

"If you can't tell him about Tanya, then at least tell him how you feel," Ralph snapped.

She shook her head. "He only sees me as his friend."

"Make him see you differently," Wilbur suggested. "You know, perfume up, put on something sexy."

"To work together at the shop?" She chuckled, unable to imagine anything more embarrassing than throwing herself at Dave to have him reject her. It would destroy their friendship. But if Tanya had her way, the friendship wasn't going to last anyway. That was if Tanya didn't kill her first.

"You have to do something," Ralph said. "You can't let this woman win. She'll destroy Dave."

"Maybe she'll leave when her car is fixed," Melissa said hopefully, only to have Ralph roll his eyes.

"That's the best you can do?" he demanded, shaking his head and ordering another beer.

"I'll think about it, but no more help from the two of you," she said, pointing a warning finger at them. A loud noise came from upstairs and they all looked heavenward for a moment before Melissa poured them each another beer.

She didn't want to know what was happening up there.

CHAPTER EIGHT

THE NEXT MORNING, Melissa was at the shop when she heard the door open. She turned, hoping to see Dave and yet worried he might not show up after his night with Tanya. The last person she wanted to see was the woman in question.

"Good morning," Tanya said brightly as she walked in. "Isn't it a beautiful day?" She was all smiles. Melissa reminded herself not to get up on the ladder while alone with the woman. She turned back to her work, keeping one eye, though, on Tanya, who moved around the room, restless as a caged mountain lion.

"Davey and I had the most incredible night," Tanya said. "The man still has it, if you know what I mean." The woman let out a loud, abrasive laugh. "What am I saying? Of course you don't know what I mean. It isn't like you and Davey have ever..." She laughed again. "Anyway, he and I had a long talk last night. I just had to come by this morning to thank you for tending bar last night so Davey and I could...celebrate."

"Celebrate?" She hated that she'd taken the bait. The moment the word was out of her mouth, she wanted to bite her tongue.

"Davey and I... Well, let's just say we're a couple now. That's why I wanted to stop by and let you know that you won't be needed at the bar anymore. I'm going to be working your shifts from now on. Sorry, but it's not like you need the money. You still have your stake, right, and frankly, you just can't be trusted."

Melissa felt her face heat with anger and embarrassment. Was that what Dave thought? She turned to look at the woman. "I'm sure Dave will let me know what was decided when—"

"*I'm* telling you." Tanya took a step toward her, but stopped when she saw the hammer in Melissa's hand. "Look, everyone knows how you feel about him. What I'm trying to tell you is, stop embarrassing yourself. Davey hates it, and it just makes me feel sorry for you. Obviously, taking that money was a cry for help."

The woman's words were like barbs piercing her heart. Was it that apparent to everyone how she felt about Dave? Tears burned her eyes, but she willed them not to fall in front of this awful woman. Tanya knew damned well who'd taken the money from the bar.

"So, do us all a favor and give Davey a way out, you know what I mean?" Tanya asked. "He told me that he feels sorry for you, so if he weakens and asks you to tend bar again, it will only be out of pity. So just say no and save us all a lot of embarrassment."

With that Tanya smiled and walked out.

Melissa slowly put down the hammer. She felt sick. She could see what Tanya was up to. But Dave didn't. Whatever had happened last night—

She quickly texted Dave, telling him she wasn't feeling well and would talk to him later. She couldn't bear facing him, and he should be at the shop any moment to pick up his tools and discuss the next building to be remodeled. Hurrying out the back door, she just had to get away before she let the tears fall.

With every step she took, she told herself there was

nothing she could do. Dave loved Tanya. He was getting a second chance with her. How could Melissa take that away from him?

But at the same time, she knew the woman would bring him only pain. Maybe Ralph and Wilbur were right. How could she sit back and let him make the biggest decision of his life without having all the information? Then, if he still wanted to marry Tanya...

First, though, she had to find out what Tanya would do once her car was fixed. Melissa still held out hope that she would leave. She realized she was already headed for the garage.

"Let me guess what you want," Gertrude said with a curse as Melissa walked in to find her working on the car. "It will be fixed when it's fixed."

"Is there any way—?"

"That I can fix it quicker?" Gertrude snapped and shook her head as if in disgust. "You're as bad as Dave."

Melissa blinked. *"Dave?"*

"He was over here first thing this morning, offering to pay extra to get it fixed sooner."

"He was?" She couldn't help smiling. Was it possible that Tanya had been lying about everything, and Dave wanted the woman out of town as badly as Melissa did?

"I can't believe the two of you," Gertrude said. "One of you needs to tell the other one how you feel and quit being so ridiculous. Honestly." She stuck her head back under the hood, grumbling to herself.

Well, Tanya had told the truth about at least one thing. Everyone *did* know how she felt about Dave. But was it possible Dave felt the same way? Melissa couldn't stop smiling as she left. Dave didn't want Tanya staying in town any longer than necessary. Why else would he ask Gertrude about when the repairs would be done?

Unless the two of them planned to take the car to Vegas to get married.

That thought made her stumble. If true, she had to know, she told herself as she refused to let go of that bubble of hope lodged in her chest.

She headed for the bar before she lost her nerve.

DAVE LOOKED UP as Melissa came in the back door of the bar. "I was just going to text you and see how you were feeling and offer to pick you up anything from the drugstore. Maybe chicken soup for lunch? I could bring it by."

She marched up to him, looking more determined than he'd ever seen her. "Did you know Tanya came by to see me this morning at the shop?"

"No. She said she was going down to the café to get breakfast. Did something happen?" He looked worried.

"She didn't push me off the ladder this time, but then again, I wasn't about to climb it with her around."

"Mel—"

"My name is Melissa," she snapped. "I'm a woman."

He raised a brow. "I'm well aware of that." He could see that she was upset, and he figured it was Tanya's doing. "Whatever she said to you—"

"She said that you—"

"Hey, I thought you were working at the shop," Tanya said as she came in holding two carryout containers from the café. "If I'd known you were joining us for breakfast, Mel…"

"Why don't we step into my office?" Dave said to Melissa and then turned to Tanya. "We need a minute. Go ahead and eat." He took Melissa by the arm and led her down the hall to his office. Once inside, he closed the door.

"Are you all right? Whatever she said to you, just ignore it," he muttered, keeping his voice down.

NOW THAT SHE was here, alone with him in the intimacy of his small office, Melissa felt her anger ebb away and the tears resurface. "Are you going to Vegas with her to get married?" she cried.

"Of course not." He looked horrified. "Mel—Melissa, I know who took the money. I didn't know, though, that she pushed you off the ladder."

Before she could speak, there was a knock at the door. Dave went to answer it. She heard Tanya say, "I think I'd better join you. Now."

Dave turned back to her. "Trust me?" he whispered. She nodded. "Then just follow my lead, okay?"

That was all he had time to say as Tanya pushed her way in, leading with a gun in her hand. "Gertrude just stopped by. My car's ready. But I'm going to need some cash."

"More than you already stole?" Dave asked.

Tanya laughed. "Is that what little Mel told you? You can't believe anything she says. She's blindly in love with you."

"Melissa didn't have to tell me. I've been onto you for some time, Tanya. I just didn't know how low you would stoop before it was over," he said, motioning to the gun in her hand. "I thought setting Melissa up as the thief was the bottom of the barrel. But trying to push her off a ladder? Now what are you going to do? Shoot us both? Is that your plan?"

"Not before you open that safe behind you and empty the cash into my bag."

"I'll be happy to open the safe, but since I saw this coming, I emptied it out the day after you arrived," Dave said.

"What?" Tanya looked shocked. "How could you have—?"

"Known? The marshal called me to tell me you were headed this way. That last convenience store you robbed in North Dakota? Someone got a description of you and the car you were driving."

Tanya smirked. "If that was true, the marshal would have arrested me by now."

"I knew you wouldn't leave without what you'd come for," Dave said. "And I promised the marshal I would keep you here until he could get a warrant for your arrest. I sent him photos of you and your car, but the judge was out of town for a few days. He should be here any minute, though. The marshal and I both figured once your car was ready you would make your move."

Tanya laughed. "You're bluffing. You always sell yourself short, Davey. I might have taken you with me if you'd played your cards right."

He shook his head. "You mean, if you'd gotten me into your bed? That wasn't going to happen, Tanya. Having you here only made me realize how much I love Melissa. But I couldn't let her know until I ended this with you. I've been anxious for your arrest so I could tell her how I really feel about her."

Tanya groaned. "You love *her*? Look at her! She's nothing compared to me."

"She's everything to me," he said and looked at Melissa. "This isn't the way I'd hoped to tell her, though."

"Really?" Tanya demanded and turned the gun on her.

"Open the safe, Davey, and you'd better hope you were lying about there not being any money in there."

MELISSA COULDN'T BELIEVE what was happening as she looked down the dark barrel of the gun the woman was pointing at her heart. Dave loved her? He'd known about Tanya almost the whole time? All of this had been about keeping Tanya here until the marshal came to arrest her?

Melissa smiled at him, tears in her eyes. This wasn't the way she'd dreamed Dave would tell her he loved her, either. Not with a crazed, desperate woman holding a gun on her. Worse, she had no doubt that Tanya would think nothing of killing them both before making her getaway.

"Have it your way, Tanya." Dave moved to the safe and began to open it.

"Surely you can open it faster than that," the woman said, clearly antsy.

As the safe's door swung open, Melissa saw that it was empty—just as he'd said.

Tanya looked wild-eyed, and for a moment, Melissa thought she'd shoot her out of anger or simple frustration. "Is this a joke? Where is the money, Davey?"

"Safe in a bank. I'm sure you checked the till while we were in here talking. Empty too. Sorry, Tanya, but what you stole the other night is all you're going to get, and you aren't going to have a chance to spend that."

"What makes you so sure?" Tanya aimed the gun at Melissa's face and pulled the trigger.

She flinched, expecting to hear the loud report in the small room. To feel pain. Or to feel nothing ever again. Instead, all she heard was a click. All she felt was sudden relief once she realized what had happened.

Tanya pulled the trigger again, then turned the gun on

Dave and continued to pull the trigger. *Click. Click. Click. Click.*

She would have emptied the gun into them, but it was becoming obvious to all of them that it wasn't loaded.

"I found the gun in your purse, along with your cell phone and your wallet full of credit cards, Tanya," Dave said. "Even as I emptied the clip, I kept hoping you weren't as loathsome as I'd heard."

Fury transformed her face into a frightening mask. She swung her arm back as if to hurl the gun at him, but the weapon was snatched from her hand as a male voice said, "I'll take that."

Melissa saw the uniform before she saw the marshal. She wondered how long he'd been out there, waiting. She felt her heart rate slowly begin to drop as she watched the marshal cuff Tanya and take her from the room.

"Mel... Melissa, are you all right?" Dave asked and quickly moved to her.

She nodded. "It would have been nice to know the gun wasn't loaded."

"I wanted to tell you everything, but I couldn't chance it. I had to let it play out, but trust me, I've been watching her. I thought I could keep you safe. I was wrong. I should have told you how I felt sooner. I love you. Can you ever forgive me?"

"I love you," she said, her voice a whisper as he took her in his arms. "I thought you only saw me as a friend."

"My best friend and the woman I've fallen madly in love with," Dave said. "I was getting up the nerve to tell you, hoping you might feel the same way, when Tanya arrived."

"You really knew almost the whole time?" she said. "Even...last night?"

Dave smiled as he pulled back enough to look into her

eyes. "Nothing happened last night. I used some of Tanya's sleeping pills on her. This morning, I let her believe it was a night to remember. But you're the only one I want to wake up next to every day, Melissa—and go to bed with each night."

"In that case, I guess it's okay if you call me Mel," she said, smiling through her tears. "As long as you see me as more than just your best friend."

"Oh, I see you for the amazing, beautiful, sexy woman you are, Miss Herbert. I can't wait to show you how much."

He kissed her with such passion and promise, she had no doubt that all of her dreams were about to come true right here, in Buckhorn, Montana.

* * * * *

Look for another great Buckhorn, Montana, novel from New York Times *bestselling author B.J. Daniels coming February 2022 only from HQN Books.*

Chapter One

Cora Brooks stopped washing the few dinner dishes she'd dirtied while making her meal, dried her hands and picked up her binoculars. Through her kitchen window, she'd caught movement across the ravine at the old Colt place. As she watched, a pickup pulled in through the pines and stopped next to the burned-out trailer. She hoped it wasn't "them druggies" who'd been renting the place from Jimmy D's girlfriend—before their homemade meth-making lab blew it up.

The pickup door swung open. All she saw at first was the driver's Stetson as he climbed out and limped over to the burned shell of the double-wide. It wasn't until he took off his hat to rake a hand through his too-long dark hair that she recognized him. One of the Colt brothers, the second oldest, she thought. James Dean Colt, or Jimmy D as everyone called him.

She watched him through the binoculars as he hobbled around the trailer's remains, stooping at one point to pick up something before angrily hurling it back into the heap of charred debris.

"Must have gotten hurt with that rodeoin' of his agin," she said, pursing her lips in disapproval as she took in his limp. "Them boys." They'd been wild youngins who'd grown into wilder young men set on killing themselves by riding anything put in front of them. The things she'd seen over the years!

She watched him stand there for a moment as if not knowing what to do now, before he ambled back to his pickup and drove off. Putting down her binoculars, she chuckled to herself. "If he's upset about his trailer, wait until he catches up to his girlfriend."

Cora smiled and went back to washing her dishes. At her age, with all her aches and pains, the only pleasure she got anymore was from other people's misfortunes. She'd watched the Colt clan for years over there on their land. Hadn't she said no good would ever come of that family? So far her predictions had been exceeded.

Too bad about the trailer blowing up though. In recent years, the brothers had only used the double-wide as a place to drop their gear until the next rodeo. It wasn't like any of them stayed more than a few weeks before they were off again.

So where was James Dean Colt headed now? Probably into town to find his girlfriend since she'd been staying in his trailer when he'd left for the rodeo circuit. At least she had been—until she'd rented the place out, pocketed the cash and moved back in with her mother. More than likely he was headed to Melody's mother's right now.

What Cora wouldn't have given to see that reunion, she thought with a hearty cackle.

Just to see his face when Melody gave him the news after him being gone on the road all these months.

Welcome home, Jimmy D.

Get 4 FREE REWARDS!

We'll send you 2 FREE Books plus 2 FREE Mystery Gifts.

FREE
Value Over
$20

Both the **Romance** and **Suspense** collections feature compelling novels written by many of today's bestselling authors.